A

Katie Daysh works in retail but her passions are writing fiction and history, which she has an Open University degree in. She is the author of the Courtney and Nightingale queer naval adventure series, set during the Age of Sail. She lives on the Isle of Wight.

KATIE DAYSH

A MERCIFUL SEA

CANELO

First published in the United Kingdom in 2025 by Canelo

This edition published in the United Kingdom in 2025 by

Canelo, an imprint of
Canelo Digital Publishing Limited,
20 Vauxhall Bridge Road,
London SW1V 2SA
United Kingdom

A Penguin Random House Company
The authorised representative in the EEA is Dorling Kindersley Verlag GmbH. Arnulfstr. 124,
80636 Munich, Germany

A CIP catalogue record for this book is available from the British Library.

Ebook ISBN 978 1 80436 703 2
Royal Hardback ISBN 978 1 80436 691 2
Paperback ISBN 978 1 80436 700 1

This book is a work of fiction. Names, characters, businesses, organizations, places and events are
either the product of the author's imagination or are used fictitiously. Any resemblance to actual
persons, living or dead, events or locales is entirely coincidental.

Printed and bound in Great Britain by Clays Ltd, Elcograf S.p.A.

Look for more great books at
www.canelo.co | www.dk.com

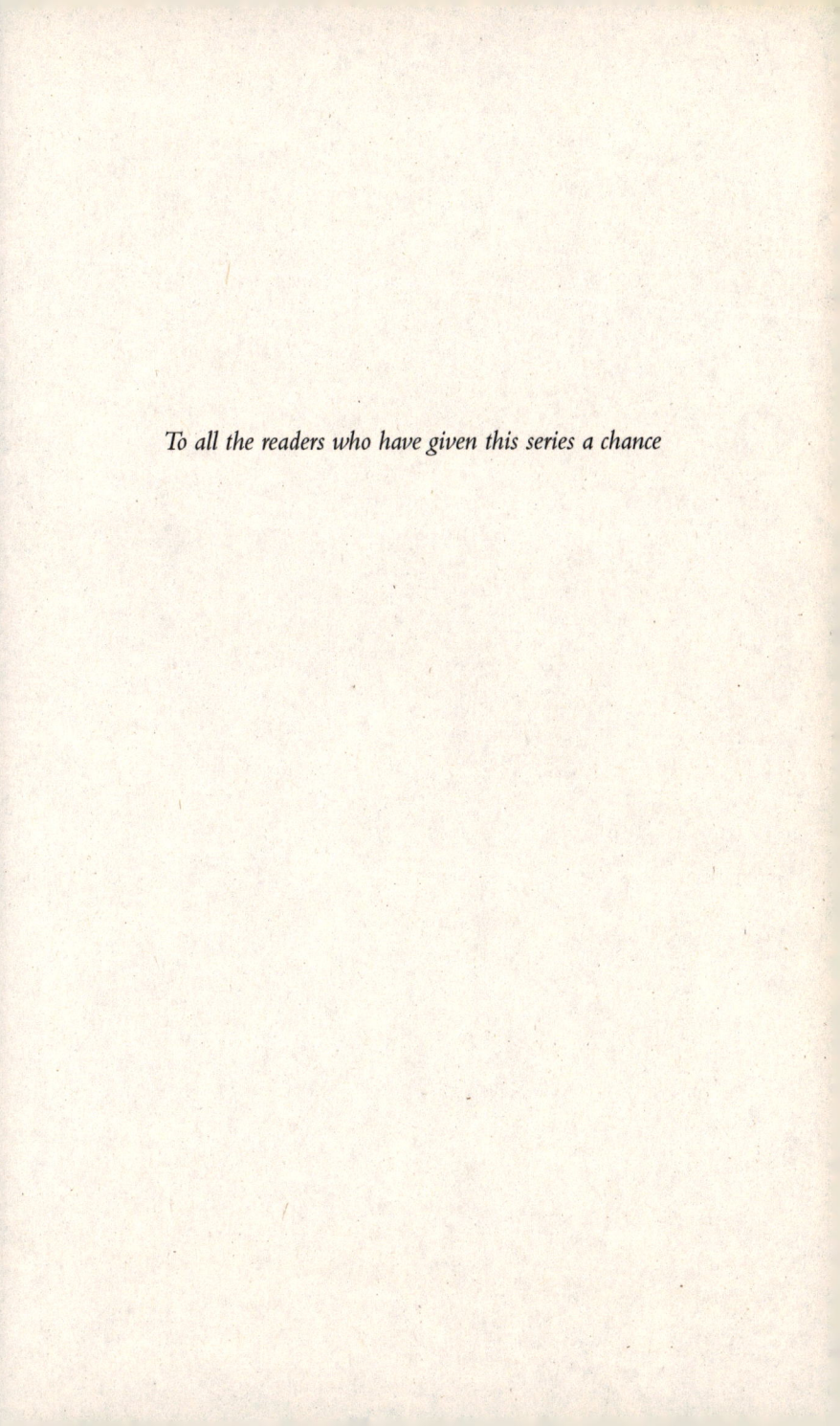

To all the readers who have given this series a chance

PART I

Chapter One: The Fire Ships

2 October 1804, nightfall

Arthur Courtney, the commander of HMS *Fearnought*, knew he should have abandoned ship by now. Through the night, illuminated by cannonfire, he could see the crew of the *Peggy* scrambling down into the launch boat. The ship, with helm lashed down and gun ports gaping, drifted along by the tide and her full spread of canvas. The *Fearnought* should have been doing the same. Forward, the double line of French ships, anchored so tightly together as if to resemble a wall of wood and iron, awaited. Their guns had been screaming for twenty minutes.

A ball smashed into the sea not a cable's length from the *Fearnought*'s hull. Courtney felt the spray against his cheek as he hurried away from the bows and towards his men. A skeleton crew stood on the battered deck. They were removing the last of the planks that opened the way into the heart of death beneath their feet. A chunk of the mainyard had fallen, cut away by French shot, and it rested to starboard. In that second when it had collapsed, Courtney had foreseen his own demise. It had only been fortune that had prevented them all being shredded to ribbons in the resulting explosion.

Below, Courtney climbed down onto the latticework deck. Rows upon rows of barrels, packed with gunpowder, sat amidst shells, grenades and reams of straw and combustible material. They were all intact, but Courtney's heart thudded at being so close to them. He told himself that the *Scylla* and the *Lysander* had both stored far more explosives than this, but that had been

3

under proper storage, always guided by Marines. Everywhere he turned now, he could see fiery destruction, waiting to be ignited. He had hated commanding this vessel over the last fortnight, knowing her fate.

Palms sweating, he laid the fuse from the explosives to the stern of the *Fearnought*. Soon, he would light the portfire which ignited the trail, but any misstep, any shift in the wind, could lead to incandescent destruction. They stood on a hellish amount of slaughter, ready to erupt at any moment.

'Captain!' Campbell, at the wheel, shouted. Courtney looked up to see the brawny man pointing to larboard. Despite the October chill, he had stripped off his shirt and gleamed with sweat. 'The *Providence*'s crew are abandoning her!'

The *Fearnought* had sailed with the *Providence* away from the safety of the British fleet. She had maintained a similar course until that French ball had cleaved the mainyard and sent them floundering in the tide. It was why Courtney had not left the ship yet; and still not now.

'Keep her on course, Campbell!' Courtney yelled back. 'She has to reach the French line! She must—'

Another ball struck the bows of the *Fearnought*. After a desperate tack, she still sailed at a strange starboard angle to the French anchorage, so the shot glanced past the bows, sending up a hail of splinters. Men staggered. Two fell to the deck. Courtney lurched forward as he noticed a barrel teetering in its iron hold. He caught it with a firm hand, pulse thundering.

Ahead, somewhere in the blackness, Boulogne loomed. There, over the course of the last year, the French had been constructing grand fortifications and batteries. Reconnaissance and agents spoke of the potential of the harbour as a launching-point for Napoleon's army, threatening the invasion of England. Attempts to scupper the port's designs had already occurred: bombardments, the sinking of vessels, even experimental floating mines from the prolific inventor Robert Fulton. All had failed. So now Lord Keith sent his fire ships, hoping to sow confusion and devastation amidst the anchored French.

With the paltry moonlight and lack of lanterns aboard, Courtney could barely see. He could only judge the distance to the enemy by the fire of their cannons and the far lights of Boulogne. In the bursts of illumination, he could discern the form of his fellow English vessels. *Providence* and *Peggy* had already abandoned ship and their little launch boats struggled against the waves. The *Fearnought* must have reached her target by now; they had wrenched her back on course and the wind had caught her sails again, ferrying her towards the French. He had to light the fuse, had to leave her to the mercy of the tide.

'All men!' Courtney cried. 'Abandon ship!'

He urged the crew aft, hurrying past the chimneys cut into the quarterdeck. They would soon funnel the night air around the *Fearnought*, spurring the flames. Courtney looked once more back at the packed barrels and combustibles. One by one, the crew disappeared through the sally door at the rear of the ship. On the other side, a chain secured their launch boat, bobbing in the dark waters, ominously and ghoulishly called a 'coffin' by some of the men. It looked so far down. Time dragged as Courtney shepherded each man down the chain and to the wooden boat. Behind him, he heard a roar of fire as another of the vessels caught ablaze. He swore he could feel the heat.

Finally, the crew sat amidst the banks of oars. Courtney looked once more back at the deck of the *Fearnought*. He felt a surge in his heart to know that she had been his first command; he would never again experience such a sensation. There had been naught but mundane routine in her before Courtney had taken command a mere fortnight ago – the blockade of Toulon allowed little more. But now, as he lit the portfire, she would end her days in a spectacle of destruction.

Turning away, he clambered down the chain and dropped into the launch.

'Out oars, men,' he ordered. 'Row like the devil!'

He kept a sturdy grip on the gunwale as the men obeyed. Ahead, the comforting line of British ships waited for them.

In the pale moonlight, he could discern Lord Keith's flagship, the *Monarch*: a hulking seventy-four-gunner surrounded by a number of other ships of the line. Their mighty firepower could not be turned on Boulogne, though. It was the duty of smaller vessels to try and approach the French harbour. Courtney knew all eyes, French and British, would be upon his *Fearnought* and the other fire ships. But Courtney's gaze drew back to the *Monarch* as a flashing beacon appeared at her bows. He squinted, trying to see what it meant. The *Monarch* was signalling some matter to him.

'Sir!' Campbell's voice cried again.

Courtney turned to where the helmsman pointed. The *Fearnought* had turned into a black silhouette, consumed with fire. Her masts stayed as firm as trees, held in place by iron bands to stop their collapse. Thick grey smoke belched from her deck, orange and red tongues lashing her timbers and spouting from her open gun ports. The tide and the wind pushed her steadily along towards the anchored French vessels at the mouth of the harbour. Too much wind. It had strengthened in the last few minutes, almost pushing the *Fearnought*'s sails aback.

The fuse, Courtney thought. With the rising wind, the fuse would burn faster. His launch boat was still in the *Fearnought*'s debris field.

'Row!' he shouted, ploughing his way amongst the crew and sitting beside them at the banks. The fire ship's crew had been so scanty that there were not enough men to occupy the launch. He grabbed an oar and heaved with them. An orange and red glow lit every man's face, making them appear like devils. Sweat glimmered on their brows and arms as they pulled with every well of strength. The sea seemed to work against them, waves rising. Courtney barely took time to breathe, only tugging at the oars, encouraging his crew, staring at the funnel of flame devouring the *Fearnought*. It grew with each passing second, a pyre that swallowed the stars.

They were too close. For a moment, Courtney considered abandoning the launch—

6

—and in the next, he felt his back slam into the hull of the boat. His men scattered, oars flying from their hands. It took a second for the sound to reach him and then the explosion turned the night into day. Blazing rays ignited the harbour into a furious dawn, raining heat and fire. Planks and timber and cordage whirled into the sky, splitting the seascape into shards of debris.

Courtney's ears rang, his eyes burnt. He scrambled to try and pull himself upright, managed to reach the banks of oars, only for a wall of water to plunge into the little launch boat. It tipped the bows upright so for a second, Courtney stared at the crest of the wave and then was consumed by it. The boat disappeared, capsized by the force of the sea. He found himself sinking, turned over and over in the chaotic rip tide. Above him, at the surface, the burning sky told him he was still awake. Dazed, moving purely through primal instinct, he groped and swam against the rolling current. Shadowy figures of his crew struggled around him, lost and confused with the destruction of their vessel.

Courtney broke the surface, gasping. A hail of detritus still fell from the sky and a smouldering hulk now sat where the *Fearnought* had been. She simmered and spat, far from the French line. Fury and disappointment tore through Courtney. For all their effort, for all his anxiety, she had not caused any damage, not even a singed brow or a split timber. She had done more harm to her own crew.

Courtney let his anger spur him on, paddling and forcing his way through the sea to his men. Only some of them could swim and the ones that couldn't clung to those still above water. Courtney could see bruises and Campbell had blood dribbling from his forehead.

'Keep close!' he shouted, getting a mouthful of salt water and spitting it out. 'Follow me to the British line!'

But the line was too far for a group of poor swimmers and exhausted men. Fortunately, as Courtney looked hopelessly back at the waiting ships, a gig swung down from the *Monarch*. Courtney raised a hand, shouting with what was left in his lungs. A great choking gout of smoke and foul air entered his throat, making him splutter and cough. Around him, he could still hear the splash and disturbance as wreckage plummeted into the sea. He could not make himself turn back again and see the shame of the destroyed *Fearnought*.

A lieutenant arrived with the *Monarch's* gig. Courtney signalled for his men to be pulled into the boat first which they were, unceremoniously and with great effort due to their sodden clothes and kicking limbs. Courtney tugged himself over the gunwale, dropping awkwardly amongst the banks of oars. The lieutenant grasped his arm to hoist him back up.

'Are you well, Captain?' he asked.

'I'm a captain no longer,' Courtney said without thought. He regretted it as the lieutenant blanched and shut his mouth, but it was no less true. Courtney's title was by courtesy only and remained as long as he had a ship to command. A commander without a vessel was just that: a hollow rank, caught between a lieutenant and a full post-captain. The time of his captaincy was over, burning in the night.

He was no more aware of it as when he climbed the side of the *Monarch* and saluted the quarterdeck. Admiral Lord Keith occupied the deck. He was a severe, white-haired man approaching sixty years of age and his cold eyes raked down Courtney's ruined uniform as he stood there before him. Courtney realised he was trailing a thin trail of ash: remnants of the *Fearnought*. He blushed at traipsing it over the admiral's ship. For a brief period, he had been the leader who oversaw all the neatness and behaviour of his own vessel. Now, he had returned to subordination, wondering if he was acting in the right way or not.

'Lieutenant,' Lord Keith addressed his flag officer, 'take Mr Courtney below and find him something to wash with. His men also.'

'Yes, sir.'

Courtney was guided off the hallowed quarterdeck before he could make any more of a mess. He was offered leave of the wardroom but Courtney chose to sit with his crew, orphans of the failed *Fearnought*. They washed the ash and char marks from their skin and the men stripped down to their drawers to rid themselves of their soaked clothes. Courtney removed his officer's coat and waistcoat and sat as a fellow man in trousers and a wet shirt. Outside, another explosion sounded, another of the fire ship igniting. Campbell glanced towards the sound and Courtney nodded to give him permission to look.

Leaving Courtney, the men gathered around a porthole, opened in anticipation of a possible night attack. He listened to their chatter, discussing *Peggy* and *Providence* which had already taken down two French gunboats. Apparently *Amity* and *Devonshire* were still nowhere to be seen, but Robert Fulton's strange catamarans, ugly and bizarre things that were meant to cling to the French ships like limpets and explode on a timed charge, still bobbed in the waves.

Selfishly, Courtney did not want to know more. His part in the attack had failed and he felt guilty for it. An officer was expected to know and understand the wind and his ship and the varying interplay between them. He had allowed the *Fearnought* to drift from her course, letting the events unfurl chaotically after the French ball had struck her mast. He had not abandoned the vessel in due time because of it and he had been fortunate there had been no deaths. It was not the start to his captain's career that he had wished for.

Now, he would return to England without a vessel or a command. It was a common feeling for himself. He felt it would remain so for many years to come.

9

Chapter Two: Spectre

The relentless rain cascaded from Nightingale's hair like a waterfall. He could feel it dripping down his throat, soaking his neckcloth and ruining his best silken shirt beneath his waistcoat. He tugged his cloak tighter around himself, keeping his arms crossed protectively across his chest.

At his feet, the dug grave gaped. He stared down into its innards where the bearers had lowered the elm coffin. The expense of that wood and this entire ceremony seemed too much. Every word that the vicar spoke seemed to be for another man, a figure that did not exist. Nightingale listened but did not take heed of them. His body might be stood in the graveyard of Portsmouth Cathedral yet his mind was far away, refusing to dignify this burial with any love or thought.

No one else accompanied him. When it came time to drop the ceremonial earth atop the coffin, he did so alone, watching those particles sift through his white-gloved fingers. He tapped his hand against his side to rid himself of the stain. Soon the rainstorm washed the earth away anyway, and began to soak the soil that the gravediggers piled down into the hole. The sludge of it covered the fine casket, hiding its sombre form and the bronze plaque that adorned its façade.

Here Lies the Body of Laurence Nightingale, Vice-Admiral of the White Squadron, it read, *Who Departed This Life 15th of November 1804, Aged 69 Years.*

Nightingale did not want to stand there in the cold and wet anymore. The vicar looked to him and gave a solemn nod. Gratefully, Nightingale crammed his hat back atop his head and walked away from the graveside. The night-time ceremony was swamped in foul darkness, and he had to pick his way between headstones decorated with sodden flowers. His father's plot would have none, not even for the sake of the ceremony. Nightingale had performed his duty by paying for this service, for the funeral procession, and for the burial, and that would be all.

The small funeral party stood outside the cathedral, wreathed in mourning black and quivering from the downpour. With Nightingale's permission, some had already departed in the waiting carriages. Barely cowed by the harsh weather, Mrs Louisa Nightingale still waited. As she saw him, she strode forward, plain skirt dragging in the grass.

'You should have gone home,' Nightingale said as she took his arm and he felt how cold she was. She held on to her hat and gave him a firm glance.

'My sex may mean I am not allowed at the graveside, Hiram, but it does not mean I will abandon my husband at his father's funeral.'

Privately, Nightingale was grateful. He had prepared himself for all manner of emotions that day, but from the hour he had heard of his father's demise to now, he had felt very little. That reaction was exhausting enough, and he wondered if he should be experiencing more. To see Louisa, a pillar of strength and certainty, soothed him. Another figure, separating from the funeral party to join them, further calmed him.

Courtney removed his hat and held it to his chest. His black curls adhered to his forehead, streaming down his handsome face. He wore his dress uniform, sparkling in gold and blue and white, but it was quickly receiving a drenching as terrible as on any voyage around Cape Horn.

'My condolences, Mr and Mrs Nightingale,' he said, though Nightingale knew he had never liked his father.

'Thank you for attending, Captain Courtney,' Nightingale replied: the first words he had spoken to Courtney in many weeks. He had seen him for the first time during the church service and his appearance had filled a terrible day with warmth.

'I wouldn't have missed it for the world,' Courtney gushed. A look of horror crossed his face as he heard his own words. 'Oh, I did not mean any disrespect. I simply meant...'

'Where are you staying, Captain?' Louisa asked, taking pity on him.

'I am at the George. I've just come from the Isle of Wight so all my dunnage is in my room at the inn. It was the last available so it's not the prettiest, and I wager the leak in the attic roof has worsened now, but...'

'Why don't you come to the hall? We have spare rooms and other guests are staying there tonight to avoid this awful weather.'

'Oh.'

Courtney's eyes flicked to Nightingale. He himself was unsure what to say to Louisa's offer. They had never had Courtney in their house for more than an hour; Nightingale did not know how the two of them would respond to the intimate experience. But Courtney was too much of a gentleman to refuse a woman's generosity, and by the time the carriage had drawn up outside Haywood Hall, Nightingale could not deny his stomach's jitters at being around the younger man again. Courtney's presence gave him joy and relief. More and more, he had wished to know where he was. After their time on the *Lysander*, they had not sailed again together and the expanse of the ocean had seemed cruel and perilous, an unassailable wall between them. He took comfort in his closeness.

And, in the hall, Courtney provided an interesting subject, being bombarded with questions and discussions. He turned as red as the claret, a boyish reaction that reminded Nightingale of the dinner in Trinidad, the lieutenant stumbling over his words to the senior officers around him.

After dinner, with the clock turning towards midnight already, Rylance guided Courtney up to Nightingale's wing of the grand manor. Nightingale had placed him in his dressing room, not far from his own bedroom. Rylance had tirelessly fetched Courtney's sea-chest from the George and beamed in his presence, telling him over and over how happy he was for his promotion. Nightingale listened to their chatter as they disappeared up the hallway then closed his bedroom door on the day.

The weight of it did not disappear from his shoulders. He had hoped that, by seeing his father's coffin covered with earth, he would be able to finally banish him entirely. But Admiral Nightingale, and the life associated with him, rose like a spectre. Nightingale turned it over again and again as he undressed and slid into his bed. His father had been the person to prompt him into the Royal Navy. He had been a seasick twelve-year-old midshipman, terrified of the world and of the fathomless ocean. The sea, and the violent service upon her, had been all he had known for almost three decades. He had won victories, suffered defeats, and lost many men he had cared for. Lieutenant Leroy Sawyer still pricked his heart upon remembering his face and manner.

When Nightingale had burnt HMS *Ulysses*, it had felt as though he had set a part of himself free. He had watched his pain and oppression smoulder into ash and smoke. Life had been rudderless afterwards; he had no clue of his course and position, operating entirely on dead reckoning. Yet it had been his choice for the first time in many years, and it had been made easier by the love of Lieutenant Courtney. Now, after almost four years of service to his brother-in-law's merchant company, he felt he had regained his feet on a stable deck. It was a career away from glory and reckless courage and unwanted celebrity. His father's death had closed the narrative that led him into and out of the navy.

Nightingale sighed and turned over. Since the Treaty of Amiens had broken down in March of the year before, France had continued to threaten England's door. French ships were blockaded in every port from Toulon to Brest to Rochefort, and the English Channel was choked with defensive squadrons. Sometimes, Nightingale climbed the rise of Portsdown Hill and looked at the distant masts. It was then that he thought of the days when he had commanded ships of war.

He did not know if he wanted to think of those days or not.

Realising he would spend another night fretting if he did not act, Nightingale rose and unlatched his bedroom door. Silence covered the dark corridor. Every guest was abed so he knew he could safely walk to the door a little way along from his own. Glancing again down the empty hallway, Nightingale knocked softly on it. For a moment, there was only the sound of the muffled rain and a distant rolling clap of thunder – then a soft voice answered. Quickly, Nightingale opened the door and slipped in, shutting it quietly behind him.

'Hiram,' Courtney breathed in relief. He sat up in the bed, hair loose, skin warmed by candlelight. The smile which broke over his face spurred Nightingale on.

'Can I join you?' Nightingale asked.

'Please.'

Courtney threw back the quilt and Nightingale gratefully slipped in. He could feel the warmth where Courtney's body had been, more so as he took Courtney in his arms. Courtney cupped his face with familiar hands and Nightingale easily, naturally, kissed him. It lingered, Nightingale sinking into homely tenderness and never wanting to part from it. This was what secured him firmly to the ground, stopping his head from drifting too terribly. When he had to pull away, Courtney kept him close, stroking his cheek, leaning his forehead against him to breathe affectations against his mouth.

'I missed you so much,' Courtney whispered, as he always did. 'Wanted ever so terribly to see you.'

'And I, you.'

'I'm sorry if I gave offence tonight. I felt so awkward around your wife and everyone else and…I find it difficult to hide how much I—'

'You gave no offence,' Nightingale chuckled. 'They were fond of you.'

Courtney smiled. He tangled his arms around Nightingale's neck and kissed him again. 'I'm sorry about your father,' he murmured as he led his lips over Nightingale's cheek and ear. 'You have acted very well.'

'Have I?'

Courtney paused, though Nightingale could see how breathless he was. He searched Nightingale's face. 'Of course,' he stated. 'Why do you think that you haven't?'

'I'm not sure.' Nightingale cradled Courtney's hand, seeking the comfort of it against his heart. Courtney always understood what he needed, and now he ceased his passionate caresses and laid back down quietly with him to listen. 'Ever since I found out about his death, I have felt…nothing. Even talking with his solicitor over his will and his estate, organising his funeral… It was as though I was organising things for a man I didn't know and had no feelings for. It's true I haven't spoken to him since Trinidad but – I don't know, I keep thinking that I should feel a shred of emotion at the least.'

'You said farewell to him four years ago, Hiram,' Courtney said softly. 'And he was a… He wasn't a pleasant man.'

'I know. But he was my father.'

'He was no father to you.'

Nightingale smiled at Courtney's reassurance. 'He did not mention me in his will. After we separated in Trinidad, it appears he became a recluse from society. He barely had anything left to his name and what he had he gave to a girl in a Portsmouth brothel.'

'Pardon?'

'To keep her quiet, I imagine. Do you know how he died?'

Courtney shook his head.

'Syphilis.'

Courtney's eyes widened. 'Good God,' he breathed.

'I saw his body, once, before he was prepared for his burial. The women would not touch him without clothing to protect them. His appearance was…awful. It seems he refused to pay for any medical treatment. His last days must have been indescribable. And still…I don't feel anything for his death.' Nightingale threaded his fingers through Courtney's, holding him tightly. 'The man who condemned me for the direction of my love did this to himself and perhaps to the women he laid with.'

'He's gone now. There is nothing you can do to change that.'

'Is this how it felt when you left your parents?'

Courtney paused. Something crossed his face, unreadable, before he nodded. 'After I had stopped feeling angry at them for what they did to me and Jane, yes.'

The both of them were so very different in ways, but much in their lives had also interlinked. Nightingale considered the two people who knew him best as Louisa and Courtney. He felt he could speak to Courtney about anything. 'Thank you, Arthur,' he whispered and raised Courtney's hand to kiss his knuckles.

'You don't have to thank me, Hiram. I've told you how I want to be a part of your life. In any and every capacity.'

With the storm still raging beyond the house, Nightingale could briefly forget about the outside world. He could ignore the judgements and hatred towards men like him and Courtney: an abhorrence that his father had carried to his deathbed. Responsibilities and duties fell away in the curtain of rain and thunder, and he was able to lie quietly in Courtney's embrace. As Courtney leant over to extinguish the candle, he took refuge in the darkness and the notion that he could do no more in this bewildering day.

He awoke in the morning as the first light broke through the curtains. A feeble sun had chased away the tempest and replaced it with bright, cold weather. Courtney still slept with his arm thrown over his eyes, snoring quietly. Trying not to wake him, Nightingale reached over and flicked open the pocket-watch Courtney had beside the bed. His initials were engraved on it: a gift from Nightingale on his last birthday. The hour was not yet eight, so Nightingale knew he had time to safely return to his own bedroom without arousing any attention.

He slowly slipped out of the bed, making Courtney roll over and groan at his absence. Quietly, Nightingale walked to the wardrobe and searched through to find what he had mentioned to Rylance to bring out of storage the evening before, now Courtney had graced them with his presence. It had been something he had considered for some time. The light weight of it brought memories flooding back. Encased in a leather scabbard, the sword had been an award for brave conduct during the Glorious First of June. Unlike the medal Nightingale had received after the Nile, it did not weigh him down with grief and guilt, but as he held it in his hands, he knew it was for a life long gone. He had disliked seeing it in his wardrobe and disliked more the thoughts of his absence from the service.

The bed creaked behind him and he turned to see Courtney sitting up against the headboard, his black curls in a mess. Nightingale gave him a smile and returned to his side.

'Good morning,' Courtney said and beckoned him over for a kiss. Nightingale accepted, treasuring their easy intimacy.

'I have something for you,' he said. 'I have been meaning to speak to you of it.'

Courtney's eyes fell upon the sword resting across Nightingale's knees. 'Hiram, I cannot accept another priceless object from you.'

'You have more need of it than I do.'

'All the same…' Courtney touched the scabbard and allowed Nightingale to ease out the blade. It shone in the dim morning light, topped with a golden lion and with a fouled anchor emblazoning the handle. Courtney's hand perfectly fitted around it. 'It's beautiful, Hiram, but I cannot.'

Nightingale had not thought Courtney would refuse. Sometimes, he could not find the words to express his and Courtney's connection, so the offer of gifts had been a material symbol of it. Courtney came from a poor background and still had little money in his pocket or saved for a future. Though his life had been emotionally broken, Nightingale had never been in want of shelter and wealth. In his society and in the service, men were rewarded with swords and titles and land.

'You do not want it?' he asked. 'It is just decoration for me now. I am not Captain Nightingale anymore.'

'Yes, you are, only in a different way. And, Hiram, I appreciate your gifts but I want to earn these things.'

'You more than have, Arthur. I know the navy. It is only because you do not have connections or patronage that you don't have the things that I had. You have done well on your own but I want to be there too.'

'I know.' Courtney smiled and laid his hand over Nightingale's. 'I want you to be there as well. But I do not need this, not now.'

Nightingale opened his mouth to say more, but eventually relented. He would not force Courtney into accepting anything; this was, after all, intended to be for his benefit. Instead, he slid the sword back into the scabbard and, as if proving its uselessness now, stuffed it back into the wardrobe amongst the uniforms he no longer wore. As he did, he thought of the other matter he had wished to talk to Courtney of. It would have to wait. Courtney did not want that conversation yet.

'I shall return to my room,' he said to Courtney. 'I shall see you during breakfast.'

Courtney nodded. A streak of worry had crossed his handsome features. 'I am going to London soon,' he said. 'I will be visiting the Admiralty in hopes of a commission somewhere, seeing as my last one burnt. Would you like to accompany me?'

Nightingale stopped with his hand on the doorknob. 'Of course,' he assured.

Chapter Three: Another Life

Guilt still touched Courtney for refusing Nightingale's gift. He had debated changing his mind, but what he had said was true: he wanted to earn these accolades, even if it took longer than it would for connected officers. He had taken many objects from Nightingale – his Nile medal, new articles of uniform, an engraved pocket-watch, and a shining modern spyglass – and he never knew how to approach the acceptance. One day, he had known he would have to tell Nightingale it felt like charity to a poor man.

So it was with his old sword strapped to his belt that he ascended the familiar steps of the Admiralty Office. The halls were full of officers like himself, ambitious men at every age, from lieutenants at the beginning of their career to elderly captains. Courtney wondered where exactly he stood amongst them, not quite at the bottom of the pyramid but nowhere near the very top. Above him, it was all blue coats and shining gold brocade. He would never be seen through all the bluster and decoration.

Half-pay and the ignominy of being cast on the beach stared at him from every wall of the grand Admiralty buildings. When he had been a lieutenant, he had known that only a grand and reckless spectacle would claw him further up the hierarchy of promotion. His months on the *Lysander* had not precisely been that, but a clandestine mission and the gratefulness of an Admiralty who had not been tipped prematurely into war had granted him the push he needed. This, he thought though, could be where he languished, caught in a strange purgatory between ranks.

The continual denial had become almost mundane. Courtney expected no more. Even with the vast blockades of the French coast and the squadrons in the Downs and the North Sea, no ship yet bore Courtney's name. He thought, with a note of spite, that if he had still been a lieutenant, he could have commanded a gunboat for one of those many blockades. A few hours loitering and lingering amongst the shining stars of the Admiralty again produced the result he expected: nothing.

He thought he would do almost anything for another push up the slippery and difficult ladder.

And more so, a new shadow had arisen, like the presence of rocks beneath the waves, subtly changing the appearance and attitude of the waters. Courtney knew it affected his mood and his thoughts. How could it not? It had the potential to throw the ship of his life onto its beam-ends and drag everyone around him down too. He had not spoken to Nightingale of it – would not bring it up if he could help it – but the notion of it hung over him.

Walking back down Whitehall with the sun hanging low in the winter sky, Courtney tugged his uniform coat around him to escape the chill. He held on to his bicorne hat and, head down, nearly collided with a man about to cross the busy street.

'Apologies, sir, I—' Courtney began to say.

'Lieutenant Courtney!'

Courtney looked around to see who he had almost toppled over. A beaming, flushed face peered back at him, rounder than when he had last seen it but no less joyful. Blonde curls framed it beneath a fine gold-trimmed hat. Epaulettes bounced as the post-captain extended an enthusiastic hand.

'Captain Harrison!' Courtney managed. Henry Harrison had commanded the *Actium* in the Caribbean and had once been tipped to supersede Nightingale's position on the *Scylla* – until Courtney had spoken up for Nightingale. Harrison had then helped suppress an attempted mutiny on the *Scylla* and been a great aid during the court martial. Courtney had thought he was still in the Caribbean – he had been when Courtney had seen the last of the *Scylla*. Courtney had had to rely on his generosity when cast onto the beach after the court martial.

'How are you, my dear fellow?' Harrison asked, shaking Courtney's hand vigorously.

'I am well. I was recently promoted to commander but I…I have been having trouble finding a commission. There are more commanders than ships.'

'Of course, of course.' Harrison had no more to say about that, or to console Courtney with. 'It is wonderful to see you! Are you staying in London?'

'I am.'

'Come and dine with me and my wife! I won't accept your refusal.'

'You are married? To Miss Jennifer Sandham, was it?'

'Miss Jennifer Sandham, that's correct. We are expecting a child within the next year!'

'Congratulations, sir.'

'And you?'

'I…' Courtney fought for words. 'I am not married, sir.'

'You surprise me. Never matter, come along tonight.'

'I am here with Hiram Nightingale. I'm sure you remember him.'

'Of course! How wonderful that you are still in communication with him. Bring him along too!'

Feeling a little run down by Harrison's enthusiasm, Courtney returned to Nightingale's rooms on Seymour Street. He was uncertain of inviting Nightingale along to Harrison's dinner; the offer of his sword had not only felt like charity, but as if Nightingale was pawning off his old life and the markers of it. Being around a shining post-captain could be setting a match to gunpowder. Perhaps that was only Courtney's own feelings though. Jealousy had become an uneasy companion.

Nightingale accepted with a strained smile. Courtney tried to insist he didn't have to come, but as the hour reached seven, he was grateful for the other man's company. They took a carriage to Bloomsbury and Courtney's mouth nearly dropped as a liveried servant welcomed them into a beautiful, grandly furnished townhouse. He should have expected it – Nightingale's manor was not exactly austere – but Harrison had been in the West Indies for years, a place detested by officers and sailors alike for its death tolls and the feelings of being at the end of the earth. Courtney gave a sly look to Nightingale, eyes wide, and Nightingale pursed his lips, warning him to be silent.

'I bet his roof don't leak,' Courtney still murmured, referring to the constant problem in his Ryde cottage.

'Mr Courtney, Mr Nightingale!'

Harrison's loud voice boomed down the winding staircase. He came hurrying down it past rich paintings of naval victories and a particularly large oil portrait of himself and his wife. The real man glittered just as much as in the pictures, almost gaudy in his best dress uniform. Courtney's eyes drew to the medal sat on his chest; he had not worn that earlier. The star design signified an accession into the Order of the Bath. Even Nightingale could not hide his surprise at that.

'How are you?' Harrison asked, shaking Courtney's hand again and then grasping Nightingale's. 'I am so pleased that you have come. I still expected to see you in your uniform, Captain Nightingale. You have not changed since the Caribbean.'

Harrison, as friendly and well-meaning as he seemed, did not seem to think of the words that came from his mouth. Courtney remembered that from Trinidad. He looked at Nightingale, knowing that the man who stood beside him was a world away from his past on that distant island. Nightingale gave a gracious smile.

'I am well, Captain Harrison, thank you – or should I call you "Sir Henry" now?'

'Oh!' Harrison laughed and gestured at his medal. 'I do not believe the Order wished to confer it on me, not truly – it

22

was in sympathy of keeping me in the West Indies for so long. That, or the French trade I interrupted. Ha! In any case, my wife makes me wear it. Here she is!'

Jennifer Harrison, née Sandham, emerged from the parlour. She wore similar colours to her husband, a fine blue gown with a golden band and hem. Anchors decorated the pleats of her long skirt and the jewellery at her ears and throat. She placed a gloved hand on Harrison's arm and lowered her head politely to Courtney and Nightingale.

'I was saying, my dear, that you impress it upon me to wear my medal,' Harrison said.

'Oh, stuff, Harry,' Jennifer sighed jovially.

'Come, let us go into the dining room. Someone is very eager to meet with you.'

Courtney cast another glance at Nightingale, again glad that he had accompanied him. They trailed Harrison and Jennifer down the hallway and into a dining room lit by candles and a chandelier polished to a mirror-like sheen. But, unlike outside, Courtney's eyes did not draw to the decorations and the furnishings. Another woman almost leapt out from her position by the windows, bubbling over with a giddy smile and flushed cheeks. It took him a moment to remember her. She had lost her babyish round cheeks and bonnet and now resembled a fine young lady with perfectly styled red ringlets and a flattering muslin dress.

'Miss Tabitha Sandham,' he recalled.

'Hello, Commander Courtney,' she said, still beaming, before she seemed to realise her social manner and dropped to a polite curtsy as her sister had. Courtney did not know what else to say. Without sounding as though he was flattering himself, there was only one reason Tabitha Sandham would be standing in front of him, looking as eager-eyed as a new bride. Surreptitiously, his eyes dropped to her hands. No marriage ring sat upon her finger.

'Miss Sandham has been staying with us,' Harrison explained. 'The London life is suiting you, is it not, my dear?'

'Yes, Henry,' she said sweetly. 'It is so very different from Port of Spain.'

Much was different from those days in Trinidad, not only the politics and the weather and the people. When Courtney had last met with Tabitha Sandham, he had been a lieutenant on half-pay, reeling after the tangled affairs of the *Scylla* and the *Ulysses*. He had been uncertain if he would see the deck of another ship as an officer and had felt a great deal of self-pity. So recently departed from Nightingale, who had returned to England, he had had no idea where his life would take him – professionally, socially, romantically. In those confused days, he had only wished for two things: another commission and the presence of the man whom his heart was beginning to ache for. Guilt always shadowed his interactions with Tabitha. She was who the world dictated his feelings should pine for. Certainly, her mind had followed that path.

He would only disappoint her.

Perhaps the circumstances were not so very different from Trinidad.

Captain Harrison was not a man who enjoyed silence. He clapped his hands, breaking Courtney's tangled and quiet pall, and directed everyone to their places around the table. Tabitha took a seat next to Courtney, Nightingale occupying his other side. Courtney had barely looked at his partner since seeing Tabitha. Being around the expectations of sexes and their proper conduct in high society always tied his stomach in knots. The accepted behaviour of boys and girls had not meant a thing when he had been young. Now, he felt the weight of it, fretting that he drew unwanted attention towards his and Nightingale's attachment.

Courtney barely tasted the soup that was served. He sipped on it, feeling the heat burn his tongue and throat. It offered a good excuse to avoid conversation – not that he had much opportunity with Harrison at the head of the table. Courtney and Nightingale were treated to a month-by-month account of Harrison's events in the Caribbean. It almost felt as though they were back there, observing his skirmishes with French merchant vessels and around the contested island of Hispaniola. The mention of the rebellion in what had formerly been Saint-Domingue, now newly independent Haiti, did not seem to prompt Harrison to remember the *Ulysses'* wretched history with it.

As Harrison carved the roast beef, the conversation finally turned to Tabitha. She expressed her love for London and the Ton, a set she was trying to take her first steps in. She told Courtney how she had come out into society and already danced sets at Almack's. Courtney had no clue what Almack's was until Nightingale explained that it was a social club of some fame and reputation that well-born men and women desired to have access to. Harrison and his family were no longer simply sea folk, but moving in circles of society Courtney was entirely ignorant of. He wondered, for a bewildering moment, what it might have been like if he had married Tabitha in Trinidad. It would be another life entirely, but perhaps he would have gained the connections he lacked.

And it would have meant that his life on the Isle of Wight would have not become so tangled. Courtney pressed down the bother. He would deal with them later.

'I do still miss being beside the ocean, though,' Tabitha said, seeming to read his mind. 'In Trinidad, I had such interesting conversations with naval officers. Here, in London, there are not so many, certainly not now the wars have begun again.'

Courtney was silent, unsure if that was directed towards him or if he should respond. In the end, Nightingale leant forward and said, 'I am certain that they would rather be here in London, ma'am.'

Harrison laughed. 'Well spoken, Mr Nightingale. That reminds me of something that I have been intending to ask you. Here—'

He paused as Nightingale and Courtney helped themselves to the next dish of carved beef and vegetables drenched in butter and a rich wine sauce. Courtney, as a gentleman of the table, also served Tabitha beside him. She primly took the proffered plate, but allowed her gloved fingers to brush Courtney's. He gave a thin smile back, flushing, and nearly missed Harrison's next words.

'—served with Nelson, yes?' Harrison was saying.

'Oh.' Nightingale shifted beside Courtney. 'Yes, I did.'

'I have not informed you yet, my dear,' Harrison commented to Jennifer. He reached over to her and laid his hand across hers. 'I was granted a commission this afternoon – the command of a seventy-four to join Lord Nelson's blockading fleet at Toulon.'

Courtney did not know who was more enthusiastic to hear that news: Jennifer or Tabitha. They both congratulated Harrison so avidly that Courtney felt uncomfortable, as if intruding on some joyous moment meant only for their family. He looked to Nightingale and realised he should be smiling, so showed his teeth in a way he hoped was cheerful, rather than betraying the envy inside.

'Congratulations, Captain Harrison,' Nightingale said when he could insert a word.

'Congratulations, sir,' Courtney echoed.

It gave another excuse for Harrison to dole out more port. Courtney accepted it, hoping that the taste of it would drown some of the shameful reactions within himself: the jealousy, the guilt, the awkwardness around Tabitha who had been nothing but pleasant to him. By the time he had eaten the main course, as well as a selection of sweet pies and a marzipan and fruit dessert, his head and stomach felt as though they were buoyant. After the dishes had been cleared away, Harrison invited both Courtney and Nightingale into the parlour for further libations and cigars. Courtney did not think he could bear another drop or crumb, so was glad when Nightingale said, 'I think that we shall leave you to your celebrations, Captain. You have been very kind in attending to us, but Arthur and I have a long journey back to Portsmouth tomorrow.'

Harrison smiled, raising his glass. 'You are very welcome, Hiram. I hope that our paths will cross again soon.'

Nightingale rose and Courtney followed, realising how unsteady his knees felt. He could never stand this side of a naval officer's life: dinners and suppers and social obligations were never by choice. All he wanted was to pull the covers around himself and Nightingale and forget about his latest failure to attain another commission.

'Mr Courtney,' Harrison said. 'Would you mind staying for a while longer? I have something I wish to talk to you about in privacy.'

The blissful bed suddenly seemed even further away. Courtney knew, immediately, what Harrison referred to. For a moment, he considered refusing. 'Of course, sir,' he said, those civic duties and expectations again weighing upon him.

Nightingale lingered. 'I shall see you in our… At Seymour Street later?' he asked.

Harrison laughed. 'I shall not take too much of the young man's time, Mr Nightingale.'

As Courtney watched Nightingale leave, he hoped that was true.

–

The hour approached one when Courtney at last returned to Nightingale's apartment on Seymour Street. He crossed the living space far too loudly and bashed open the door to his and Nightingale's bedroom. The candle still burnt but Nightingale had obviously been sleeping for he jerked awake at the sound of Courtney's footfalls. Courtney's head still span with Harrison's words; he had barely thought to be quiet.

'Apologies, Hiram,' he rushed. 'I didn't mean to wake you.'

'No, no. I was only resting,' Nightingale lied. He stretched and sat up against the headboard, setting aside the book lying flat on the quilt. 'Did you speak with Captain Harrison?'

'I did.' Courtney sat on the edge of the bed, removed his coat and tugged at his neck-cloth. It unwound easily and he threw it in the direction of his chest before irritably pulling at his waistcoat buttons.

'I assume that you did not like what he had to say?'

Courtney did not reply for a moment. He shucked off his waistcoat and tugged his shirt over his head. Though the talk with Harrison and the cool night air had chased away most of the effects of the port, his fingers still fumbled with his buckled shoes and the buttons of his breeches. He did not respond to Nightingale until he had managed to don his nightshirt and had climbed into bed beside him. Then, he wrapped his arms tightly around Nightingale's waist and buried his face in his neck.

'I wish we could always have this,' he murmured, choked with sudden emotion. He thought of the thorn currently in his heart and started to wonder if he should mention it to Nightingale – he knew what they would talk of would stir it up.

Then, Nightingale pressed his lips to the top of his head, winding his fingers into his black curls, and Courtney only selfishly wanted to cling to him. 'What do you mean? Of course we can.'

Courtney sighed. Keeping Nightingale in his embrace, he laid his head against the pillow and tried to achieve the correct tone for the words he was about to say. He kept his former pains to himself and said, 'Captain Harrison offered me a position on his seventy-four.'

Nightingale's eyes lit up, but, seeing Courtney's deadened expression, he wiped the smile from his mouth. 'That is wonderful, is it not?'

'Yes. He is missing an officer who's been taken grievously ill. I would be a volunteer, but it would be a good addition to my record of sea service. And a seventy-four... It has been a long while since I served on a ship of the line.'

'Then why this brown study?'

'Miss Sandham…' Courtney shook his head. 'Captain Harrison wants me to wed her. He even went so far as to call me his future brother-in-law. This position on his seventy-four would be a favour to me and… That would be how I repay him.'

'Ah.'

Courtney could not read Nightingale's reaction. If Nightingale had not already been married when they formed their bond, Courtney knew he would have been very jealous of any woman who attained the open love he and Nightingale could not. Having met Nightingale's wife and understood their untraditional arrangement, he was fully aware he could never hope to have such fortune with a wedded partner. But Nightingale was too honourable to experience envy.

'I don't believe Captain Harrison is like that, Arthur,' Nightingale said in a measured voice. 'He would not expect such a thing.'

'I'm not so certain. He might not think before he opens his mouth but… Even in the Caribbean, he was trying to play marriage-broker. If I accept this position, I feel I would be accepting Miss Sandham's hand as well.'

'Do you wish to marry?'

'Do I wish to marry?' Courtney stared at him, frowning. He was about to answer vehemently in the negative, then remembered one of the reasons for his heartache. He hesitated and asked, 'Why would you think I want to marry?'

'I don't know. I…I did not wish to marry either, but I did. And this world is difficult for one who is unattached, one who is like us. It draws questions, it…' Nightingale's response trailed off. Courtney tried to hide how much it had struck him, and how much he knew it to be true – however much he hated it to be so.

'I don't want to marry, Hiram,' he said, more firmly now. 'Not if I cannot marry the one who is in my heart.'

'Arthur…' Nightingale lowered his eyes. Courtney could almost see the cogs of his mind working. He was about to add more when Nightingale said, lightly, 'You've been drinking and now you're talking rot, Arthur.'

'I'm not,' Courtney insisted, but he could already tell that this conversation would not happen now, not when he was so conflicted about Harrison and Tabitha.

'How about we sleep and speak more about this in the morning?' Nightingale offered. 'But I truly think this would be a good opportunity for you. Captain Harrison is the connection in the navy that you need and have often said you do not have. His association with the Sandhams has only increased that standing. They come from very good stock. I think you should accept.'

'Accept what?' Courtney asked. 'The position? The marriage? How can you...'

But Courtney did not want to continue. The idea that Nightingale would let him go so easily hurt him. He loved Nightingale more than anyone else in the world, except for his sister, Jane, and he wanted their lives to be as one. He knew, though, that the perils were terrifying. They could never truly be united with the hatred of the world permanently at their backs.

Courtney said no more to Nightingale. He turned over and blew out the candle. For a while, he stared at the tendril of smoke as it dissipated into nothing. Nightingale's advice was always sensible. He tended to choose the route that gave the least grief and the least trouble. It had been a calmness that had mellowed Courtney's youthful arrogance and passion – though Courtney could never forget how Nightingale had shocked everyone by setting fire to the *Ulysses* and loudly condemning those who had forced him into places he did not want to be. Courtney had admired that, just as much as he now admired Nightingale's talent at keeping him on an even path. Neither of them was the same man from years before. They had become more alike without losing their individual hearts.

But he did not know how he felt about Nightingale's words that night – about marriage, about connection, about accepting

Harrison's generous offer. He did not even know what he felt inside his own heart. Recently, the danger of their connection had become even clearer. At his cottage in Ryde, letters had started to arrive. They made it plain that his true feelings, his true inclinations, were known. It stung even more knowing who the author was.

Courtney had not believed it at first but the reality was unshakable and undeniable. It frightened Courtney, unmoored him from his usual foundations. And more than that, it terrified him to think of Nightingale being caught in such a storm. He had to find a way to remedy the danger of the notes, and, worryingly, Harrison's offer and Tabitha's presence seemed to promise a convenient measure. But the idea of it stuck in his throat, made him feel unfaithful and nauseous.

Harrison, and Tabitha Sandham, had starkly shown that the world and the navy were changing quickly. At these times, he could barely keep up the pace.

Yet as Courtney reached back to try and find Nightingale's arm to pull around himself, he knew what the true heart of the matter was.

He loved his career and he loved Nightingale. And he did not want to have to choose between them.

Chapter Four: Anchorage

21 December 1804

The low December sun had done little to take away the winter chill. A thin layer of snow covered the heathlands and clung to the trees. The passengers Nightingale had travelled with in the carriage had been wrapped up tightly in thick coats and mufflers, but their breath still puffed before them. He had had to watch his footing as he meandered along the high street, avoiding pockets of frost and ice. Outside the George, a throng of naval and army officers, bedecked in blue and red, shivered. Nightingale raised his hat to them and wondered about entering the inn, if only to warm himself by the fire for a moment.

He decided to wait in the courtyard.

Fortunately, he did not have to linger for too long. In fifteen minutes, Courtney emerged, boat cloak around him. Nightingale smiled and raised a hand, once again filled with admiration for Courtney's fine looks in his uniform: a blue frock coat with an epaulette on the left shoulder, a silver-buttoned white waistcoat and white breeches. Nightingale had not seen many men who fitted the appearance so well.

'Would you still like me to walk with you?' Nightingale asked.

Courtney nodded. He had been in Portsmouth for the last few days, sorting his affairs, but had refused Nightingale's offer to stay at Haywood Hall. Neither of them had spoken much since the discussion in London, which had been a fortnight ago now. Nightingale knew he had phrased himself wrongly.

He had truly meant that Courtney should accept the offer of such a momentous position on the seventy-four, but he had not considered the matters of the heart around it. Frankly, he had not thought of Harrison's offer as binding. Many women surely desired Courtney's companionship: he was handsome, kind, and passionate. The prospect of marrying him must have crossed many minds.

The idea of having to part from such a man agonised Nightingale, suddenly making him feel cold. Harrison could not have been serious.

Now, Courtney was quiet and contemplative. Nightingale tried to consider it merely as his nerves. He remembered feeling a similar way when he had become a commander, that tenuous rank in which an officer could either stagnate or advance to the heady pinnacle of being made post.

So far, Courtney's options as a commander had been very limited. Nightingale thought he should have been ecstatic over the notion of serving on a seventy-four-gunner.

But, whilst they walked down to the docks, he did not say these things again. He kept to safer ground, asking about the cottage on the Isle of Wight and noting how the problems continued: not only the leaking roof, but the attempts Courtney was making to settle his debts there. Hearing about Courtney's financial issues drew up the matter Nightingale wanted to speak to Courtney of – yet, once more, the moment did not seem right.

'Captain Harrison said he would meet me,' Courtney said as the familiar smell of the docks began to creep over them, the tar mixed with timber and fishes dredged up from the harbour. 'You do not have to come any further. It's getting cold.'

'I want to see your ship,' Nightingale replied, a little hurt. 'Captain Harrison said he would give us the tour, did he not?'

'The business of setting sail…'

But Courtney must have known he could not tell Nightingale the ways of the service. He relented to Nightingale walking with him past the docked ships: schooners and fishing smacks alongside brigs and sloops. The larger vessels were anchored further out, and amidst them must have been Harrison's command. The captain appeared suddenly, jumping up from a launch boat and tilting it dangerously.

'Commander Courtney!' he cried, waving his hat. 'Mr Nightingale!'

They made their way over, Courtney aiding Nightingale down into the little launch. Harrison beamed at them as he ordered his men away from the pier. 'I am so pleased you accepted, Commander Courtney,' he said. 'It is an honour to have you aboard. And, Mr Nightingale, I promised to give you the grand tour of the *Actium* in Trinidad but never had the chance. I think you will enjoy this grand tour – if you can stand the havoc.'

'I know well the mania of a ship of the line, Captain,' Nightingale said.

'Oh, that is not what I mean! You shall see.'

Nightingale pulled his coat tighter around himself as they drew further from the shore. Though the sun struck through the hard blue sky, the rays did not touch him. All they did was attack his eyes. His vision had not worsened since treatment after the Nile, but neither had it improved. Bright lights still made his head throb, so he tugged his hat down for a little shade. Harrison talked at them and Nightingale nodded politely along, noticing that Courtney still said very little.

'We are all here, present and correct, apart from poor Lieutenant Oakley, of course, which means we've had a bit of an upset in our hierarchy. Oh, and I am still awaiting my new bosun who will join us in Toulon. Our previous fellow took a frightful tumble. Two men down! The hands will be saying we are cursed.'

Courtney winced. Sailors were superstitious creatures; not much bad fortune had to hit a ship before they started believing in curses. 'Don't say that, sir,' he said, hoping it sounded good-natured.

'Oh, I am only jesting. A ship is her men, not her frame. And good news – we have only this morning brought a shoal of bass into our stores. We'll have sea-pie until we are tired of it. Mr Nightingale, you'll know the tedium of blockade duty, but I refuse to relent to dull food. Ah, here she is!'

Harrison swept his arm to the beautiful two-decker which appeared through the curtain of other vessels. She was freshly painted in yellows and blacks, anchored at her head and stern, prim and proper and beautiful. But, even as he admired her style, cold familiarity crept over Nightingale's spine. Memories of a distant past floated up in him, trailing a sense of dread. He knew her, knew that rig, knew that way of leaning slightly astern, knew the slope of her decks, knew that figurehead. She was captured in a globe in his study at home.

Without thought, Nightingale had reached over the bench towards Courtney's hand. He stopped himself at the last instant.

Obviously expecting praise, Harrison looked between them. Nightingale could not speak. At last, Courtney rose from his silence.

'The *Lion*,' he said. Those two words wounded Nightingale more than he thought possible. 'You command the *Lion*?'

'I do,' Harrison replied ebulliently. 'I thought you would remember her, Mr Nightingale.'

Nightingale nodded, all that he was capable of. He had not seen the *Lion* since leaving her, invalided from service, after the Nile. He had been glad, when being taken across to another ship that would sail him home, that he could not see the *Lion* through the bundle of bandages around his eyes. He had destroyed her in the hail of fire which rained. He had not anchored her far enough away from the halo of death that the *Orient* became. He had not been able to prevent Lieutenant Leroy Sawyer's death.

Now, her high sides rose above him. Not a scratch marred her hull. Her masts had been refitted and her bowsprit, which had been a measly twig after the Nile, sprouted proudly over the painted figurehead of a roaring lion. No trace of the inferno or the cannonfire remained upon her. She almost seemed new, every remnant of that past scrubbed away and repaired and consigned to the waters of Aboukir Bay. Was that who he was now? Every part of his former life stripped like rotten timber and patched together in a new order?

Harrison scaled the tumblehome ladder with ease. Nightingale nodded for Courtney to follow, but the man lingered, searching his face.

'I did not know,' Courtney whispered. 'If I had known...'

'Go,' Nightingale said. 'I shall be fine.'

The climb took an age. Nightingale had performed this action during battle before, moving against pistol shot and carnage, but each time he set his feet and hands upon the ladder, it felt as if he dragged himself through tar. At last, the gunwale came within grip and he pulled himself up and onto the deck. His legs wobbled, the water suddenly seeming so far below. Above him, the masts towered, little dots of men aloft. The crew crowded the deck as well, heaving the last of the stocks aboard and moving barrels and chests below. Harrison spoke to them jovially.

But, amidst the drama of preparing to set sail, Nightingale felt alone. Around him, the business faded away. The shouts of the officers, directing the working sailors, became screamed orders; the bump and clatter of the barrels transformed into the rumble of guns; the stationary set of the ship changed into her imprisonment, staring at the flaring aura of the *Orient*. And down the deck, the puddles of water darkened into bloody pools, trailing back to...

Nightingale's eyes were irresistibly drawn to the foremast. Now, it was sturdy, the iron rings repainted. But six years before, he had knelt there, Leroy's cold hand in his own. He had watched him take his last choking breath before the entire world had gone dark. Six years. Had it only been six years?

'Hiram.'

That voice was not Leroy's. Leroy was dead. Nightingale had allowed him to die.

'Hiram.'

His name came firmer. Nightingale blinked and turned back to the *Lion*, as she was now in 1804. Courtney stood beside him. He had placed a hand on his arm, peering at him with soulful, worried eyes.

'Are you well?' Courtney murmured.

'That's where he died,' Nightingale heard himself say. 'I thought I… I don't know what I thought.'

Courtney stared at him, searching his face. 'Are you coming below? Captain Harrison and Lieutenant Appleton are waiting.'

'Appleton?'

'The acting first lieutenant. We were just introduced to him. Are you… Are you all right?'

Nightingale did not remember that. 'I don't… I don't know what has come over me, Arthur. I'm sorry. I don't think that I can come below. I can't…'

'I shall inform Captain Harrison,' Courtney said decisively. 'You stay here. I should have asked him about this ship first. I did not mean for you to see this.'

Nightingale could only stand, frozen, as Courtney disappeared below in search of Captain Harrison. He pressed himself to the gunwale as if the deck was still flooded with debris and corpses. He could feel his arms shaking as he clung to the rail, his palms sweating. He had conquered these fears, he told himself. Though he knew they could not entirely be lost, he had prayed they had ebbed away like the receding tide. But the waters swept over him again, all the colder and all the more forceful for being absent for so long. He had once commanded men such as those on the deck, giving him strange looks and moving around him as if he were an invalid. All he could do now was to try and not weep.

Courtney re-emerged, a rock in the growing storm. He steered Nightingale away from the sailors and beneath the eaves of the raised poop deck. Leroy had once stood beside him at the nearby helm, his last moments alive.

'Return to the shore,' Courtney ordered. 'Go home. I'm sorry that you had to be here. I wish I could return with you but I must stay, you know that.'

Nightingale nodded. He wanted to reach out and touch Courtney, prove to himself that he was truly there and he was not another phantom, but he could not do that here. 'It is not your fault,' he said, voice thin. 'I thought that I had recovered. I thought this was behind me.'

'There is no shame in it,' Courtney insisted. 'Tell me how to help you.'

Nightingale forced himself to smile, touched at Courtney's care, even through the unspoken tension between them. He loved him, with all his heart, so much that it started to turn to pain. 'Just be careful,' he managed. 'Please. Come home to me.'

Courtney blinked. The issue of Courtney's future – professional, romantic, social – flickered before them. 'Of course,' Courtney said.

Insisting to Courtney that he should apologise to Harrison on his behalf, Nightingale descended down to the launch again. He wrapped his arms about himself, staring ahead at the distant docks. He knew Courtney would be watching him depart but he could not make himself turn around and see him there on the deck.

The shadow of the *Lion* still followed him through the docks and back into Portsmouth. It did not cease even as he took the carriage to Haywood Hall and shut the door of his bedroom behind him. He stood for a long while with his back pressed to the wood, breathing through a shaking throat. The anchor around his neck had returned. He felt the weight of it, threatening to drag him back down into the cradle of fire that he had worked so relentlessly to claw his way out of. He tried to stop it but the more he wrestled, the heavier it became.

As sudden as it had felt, he knew, truly, that there was no abruptness about it. The seeds had always been there, and recently, they had begun to bloom. Doubts had festered. Questions had plagued him. He had not confronted the issues, as he had vowed to do in Trinidad. The result of such ignorance broiled within him now.

And he knew where the kernel of it lay. He had not been able to turn and look at Courtney on the deck of the *Lion*. He had not been able to face seeing him in the place where Leroy had once stood.

Chapter Five: The Fleet

19 January 1805, south-east of Corsica

For the third morning in a row, Courtney had been awoken to the sound of brawling in the mess deck. Throughout the first nights, he had dismissed it, thinking it must simply be rats or one of Harrison's menagerie of animals: the 'mania' he had referred to in Portsmouth. When the scuffling and harsh words interrupted the early hours of the morning watch, a time where the men should have been seeing to their cleaning, he had been on the verge of rising and threatening them all with a lashing, but Lieutenant Ralph Appleton had time and again beaten him to it. The man never seemed to sleep or come off duty.

The broken hours of sleep did not help the quagmire in Courtney's mind. He had had no time to organise affairs on the island, not responding to any of the notes that came to the cottage and only briefly mentioning them to Mr and Mrs Woods, the couple who had helped raise him as a child, without revealing their author. He should have talked of them to Nightingale, he knew, but it would uncover notions and grievances that he could not stir up and simply abandon. Courtney had seen Nightingale's reaction to the *Lion*. He would not give him more reason to suffer.

Instead, he suffered himself, giving up any chance of rest and sitting in the empty wardroom. Captain Harrison had offered him the freedom of the great cabin, but Courtney had refused. He had spent his career, from forecastle man to lieutenant, thinking envious things about the men who berthed in better places than himself, so had chosen the empty cabin of the absent Lieutenant Oakley.

However, four weeks into the journey, he felt useless within the *Lion*'s walls. As a volunteer onboard, he had no true, dictated place and so did not have to adhere so thoroughly to the four-hour watch structure, but life on a British warship had a rigid familiarity. Now, like clockwork, Harrison's steward, an elderly man named Gainsborough who was as morose as his captain was merry, looked into the room. Courtney interpreted his mumble as asking if he required anything. He could never accustom himself to the business of servants, but Harrison had been insistent on Gainsborough aiding him. The steward disappeared and returned soon afterwards with toasted cheese and black, charred coffee, neither of which appealed to Courtney. He had no energy to argue, though, so ate and drank with a grimace.

Lieutenant Appleton, as expected, already manned the upper gun deck when Courtney entered. Courtney thought about avoiding him and heading up the companion-ladder, but chose to rise above his awkwardness around the lieutenant. The lieutenant was younger than him by some years, fair-haired and handsome, and Courtney would not let his youthful attitude bother him. Appleton gave Courtney a cursory glance, barely moving to allow him to stand at his side.

'Good morning, Lieutenant,' Courtney offered.

'Good morning, Commander,' Appleton said tonelessly.

'The men were boisterous again this morning,' Courtney said, not knowing what else to utter.

'I reprimanded them,' Appleton replied simply, almost as if he took Courtney's comment as a personal insult. Courtney went to say more, only for Appleton to bawl, 'Mr Bowles! All possessions stowed with your hammock, please! And take that cat back to its proper home below!'

'Yes, sir,' came the young man's distant answer, somewhere in the depths of the long gun deck, a far greater span than that of the *Scylla* or *Lysander*. Courtney wondered how Appleton had spied him from so far away. But, true to his order, Bowles hurried past them, ginger cat about his shoulders. He held a ball of string which the animal kept batting.

'The cat is another of Captain Harrison's menagerie?' Courtney asked Appleton.

'Yes,' Appleton said curtly. 'Sometimes they distract the men. I know this crew's offences well. They'll try anything if they can. Lieutenant Martin will confirm that.'

Martin had hardly said a word to Courtney either. But Courtney knew Appleton's trick: proving to him how familiar he was with the crew and their quirks. He had been guilty of doing such a thing to his own superior officers. In any case, he was saved from replying by the sound of boots descending the companion-ladder. Harrison appeared, Mr Fitzroy nestled on his shoulder. Courtney had recognised Fitzroy, the capuchin monkey from Trinidad, and had been surprised it was still alive.

'Good morning, Mr Appleton,' Harrison greeted. 'Good morning, Mr Courtney. How is everything this morning?'

'Fine, Captain,' Appleton responded, surprising Courtney that he did not mention the ongoing disturbances. 'Mr Bowles will be back presently. He is stowing the cat below.'

'Hephaestus, I assume, not the cat o' nine tails.'

'Yes, sir,' Appleton said without a trace of humour in his voice or face. Courtney felt his cheeks warm at the discomfort.

Harrison did not seem to mark any issue. He cast his eye towards where the men had ceased their cleaning and stowing of bags. With Appleton at his side, he grasped his hands behind his back and walked along the deck. Courtney followed. They had been weeks at sea and he was yet to remember many of the men's names. It was unlike him; he prided himself on knowing the individuality of each sailor, his strengths and his talents. But it had been a long while since he had served on a vessel as large as the *Lion*. Her complement was for six hundred men, more than double that of the *Scylla* and the *Lysander*.

Appleton was the one who whispered names to Harrison as they inspected the cleanliness of the deck. Harrison smiled and nodded. They passed the eighteen-pounders of the upper gun deck, partially covered by the mess tables which had been pulled down in readiness for breakfast. The timbers had been swabbed and brushed, but even Courtney could see the marks of messed powder and damp patches of grog on the floor. Appleton's eye kept drawing to the smears, but Harrison either did not notice or gave it no mind. When Bowles returned, missing the tomcat, Appleton started to reprimand him, only for Harrison to step in, his grin still present.

'It is no matter, Lieutenant Appleton,' Harrison dismissed. 'I assume Hephaestus is settled?' he asked the young sailor.

Bowles frowned. 'Heph— Sir?'

'The little tom.'

'Oh. Yes, sir. In the cable-tier, sir. Catching rats, sir.'

'Very good. Lieutenant Appleton, I believe the men have done good work. Inform the bosun to pipe them to their breakfast, please.'

'Yes, sir,' Appleton replied.

Jasper Baker, the bosun who had arrived to them near Toulon, had already been loitering about the men as he had taken it upon himself to do as if he were their master-at-arms searching for misdemeanour. He had seemed friendly enough when not reprimanding the crew – he had been one of the only officers, petty or not, to not look Courtney up and down as if judging him against Oakley's worth – but Courtney would not have wanted to be a man under his rattan cane. Courtney was surprised that Appleton too acted as though he feared receiving a strike from it. He gave the orders to Baker tersely, looking at him askance.

As Baker's pipe blew, Courtney dodged the hurrying men who only stopped to give him a brief salute. Harrison signalled to him from the companion-ladder.

'Come and join me on deck, Mr Courtney,' he said. 'Lieutenant Martin will want a second, and third, pair of eyes on our trim.'

The sky, from a firm blue, had turned to a murky grey. A growing breeze ushered heavy clouds in from the north. Lieutenant Christian Martin occupied the deck, watching the heavens. He had been the most junior of the lieutenants before the first lieutenant, Oakley, had become ill and departed the ship. Now, the hierarchy had been shaken and, in the way of Appleton, Martin had an acting command. Below him, the oldest midshipman, Simmonds, had been bumped into the job as third. On deck, Martin had the topsails and courses set. Harrison, observing the weather, ordered a reef in the topsails, then wandered over to the binnacle to inspect the compass and barometer.

'It has been rising and dropping,' he said to Courtney. 'We shall have a storm on our hands soon. Perhaps that will be for our benefit. It might chase the French back into Toulon.'

The *Lion*'s destination had been the southern French port of Toulon, where Lord Nelson had Admiral Villeneuve's fleet under blockade, but upon arrival, she had found the harbour empty of any vessels, French or British, aside from a handful of sloops. Only a day or so earlier, the French had slipped through the British net and put to sea – with Nelson firmly on their tails. Now, the *Lion* searched the Tyrrhenian Sea for any sightings of the two fleets.

'Where do you suppose the French have gone, sir?' Courtney asked Harrison.

'With Spain in war with us also, I would say that Villeneuve aims to combine his blockaded fleets and join with the Spanish. Their rendezvous point, however, could be anywhere.'

The *Lion*'s head pointed towards Sardinia. Beyond the island, the northern coast of Africa loomed. Bonaparte had already attempted to take Egypt once. This very ship had taken part in the crippling of his fleet at anchor in Aboukir Bay. The thought of returning to the mouth of the Nile drew Courtney's mind to Nightingale. He had been unhappy with how he had left the man who had obviously been holding himself together after unexpectedly setting foot again on the *Lion*. He regretted separating from Nightingale whilst staying in Portsmouth, but it had felt a necessity. Harrison's offer had driven a wedge into Courtney's stomach and he did not know what to do. Soon, he would have to speak to Nightingale about it – but not now, when Nightingale was in pain.

The idea of not helping him through it wounded Courtney almost as deeply.

'Do you then, Commander Courtney?' Harrison suddenly asked. Courtney blinked and realised he had been staring out into the blue sea that surrounded them.

'I'm sorry, sir?'

'You have been quite distracted, Commander. I hope the French will bring your attention back.'

'Apologies, sir.'

Harrison smiled. 'I was not reprimanding you, Mr Courtney. All I asked of you was: do you believe the French will invade England?'

Courtney did not know why Harrison, his senior officer, asked such a thing of him. 'Yes, sir,' he still said. 'If they have the chance, they shall. I was lately at Boulogne, as part of the squadron which tried to destroy the fortifications being built there, perhaps in readiness for the Armée l'Angleterre.' As he always did, Courtney stumbled over the French language. 'The French have already defeated Austria, occupied much of Italy and made agreements with Spain. I see no reason why Napoleon wouldn't want to add England to his empire.'

'I agree,' Harrison said. 'But we shall fight them wherever they sail and land.'

It was a situation Courtney should have felt familiar in. Since he had been a lad, running from home, he had battled the French, and the Spanish, on the high seas. He had seen his first action as part of a convoy protecting British trade and from then had progressed from forecastle man to junior officer and up to first lieutenant. Now approaching thirty, he knew he had spent more time on the water than on land. Yet, as he supervised the deck that winter's day, he had barely felt more out of his depth. He tried to tell himself it was the unfamiliar sensation of sailing upon a ship of the line. Both the *Scylla* and the *Lysander*, upon which he had served his most memorable commissions, had been below that vaunted rating. Here, upon the weather deck with two decks of guns below him atop the orlop and the hold, he could not accustom himself to the height above the waves and the monumental mass of her. A small town floated below his feet – and they sailed towards a whole fleet of these vessels.

That town, he knew, had had its foundations rattled with the changing of the officers and Courtney could already see the upset in its upper works: the brawling and the general feeling of laziness on deck. He observed the men talking familiarly as they worked, some of the waisters lingering with their hands in their pockets. Martin said nothing but Courtney could not bear the sight. He found himself barking a rebuke at a gang of them as Appleton joined the watch when Martin went below. Appleton, at least, did not follow such a bizarre approach as his fellow lieutenant, instead taking up Courtney's scolding.

Courtney occupied a strange space with his rank, but he chose to stand on as the bells rang out. Appleton updated the logboard and, after doing so, decided to adjust Martin's trim, despite Harrison's approval of it. In the light airs, the topsails were double-reefed. This time, Courtney raised his head to watch the men high above in the tops, little dots against the bright sun. The mizzen-topsail yard came down as the halliards were let go, the spar dropping onto the cap with more speed than Courtney would have liked. That was the overall impression he received from the following operation: everything a little sloppy, a little jagged whilst they hauled out reef-tackles and steadied the yard before the topmen laid out upon it to reef the canvas.

Quite without realising, Courtney had retreated to the lee side of the deck and handed the weather side to Appleton. He did not know why he did; he outranked the younger man and even if he had retained the title of lieutenant, his seniority in experience would still place him above Appleton. But the proxy title of 'captain' meant very little without a ship to command.

Courtney wanted to ask Appleton more about the disturbances that morning, but the observance of noon brought the midshipmen to the deck, alongside Harrison. The *Lion* carried ten midshipmen, now technically nine with the raising of Simmonds: some of them still red-cheeked, wide-eyed boys on their first vessel, some of them approaching the age where they would take their lieutenant's examination. Mr Midshipman Fox was the youngest, aboard his first ship at the age of thirteen. He stood slightly separate from the rest of the berth, turning his navigation book in his hands.

'Commander Courtney,' Harrison said. 'Would you grace us with your presence? I wondered if you would be so kind as to support the young gentlemen with their readings.'

'Yes, sir,' Courtney had no choice but to say.

Courtney's time as a midshipman had been short and tangled. He had experienced hellish conditions ever since then, but few quite matched the practice of navigation and noon sightings. Even as a junior lieutenant, he had struggled to grasp the concepts and had often forgotten his schooling, leaving it to the master, the true expert upon any ship. But now he tried his hardest to follow along with Harrison.

To locate the position of a vessel, speed – dictated through heaving the lead – and calculating leeway were essential, but these could be inaccurate at the best of times. Measurement through astronomical navigation could be far more precise, only this came with complex mathematics which Courtney had always detested. Courtney bent down to help some of the mids with the sextant, hastily setting the shades on it before they could blind themselves in the sun's light. Together, they aligned the sun in the telescopic sights and then dropped it to the horizon, ensuring the reflected image of the celestial body sat squarely in the centre, thus finding its angle of altitude. He allowed Harrison to guide them through the subsequent calculations to discover the latitude.

With aid of the new chronometer Harrison had applied for, and the meticulous tables and logs from Master Moore and Appleton, and the not-quite-as-meticulous account from Martin, the mids stumbled through longitude calculations, using the prime meridian at Greenwich as their base point. Fox somehow managed to place the ship somewhere in the wilds of Canada which led to snickering and teasing from Mr Midshipman Ramsey and a gang of others whom he encouraged. Harrison said nothing about the torment, even when Fox morosely resorted to observing through the far simpler spyglass. Courtney left him to it, but was unable to stop himself making a sharp remark to Ramsey to quieten down.

The rest of the noon observation involved the mids scribbling in their logs and journals whilst Harrison chatted familiarly to Courtney about his career as a midshipman himself. Courtney did not relish the casual talk, though none of the young gentlemen seemed to realise anything out of the ordinary.

'Sir,' Fox suddenly said, lowering his spyglass. 'What is that?'

'What is—' Harrison began, only to be interrupted by a cry from a topman aloft.

'Boat ahoy!' the man called. 'Forward of the starboard beam!'

The mids peered curiously to starboard. Without a glass, Courtney could only see a small mass on the waves. Before Harrison had a chance to examine it properly, Appleton hurried to the poop deck with his own assessment. 'It's abandoned, sir,' he said. 'The hull is shredded to pieces.'

The boat could not have been entirely decrepit for it bobbed past the *Lion*, still partially afloat. As it came closer, Courtney saw it was a cutter, around twenty-four feet in length, and painted not in the white, yellow, and black of the Royal Navy, but a dull, chipped blue.

'French,' Appleton commented. 'Permission to train a great gun on her, Captain?'

Harrison shook his head. 'We'll not waste the powder, Lieutenant. We shall have ample time for the lads to practise if we are to join the blockading squadron.'

Appleton opened his mouth to say more, then seemed to think better of it.

Soon, however, other wreckage stole his attention. Flecks of black transformed into ruined spars and broken planks, ferried forlornly along by the waves. An entire foreyard split from the cloud of debris and had to be knocked away from the *Lion* by men hanging out the gun ports with pikes.

'Perhaps we have missed the battle,' Harrison said with a touch of envy in his voice. Courtney did not know how he felt about the suggestion. In his heart, he understood that officers should not long for conflict, but he had to admit that the resumption of the war with Napoleon had given direction back to his life. For a man like himself, a grand naval victory was the only chance for promotion and for that hallowed post rank. How easily such a thing could lead to recklessness.

But within the day, another call came from the tops. Courtney had been below, writing a note to his sister, Jane Wainwright, but the cry had him hurrying up from the wardroom. Night fell early in the short days of the winter, the sky turning purple and dull stars piercing the clear heavens. Across the sea, though, as plain as a rising dawn, lights burnt. Even from a distance, Courtney could make out the glow of ships' lanterns and the illumination of their stern gallery windows. By his count, there were at least four, with more certainly ahead of the rear vessels.

Appleton, who apparently had not left the deck since that morning, was at the forecastle. In the darkness, signal flags would be invisible so a system of lights had been rigged to be hoisted into the forestays and at the signal halliards at the stern. Courtney watched as a ghostly blue glow appeared above his head.

'Is Lieutenant Martin about?' Appleton asked when he noticed Courtney.

'I'm not sure. We have found the Toulon fleet?'

'Would you fetch Lieutenant Martin, send him to deck, then I shall inform the captain.'

Courtney dismissed the fact that Appleton had ignored his question. 'I shall remain on deck, Lieutenant, whilst you inform Captain Harrison.'

Appleton barely reacted, but Courtney could tell he was unhappy with the suggestion. He wanted to say something about providing additional assistance to the *Lion* in a time when she needed the extra hands and officers, yet stopped himself. Appleton wished for a response of that attitude.

'Very well,' the lieutenant said. 'Keep your eyes on the men.'

Courtney tried to pay it no mind. He had been doing nothing but keeping his eyes on them, following their discomforting behaviour. He looked down the deck where the men and Fox, the midshipman on watch, lingered, some of them watching the approaching lights and most of them within earshot of him and Appleton. Courtney swallowed his pride. Ahead, the sternmost ship's aft lights were flashing in recognition of the *Lion*'s signal. It would take some time for the *Lion* to fully catch up with the fleet but a single ship was faster than a squadron of them. Courtney observed them as the *Lion* approached, anticipation building in his chest. The British vessels sailed on a southerly course, their heads directed towards Sicily. He wondered if they had seen any sign of the French fleet, or if the *Lion*'s observation of the French wreckage would be a key clue in where the enemy had disappeared to.

As Courtney watched the distance slowly close, he thought of how if anyone was to know, then Lord Nelson would. His stomach tightened at the idea of Nelson being amongst that squadron ahead. He had never met the man but had followed the reports of the admiral's grand victories at the Nile, Cape St Vincent, and Copenhagen. The years had already moulded

Nelson into an impressive figure whom England had pinned their hopes upon – and now Courtney sailed in his wake.

Harrison was still chewing on the last of his dinner as he arrived on deck with Appleton. He gave a beaming smile at the sight of the ships. 'With the approaching storm,' he said, 'I had my doubts of finding the fellows. Let us pray the French are as easy to locate.'

Courtney was not so sure. They had found the British because of knowledge of their own fleet and the locales they frequented. The French, as Harrison had said earlier in the day, could be anywhere. Intelligence from Nelson's ships, as the *Lion* gradually took her place, did not sound any more hopeful. Nelson indeed aimed for Sicily in order to probe for more information at the port of Palermo, but beyond that, Admiral Villeneuve's movements were the work of guesses and questions without answers.

Yet, with the *Lion* welcomed into the bosom of the British fleet, Courtney felt the first flickers of something other than bewilderment. He stayed on deck, no longer looking at the stern lights of the ships but at the massive, gorgeous beasts, sailing with courses and topsails set. He had counted eleven within sight, plus a forward set of two frigates which lingered on the distant horizon. Many of them were of the *Lion's* ilk: third-rates of sixty-four to eighty guns, great ships of the line that formed the valiant heart of the Royal Navy. For the past few years, Courtney's only experience with them in this mass had been looking at them laid up in harbours. Now, he was amongst them, on a vessel which had already fought famously at the Nile and which Nightingale had given so much of his life to.

He wished Nightingale was with him so he could see the elegance of the fleet as it cut through the black waters. The moonlight bled into the taut canvas and reflected off the iron hoops of masts and pulleys. Each vessel moved with the ease of hundreds of men who knew her intimately. But one eclipsed them all, and Courtney's breath caught when he first saw her. The *Victory*, Nelson's flagship, could be distinguished by her three decks, towering above even the *Lion*. She commanded the British squadron as it pierced through the eastern Mediterranean, the symbol of all that awed Courtney about the Royal Navy. He had not joined for the pomp and the bluster, but for an escape out of his poverty-stricken childhood, the same as many sailors. These ships, though, had given him homes and had become markers of his journey through life.

This was all he knew.

And now, with Bonaparte threatening Europe and potentially England, Courtney thought he headed to the heart of the coming conflict.

Chapter Six: Shifting Fortunes

Nightingale had spent weeks feeling as though he stood upon a cliff edge. The last few years had witnessed him climbing the slow rise, leaving behind the grief and turmoil of his past, shedding much of which had weighed him down. It had been a perilous ascent and he had stumbled a few times, but overall, he thought he could look down and see how far away his troubles had seemed. Now, one moment, one single hour, had churned the dust up again, getting into his lungs, making him teeter on the rim of all that he had built.

He feared to fall, so he had barely taken a step, barely put himself into a situation where that distant ground could rush up to him. Louisa had noticed – how could she not, when Nightingale had sequestered himself away in his wing of the manor, making all of his interactions by writing? He had appeared for luncheons and suppers, sometimes had toured the gardens, but with barely a word. His head had turned once more into a quagmire, thoughts and ideas spiralling, and to invite any other conversation seemed far too loud.

The sword he had extracted from the attic rested against the wall in his dressing room. He spent many hours gazing upon it with a pen in his hand, writing and re-writing the document he knew he could not ignore any longer. As an officer in the Royal Navy, notions of death had never been far from his mind: it could come not only from pistolshot and cannonfire, but from disease and accident and fire, every waking second fringed with danger. He had never fretted about it snuffing out his years, only those of the people around him. Now, he had to confront it and, infinitely more terrible, the thought of Courtney's.

Even the whisper of it turned his blood cold. Neatening the clauses on the sheet of paper before him brought the images over him like a continual high tide.

He nearly jumped out of his skin when he felt a hand upon his shoulder. He had not heard Louisa enter.

'My dear,' he breathed. 'You startled me.'

'My apologies,' she said. 'There is a gentleman to see you. I've had him wait in the parlour downstairs. What are you writing?' He could feel her eyes moving over the paper before him. 'Your will,' she continued softly. 'Should we not speak of that together?'

'We shall. I simply wanted to put some of my thoughts to paper.'

He knew she must have read the item he had just noted down, but she said nothing more about it. After more than twenty years of marriage, she understood when to press and when to retreat. Nightingale was aware he had never been the ideal husband, yet he and Louisa had found their own path, unfettered by convention. This will, however, could dislodge some of that work. He wanted to explain, but words would not come to him – not yet.

'Shall I tell him that you are occupied?' she asked, voice without a hitch.

'Do I know him?' Nightingale questioned. He wanted to know whether he, whoever he was, was aware of his background and shifting fortunes.

'You do. Please, Hiram. He has come a long way.'

Nightingale relented, taking Louisa's arm as she led him downstairs and into the parlour. A tall figure stood by the fireplace which blazed in the January chill. He was dressed in a lieutenant's uniform: a blue frock coat with white waistcoat, gold-brocaded hat beneath his arm. His fair hair was tied in a neat tail, every stitch of his clothing brushed to fastidious perfection. When he turned at Nightingale's entrance, it took Nightingale a moment to recognise him.

'Mr Smythe!' he greeted, joy flooding his chest – to see the boy again and to note the lieutenant's rank he now had. He had been a shy fifteen-year-old midshipman on the *Scylla* when Nightingale had first met him. No longer was he a boy, Nightingale corrected himself, but a young man.

'Captain Nightingale!' Smythe said, and did not amend the title. 'My apologies for springing upon you unannounced. I was passing this way on my journey down to Spithead. I am to join my first ship commissioned as a lieutenant!'

'Congratulations, Lieutenant. I am so very pleased for you. Louisa, my dear, would you fetch the port?'

'Oh, no, I could not, Captain,' Smythe said. 'I have to be with my ship soon and my health has been drunk so often I feel as though I've caused irreparable damage to my friends and family.'

Nightingale smiled. 'What is your ship?'

'The *Reliant*, sir. She's a thirty-six-gun frigate, Captain Newman. I am her second lieutenant.'

'That is wonderful news, Mr Smythe.'

Smythe nodded, squeezing his hat beneath his arm. The old captain in Nightingale wanted to tell him not to make creases, but he no longer commanded Smythe. The last time he had seen him had been at Jane's wedding. 'Is… Is Commander Courtney here?' Smythe asked.

Nightingale's first reaction almost made the smile fade from his face. There could have been a thousand reasons for Smythe assuming Courtney would be with him, but Nightingale always leapt to the most damning conclusion. 'No,' he said, schooling his voice as ever. 'He is serving on a seventy-four.'

'Oh. How fortuitous for him. I only wished to convey my thanks to him. He helped me ever so greatly on the *Scylla* and on the *Lysander*, not only teaching me what I would need for my lieutenant's examination but… Well, providing a model for me. Commander Courtney and yourself have been great ideals.'

Affection rolled through Nightingale. He had not realised Courtney had done so much for Smythe – and neither had he thought it possible to love the man any more, but he kept finding more reasons. 'You are more than welcome, Mr Smythe,' he managed to respond. 'I am pleased that your efforts have borne fruit. Long may it last.'

When he had safely sent Smythe off to his ship, Nightingale lingered by the window and watched the lieutenant disappear down Portsdown Hill. He had never desired children, but a career of commanding ships and tutoring midshipmen and junior officers had given him a string of simulated fatherhoods. He could only wish their journeys would be smoother than his had been. With that thought, the old chill crept over him again. He had left that life behind, yet thorns of it were still embedded in his flesh and heart. Seeing the *Lion*, repainted and re-manned but ever the same ship, was the symbol of it all.

'He shall be fine,' Louisa whispered from behind him with a hand on his shoulder. 'The dear soul thinks the world of you. I pray you can see that inside yourself again.'

Nightingale laid his own palm over her knuckles and felt the ring that bound him to her. 'I am fine,' he insisted softly.

'I know you, Hiram. I told you not to shut me out of your mind.' She paused. 'He…will return.'

'I am sure the *Reliant* will treat him well.'

'I…I did not mean Mr Smythe.'

But Nightingale could not bring Courtney's name to his lips, not now. He could not broach the sensitive subject with Louisa. 'I am returning to my will,' he said, extracting his hand from hers. 'Inform me if anything else requires my assistance.'

He did not expect more but, as if the first emergence from his solitude had provoked the world to turn its eyes back upon him, Louisa again appeared before the afternoon was over. Nightingale looked up, resisting the urge to make an irritated comment. The look on her face, and the note in her hand, stopped him. 'What is it?' he said instead.

'I'm sorry, Hiram, I would have waited until you came down later, but I thought it best to show this to you as soon as possible.'

Nightingale frowned and took the note. It was folded crudely, without a wax seal to hold it together, and the thin paper meant he could decipher the writing on the inside. His name and address had been scrawled upon the front in an unsteady hand. Standing and walking to the candle, he opened it and held the spidery handwriting to the light, looking over the short sentences and spelling errors. Louisa lingered but he did not tell her to leave.

Mr Hiram Nightingale, the words said,

> *Our sorries for disturbing you in this way. But we did not know who else to tell. We have had trouble. We have had notes from an unknown person. They have been sent to Artie's cottage. Please, we ask, can you help us?*
>   *Mr and Mrs Woods, the Fisherman's Catch, Ryde, Isle of Wight*

A cold hand gripped Nightingale's spine. He re-read the desperately scribbled note and tried to make sense of it. He had visited Courtney's cottage some months before and nothing had seemed unfriendly. Everyone who Courtney had introduced him to in his childhood home had been civil. Though Courtney had made a handful of enemies in his career – and not all of them on the opposing side – the island had felt a world apart from that, a place he and Courtney could escape and have their own life, as one. It was why Nightingale's stomach now tied so tightly.

'What is it?' Louisa suddenly asked.

'It is Mr and Mrs Woods.' Nightingale had not spoken to Louisa often of the island and Courtney's cottage. 'They were Arthur's guardians when he and Jane were young. They've been having some trouble.'

'I hope it is not serious.'

'I'm not sure. I must go over there.'

He had made the decision quickly and only realised how drastic it sounded when he saw Louisa's reaction. But she tempered her surprise and said, 'I shall accompany you.'

'No,' he said, perhaps too harshly. 'No,' he repeated, softer. 'I know the island and these people. If Mr and Mrs Woods are endangered, I don't want them to be overwhelmed – and neither you. I don't know what this "trouble" entails.'

'I don't want you to hurt yourself, Hiram.'

'I shan't.' Nightingale forced a smile, though he knew he could not fool Louisa. 'I've commanded ships of war, my dear. I think I can weather this.'

'This is not the same enemy.'

'Perhaps not. I shall be careful nonetheless.'

But he knew, when he left the following day, paying his way on a schooner of a local fisherman he knew, Louisa was still unhappy with him. She had a right to be displeased. She had been loyal to him in her nursing and care, had barely wavered throughout his entire career on the sea when he had been a single moment away from death. Now Courtney was gone, Nightingale experienced some of the worry that she must have felt for him. He had been unfair to her by leaving so suddenly for the Isle of Wight with little explanation, but his desire to support Courtney and his family ate away at him. More and more, he had felt torn between his life in Portsmouth, a life he barely felt settled in after departing from the seas, and his new, budding days with Courtney. He detested that Louisa was caught in the middle – not her presence, but the pain that could await her.

He knew he should have been honest with her.

That day would have to come, but when arriving in the port of Cowes, he set such frets aside and took a coach to the Fisherman's Catch. The little tavern, nestled at the edge of the hamlet of Ryde, had been a frequent haunt for himself and Courtney. Courtney had spent much time there as a youth, under the care of the owners, Mr and Mrs Woods. His parents had often been absent, meaning he mostly had had to raise himself and Jane, his younger sister. The Catch had been a refuge for them.

On Louisa's insistence, Nightingale had brought Rylance, his loyal steward, with him. The man had been with him as a captain's servant and had never parted from him since. He seemed to already be looking for dangers and hurried to open the door of the Catch before Nightingale could. 'I think we shall be safe here, Rylance,' Nightingale said.

'Never know, sir,' came the man's response.

Heeding Rylance's words, Nightingale glanced around the tavern as they entered. A cluster of men sat by the fire, tankards of ale between them. They were deep in conversation and barely looked up at Nightingale's presence. Nightingale could not shift the impression of stepping into a world where he did not belong. It was true that he had spent summers on the island as a child before his mother had left for Portugal, but they had stayed in a plot of their own, away from the locals who his father had often disparaged. Courtney's presence had always eased what he saw as his own jagged impression but, without Courtney, he felt a stranger.

At the bar, Mrs Frances Woods nearly dropped the mug she was holding and hurried around to greet Nightingale. Her round cheeks flushed and her greying curls nearly fell from her bonnet as she curtseyed to him. Nightingale reddened.

'You don't have to do that, ma'am,' he said, not for the first time, but Mrs Woods was already speaking.

'Mr Nightingale,' she rushed, 'thank you for coming. I am so very grateful.'

'You do not need to thank me. I could not leave you and your husband to deal with this alone.'

'With Artie gone, we didn't know who else to turn to. He said he would arrange things but was called away before he could.'

Nightingale paused. 'Arthur knew of the notes?'

'He did. They began to arrive only a few weeks before he departed. They startled him.'

Nightingale did not know how to react. It explained some of Courtney's behaviour: his malaise, his frustration, his reticence around Nightingale. Perhaps it even explained his hesitation when they had spoken of Miss Sandham and Harrison's offer. But why had Courtney not spoken to him of the notes? It must have been a weight upon him.

'We did not wish to disturb you, Mr Nightingale,' Mrs Woods continued, 'but the notes kept arriving. Owen and I… Well, we fear—'

'You did not disturb me, ma'am. I was happy to make the crossing. Do you have the notes? Can I see them?'

A flicker of worry crossed Mrs Woods's face. She looked around at the patrons but all were still engrossed in their own affairs. 'Here,' she said, beckoning to Nightingale. 'I have them in our lodgings.'

She guided Nightingale out of the common area and through a door to the private rooms. 'We have only two vacancies,' she explained. 'The lads have been training nearby.'

'Training?'

'For the local Sea Fencibles. There have been other upsets aside from the notes.'

Nightingale had sometimes seen the Portsmouth Sea Fencibles at the docks: an assortment of local fishermen, merchant skippers, colliers and sailors who manned the coasts of England to ward off enemy ships. They were not as rigid and formidable a force as Cornwallis's Royal Navy fleet in the Channel or Lord Keith in the Downs, but many of the small vessels were armed and the men ready to fight, work in the signal towers, and defend the shorelines.

'Here,' Mrs Woods said, opening a door into a cramped parlour area that led into a small bedroom. Nightingale felt he was invading her privacy so waited as she entered the bedroom and searched through a cabinet. He looked around at the little space with its sparse furnishings. One picture sat on the wall above a ragged armchair. He stepped nearer to observe it closer, seeing it was a pencil drawing of a young boy and girl, dressed in clothing too large for them. He thought he recognised the black curls of the lad and the wild untamed hair of the girl.

'This is Arthur and Jane,' he said as Mrs Woods re-entered. For a moment, the worry left her face with her smile.

'Yes. That's them when they were children. My husband is quite the artist.'

'Arthur said he used to stay here often.'

'He did. His and Jane's parents were…neglectful and could be harsh. When they were not in the debtor's cells, they drank and could barely look after themselves, let alone two young children. Owen and I were happy to care for Artie and Jane. Then, as they got older, Artie took Jane to their mother's brother and eventually left for the sea.'

'The *Grampus*,' Nightingale said. 'He told me of her.'

'Artie always liked to follow his own way. I'm glad that he found his way back here.'

'As am I.'

'I do pray that these messages won't stop that,' Mrs Woods said and looked down at the paper in her hand. Sighing, she offered the small collection over to Nightingale. They had been folded over and he barely wanted to open them up and read the writing. He took a breath and did so. He did not know what he expected – perhaps a demand for money, perhaps for some other service, perhaps a bribe – but he found seven words.

Wives and sweethearts. May they never meet.

The same message was scrawled on each of the notes. Nightingale recognised the missive. It was the traditional toast taken on a Saturday in the King's Navy and its pithy reply. Nightingale had never found it very comical or witty – and he certainly did not now.

As it ever did, Nightingale's mind leapt to the worst of the interpretations. This time, though, he could not see any other way of reading it. Many sailors had wives, and those same sailors often had sweethearts. Nightingale was no different, although the sex of his sweetheart was different to the loves of the other mariners. His thoughts went immediately to Louisa. She knew of the direction of his heart, although... Nightingale swallowed. She did not yet know about Courtney.

And Courtney had tried to shield these notes from Nightingale's knowledge. Did he wish to protect him? Was he ashamed of them? His heart hurt for Courtney, having to bear this and then ship aboard the *Lion* without concluding the troubles.

'Have you seen who delivers these messages?' Nightingale asked.

Mrs Woods shook her head. 'Their delivery is random, and they always come from the post-boy. The sender never delivers them himself. I say "himself" but...I don't know. I would like to think a lady would not do such a thing.'

Nightingale nodded. 'Has the post-boy been questioned?'

'It is our Walter, mine and Owen's ward. He delivers to many houses in the area.'

'I shall talk to him,' Nightingale said, 'and then I shall go the cottage.'

'We cannot trouble you so, Mr Nightingale. You have your own life.'

A life, Nightingale thought, which had recently split at the seams a little. It had not been entirely the *Lion*'s reappearance that had struck the hammer-blow, but a slow, creeping force that made him doubt his own past and present. He wanted direction again. He wanted a purpose in a burning world.

'I have informed my wife I shall be staying here,' he said with a strained smile. 'After your care to Arthur and your hospitality towards me, I would be very glad to help you. And please, call me "Hiram".'

With the messages stowed in his dunnage, Nightingale exited into the common area. Rylance had joined the men by the fire, a tankard before him. He leapt to his feet as Nightingale entered but Nightingale waved him down. 'By all means, finish your drink, Rylance,' he said. 'The cottage shall be cold.'

Rylance smiled and sank back into his seat. Nightingale took a chair by the window, looking out into the dark night. He had dined here many times with Courtney, a quaint and homely place away from the cares of the world and the brewing wars on the continent. But, with the presence of the Sea Fencibles and the appearance of these messages, Nightingale realised that no town, no island was untouched by the ugliness of society. He simply hoped Courtney was safe out there, sailing on his old command – safer than he had been, safer than Leroy Sawyer had been.

Nightingale knew he would have to find his way here on the island. Courtney had excluded him from knowledge of the notes for a reason. But Nightingale would not allow an anonymous figure to ruin what they had created here, away from the world, away from frets. Whatever Courtney's decision was when he returned, he vowed to make their home safe.

Chapter Seven: The Watch

29 January 1805

Charlie Bowles could not have been more than twenty years old – he certainly behaved like a seaman on his first cruise, with the fear of the sea and the huge height of the mainmast not yet instilled in him. He barely looked down as he thrust his bare feet into the main t'gallant rigging and scaled the lofty peak. Courtney found his chest tightening and his breath shortening with the scramble between each yard. He had never had a head for these stomach-rolling elevations, but he had always managed it like a young man: blustering and without aching muscles. Now, he was reminded of the time he had climbed with Nightingale on the *Scylla* to view the distant *Fénix*. He had made an unkind remark to Nightingale about his older years: 'You should be careful at your age.'

Perhaps such a comment was currently in Bowles's mind about him.

Courtney knew, as he clambered up, that he did not need to do this. Bowles, a topman, was perfectly capable of making an observation from the masthead. But the alternative was sharing the deck with Lieutenant Appleton and spending another after-noon watch helping the midshipmen. Most of them were onboard because of their fathers' patronage and with little knowledge of weather or navigation between them. The only unconnected member of the number was Fox, and he, as Courtney had seen during their lesson, was the brunt of the others' jests. Harrison had not said a word about it but Courtney had seen the hurt in Fox's eyes.

The masthead loomed above Courtney. He dug into the reserves of his strength and made the final climb, up through onto the highest yard. The past week had been full of gales and dirty weather, so much that the fleet had had heave-to and cease their ever-moving search for the enemy. Now, the dark skies had ebbed and, in the fair winds, the *Lion* had her royals set. Canvas and rope had shielded Courtney's view until he reached the very summit, stabilising himself about the main truck. Only the *Lion*'s pennant flew here, streaming away aft.

Courtney took a breath and ensured his balance was set. Beneath him, around one hundred and eighty feet dropped away to the quarterdeck. Appleton and the men about the waist of the *Lion* were mere dots. Courtney closed his eyes, regretting his glance downwards.

'All right, sir?' Bowles asked. He had one arm casually about the spar, bandana and loose shirt flapping in the breeze.

Courtney swallowed. 'Fine, Mr Bowles. I'm more concerned about the Combined Fleet.'

The Combined Fleet: the potential unification of the Spanish and French ships which yet prowled the Mediterranean. The disappearance of Villeneuve from Toulon had plagued Nelson's squadron and with no definite knowledge of the French admiral's destination, the *Lion* and her sisters had been relentlessly searching the seas around Italy. Now, Courtney looked out across the blue expanse. To the west, somewhere over the horizon, was Palermo, and to the south Messina and the perilous strait waited. Courtney looked that way, seeing the forms of the other British ships in a loose crescent formation. Other topmen would be watching for any sign of their foes.

The only rupture in the flat azure was the squat black shadow of the nearest island. Courtney knew it to be Stromboli. More than two years previously, he had observed the same sight from a far smaller ship, scheming to trap a marauding polacre and rescue the prisoners onboard her. The piratical *Barbarossa* had succumbed to the ash of the volcano. Perhaps her skeleton still sat on the seabed.

If so, she was the only enemy vessel within proximity of the British.

Fighting his disappointment, Courtney clambered back down, leaving Bowles back amongst the other topmen. They were all too occupied to salute or acknowledge Courtney other than to give a look in his direction. Gone were the days, Courtney thought, where he had laboured amidst the cordage and canvas of a ship, always listening out for officers' orders and their roving eyes searching for missteps and disorder.

He jumped back to the deck and found his coat still hanging upon a belaying pin. Appleton, though, was nowhere to be seen. Lieutenant Martin had taken his place, pacing with his fist curled far too tightly about the handle of his sword. He was not the only man armed; each of the warrant and petty officers had their firearms and hand-to-hand weapons close by. Baker prowled with one hand around his rattan starting cane, the other on a dirk in his belt – not a comforting sight for men who feared a bosun's authority. Courtney collected his own cutlass but knew, from his own observations at the top, that the chances of using it were slim.

'Where's Lieutenant Appleton, Mr Martin?' he asked.

'He's with the captain and Master Moore, sir. He asked for you to join them at your convenience.'

Harrison's great cabin, in the way of the rest of the ship, had been cleared and turned out for action, as it had been for the past few days in anticipation of meeting the French. Partitions had been struck down and the eighteen-pounder and thirty-two-pounder guns had been run out to the portholes. In Harrison's cabin, a single table remained on the chequer-board floor, upon which lay a number of charts. Appleton and Moore were in deep discussion when Courtney entered, Harrison watching with his arms crossed over his chest. Fitzroy, the capuchin, perched on the locker by the gallery windows, a chunk of apple in his hand. Moore, a short and stocky Plymouth man in his late middle years, glanced over at Courtney's approach and greeted him with a dip of his head. Appleton turned and gave no such welcome.

'Courtney,' Harrison said, smiling. 'What news from the top?'

'Nothing very favourable, sir,' Courtney replied. 'There are no signs of any enemy vessels.'

'That is hard news. The men have been itching for a fight for almost a week.' He returned to the chart of the Tyrrhenian Sea alongside one of the inked coastline of Egypt. 'We have been speaking of the potential destinations of the French. Mr Moore believes the gales have frightened them back into Toulon and we are chasing phantoms, but Lieutenant Appleton thinks they are headed for Alexandria.'

'Bonaparte is still avid to reclaim Egypt,' Appleton explained. 'Napoleon has long had his eye on Egypt as a place of operation against British interests in the Mediterranean. He has lost his hold there but would, I wager, be eager to gain it again.'

'What we know of Villeneuve's character points to a certain timidity,' Moore countered, 'and these gales are unkind to any man, especially to a French fleet which have been blockaded in port for some time – with detriment to their seamanship. The safety of Toulon would have been too much of a temptation.'

'Lord Nelson believes that the French have Egypt in their sights.' Appleton refused to surrender his argument. 'If there is any man who understands the enemy and their ideas, it is he.'

'What are your thoughts, Commander Courtney?' Harrison asked. 'You have sailed these seas before, I believe.'

The Mediterranean was a frequent location for the Royal Navy. Even though both he and Harrison had been stationed in the Caribbean for some time, surely they had all sailed the Mediterranean Sea in some capacity. 'I agree with Lieutenant Appleton,' Courtney said, surprising himself. He did not miss Appleton quickly raising his eyebrows, before schooling his expression again. 'This very ship battled the French fleet at anchor in Aboukir Bay. Villeneuve was at the Nile and knows the importance of Egypt to his master and his country.'

'There you have it,' Harrison said. 'Let us hope we find them as the *Lion* did before.'

The *Lion* had taken a fierce beating at the Nile, so Nightingale had told Courtney. She had been towed, with great difficulty, into harbour for repairs. Nightingale himself had believed she would not recover from her wounds. But she, and Nightingale, had been patched together, ready for war and grief again.

Courtney's thoughts were interrupted by a knock upon the bulkhead where the partitions had been removed. Harrison glanced up and Courtney was surprised to see Fox there.

'Mr Fox,' Harrison greeted. 'Is there trouble?'

'Uh, no, sir. I mean to say, perhaps, sir.'

Harrison waited but Fox, in the presence of the captain, seemed to have mislaid his tongue. Eventually, he managed to say, 'I have a…petition for you regarding my station, sir.'

'Your station, currently, is to man the ship in anticipation of meeting the enemy.'

But each of the officers in the cabin must have known the chances of that were looking slimmer by the hour. The crew, from captain to powder boy, had been strung out in a manner of high alertness and they were understandably becoming restless, something which had not helped the worrying behaviour Courtney had noticed before. *Cursed*, Courtney thought, and regretted it immediately. Harrison's jest before boarding the ship was infecting his mindset.

'If you permit me, sir,' Appleton said, 'I shall hear Mr Fox's petition.'

'If you think it best, Lieutenant,' Harrison agreed. 'Do not keep him for long, though.'

'Go to the wardroom, Mr Fox,' Appleton said. 'I will be there promptly.'

'I shall accompany you,' Courtney added.

He wondered over his reasons for saying such a thing, especially as Appleton seemed disgruntled to have him at his side.

But as he descended the companion-ladder and walked the upper gun deck, crunching through the sand which had been scattered over the timbers in preparation for battle, he knew why. The men and boys who hung in the doldrums between the order to clear for action and to occupy their stations for battle were still unknown to him. He did not know their names as Appleton did, and they barely knew his. Whereas Appleton, acting Second Lieutenant Martin and acting Third Lieutenant Simmonds had responsibilities for their divisions, Courtney felt only a loose connection to them. That, he knew, was a certain path to disaster. An officer who did not understand his sailors could not inspire loyalty or confidence – and he certainly would not know how to position them in either normal routine or during conflict.

He perched upon a gun carriage as Fox lingered in the cleared wardroom. He was a tall lad for his age but his fair hair still curled boyishly and his face was full of the uncertainty of youth. Men often sent their sons and relations to sea at a very young year, hoping they were on a path to becoming stalwart officers. Courtney wondered if Fox had had any choice in the matter. Appleton observed him silently. He stood where their mess table usually existed, now stowed below to avoid potential splinters if the French were to suddenly appear and blow a hole through their stern windows.

'Mr Fox,' Appleton said. 'What is the meaning of this?'

'Apologies, Lieutenant,' Fox said, twisting his hands before him. 'I know it isn't the best time, sir, but I was wondering, sir… I was…'

'We do not have long, Mr Fox. Find your tongue, please.'

'I was wondering if I might move my berth from the gunroom and to the older midshipmen's space in the after cockpit.'

Appleton paused. 'It is not at the behest of a midshipman to change his berth, his watch bill or station. That is a mark of your experience at sea and was decided for you.'

'No, sir. Sorry, sir.'

'What are your reasons, Mr Fox?'

'My reasons, sir?'

'Yes. You must have your reasons.'

Fox shifted on his feet, playing with the rim of his hat. 'I...
I don't like the other midshipmen, sir. They're up all the time
and moving around at strange hours and tormenting each other
and me. It's not friendly.'

Appleton hesitated but then continued, 'A midshipman's
mess is often boisterous. I remember it well myself. It can teach
you to stand up for yourself. Has someone taken a particular
offence to you?'

Fox visibly paled and glanced over his shoulder. The normal
state of the ship did not allow much privacy, but a ship with
all her partitions stripped down meant just that: no places to
whisper or have confidential discussions. The absence of those
walls suddenly seemed to sweep over Fox and his own defences
came up. He shook his head tersely, muttering a, 'No, sir.'

Courtney thought of Ramsey and the other mids during
the navigation lesson, how they had followed Ramsey during
his needling of Fox.

'Well then, if there are no issues, then there is little that I can
do,' Appleton finalised. 'As you were, Mr Fox.'

The young midshipman gave a small salute and hurried off
before more could be said. Appleton watched him scamper
away then sighed. Courtney realised, peculiarly, that his hands
trembled but he quickly grasped them, tucking them behind
his back.

'You could have assured him we would speak with the
captain,' Courtney suddenly decided to say.

Appleton barely reacted. 'You do not agree with my
decision?' he asked.

'I simply don't think it is right for the boy to suffer needlessly.'

'I drew up the watch bills and the divisions of the men before
we sailed, months ago, from Spithead,' Appleton continued. 'I

had to adjust them after the changing of our officers, but there is not a man who knows them better than I. I have come to know the midshipmen also and where they would be best placed. The younger ones must stay with the gunner and his mates in the gunroom and the older ones must stay in the after cockpit. That is the way of it.'

'Mess mates can be tough to deal with,' Courtney said. 'A man either bonds with them until death and is loyal throughout all hardship, or…they treat him with less care than a mangy dog.'

'Men can be harsh,' Appleton agreed, surprising Courtney. 'And boys. We officers were all midshipmen once.'

Courtney thought it best not to disagree. He had only very briefly been a midshipman before lying his way through his lieutenant's examination. Appleton did not need to know that.

'The midshipmen,' Courtney stated. 'They were not very pleasant to Mr Fox during a recent navigation lesson.'

Appleton paused. He stood, adjusting his waistcoat and uniform coat which had crumpled beneath him from the bench. 'None of this ship is very pleasant, Commander.'

The nakedness of such a statement shocked Courtney. He wished to ask more – a lieutenant did not simply admit such a thing with no qualms – but Appleton's eyes had suddenly drawn to the rest of the deck. Courtney looked around and noticed another figure by the struck-down partition.

'Mr Baker,' Courtney said. He, at least, was a man he knew the name of. Bosuns often left a marked impression on their ships. As one of the most senior petty officers, they were responsible for much of the crew below them, keeping them in line as much as their maintenance of rigging, boats and other equipment aboard. They were expected to know everything about their men. Baker, an older man in his sixtieth year at least, must have had a wealth of experience in his role. 'Can we help you?'

'That Mr Fox, sir,' Baker said, deferentially knuckling his forehead and dipping his hat, 'him and Mr Ramsey have had arguments. Mr McPherson complains all about it.'

'Who is Mr McPherson?' Courtney asked.

'One of the gunner's mates,' Appleton explained. 'And, standing officer or not, Mr Baker, it would be wise for you to not comment on the behaviour of the young gentlemen, who, I will remind you, are above you in rank.'

Baker dipped his hat again. 'Yes, sir. Sorry, sir. Was only concerned for the ship, sir. Won't have it embarrass itself.'

That was something Courtney agreed with him on. But Appleton said firmly, 'That will be all, Mr Baker. Return to the deck.'

'I shall also, Lieutenant,' Courtney said, intending to find Fox before he could disappear into the bowels of the ship. He could not allow the boy to be aggrieved, regardless of what Appleton said. Courtney found him walking swiftly forward, about to descend a companion-ladder. 'Mr Fox!' Courtney called and he jumped, freezing to a halt.

Courtney reached him, surprised to note the tears on the lad's cheeks. He tried to wipe them away with the cuff of his sleeve, a childish gesture that reminded Courtney how young and vulnerable these potential officers truly were.

'Don't mar your uniform, Mr Fox,' Courtney said. 'Here.'

He handed Fox his handkerchief and drew him beneath the shelter of the ladder, away from the prying eyes of the men he would have to govern.

'Thank you, sir,' Fox managed with a sniff.

'I believe,' Courtney continued, 'that Lieutenant Appleton and I did not give your petition a fair look. You may tell me truthfully now. How are your fellow midshipmen treating you?'

Fox swallowed. 'Tolerably, sir,' he answered.

'I have noticed their cajoling of you. It is not honourable behaviour from boys aspiring to be officers.'

'It is nothing, sir. I can ignore them.'

'But you wished to have your berth changed.'

Fox shook his head. 'It was not proper of me, sir. I must bear it.'

Courtney knew he had not seen the extent of it. He supposed it was worse in the gunroom below the wardroom where the younger mids berthed. He only witnessed the nasty behaviour when it came to the surface, when it touched the upper decks of the Lion. He considered what he had half-planned to say to Fox, turned it in his head again and thought of dismissing it, but the image of the poor lad being tormented by his peers sat so very foully with him. He knew the effect of horrid midshipmen, having felt the harshness of Mr Midshipman Lowe towards himself and his former friend, Walker, on the *Grampus*.

'Would you help me with a matter, Mr Fox?' he asked, then cursed his phrasing. 'I require your aid with a matter,' he tried again.

Fox's expression still did not ease. But he said, slowly, 'Yes, sir,' as if Courtney was about to ask him to scrub down the heads.

'This ship is…' How to describe it to a young, wide-eyed midshipman first entering the navy? 'She is not operating as best as I would like. I feel there is some…disorder on the lower decks. An officer must know his crew by the sound of their voices and feet on the timbers if he is to succeed. Do you wish to be a successful officer, Mr Fox?'

Now, Fox's gaze lightened. 'Oh, yes, sir.'

'I need you to watch over the men. To be a fine officer-in-training and observe their errors and moods.'

Courtney felt vaguely ridiculous asking such a thing. Here he was, resorting to relying on a midshipman on his first cruise, taking advantage of his desire to be an accepted member of the midshipmen's mess. But, away from the wardroom, and even within it, Courtney felt he had no allies. He had to do something.

With Fox drying his tears, Courtney ascended the decks again, keeping one eye for the ship and one for the open stretch of water about them. Perhaps that was the trouble: with such a wide seascape about them, marred only by the other ships and the disappearing forms of the Aeolian Islands, concentration turned inward. The constant flux of being cleared for action did not help matters, maintaining a high fever about the crew, itching for action. He hoped that when it came, it would unleash the tension he could already feel simmering through them all.

Not a pleasant ship, he suddenly thought, remembering Appleton's words. Surely it had not always been that way, not when Nightingale had commanded it. So what had changed?

Courtney sighed as he watched the sea. If officers and men were willing to damn the *Lion* out loud, what could that possibly mean for events beneath the surface?

Chapter Eight: Incoming Tide

Nightingale watched as Walter walked down the garden path of the cottage, his post-bag slung over his shoulder. Before today, Nightingale had only exchanged a handful of words to him when visiting the Catch with Courtney. The boy, aged around sixteen years, had a similar background to Courtney: a neglectful father and mother, taken in by Mr and Mrs Woods for guardianship and protection. He obviously felt an affinity with Courtney for it because his face had crumbled at the knowledge of the messages.

'I had no idea I delivered them horrible things,' he had promised Nightingale. 'I never would have...'

'No,' Nightingale had assured. 'It is best that you did – otherwise we never would have known that someone is angered. We can be alert to it now.'

But, with Walter gone and promised to secrecy, Nightingale was still no closer to knowing the perpetrator. He wondered if it were, perhaps, someone he had not been acquainted with. That, though, did nothing to narrow down the suspects.

Rylance emerged into the parlour with a silver tray, a teapot and mug perched on it. 'Reckoned you must be wanting something to drink, sir,' he said. 'Are you hungry?'

Nightingale allowed him to pour out the steaming tea. Many a time he had shared a drink with Courtney in this parlour, reading, watching the open fields outside or enjoying each other's company. That seemed long ago now. 'What is the hour, Rylance?' he asked.

'Coming onto four bells in the afternoon watch, sir.'

'Two,' Nightingale corrected.

'That's what I said, sir.'

Nightingale smiled. 'I need to be along to the Catch soon. You can stay here if you'd like, and see if anyone comes along.'

'Last time we was at the Catch, sir, I spoke to some of the locals. Good lads, but they said there was trouble afoot.'

Nightingale thought back to what Mrs Woods had said to him: trouble beyond the matter of the threatening notes. He had had no time to ask more and did not think it was even his place to enquire. Now, he prompted, 'Trouble? Of what manner?'

'They said there was to be a hanging, sir. Something about smuggling. A man had been caught ferrying goods ashore from a ship that was wrecked – or he was the only one to be snatched by the riding officer.'

'My God.'

Nightingale had heard of the tales of smuggling as a youth on the island and also afterwards, as a captain to men from a myriad of backgrounds. The south coast of England, including the Isle of Wight, was a particular centre for smuggling, owing to its rugged shores and residents with intimate knowledge of the sea. In these times of war and heavy taxation, the industry of free trade, as it was so euphemistically named, increased.

'Apparently, there's a right bastard attached to the customs service,' Rylance continued. 'Wants to wipe out all the illegal trade between here and France. Thinks it opens the door to French agents coming across the Channel.'

'When was this hanging to take place?' Nightingale asked.

'Oh, today, sir. The trial's already been had and the poor sod's been found guilty. They're to make an example of him at the top of Union Street.'

Within the hour, Nightingale found himself trudging up the long, steep hill Union Street ran down. A crowd had already gathered, people from the hamlet and further afield come to watch the death of the man who had been judged by the court. Nightingale spied a few men who had been at the Catch and they nodded towards Rylance. Nightingale received no such greeting.

His attention was soon drawn, though, to the gallows which had been constructed at the brow of the hill. There folk congregated, amassing together with some of them climbing onto carts and barrels to get a better view. An official was already speaking, addressing the men and women and children who murmured and whispered amongst themselves. Nightingale, not tall enough to see from the rear, had to ease his way through the bodies, getting sidelong looks in the process. This was not a friendly crowd, he interpreted, and perhaps not a docile one either. He had to strain a little to hear the official's words.

Before the gathering, a young man stood with hands tied behind his back. He was perhaps Rylance's age or a little older, a lad moulded by the sea in his weathered skin and long, pigtailed hair. He wore a loose, dirty shirt and open waistcoat and his feet were bare on the timbers of the gallows. His head drooped, eyes staring at his blackened toes. Nightingale thought of what Rylance had said: the customs service had feared French agents and French influence on the smuggling routes. This man did not seem a threat to anyone.

But still the representative of the law spoke of him as if he had committed treason. Smuggling was a thorny issue. Many residents of the coastal regions, certainly those suffering in poverty, saw it as their immemorial right and were skilled at creating their own economy, with everyone from tavern owners to fishermen to blacksmiths involved. But it undermined official channels and conveniently stepped around the revenue the customs service dealt with.

Nightingale wondered if the speaker was the man Rylance had called a right bastard. To his surprise, he wore a lieutenant's uniform rather than any clothing of another service. Nightingale now spied other men of the sea, sailors dotted about the front of the crowd.

'With incontestable evidence that Mr Hodges was involved in the crime of smuggling and wrecking, he will today hang,'

77

the officer narrated. Behind, Nightingale heard the grumblings of the crowd rise. It did not deter the lieutenant. All had been set in place; the gallows already loomed.

Nightingale watched as Hodges was guided firmly up the steps to the platform. The noose swung lightly in the breeze. As it ever did in sight of these foul things, a deep chill rolled through Nightingale. No matter how many sailors had been condemned before his eyes, no matter how many had been executed from the yardarms, he only ever saw Tom. He only ever felt the iron hand of his father clamped upon his shoulder, making him watch.

Now, though, he did not have to. He lowered his eyes as the rope was placed around Hodges's scrawny neck and had to be tightened such was its thinness. Then he only listened, to the fragile groan of the lad, the resulting hush of the crowd, and then the thud of the barrel as it was kicked from beneath Hodges's feet. The snap of his neck made Nightingale wince.

It was done. Rylance caught his eye as Nightingale raised his head again and he nodded. Together, they attempted to escape the crowd, but as if the breaking of Hodges's neck had severed something in them, the bodies only pressed closer. Too late Nightingale realised the ruckus growing at the rear of the mass. Something flew over his head and nearly wrenched off his hat. He heard the lieutenant curse and he looked around to see blood had emerged on the man's cheek. Before Nightingale could react, another stone hurtled through the air. Within a few moments, a hail of them soared towards the lieutenant, pelting around Hodges's swinging body.

'We should get away from here,' Nightingale heard Rylance urge. The steward gripped his arm and yanked him without ceremony towards the fringe of the rumbling crowd. They reached a cart, stacked with burlap sacks, and Nightingale caught the side of it to balance himself. Behind, what had begun as stone-throwing had swelled into pushing and shoving, the local men trying to reach the gallows. Harsh cries spouted from the throng. Nightingale only heard the odd word, dissent related to food and grain and laws.

The lieutenant struggled to get down from the platform. When he did, the angry men attempted to surge forward. Constables and the sailors Nightingale had spotted formed a loose barricade, thrusting themselves against the crowd. In the midst of it, Nightingale spied a lone woman, her dark hair coming loose beneath a cloth tied about her head. She stared angrily at the advancing lieutenant before shouldering her way through her fellows and disappearing behind the mass. Nightingale thought of finding his way to her, ensuring she got home safely.

Then the lieutenant was set upon by a gang of men breaking loose from the cordon. He did not crumble beneath them but fought back, his sailors rushing to his aid again. When he managed to extricate himself for a moment, Nightingale hurried forward, ignoring Rylance's protests. Praying that his own presence would still the crowd, Nightingale grasped the lieutenant's arm and urged him away. Fortunately, the furious locals continued to brawl with the sailors.

'Where are you going?' Nightingale asked the lieutenant.

'To my vessel,' he replied. 'The *Racer*. Her launch is waiting for me at the beach.'

Nightingale guided him away down the hill. The fight did not seem to follow them but Rylance kept a firm eye backwards. They took a route along the muddy, weaving path and hurried down to the duver, the narrow strip of sandy land that buttressed the beach. Dirty grains and gravel churned beneath their shoes. Nightingale looked out to the Solent's waters and saw a gunbrig anchored further out. A lieutenant could command a non-rated shallow-draught vessel such as her.

'You are a lieutenant attached to the customs service?' Nightingale asked.

'Yes. Lieutenant Osborne. The Navy is stretched as it is and many of the vessels diverted into the customs service have been sent to war. I'm the last of a dying breed, trying to calm these damned people and trying to patrol these cursed waters.'

Nightingale did not comment on that. *Yes*, he thought, *this must have been who Rylance had termed a right bastard.*

A launch boat waited for Lieutenant Osborne, but his sailors were still caught with the crowd.

'Perhaps we should wait at an inn,' Nightingale suggested. 'I don't wish for anyone to be harmed.'

'I won't skulk away, sir.'

There was no chance to escape the advancing mob, though. Nightingale waited, helpless, by the gig as they spilled down onto the rocky beach, refusing to give up the sailors in their midst. Someone was shoved to the ground and trampled over by careless boots.

'For God's sake!' Nightingale boomed, using the voice he had perfected in the wild teeth of gales. 'Let them go!'

'I shall hang them all,' Osborne threatened at his side.

'No,' Nightingale said, holding up his hand to him. 'Get to your *Racer* and let this be the end of it.'

'Who are you, sir?'

Nightingale could not respond. A handful of the Racers had broken free and rushed towards the gig. Osborne heaved himself into it and they tried to shove off from the shore. The tide took the launch but it still struggled to balance itself. A few of the local men approached the waves as they crashed onto the beach and Nightingale tried to draw them back. He did not doubt Osborne's words that he would try to hang them all.

'Sir!' he heard Rylance cry somewhere behind him. 'Watch your—'

A deafening shot cracked. The men about Nightingale cringed, covered their heads, and swore. Ahead, the launch boat lurched as its crew shifted and nearly overbalanced. The larboard gunwale of it tipped and Lieutenant Osborne's voice echoed over to them.

In shocked silence, Nightingale turned to see a man watching from the street. An ancient musket smoked in the wan light. He was reloading and re-priming the gun for another shot.

'No!' Nightingale shouted. 'Lower your weapon, man!'

The damage had already been done, though. The gig careened awkwardly in the waves as the water rushed through the hole in the hull. The mob stared without movement as the gig's crew tried to return to the beach. But the sea had already marred their vessel and tossed it mercilessly. Nightingale hurried forward into the surf as the men were tipped into the cold water. It was not deep, but enough for their feet to not touch the bed, and Nightingale knew a sailor's deathly fear of drowning and bottomless seas. During the peace, and their times on the island, Nightingale had had Courtney teach him the finer points of swimming. Now, he had no care for his clothes as he waded as far as he dared, providing an anchor for the sailors to swim towards. The other locals started to join him, a line of people and safety.

Gasping, shivering seamen were thrown out onto the sand. From lower Ryde, residents had run to the beach to stare. Nightingale spied Lieutenant Osborne in the water and, against his better judgement, yanked him out of the embrace of the foam and surf. By the ruined arm of his coat, he ferried him towards dry land. If he drowned, the locals would reckon justice had been served – but that same justice would then fall violently upon their own heads.

Osborne coughed and spluttered, spitting out salt water. He tried to stand, but his breeches were waterlogged and limbs too unsteady. Nightingale grabbed his shoulder and pulled him to his feet. He had lost his hat, so his black hair was plastered about his forehead.

'I told you…I would…hang them…' he croaked to Nightingale.

'Let us get someplace warm,' Nightingale said. 'You'll all catch a death of cold here.'

Osborne seemed to have other ideas. He threw off Nightingale's arm and tried to straighten his soaked uniform. 'Which man of you fired the shot?' he asked fiercely. 'I'll have you brought before the magistrate!'

'It was I.' The man had leapt down to the beach, musket still under his arm. He kept it trained upon the breast of Osborne, who reached for his own sword-belt. Nightingale saw there was no pistol there, and the threat did not frighten the local. The rest of the men looked askance at him, muttering amongst themselves and stepping away. The reality of death, so near, had sapped their ire.

Now, Nightingale gained a better look at the shooter: a man with lank, grey hair to his shoulders, of an indeterminate age, skin marked with pocks and scars, including a livid one across his nose.

'Put your gun down, sir,' Nightingale said firmly.

'No, sir. Reckon I'll need it. The fucking Navy and the fucking customs service, robbing us of what is ours.'

'Mr...' But the man did not give his name to Nightingale. 'The Navy are also overseeing the defence of the English coast. They are here to supervise your own Sea Fencibles.'

'And hanging our men,' came the hissed response.

'Damn your eyes, sir!' Osborne cried and stepped forward to strike the man. The musket came up. Nightingale stepped forward and knocked it towards the sky. With Osborne blaspheming in one ear and the gang of locals clamouring to hold back their comrade, he tried to make them cease. In the din, a fist emerged from nowhere and collided with his right cheekbone. He staggered, holding it, and for a moment broke from the fight. Through blurred vision, he saw two figures hurrying across the sand. One of them, a man dressed in a dark cutaway coat and riding boots; the other, a broad-shouldered woman with brown hair wound back into cloth, kicking her skirts away as she ran. Nightingale recognised her from the hanging.

To Nightingale's surprise, the woman grasped one of the men by the arm and pulled him out of the riot. He span and immediately froze. 'Lucy,' he gasped.

'I've brought the damned constable to you,' she said with venom in her words. 'Why are you fighting like rats in front of every man, boy and girl?'

The men had no response. The only one to move was the shooter, dashing across the beach and away.

--

Nightingale sat by the fire in the parlour of Harry Castle, the local magistrate's house. He could feel his cheek throbbing and could not wait to return to the cottage and nurse it. It hurt viciously, even more with the shame coursing through him.

Lieutenant Nicholas Osborne stood with a brandy in his hand. His uniform had dried since the events of the afternoon, but he still wore his wet shirt and breeches, as if to remind Nightingale and their host of what had happened. It was impossible to forget, though, considering it was the sole reason Nightingale had travelled to Harry Castle's home, hoping to plead the case of the men.

Castle sat in the armchair opposite Nightingale, fiddling with the ring about his finger. He barely looked old enough to be a magistrate. He must have been Courtney's age, with fair curled hair and piercing blue eyes. They kept darting towards Osborne, who towered over them both.

'You say that the men meant no harm,' he said now to Nightingale. 'Yet they tried to set upon the lieutenant and his men at the hanging and then marched to the beach and fired a shot at the launch boat.'

'Precisely,' Osborne interjected. 'One of the *Racer*'s gigs was lost. They caused damage to the property of the Royal Navy and to one of its officers.'

'The gunshot did not wound anybody,' Nightingale said calmly. 'If the gentleman had wished to, he could have harmed one of your crew or yourself, Lieutenant. Yet he aimed low, at the hull of the gig.'

'Do you suggest that he had any accuracy to his shot? It was only fortune that saved us, not by anything deliberate.'

'When the men saw that your gig crew were in danger, Lieutenant,' Nightingale continued, 'they rushed forward to help pull them from the waves. If they meant malice, they could have let you founder.'

'We would not have foundered if they had not discharged the shot.'

'Only one man fired any weapon.'

'Yes,' Castle said, leaning forward before Osborne could argue further. 'Yet we do not know where that man has gone to. He fled the beach and has not been seen since.'

'It is a small town – a small island. Some person must have seen him or know of his identity,' Osborne argued. 'What did the prisoners say?'

'They are not prisoners by a precise definition,' Castle said. 'They are being held whilst we discuss this incident. If I see fit, then they shall be brought before the court and then perhaps on to a formal trial. They say they did not get a firm look at the man.'

Nightingale did not wish for another formal trial. One man had already been hanged. He could not shake the feeling that the townsfolk were covering the identity of the shooter. No one wished to turn on one of their own, especially when such a heavy-handed officer was on the opposite side.

'Regardless,' Osborne spat, 'they brawled with my seamen. I am here to protect these coastlines and to work closely with the customs service. I won't tolerate such blatant disrespect to myself and by extension, the customs officials and King's Navy.'

'The brawl was unfortunate,' Nightingale conceded. 'But you must understand that feelings run high and angry in such an intimate community. They do not like to see one of their own at the end of a noose and certainly not when times are as they are.'

'That does not excuse their behaviour. They injured me with their weapons—'

84

'Stones, sir.'

'The Articles of War,' Osborne continued, ignoring Nightingale's interruption with a flare in his eyes, 'state that such actions towards an officer of the King's Navy warrants death.'

'The Articles of War are for members of the fleet, Lieutenant – and Article Thirty-Two states that any flag officer, captain, commander or lieutenant behaving in a scandalous, cruel, oppressive manner, unbecoming himself, shall be dismissed from the service.'

Osborne shut his mouth, his face falling from the pinched anger it had been curled in. Nightingale, buoyed by the reaction, continued. 'The men took issue with Lieutenant Osborne because of the hanging. They do not see justice in the same way. It is punishment enough to watch their fellow swing from the noose. I do not think they need to be reprimanded further.'

'Do not think?' Osborne seemed to inflate with his anger. 'Who are you, sir, to give any voice to these matters?'

Nightingale did not answer, knowing he could only stoke Osborne's fire. He had dealt with enough angry officers in his life.

'I can view this matter from both of your perspectives,' Castle said. 'But my role is not to alienate those amongst our towns. It is a difficult enough issue to gain their enthusiasm for the Fencibles. You are correct, sir, that emotions are frayed because of the war and the austere conditions.'

Osborne opened his mouth to say more but the young magistrate continued, 'I will not say the matter is settled, for the gentleman who fired the shot is still missing. I shall keep a close watch for him and for the behaviour of the men who caused the conflict today. You, Mr Nightingale, can accompany them back to their homes.'

Nightingale breathed out, shoulders loosening. 'Thank you, sir. I will also keep a close watch on them.'

It was a more preferable conclusion to what Nightingale had feared. He had not expected such leniency from a magistrate, but perhaps Harry Castle's age had acted in their favour. He still seemed somewhat hesitant, new to his station and role. Nightingale would have to enquire further about his character when back at the Catch. He wished to return there with the men as soon as possible, but as he exited Harry Castle's house, into the late, cold night, Osborne caught up with him. He had tugged on his uniform coat again, the wool still a little dark with seawater.

'Who are you, Mr Nightingale?' he asked without any further remark. 'What business do you have here?'

Nightingale held out a hand, but Osborne did not take it. Nightingale retracted it, thrust it behind his back, and stared at the lieutenant in the way he often had to a misbehaving young midshipman. 'My name is Hiram Nightingale, Lieutenant. I was a post-captain in the Royal Navy which I served for almost thirty years. Good night, sir.'

With the fortunate Ryde residents in tow, Nightingale journeyed back to the hamlet. A man named Graham Browne awkwardly thanked Nightingale, but Nightingale did not know if that gratitude came from the entire group. They did not converse with him much and he did not blame them. Regardless of his actions with the magistrate, he had guided Lieutenant Osborne away from the fray and tried to protect him down to the beach. Perhaps he was seen as another representative of the 'fucking Navy', as the shooter had accused.

That, or he was still an outsider to them.

Mrs Woods was the first to truly acknowledge him when they reached the Catch in the cold night. She rushed out of the door and hurried around to each man to reprimand them as soundly as any furious captain. She ushered Nightingale into his usual table and, regardless of the late hour, emerged from the kitchen with his favourite meal: a cod pie and ale.

'I have been up all hours,' she said, 'fretting there'd be another hanging. If they ain't careful, the whole lot of them'll be shot like dogs.'

'Lieutenant Osborne certainly seemed to be on the verge of ordering such a thing,' Nightingale replied morosely. 'It was only the magistrate's mercy which saved them.'

'Harry Castle is from an old family. They weren't always magistrates and law folk. The son is a good lad from what I hear, had to take over from his father when the fever took him before his time.'

'I wondered about his age,' Nightingale said. He raised his fork and winced as he opened his mouth.

'That looks a great hurt,' Mrs Woods commented about the mark on his cheek.

'I should know better than to come between men whilst brawling. Do you know, when I first met Arthur, he had a great black bruise around his eye from involving himself in a fight.' Nightingale smiled. 'Arguing with naval officers and fighting... I think Arthur has had an influence on me.'

'I shall fetch you something to cool the pain.'

'I am fine. I have experienced worse than this.'

But she soon returned with a cloth and a bowl of water. Nightingale caught a sight of himself in the shimmering reflection and saw the truth of his injury. A foul-looking bruise had already formed about his right cheek, slightly swollen. He hoped no bones had been fractured and knew he would have to write to his doctor to confirm.

As he soaked the cloth in the water and felt sorry for himself, he watched the other residents slink back to their homes. At the door, Browne paused, looking around with his hat in hand. Nightingale wondered if he searched for him, but then a woman appeared at his side. Nightingale recognised her as the one who had been at the hanging and who had brought the constable to the fighting men. Browne spoke to her in low tones before they departed into the night.

'Mrs Woods,' Nightingale said when the landlady came near again, 'who was the woman who left with Mr Browne? I saw her earlier but did not have time to speak with her.'

'Oh.' Mrs Woods glanced towards the door, as if checking for the woman's presence. 'That is Lucy,' she said quietly.

'Lucy?'

'Yes. She came to Ryde recently from the other side of the island, St Lawrence I believe. Mr Browne has taken a liking to her and she to him. But we don't know much about her and the things we do know, or rather the things we suspect...'

Nightingale frowned. 'What do you suspect?'

'Ain't my place to say, Mr Nightingale, sir.'

'Should I be wary of her? She seemed quite sensible to bring the constable to the mob today.'

'I haven't spoken to her often. She simply is always there when trouble brews.'

Mrs Woods could not be pressed to say more. Nightingale knew she was implying that he should avoid Lucy, but his curiosity ran too high. Ryde, and the island, still seemed strange to him, and he to it.

'Thank you for speaking with me and aiding me,' he said by way of assuring her she did not have to go on. 'I know that I am somewhat of an outsider here.'

'You are Artie's dear friend. I would not treat you any differently.'

That was how he was known, only through Courtney. Courtney was far away now, no doubt trying to find his own feet amongst a new crew. The distance between them sometimes felt so vast, even vaster when Nightingale's head was hazy. He had come here to find a use for himself, to try and alleviate the dawning pains that emerged from under the *Lion*'s keel, swelling up from deeper waters. He did not want to appear as though he was utilising these people for his own means, but he wanted to feel purposeful again, in command of his destiny.

Perhaps that goal would take some time.

Chapter Nine: Partitions

19 February 1805, off Malta

Captain Harrison arrived back on the *Lion* with none of the pomp due his rank. He had departed and returned to the ship so often in the past few days that he claimed Baker's shrill pipe was starting to grate in his head. Now, in the middle of February, with Valletta to starboard, he climbed the ladder onto the quarterdeck in silence. Still, the entire company of men were present to stare, awaiting the news they knew he would be coming back to the *Lion* with. Courtney watched his face closely but he revealed nothing in his expression. Harrison always smiled to the crew like he did now, as if he were the docile seaman and they were the officers.

Appleton, who had obviously been waiting for the captain's return below, emerged from a hatchway and shouted at the men to disperse back to their work.

'Have us fill away,' Harrison said. 'Our course is set to be re-victualled off Sardinia and then back to Toulon.'

Disappointment rolled in Courtney's gut. He followed Harrison to the great cabin where the captain walked to the gallery windows and looked down to the waters with the *Lion*'s churning wake. Fitzroy emerged from Harrison's night cabin and hopped up onto an epaulette. Harrison idly stroked his scrawny stomach. 'Word has come from Captain Blackwood's *Euryalus*,' Harrison said. 'There is confirmation that Villeneuve has been driven back into Toulon. We have missed the enemy and now he is safely back behind the blockade.'

'We are to return to blockading duty, sir?' Appleton asked.

'Indeed.'

Appleton's expression darkened, so much so that even Harrison marked it.

'Well, it is a sore mission, Lieutenant, but you do not have to look as though you have lost a childhood sweetheart.'

'It is...' Appleton shook his head and schooled his face back to its usual stoic appearance. 'Yes, sir. Of course, sir.'

'There is no need for us to be cleared for action now,' Harrison continued. 'Have the men return to their normal stations and allow them to breathe easy for a while.'

When Appleton left, he cast a look in Courtney's direction: a look Courtney thought he should have read something in. He did not, having been subject to various glares from the acting first lieutenant. Courtney thought he understood what Nightingale had felt when first coming aboard the *Scylla*.

The disappearance of the lieutenant seemed to relax Harrison's shoulders, perhaps for the same reason the men could now rest: partitions were re-erected, sea-chests and possessions could be brought back up, and the atmosphere of anticipation could dissipate. The *Lion* returned to her regular state, away from looming battle. As Gainsborough and the officers' stewards assembled the furniture again, Harrison hurried Fitzroy away and motioned Courtney to sit. Courtney tried to ignore the awkwardness of the men flitting around him, fussing over the captain's cabin. Harrison sent for coffee and Gainsborough returned with two silver cups of it, but with no available table, Courtney cradled his and tried to bear the heat.

'What do you think, Courtney?' Harrison asked. 'Are the French in Toulon to stay or shall they make another run?'

'They've succeeded in evading the fleet once, sir. There is no reason to think they won't try it again. By coming out they obviously had some end that they did not meet.'

'Hmm.' Harrison sipped the coffee. 'How do you find the experience of the *Lion*? It has been a while since you served upon a ship of the line, yes?'

'Yes. The last third-rates I set foot upon were for…unpleasant reasons.' The *Leviathan* and the *Mallard* had both served the purposes of holding court martials in their great cabins: the first for the *Ulysses* mutineers and for Nightingale's own conduct, and the second for the accusations of ill behaviour and sodomy between Paterson and Arnold on the *Lysander*. 'There were some matters I wanted to speak to you of, though, Captain, if you'll permit me?'

Harrison smiled. 'Of course, of course! You are our guest aboard the *Lion*.'

'That is the heart of it, sir.' Courtney could not bear the heat permeating the metallic cup anymore. He looked for somewhere to set it down and Gainsborough appeared with his platter. Harrison waved the man away, out of hearing distance. 'What happened before I came aboard? You mentioned your lieutenant had been taken ill.'

'Oh, yes, Lieutenant Oakley. Poor soul. He had a bout of the ague fever. Lieutenant Appleton tells me he contracted it when serving in the Caribbean and it continues to bother him.'

'The Caribbean is a wicked place for diseases,' Courtney said. 'My former captain, Carlisle, on the *Scylla* died of the yellow jack.'

'I remember Captain Carlisle. A good man.'

Carlisle had promised to aid Courtney in his career; an influential officer with connections was what Courtney needed. When he had died, that potential had been snuffed, without mentioning the grief Courtney had felt for his demise and the demises of so many other men amongst the *Scylla's* crew. He had felt listless and angry afterwards, unsure where his feet could tread upon the *Scylla's* boards and if each step would bring him physical or professional death. He experienced a similar churning sensation now, an officer caught between ranks and responsibilities. Perhaps he was doomed to always live in this purgatory.

And, more, he knew the resentment a person could harbour towards a man that stepped into a coveted position.

'Lieutenant Appleton seems to command well,' Courtney said. 'He is taking the mantle of Lieutenant Oakley as well as his own duties, isn't he? He has stood many watches and that is not necessarily the responsibility of a first lieutenant.'

'Lieutenant Appleton is a diligent officer,' Harrison replied. 'He assured me that he bore no hostility towards his role or the loss of Lieutenant Oakley's.'

Did he? Courtney thought. He nearly said it, but stopped himself. However affable Harrison was towards him, and however open Harrison seemed to be towards his officers and crew, there were lines Courtney had learnt not to cross. 'I am grateful that you permitted me to come aboard, Captain,' he continued. 'This ship has a certain connection to me through Captain Nightingale. Yet I am not used to…being so useless. If it is needed, I would not decline to step into Lieutenant Oakley's rank and act as he would.'

Harrison frowned. 'You are a commander, Courtney. Your coat proves it.'

'Yes, sir.' Courtney knew he should have left the conversation there, but he continued, 'Assign me the duties of an extra lieutenant and I would feel some utility about the ship. I have no qualms over standing watches.'

'You are a very zealous man,' Harrison said with a chuckle. 'Truth be told, I did consider a similar situation when I invited you aboard. Circumstances stopped me.'

Courtney wondered what those circumstances had been. Perhaps Harrison had felt uncomfortable asking Courtney – and such a notion unsettled him. A captain should not doubt his decisions or his ability to make them. Then again, perhaps Harrison already considered Courtney as a member of his family and was trying to settle him into these ideas of favours and positions granted by connection. *A member of his family*, Courtney thought, and bristled at the implications of it. Soon, perhaps, he would be, by way of Miss Sandham.

'I shall consult Mr Daniels, the purser, but I cannot foresee his refusal. He is having a grand day because of the prospect of new victuals and new accounts. His diligence is a great boon, as it yours.'

'Thank you, sir.'

'Not at all, not at all.' Harrison waved his hand and Fitzroy took it as a signal to scurry back to him. 'Oh, this pestering creature. Do you know that Miss Sandham was the one to beg me to keep him? I am fond of animals, but this one is a menace.'

Harrison said it with an affectionate smile, helping Fitzroy up to sit amidst the corners of his hat. Courtney hoped Harrison would not think of what he had just said but regrettably, the man continued, 'Speaking of the girl, I shall write home to my dear wife soon. I mean to arrange a meeting between us all, every member of the Sandham family and I together. I shall attend with you to soften the fright of it, although truly they are not so terrible and blood-curdling. I should think to invite your family too but...'

'I only have my sister,' Courtney said.

'Ah yes, Jane. Mrs Wainwright now? I remember her from the trial. Perhaps it is best not to invite her along.'

Perhaps it would be best not to invite me either, Courtney thought. He had heard of the ways of the upper sets of society, arranging nuptials without considering the true hearts of the partners. Though Nightingale did not occupy the same echelons as the Sandhams, Nightingale and his wife had had no choice in their marriage – it had simply been a convenient and seemingly proper match between a successful captain and a daughter of merchant shipping and politics. Then again, Courtney was not a man of property or wealth. He would not be the first logical choice of a woman such as Tabitha Sandham. He should feel pride and gratitude. He did not.

As Harrison said, Courtney's coat might prove his rank, but, as difficult as it had been to attain it, it could easily be stripped from him. When dressing in the mornings, Courtney had to face the awful truth that he disliked the epaulette on his left shoulder. It seemed to be a useless scrap of lace and golden fabric. He had been a lieutenant for over a decade and he knew the expectations of such an officer, what he could amount to and what he should sensibly keep his mouth sealed about, even if he had not always done so. Sometimes, he looked over the sea and out to the vanguard of the fleet where the frigates sailed. A frigate officer's life did not feel so confined. During Courtney's years on the *Scylla* and then the months on the *Lysander*, he had relished their speeds and manoeuvrability of sailing.

Yet then as soon as he had fallen into these blackened moods, he cursed himself again. He had gained what he desired: a step further up the ladder of promotion, closer to attaining his name being posted in the Naval Gazette as a captain. Perhaps it was not the sight of the frigates or the memory of the *Scylla* which ate at him. Perhaps it was what Harrison had discussed with him before coming aboard and what he had mentioned in the great cabin. Courtney felt he had made a deal that he could not rescind on.

Or perhaps it was the notes that had arrived at the cottage. He knew he should have spoken to Nightingale about them, but the words had not come and the *Lion* had offered him a good excuse not to mention the subject. Soon, he swore, he would write to him and offer his apologies, but he wished, ridiculously, to pretend that his life with Nightingale was still light and hopeful – a marked, but welcome, change from the mood onboard this seventy-four-gunner. So, instead of sifting through the problems back home, Courtney tried to tease out an answer to those that existed here, amidst these timber walls.

—

Courtney stood at the bottom of the aftmost companion-ladder, surveying the lines of the twenty-eight eighteen-pounders. Beside him, Harrison and the master gunner, Greene, watched silently. After speaking with the captain, Courtney had gained the authority of the upper gun deck which Appleton had been entirely caring for in the absence of Lieutenant Oakley. Almost instantly, Courtney had asked permission to exercise the great guns. The men needed a distraction from the disappointment of losing the French and the tedium of blockade which awaited them – and perhaps with the firing of the guns, it would unleash some of the tension which had obviously been bottled within some of them. Again, Courtney had been woken by brawling and again, Appleton had dealt with it in lieu of Harrison.

Observing the men organising themselves under the eyes of the petty officers, Courtney tried to forget such disquiet. The British fleets under Nelson, Cornwallis and Lord Keith might be watching the French and Spanish fleets at Toulon, Brest, Rochefort and in the Downs, keeping a stranglehold on the trade and wellbeing of the enemies' economies and freedoms, but soon, they would try to fight again. Then, superiority of firepower and of techniques amidst the gun decks would gain the victory. This, more than worrying over marital problems and navigating the tentative and uncertain pyramid of the *Lion*'s officers, was what Courtney knew.

Courtney had also requested the presence of a number of the midshipmen, as would occur in battle. Five of them, including Fox and Ramsey, stood nearby the cannons they would oversee, eagerly awaiting Courtney's orders. Courtney made a note to seek Fox out soon; the boy had not yet come to him with any information. Now, Fox should have been putting a stop to the rumble of low murmuring that rippled through the deck. Neither he nor Ramsey said a word.

'Silence there!' Courtney called and heads whipped around to him. Courtney regretted he did not know the men's names. He turned to Greene. 'Is this everybody, Mr Greene?'

Greene hesitated for a moment. 'This is everybody available, yes, sir.'

'How do you mean?'

'Many of my men are ailing. A stomach complaint that the doctor is administering to.'

Courtney had noticed empty spaces amongst the gun crews. Eighteen-pounders required at least ten men, and, even if in battle some would be pulled away for other necessary duties, it would be sensible to have the full complement during drill – certainly the important gunner's mates. Harrison, however, did not comment about them, so Courtney continued, 'I wish to see a clean and rapid rate of fire, no careless shooting without proper targeting. I know that, when trained well, we English can fire three broadsides to every one of the enemy's.'

When Nightingale had taken command of the *Scylla*, he had instituted a competition of larboard against starboard battery. Courtney had decided not to pit these men against one another – not yet, when enough unrest already simmered between them – but he wished for at least a little enthusiasm. Aside from the mids, the faces that peered back at him were unreadable, certainly not spurred by his words. He tried to ignore the lack of reaction, ordering for the guns to be cast loose and then seized to the ringbolts.

As the men obeyed, footsteps sounded on the companion-ladder and Appleton appeared. He glanced at both Harrison and Courtney and directed a question towards the captain: 'Should I be present for this, sir?'

'If you will, Lieutenant,' Harrison said.

Appleton joined them to watch over the drill. Courtney had wanted the gun captains to take command, and they tried, but not with the urgency and precision Courtney wished for. He ordered for cartridges to be pricked, guns to be primed, and handspikes to be grasped, as well as the details he should not have had to stress: powder horns drawn away from the guns when not needed, vents covered before coming to fire. To his satisfaction, the men were a little better at targeting the things, the captains accurately addressing their crews by peering out the portholes, through which they could see a barrel bobbing to starboard and larboard.

'You may fire at will!' Courtney prompted, wishing to see if the men would leap too quickly at the chance or more finely tune their aims. He was answered by a succession of bangs, then a handful more, as if the sound had pressured other crews to follow. Fox instinctively clapped his hands over his young ears, this obviously being his first time hearing such a din. The rest of the gun deck touched off their powder at a haphazard rate, like an orchestra unable to follow their conductor. Some of the crews were preparing to reload their cannons before the final round had ceased.

'Sponge your guns!' Courtney snapped, seeing how some men had not even taken that essential step to prevent any hot embers prematurely igniting the powder.

The previous process repeated, this time a little smoother but with far more jagged edges than a British crew should have. Mistakes were made, leading to Courtney stepping in more times than he would have liked, and by the time the final shot had sounded, he was more down-hearted than when he had begun. He tried to consider it in light of the missing gunner's mates, but they should not be responsible for the entire gunnery of a ship. Every man had to know the drill, for in battle, a single error, a single slip, could be the difference between life and death – either from the enemy or from the cradle of danger that was a gun deck.

'It is the first time we have truly exercised the great guns, sir,' Appleton said to Harrison as the mids supervised the men cleaning the cannons and re-stowing the powder horns, rammers and spongers. 'They may be a little tardy now but more hours honing their speed and efficiency in their gun crews will see them right.'

'They shall have ample time to practise,' Harrison replied lightly.

'I shall ensure it, Captain,' Courtney interjected. He could not deny the spark of shame within him. Regardless of if the men had had little opportunity to test themselves, they had not behaved with the tightness and discipline Courtney had grown to see, and expect, amongst the crews he manned. 'I'm concerned about the missing gunner's crew and the other empty spaces. These eighteen-pounders require at least ten men.'

'Some are in the sickbay,' Appleton replied, as Greene had.

An inordinate amount, Courtney thought. 'I shall visit them, with your permission, Captain,' he said.

Harrison hesitated for a moment. 'I shall accompany you,' he said and then changed his mind. 'No, perhaps I should ensure the men are cleaning sufficiently. Thank you for your enlightening exercise, Commander Courtney.'

Courtney smiled stiffly, a little unsettled by Harrison's indecision, but pushed it from his mind as he left the upper gun deck and found his way to the screened bay beneath the forecastle which constituted the sickbay. When entering the *Lion*, it had taken a while for Courtney to become familiar with every officer. Harrison tried to invite them all to dinner each night, but those who arrived were few and far between, considering the harried state of the ship. Courtney had been surprised, and very pleased, to realise the *Lion*'s doctor was none other than Dr Francis Archer, the same man who had cared for the *Scylla*.

Next to the open companion-ladder and nestled in the bows, the choking pall of gunpowder and smoke had not permeated Archer's small area – a confined space which seemed even narrower with the robust bill of men currently there. The scent of vomit and excrement turned Courtney's stomach. He had wondered if the seamen had been falsifying their illness to avoid duty, but he saw now that was not the case.

Currently, Archer attended a crewman who was deathly pale, mopping the sweat from his forehead. The man groaned pitifully.

'Cease this griping, Mr McPherson,' Archer murmured. 'You'll recover, man. I've told you this.'

McPherson. Baker had mentioned that the man had often complained about the midshipmen's berth's noise and clamour. He had no real reason to gripe, both because of his rank and because he should not have been near enough to hear such disturbance, not as his superior, the gunner, would be.

Courtney looked over the rest of the sickbay. Each of the hammocks and cots had been filled, a couple of them even holding two men lying at odds to each other. Archer's loblolly boy, Ellis, moved between them with bowls of thick oatmeal gruel. The last time Courtney had seen a sickbay this full had been on the *Scylla* when she had succumbed to yellow fever. Dr Archer had been the surgeon then, too, and he had been shoving the dead aside with every new patient that entered.

He glanced up at Courtney now and nodded. 'Beg your pardon, Commander, I shall be with you directly.'

Setting the cloth aside, Archer finished with his patient and, with a word to Ellis, followed Courtney beyond the canvas partition of the sickbay.

'They seem devilishly ill,' Courtney said. 'Should I be worried about the state of it?'

Archer removed his spectacles and cleaned them on the edges of his black smock. He seemed a good deal older than he had upon the *Scylla*, although less than five years had transpired. Deep lines decorated the creases of his eyes and forehead and his bird-like face had sunk a little into the cracks of age. A naval doctor's career was not a smooth and simple one. 'It is not the plague, Commander, nor the pox. I would not wish to fumigate the ship in any haste. But it does give me cause for concern.'

'What are the complaints?'

'A distemper of the stomach primarily. The men are purging themselves quicker than I can administer any emetics. It may be an issue with their diet.'

'They eat and drink the same things each day, each week. Their diet has not changed.'

'When we re-victual and then reach Toulon, fresh fish and vegetables might answer – though I think the illness should have worn itself through by that time, if the problematic stuffs are not still afoot. I shall keep a close watch and see if the ailment spreads amongst close fellows, or if the issue is with what they consume.'

A part of Courtney doubted it; English seamen had stomachs and other internal organs made of lead – or perhaps sponge, with the amount of drink they could imbibe. 'I have just drilled the men at the great guns. Mr Greene, the master gunner, says that many of his men were taken ill. Might I have the names of the ailing crew?'

'Of course. I shall have Mr Ellis draw one up for you.'

They were interrupted by a moan from beyond the partition, one of the suffering men. Archer reached to draw the curtain back again, but Courtney stopped him.

'What are your thoughts of the men, Doctor? How do you mark their behaviour?'

Courtney had served with Archer in the debacles that swept over the *Scylla*, from yellow fever to the pursuit of the *Ulysses* to Nightingale's trial. He knew the doctor to be an astute man, someone reliable and trustworthy – and someone he could ask this question of without reproach.

Archer sighed. 'As their doctor, I think it best to deal with the men solely on the other side of that canvas. I don't probe too deeply into their reasons and motivations, unless it is relevant to their treatment. But you and I both know the ways of sailors, Commander.'

'We do indeed.'

'I do have one matter that gives me some concern, though.'

'Go on.'

'My stores are…not as they should be. I thought perhaps I had made an error in my note-keeping but worryingly, I don't believe that is so. I am missing two bottles of laudanum.'

'Laudanum?'

'Indeed. In the last fortnight, they have disappeared. The matter has not recurred since my sickbay has swollen in number but I will be keeping a closer eye on the stores and I have ordered Mr Ellis to do the same.'

If it had been any other tincture, perhaps Courtney would have paid it less mind. But laudanum could be in the way of beer and gin. Too much of it could cause a deep-rooted addiction in men, driving them to drastic action to obtain it. With the ill discipline already festering in the ship, Courtney could not help but fall upon accusation. He could not allow the matter to worsen.

'I shall have Mr Ellis bring the list along to you, Commander,' Archer continued. 'Now, I best return to my patients.'

Courtney let him go. With the upper gun deck scrubbed and maintained again, he sought out Fox, but the boy did not brighten the mood descending over Courtney after Archer's words. He shied away from Courtney's questions, something Courtney knew he could have alleviated by talking to Fox away from his fellow mids. He barely met Courtney's gaze, cheeks reddening the more he mumbled his answers – answers that proved the torment still continued, or that a new incident had rattled the poor lad. With the absence of the gunner, Greene, performing extra duties in the wake of his mates' ailments, perhaps the situation had worsened. Courtney resolved to speak to Harrison about Fox's pains, but was still too irritated by the gun exercise to do more that day.

It had proved that there was still much to be learnt. Courtney was unhappy with the gunnery, unhappy with the behaviour of the men, and just as much as that, unhappy with his own outlook. He did not know this crew or their officers very well. They would not enthusiastically go to a gun exercise, or a tacit assignment in Fox's case, for a man they had no respect for. He had to unite them and show his worth to them and those he shared the wardroom with. The partitions may have come down, the battle stations unmanned for now, but more barriers than simply bulkheads and timbers existed.

It would be a long journey back to Toulon – and then, a long blockade.

Chapter Ten: By Another Name

True to Nightingale's estimations, Louisa had been very displeased by the state of his face. She repeated that she had told him to be cautious and did not cool even as Nightingale told her of the events which had led to his injury. Considering it had naught to do with the offensive messages sent to the cottage, Nightingale relayed everything to her about Lieutenant Osborne and the hanging of Mr Hodges.

'These people are not the crew of your ship, Hiram,' she said over their supper one night back at Haywood Hall. 'You do not have a responsibility for them.'

'I feel I do,' Nightingale said. 'Though some of them have treated me less than favourably, Mr and Mrs Woods have been so welcoming and warm. I don't like to see them being worn thin and treated cruelly by Osborne.'

'You have a soft heart. It is not a detestable quality, but your attention should be on your own health. Neither one of us is in the spring of their youth any longer.'

Nightingale huffed, an immature response he knew was at odds with Louisa's statement. 'I am turning forty-five this year, my dear. I like to believe I have a few years yet to live.'

'Years that will not be pleasant if you spend them like a pugilist.'

'In all my life, I have taken a fist to my face on one occasion, I hardly think that warrants...'

But Nightingale knew that he would not be victorious in this quarrel. He hated raising his voice at Louisa or even stepping close to an argument with her. She did not deserve that, after all she had borne from him and his moods and melancholy. Yet it was clear, even without considering their terse words, that she had been hurt by his behaviour and the consequences of it. Nightingale was equally wounded that she did not trust him to follow his own path and methods. Then again, he thought as he lay beneath the quilt in his lonely bedroom at the hall, she did not truly know what drew him back to the island. She did not understand the attachment he felt to that little cottage and the life he shared with Courtney there. He wanted desperately for those people there to accept him and like him.

But, never had he admitted his bond with Courtney to Louisa, not as he had the love he had once felt for Leroy Sawyer. She deserved his honesty, as did Courtney.

He could not sleep for want of wondering how he would broach the sensitive subject with her. She did not wish for his romantic pursuits or his carnal desires, for which Nightingale had none, but his connection with Courtney stretched beyond a simple amorous tie. Many years had passed with Louisa as his only ally and friend – against his father, sometimes against her father, and against the rest of the world which shackled them both to accepted traditions – and his love for Courtney had not diminished his affection for her. Though she had never been an envious woman, she would be entirely vindicated if she felt pained or affronted by Nightingale bringing Courtney so closely into his world.

Yet, where he and Louisa could pronounce their marriage and wear each other's ring, he could not announce such things about Courtney. He could not have a material and lawful union with Courtney.

And so, in the dark of the night, Nightingale teetered between emotions and decisions. When Louisa came down to the morning room for breakfast the following day, he had been awake for some hours already, trying to concentrate upon his correspondence. He had listened to Louisa's lady's maid take her a mug of hot chocolate at nine, and wondered if he should join her in her rooms, only to forgo it. He nonetheless gave a welcoming smile as she entered the morning room and took her seat opposite him.

'Good morning, my dear,' he greeted.

'Good morning, Hiram.' She sent for tea and two slices of buttered toast then considered the newspapers on the table. Nightingale wondered about raising some of the events within, when she said, 'I have been pondering, Hiram. I cannot prevent you from visiting the island. It is simply strange to think of you having a life there too.'

'It does not mean that my life here is any less,' Nightingale insisted.

'I know that. It is in the way of your life at sea. Those ships were where you belonged at the time.'

Nightingale was silent for a moment. 'I sometimes wonder if they are where I still belong,' he heard himself say.

'Don't be absurd. You were firm with your intentions to leave the service. This has been your own path for a few years now.'

Nightingale nodded. For the first time, he did not believe Louisa knew him as well as she once had. But that was not her fault; Nightingale had retreated from his honesty, not sharing it with anyone. It was unfair of him.

However, he still travelled to the island next without finalising their growing troubles. He found his old habits returning and hated it. It made him feel helpless, as if it was a tide that he could not prevent from washing up the shores of his life and taking him under.

As he ever did when these forces darkened him, he set the *Larkspur* away from her moorings. It pleased him to command the vessel, though she was not of the same breed as the ships he had once captained. She was but a two-masted brig, not by technical terms a 'ship' at all which was defined as having three masts. But she sailed calmly and sweetly, an ideal companion in the twilight of his old career. He could walk her short deck in a minute, and the close spaces below did not swamp him with their magnitude or crush of crew. A sparse complement of guns furnished her, six six-pounders and two carronades, but Nightingale had not found cause to use them.

His crew ever changed, men brought on by Robert Haywood's company, but he had managed to retain a handful from his former days of glory, and his first mate was sturdy and dependable. Obi had been a former slave, escaping from an Antigua plantation, when he had joined the *Scylla* prior to Nightingale being her captain. He had served in the *Lysander* crew, helped to rescue the prisoners from the *Barbarossa*, and since then, Nightingale had kept in communication with him. He had been overjoyed to accept the position of the *Larkspur's* first mate and took great care of the brig in Nightingale's absence. He eyed their trim diligently as they crossed the Solent, heading for Bembridge – but before they could reach there, in view of Appley, a fishing smack hailed them. The little single-masted tub, with the name *Marian* painted upon the side, passed under the *Larkspur's* lee. Approaching the rail, Nightingale was surprised to see the figure of Lucy on the deck, sifting through the nets which had been dragged in. Mr Browne accompanied her.

'Captain Nightingale!' Browne called.

'How are you, sir?' Nightingale asked, then raised a hat to Lucy, realising he did not know her surname. 'Ma'am.'

Lucy said nothing, but gave Nightingale a slight nod.

'This your ship, sir?' Browne asked, eyeing the *Larkspur*.

'My *Larkspur*, yes,' Nightingale replied.

'We've had good day's catch, Captain,' Browne said, indicating the baskets and barrels full of plaice and bream. 'We even seized an eel.'

A long, thin silver eel still sat in a wicker cage.

'My congratulations,' Nightingale commented.

'You heading to Cowes, Captain Nightingale?' Browne asked.

'No. I thought to sail down to Bembridge.'

'Reckoned you'd want to find out about the ships, sir.'

'The ships?'

By the glance which passed between Browne and Lucy, Nightingale knew something had occurred in his absence.

'We heard word of a French attack,' Browne answered. 'Lieutenant Osborne was drawn away to join the squadron which repelled it.'

Their course changed, Nightingale set the *Larkspur* towards Cowes. He wondered if he would find anything at the harbour or if it was another rumour spread to instil fear and worry in the populace. Tales from the sea could take months to reach land and that time could stretch and conflate the truth.

There, in the busy harbour, merchant and private vessels sat side by side. It was the view of any port along the English coasts, but to Nightingale's shock, this one had what seemed an awkward thorn stuck into it. He had seen such things in Portsmouth and had not thought to meet one here. A great, heaving prison hulk loomed over the blue waters, out of place, untidy. Nightingale kept a wide berth of it but could not stop his eyes from looking back.

'I did not know a prison hulk was moored here,' he remarked to Obi.

'An ugly thing,' Obi commented, and Nightingale agreed.

Not wanting to loiter, he anchored the *Larkspur* head and stern and took Obi ashore. After dealing with the harbour authorities, he waited, enquiring of other men if they knew anything about the squadron. It seemed a disturbance had called all nearby naval vessels away, just as Mr Browne had said. Nightingale had not been there long when Obi pointed out a small flotilla of ships. It took a short while for Nightingale's eyes to adjust in the low sun and to decipher their form. A brig and a single frigate were the largest vessels amongst them, the others being smaller gunbrigs. Nightingale thought he recognised Osborne's *Racer*.

The squadron navigated the headpoint until the brig and the frigate heaved-to and backed their topsails. Nightingale observed them and their prim, precise manoeuvres, eyeing the state of their cordage and canvas. The brig had had her course fettered and the standing rigging of her foremast was partially shot away. The frigate, most likely by dint of her size and firepower, seemed the least damaged of the few but to Nightingale's surprise, they were all wounded.

He felt curiously ashamed to see such harm. His own *Larkspur* had not discharged her guns before. Other vessels fought and suffered, not only in the Mediterranean where Courtney served but here, close to English shores too. But Nightingale was no longer commissioned by the navy and could not raise a hand against other countries unless provoked. The wanton capture and conflict with enemy vessels could lead to accusations of piracy.

Obi spoke of the squadron's damage as Nightingale watched the gunbrigs. The shallow-draught *Racer* sailed further into the harbour, mooring in the same manner as the *Larkspur*. A small launch peeled from her. With Obi at his side, Nightingale made his way down, curious to hear what had occurred. As he had supposed, he spied Lieutenant Osborne coming ashore, an older post-captain beside him. To his shock, he recognised the man: Captain Lovett, the officer who had helped ferry Nightingale to Portsmouth's harbour after he had been invalided home from the Nile. He had assumed Lovett had retired but there he was, noticing Nightingale's arrival at the docks and frowning as if in dim recollection. Then, clambering up upon the pontoon with the aid of his steward, he grasped Nightingale's hand and greeted, 'Hiram, isn't it? Hiram Nightingale!'

Nightingale smiled and felt a spark of satisfaction at Osborne's surprise. 'Yes, sir. Captain Lovett, sir. How are you?'

Any joy at reuniting with Nightingale left Lovett's face. 'Sickened, my good man. Sickened am I. My *Uriel*,' which Nightingale guessed was the frigate, 'a brig and three gunboats, and yet we could not stand firm against three French frigates.'

The firepower of the opposing sides could have been more or less even, but Nightingale knew the British insistence on always besting the French in seamanship and gunnery. 'Where did this occur?' Nightingale asked.

'Sir,' Osborne suddenly said, directed towards Lovett. 'I feel it is my duty to ask if it is wise to allow such questions. We do not know this man well.'

Lovett cast a harsh look at Osborne. 'Do not take offence, Captain Nightingale,' Lovett said. 'Our trust has been shaken somewhat. Are you staying in Cowes?'

'No, sir. I have a… I am at a friend's accommodation in Ryde.'

'I must report to our commander in Shoreham on tomorrow's tide, but I would relish speaking with you again. Shall we dine at the Dolphin this evening?'

'I…' Nightingale was a little taken aback by the offer – he had intended to be back at the cottage before nightfall – but he had come to Cowes with the intention of finding information. 'Yes, sir. Obi, do you mind seeing to the *Larkspur*?'

'Of course, sir.'

Obi departed, Lovett's eyes following him. 'He is your officer?' he asked.

Nightingale bristled, always ready to defend Obi and his good character. Most of the world only saw the colour of his skin. 'He is my first mate, yes,' he said.

'My word. What a modern world we live in.'

A little after six, Captain Lovett entered the Dolphin Inn where Nightingale had been sitting for the past hour. He had been perusing *The Times*, reading of the French's recent escape from Toulon. Lovett, raising his hat to the landlord of the inn and loudly asking for his usual order, indicated it as he sat opposite Nightingale.

'You are not part of the Mediterranean Fleet, eh, Hiram? I read that the *Lion* has taken up station there.'

Nightingale reddened. 'I am not in the navy any longer, sir.'

Lovett sighed and shook his head. He held a hand to his chest. 'My apologies, Hiram. I did read of the court martial after the *Ulysses* affair. I only struggle a little not to imagine you commanding a king's vessel. I hope I did not offend.'

'No, sir,' Nightingale assured, though it still stuck in his throat. To lighten the atmosphere, he continued, 'My former lieutenant serves on the *Lion*. Arthur Courtney. He also spoke up at the *Ulysses* trial.'

'I do not remember the name.'

Nightingale smiled thinly, slightly affronted for Courtney. He did not pursue the topic, but ordered a broth and he and Lovett talked of the island and of Nightingale's growing familiarity and love for it. When the meals were brought from the kitchen, and the rest of the inn also engrossed themselves in their meals, Lovett returned to the events of that morning. 'I apologise for Lieutenant Osborne's comments towards you,' he started. 'His *Racer* was troubled quite severely by the French frigates. He lost a carronade onboard and when coming to his aid, another of our gunbrigs was nearly disabled.'

'It is no matter. He and I have had some harsh words in the past.'

'Oh?' Lovett's eyebrow quirked in interest. 'I know that he takes his work with the customs service very seriously indeed.'

'The issue was settled, as much as I know.'

'Without disparaging him, I know that he can be a little hard-headed. He takes after his father, my brother-in-law.'

'Ah.' Nightingale had not realised the family connection. Perhaps that had had an influence on Osborne's multi-faceted roles. Nightingale felt he should apologise for his unkind behaviour but found he could not find the words – and, after a moment's thinking, determined that he had no obligation to retract his treatment of Osborne, following the lieutenant's own actions.

Lovett moved on without any outrage. 'You asked me earlier where the skirmish had occurred. A number of the Channel Fleet have required our presence over the last days.'

'I am confused. You are not part of Lord Cornwallis's Channel Fleet?'

Lovett chuckled. 'Now you give offence, Hiram.'

'My apo—'

'No, no. I am one of three commanders of the Isle of Wight Sea Fencibles. The squadron you saw is almost the sum total of our defensive force.'

'I have met a handful of the men training for the Fencible squadron,' Nightingale said, thinking to the folk Rylance had spoken with at the Catch. Surely some of them had been involved in the brawl at the hanging as well. 'I have heard that there is little enthusiasm for it in these lean times.'

'We are indeed stretched very thinly,' Lovett admitted. 'With the island being so close to the Channel, we are often attached to other business also. As I said earlier, I have to report down to Shoreham tomorrow and that means that the Fencibles here shall be missing one more officer.'

'Are the skirmishes with the French frequent?'

'On a scale such as that, no. It is not customary for my small squadron to accompany a contingent of Cornwallis's vessels. Our action is mostly against merchant vessels, although our attention has been focused recently around the Solent and Spithead.'

'Why is that? If the French are in the Solent already, I think I would have read something of it in the papers.'

Nightingale meant it lightly, but Lovett continued seriously, 'There are prison hulks in the Solent. We are concerned for the prisoners within.'

'Ah. I saw that there is one in Cowes harbour also. I did not expect that here.'

'The *Impregnable* is a new addition to the harbour. With the wars against France and Spain, the numbers in our hulks are swelling. Cowes is a growing harbour and the *Impregnable* prisoners are being put to work.'

Doubtless another focus for Osborne's scourge against smuggling also, Nightingale thought, but did not say. He digested this information along with the rest of his soup. He had seen the prison hulks at Spithead and knew of the many other anchorages around Britain's coasts and docks. The decommissioned hulk ships were unpleasant things, stripped of masts and rigging, rife with disease and malcontent, and currently holding masses of French prisoners as well as those bound for transportation to Australia. Many men had attempted escapes, a handful successfully but most to no avail. They were each as ugly as the *Impregnable*, just as Obi had commented.

'Do you know,' Lovett suddenly said, wiping his mouth with a handkerchief, 'you would be a fine addition to the Fencibles' officers.'

Nightingale nearly laughed. 'I do not believe I would be welcome. I was dismissed from the navy.'

'You served the King's Navy for nearly thirty years, Hiram. Many of the captains who care for each of the Fencible companies are men at the end of their careers, with sea experience but with no commissions in the larger fleets. We are eligible for prize and salvage money and our men are protected from impressment. How long have you lived on the island?'

'I do not live here, sir, but I have spent much time on the island, both in the last few years and before, when I was a child.'

'You are familiar with the people of Ryde?'

'In a manner of speaking, yes.' He did not mention their questionable feelings towards him. At times, he thought he imagined such things.

'Then, there you have it.' Lovett waved his hand but Nightingale did not grasp what 'it' was. The captain saw his bemused expression. 'Lieutenant Osborne has lent his hand to the training of the Fencibles but, well, perhaps you have seen it yourself as you say you have shared harsh words: he is not popular. As his uncle I can say it freely. He does not necessarily inspire their loyalty and motivation, and his main attention goes to the customs service. I know that he sees the local populace as criminals waiting to put a foot wrong and be hanged. But I know that their trades would turn them into valuable assets – knowledge of the seas, of the bays and their own charters. You have the heart they might need.'

Nightingale thought of what Louisa had said to him: *You have a soft heart.* 'I am not sure,' he said and detested himself for it. Where had the captain's spirit within him disappeared to? He had been an officer since eighteen years of age and had had to always ensure his men felt hearty confidence in him and his actions. After Leroy Sawyer's demise, that faith in his own ability had declined, but the *Scylla*, and Courtney, had reawakened it. When he now considered it, it felt like an ember, flickering in the pit of a fire, unable to struggle back to life. It had been doused by the *Lion*'s reappearance and the doldrums he sometimes considered himself to be in.

'I suggest that,' Lovett continued, regardless, 'when I travel to Shoreham in the morn, you accompany me. I shall request your audience with Admiral Nagle. Speak to him of the matter and he shall be able to advise you.'

'That seems an awful imposition.'

'Not at all,' Lovett said dismissively, and then when he saw Nightingale still hesitated, said, 'Accompany me anyhow. Your actions at the end of the journey will be your decision.'

He may have said that, but Nightingale still felt a shade of the same motives Sir William and his father had claimed when sending him to the *Scylla* in the Caribbean: kindly on the face of it, but with an undercurrent of misunderstanding of his own desires. Still, Nightingale was uncertain of those desires himself. Hadn't he prevaricated over his career recently, wondering if he had done the correct thing? Hadn't he stared at his old uniform and sword, only to try and give it away to Courtney? A part of him could still not shed those old entrapments. He wanted purpose, again – and he had thought that, by coming to the island and helping Mrs Woods, he would find it.

Therefore, he sent Rylance back to Ryde to return with his chest and a change of clothes. The next morning, Lovett returned to him and during the journey down to Shoreham, spoke to Nightingale in such a way that he had almost started to feel confident in the captain's ideas. But, when they reached the coastal town and Lovett informed Nightingale that they would be dining with Admiral Nagle and his local Fencible commanders and a host of militia officers, he had to convince himself that he was not in the same position of a few years before: passed around for commissions that he had no choice in, in waters he did not know, and with the shadow of the *Lion* still hanging over him.

Dressed in the best clothes he owned as a civilian rather than the uniform he would have felt more at ease in, Nightingale sat at the admiral's table and bore the curious looks of his fellows. Even the militia men knew his name and what he had done. He described the battle with the *Ulysses* and the court martial, hating that the almost five years that had passed were not enough to blot the memory of it. *Yes*, he said, *I was indeed wounded by a gunshot from my own lieutenant. No*, he said, *I did not anticipate the rising up of the* Ulysses *prisoners on the* Scylla. *Yes*, he said, *I did board the* Ulysses *from a reef of coral. No*, he said, *I had no clue of Lord Fairholme's machinations over Saint-Domingue and his own purse. Yes*, he said, *I set the* Ulysses *alight. Yes, I burnt her. Yes, I burnt her. Yes, I burnt her.*

Within the space of the two hours of supper, he was having visions of gutting this ship with fire also. As the health of the king was drunk, alongside confusion to the enemy, ourselves, and, much to Nightingale's discontent, wives and sweethearts, he cursed Captain Lovett and wished, more than anything, that Courtney was there. When they had dined in Trinidad, and too much attention had fallen on Nightingale, Courtney had given an account of the *Scylla*'s history with the mutinous *Hermione*. He had adored Courtney in that moment.

But, as the guests filtered out of the cabin later in the evening, Lovett indicated for him to stay. He leant across to him and muttered that he had spoken to Nagle earlier, making an entryway that Nightingale could exploit. With sea-pie in his stomach and port swarming in his head, Nightingale did not want to open or exploit anything. Yet he made himself stay, if only to say that he had not travelled all this way without meaning.

Stewards came to clear away the cutlery and the plates. Nagle requested more port, to which Nightingale regrettably agreed. He had not missed this side of a naval officer's life.

'Captain Lovett informs me,' Nagle said, his Irish background seeping into his accent, 'that you had an encounter with the customs service on the Isle of Wight.'

'That's correct, sir. There was an unpleasant execution and some of the residents took issue with one of the lieutenants attached to the service.'

'I see. Was there violence?'

'A fight broke out between the lieutenant's sailors and some of the residents, yes. One man fired a musket, but no one was harmed, only pride, I believe. I spoke with the local magistrate, Harry Castle, and the matter was resolved.'

Nagle considered his words. 'Captain Lovett also informs me that you have been residing on the island recently. Do you have merchant business there for Haywood and Co.?'

So Lovett had spoken of Nightingale's current career with his brother-in-law's shipyard. 'No, sir. I have been assisting a friend of the family. I have accommodation there.'

Nagle nodded. 'Well, I know that you did not travel to Shoreham only to tell me this, Mr Nightingale. There is no sense in stepping around the subject any longer. You wish to hear my opinion on whether you should be accepted as a commander in the Isle of Wight Sea Fencibles.'

'I—' Nightingale glimpsed Lovett's face, flushed with the port but encouraging him with a sly smile. He did so hate being strung into these awkward positions. He decided not to speak the exact words Lovett wished for him to say. 'I am not certain my personal and professional position would allow such a thing,

Captain, but I admit that I have felt a desire to become useful again, certainly with the growing threat to England's shores. My old ship, the *Lion*, which I commanded at the Nile under Nelson, is sailing once more and I stood on her decks only recently. It made me consider where I am and the path that led to me to this point. True, I have spent the last two hours discussing my actions on the *Scylla* and the fate of the *Ulysses*. I am not ignorant of the discomfort and perhaps the malice men feel towards me. If I were still an officer and another man had done what I did, I would feel the same thing. I therefore know that I would not be allowed into the position of a captain of Sea Fencibles. That is for men who still serve the Royal Navy. I, whatever my feelings towards it, no longer do.'

It was the deepest Nightingale had talked of his inner thoughts for a long while. He had fretted that he still stood in the same position as he did years before when confronted with the commission on the *Scylla*. Now, he spoke with the honesty he should have back then. Nagle, to his credit, did not immediately dismiss it as sentimentality and conjecture.

'Mr Nightingale,' he said, 'I appreciate your candour. I understand your uncommon situation and the troubles you feel for it. I am an Irish officer and for many men like me, ostracism is a familiar fellow. What precisely, then, do you require from me?'

Nightingale looked again at Lovett. Behind him, the night had fallen over the water. Moonlight glimmered off mast-rings and the gaskets of furled sails. A diverse host of vessels occupied the harbour, but all with a solid, collective purpose: the defence of England and all who lived on her green fields and in her towns. Hadn't Nightingale vowed to act towards this aim when travelling to the island?

He turned back to Nagle and said, suddenly so sure, 'I wish for a letter of marque and to be commissioned as a privateer.'

That had obviously not been what Nagle expected to hear, for he lowered his cigar and sat back in his chair. Lovett cleared his throat and looked similarly discomfited.

'I have my own charter,' Nightingale continued. 'The *Lark-spur*, from my brother-in-law's Bristol shipyard. With a letter of marque, I would be free to disrupt the trade of our enemies and protect the coastlines of the Isle of Wight and, by extension, England. Although the approval would come from the Admiralty, I would not, by technicality, be countermanding their prior decision to dismiss from the service.'

The suggestion hung thickly in the air. Finally, Nagle said, 'I understand your reasoning, Mr Nightingale. It...seems sound. I shall see what it is I can achieve.'

When leaving with Lovett, the man turned to him with hesitant approval. 'The notion of privateering had not crossed my mind, Hiram,' he said. 'I would not have considered you to be a man with such an inclination. But, Admiral Nagle has a firm connection to the crown prince. I am certain that your request has a fair chance of being granted.'

Privateering could either be a dirty business, or a glamorous one. Although sanctioned by the government and Admiralty, enemy nations would still consider him as a pirate by another name. Certainly, many true pirates had started their careers as privateers before turning their backs on their letters of marques and the Crown. Nightingale could not forget that he had been a part of the *Ulysses* trial, where the mutineers had been tried, and hanged, for piracy – and so recently, Mr Hodges had been executed for smuggling, another activity outside the law.

This course, however, seemed a balance between what Lovett had wanted for him, and what Nightingale himself desired. He knew suddenly, faced with such nearness of gaining another commission, that he did not want to return to a naval ship. It had been something he had fretted over, puzzling over his old sword and uniform. He had not wished for acceptance by those old employers anymore, though. He simply wished for the purpose of it, a direction in his life, something he could control and command.

Such abrupt confidence buoyed him, made him travel back to Portsmouth with a certainty in his heart that he had not experienced for some time. Louisa's response, at Haywood Hall, was as Nightingale expected. 'A privateer,' she repeated back to him. 'Is this what you desire?'

'It is.'

'Truly?'

'Yes.'

Nightingale had arrived late in the day. Louisa looked uncommonly informal, sat in her bedroom with her thick black curls loose about her slim shoulders. She had been drawing a whalebone brush through them when Nightingale had shyly knocked at her door, and she now ran her thumb along the bristles. Nightingale was unaccustomed to seeing her in her nightgown. The only time they had shared a bed, even shared a room to sleep in, had been their wedding night, so long ago.

She waited for Nightingale to continue, to explain his drastic decision.

'May I sit?' he asked.

'You are my husband, Hiram, you do not have to ask permission of me.'

'This is your space, my dear.'

'It is not a quarterdeck and I am not your superior officer, come now.'

Nightingale smiled at her jest and sat on the edge of her curtained bed. He could feel the heat of a bed-warmer through the quilt. 'For a while,' he said softly, 'I have wondered – not if I acted rightly by destroying the *Ulysses* and my career but… It is not a regret, you see, more a drive for purpose. When I saw the *Lion* again, it frightened me. It reminded me of those times and what I struggled through. I felt myself slip, in danger of returning to my old self, but going to the island and seeing their troubles and thinking that I could perhaps help them a little… I believe I am ready to face the sea again.'

Nightingale saw she was still uncertain. There was a sadness in her face that he did not like. She took his explanation without comment and he felt instantly ashamed for the past couple of months; she had had little choice in his actions and decisions.

'I'm sorry, my dear,' he said. 'I know that I have been leaping on sudden ideas without much notice. It most likely appears as though I haven't considered you.'

Louisa shook her head. 'You have been to sea again,' she replied. 'You skipper the *Larkspur*.'

'I know. She is so very different to the ships I used to command. As a privateer, she will be outfitted with heavier guns and Obi and I shall have the consent to battle against the enemies of England again. It will be similar to when I served the King's Navy. Although…not entirely.'

Louisa considered that for some time. Eventually, she set her brush down and walked to her window, which looked down over the fine gardens of the hall. She kept a small box there, locked with a tiny key, a personal and private thing. Now, she opened it and extracted a small sheet of paper. Nightingale thought of a day years before when Louisa had found another note of his, asking Alexander Davison if a medal could be crafted for Leroy Sawyer as a memorial for his sacrifice at the Nile. He did not feel the same cold uncertainty as he had when Louisa had gently confronted him about it, only guilt that he had done something to offend her. He had never felt worthy of her, and neither her kindness nor patience with him.

'Is it the *Lion*?' Louisa asked.

Nightingale frowned. 'How do you mean?'

'You said that the *Lion* was the catalyst of your worries. But I have noticed it in you for a while, perhaps since your father's death or before.'

'My father's death did not grieve me,' Nightingale said honestly. 'I said farewell to him years ago.'

'I saw your will, Hiram. And, whilst you were away, this note came for you.'

Any explanations Nightingale had been concocting about his last will and testament faded. Louisa handed the note to him and he saw his name and address upon it.

'I do not make a habit of prying in your mail, Hiram. I never have. Do not think badly on me. But I noticed this was written in the same hand as the letter your friend, Mrs Woods, sent you. I feared it was something terrible that had happened on the island that would need your attention – or perhaps mine, if you were to be some time away.'

'I would not ask you to solve my problems, my dear,' Nightingale said. Louisa had her own life, supporting her father, often travelling to London and Bath to converse with and entertain his colleagues and friends.

Now, Nightingale opened the note as Louisa already had. There were precious few words within, only a message from Mrs Woods that the frequency of the threatening post had decreased. The relief at such news balanced with Louisa's knowledge of his purpose on the island. He had not wished to draw her into the tumult, not when it pricked at the very sensitive heart of the matter.

'This is the trouble that you spoke to me of, is it not?' Louisa asked. 'You have been receiving threatening notes at the cottage.'

'Not I. Well, perhaps they are addressed to me also. I did not want to tell you and worry you.'

'Worry me? Hiram…'

To his surprise, she sat upon the bed beside him and laid a hand over his. Nightingale put aside the letter and gratefully cradled her soft fingers. She wore their wedding ring, still, despite the falseness of their romantic union, and he rubbed his thumb over the diamond set within it.

'I am your friend,' Louisa said. 'We spoke of this. I love you, not as a wife may but not any less because of it. We understand one another and trust one another. I know you very well, Hiram, and so I know that it is not the *Lion* and it is not your father's death that plagues you. It is not these notes either, but rather the wider implications of them.'

In a rush, Nightingale's heart suddenly beat faster. He fought to try and find the words and could only manage, 'I wish it were not like this.'

'In an ideal world, Hiram, we would not be married. But I do not hate you for it, and I do not resent you for the decisions you've made and what you've had to do. You underestimate me.'

'But my life has been your life, my dear. I do not want you to feel half of the pain that I have. All I desire is for the people that I love and respect to be safe.'

'My love, I am a woman with uncommon desires and with an uncommon outlook to the physical and to the romantic. Pain will always come to those who do not fit into the world.'

Nightingale admired her words, as he had admired so much about her. He squeezed her hand and drew it closer to him. 'And yet I feel I never comfort you. You are ever the one with the assuring and encouraging words.'

'I do not need comfort or sympathy, Hiram. You have done more for me by simply allowing me to be as I am, not only as a wife but as a woman who can run her own household without interference and who can travel as she pleases. Not every man, whether he is attuned to his marriage or not, would allow that.'

Nightingale smiled. 'Do you want to know about these notes?' he asked.

'They are to you and Commander Courtney, yes?'

A pit shivered in Nightingale's stomach. He took a breath to press it down and said, 'They are.'

'And Commander Courtney – Arthur – is a great friend to you.'

She was prompting him; he could see it in her eyes. He nodded. 'I love him,' he said.

Relief crossed Louisa's face. 'As you loved Lieutenant Sawyer?'

'No.' Now this Nightingale had barely even admitted to himself. But it felt right and comfortable to say, 'I love him infinitely more.'

The statement echoed within him, every beat of it strengthening his certainty. He loved Courtney, wanted to spend his life with Courtney, appreciated that with so many important realisations, the other man had been there to set the pace. He wished that they could have the openness to express such a thing.

'I worry for him,' Nightingale continued. 'Not only for his place on the *Lion* and on the sea. That I know he can conquer and face. He's a skilled and conscientious mariner – but he does not have a shield like you and I have. Our union, I believe, helps us to be true in relative protection. These notes show how tenuous and dangerous it is. Someone, I don't know who, may be aware of what we have, and that is terrifying. My father, when he found out about me, he...'

Nightingale would not talk about it again. Louisa knew what his father had done, binding him to a tree in the shelter of their garden as a youth and having him flogged for the crime of sharing an embrace with Tom, their groomsman. Tom had been hanged; Nightingale's father had claimed his own fate was a mercy. Courtney's own childhood awakening, a tryst with a boy on his first ship, the *Grampus*, had nearly ended with a worse fate, but he had been saved by the sinking of the ship and all the evidence against him. But now, no sinking ship and no vanished proof would arise to save him. He was a bachelor – growing older with every year – and Nightingale feared the world would see through the façade. Perhaps somebody already had. It was why Nightingale had felt so very torn about the matter of Courtney's potential matrimony. It was such a painful admission to think that might be what they must resort to.

'He will return,' Louisa insisted softly. 'Arthur will come back to you and he shall find his own way, as you have, as I have.'

'I have included him in my will,' Nightingale said, reverting to what Louisa had mentioned earlier. 'When I die, I wish for everything I have to come to you and to Arthur. He grew up with nothing and this is... It is all I can give him, in a world which won't allow much more. I have not spoken to him about it, but I'm not certain he wants to hear it yet.'

Courtney had rejected the offer of his sword. Nightingale thought that discussing his last will and testament with him might frighten the other man: a marker of the seriousness of their bond, or perhaps Courtney did not wish to hear of Nightingale's death.

'I shall aid you,' Louisa said. 'In both the drawing up of your will and by allowing you to be as you are, just as you have for me. We may not have a traditional marriage, Hiram, but your happiness is also my happiness.'

'And your happiness is mine,' Nightingale vowed.

He meant it, truly. Although the mire of his head sometimes felt too murky and deep, he knew he was fortunate to have Louisa and Courtney by his side: two people who understood him in both his sadness and his joy. He considered Courtney the partner in his life, although there were no names for their union. Nightingale had feared he was in the same place as years before, but with the day that had passed, he knew it was not entirely true. He had admitted the truth about Courtney to Louisa and he had dictated the terms of his engagement again with the sea. The *Larkspur* awaited and he remained her captain.

Chapter Eleven: A Lieutenant's Word

March 1805

My dear Hiram,

The fleet has returned to the waters off Toulon. After twelve weeks at sea, entering the Mediterranean through the Strait of Gibraltar, searching the bounds of the Tyrrhenian Sea and squeezing through Messina to Alexandria and then back to Toulon by way of Sardinia, it has taken some accustoming to being stationary in this loose blockade. The view from the quarterdeck does not often change. Though we are out of sight of Toulon and Villeneuve's ships, I can imagine the scene amongst the French. It will be the same for Ganteaume at Brest and Gravina at Cádiz. Villeneuve has already escaped once, and I cannot forget that Admiral Missiessy is not at Rochefort where he should be holed up. The enemy will be scheming, no doubt, or perhaps this is already part of a bigger plot.

Here, at Toulon, there is little to do but watch and wait. Our excitement mainly comes through the arrival of packet vessels and storeships. I am certain that the officers are especially pleased with the latter. Through issues with the quartermaster, our wardroom has had fewer luxuries as might usually be the case.

I have been trying to understand the Lion and her crew more familiarly, not only as a ship of the line but as a vessel full of nearly six hundred men, every one *hailing from a different background and station. I have read the muster books, consulted Lieutenant Appleton's watch bills and have tried to talk with my fellow officers, but am finding it difficult for anything to adhere in my mind. The lieutenants treat the crew as if they are a closed secret for only them to comprehend. All that I know is that they have struggled to maintain the desired rate of fire when in gunnery drill and I see rumblings amongst them that I cannot grasp the kernel of.*

Perhaps I am being overly harsh on myself and the ship. I know that she has a connection to you and I wish to have her represented in the most orderly and impressive way possible. Now that Captain Harrison has allowed me more of an official position and role aboard, I feel I can try and work towards that end.

I hope that the island is treating you kindly. You must ensure that Ma and Pa don't wear themselves too thinly by providing accommodation and resources to the Fencibles. I was sorry to hear of the mistreatment by Lieutenant Osborne. We both know the trouble when officers try to play it high and mighty. I hope that...

Courtney allowed the sentence to trail off, wondering what precisely he hoped. Nightingale's most recent letter had mentioned the notes that were still arriving at the cottage. Courtney had known they would; it was too much of a hope to think they would relent. But Nightingale had not indicated he was aware of the notes' author.

Regret, worry, churned in Courtney. He should have told Nightingale about the notes. Now Nightingale had come to the island, doubtless to locate the source of them. What must the man think of him after discovering he had hidden such a thing?

Courtney scrubbed out the start of the previous sentence and continued.

I apologise for not mentioning the notes to you. They started arriving not long before I came to your father's funeral but I thought that I could sort the problem myself, before circumstances overhauled me. I did not intend for you to become embroiled in them also. I did not wish to unduly worry you. Please, do not involve yourself too heavily. I shall make arrangements when I return.

Be assured that you may make use of the cottage whenever you need. It is not entirely mine. I wish that…

He wrote ridiculous things again, wishing, hoping. What did he wish? That he was back at the cottage with Nightingale. Whenever they were there, the walls seemed to bar the rest of the world. Miles of countryside and emptiness separated them from society. They had dined without servants and stewards in the kitchen; they had furnished the rooms together; they had kissed, held and lain with each other in the bedroom. It was theirs, and the idea of the notes tainting it galled Courtney.

Courtney shook his head and tried to formulate his thoughts into sensible sentences, but could not find any. He tried to scrub the words out. The ink smeared, leaving an unsightly black blur. The look of it sapped Courtney's desire to continue. He decided to finish with,

I pray I shall see you soon. Ensure that you do not wear yourself too thinly also.
Ever yours,
Arthur

The week of blockade had already cast cobwebs into Courtney's head and the rest of the crew's. Courtney had kept a closer watch on the men, certainly following the visit to the sickbay. The ailment slowly lost its grip, but Courtney found causes to be unhappy with the men almost every day. Little irksome issues, against the backdrop of languishing without much action, were magnified into larger troubles. Snide comments passed between messes; the midshipmen continued to fail in their education; and no matter how often he employed the men with their holystoning, he continuously found scuffs and dirtiness about the decks. Baker, the bosun, stalked the ship with cane in hand, unafraid of utilising it. Courtney often watched the harsh snap of it on backs and limbs.

'Has Mr Baker always been so free with his use of the cane?' Courtney asked Appleton in the wardroom one evening.

Appleton turned over the piece of beef on his plate and seemed to hesitate. 'Mr Baker keeps the men in line,' he said. 'You have doubtless seen that they need it.'

Courtney did not know how to respond to that. He had considered, perhaps, that it was his own conflict enlarging the problems. Appleton's comment, at least, confirmed it was not within his own head. 'There was upset in Dr Archer's sickbay,' Courtney said. 'I wanted to believe that it was merely their illness affecting them.'

'Perhaps,' Appleton said without commitment.

'There was upset in Dr Archer's sickbay?'

Lieutenant Martin looked curiously over at them from the other end of the table, worrying his bottom lip between his teeth. He had barely said a word to Courtney since embarking.

'Yes, an illness of the stomach, in Dr Archer's words,' Courtney said.

Martin considered that. 'I have been feeling out of sorts,' he commented. 'Do you think I should turn myself over to Dr Archer?'

Courtney wondered why people kept asking his own advice. The *Lion* seemed to be built on a foundation of uncertainty, and that was dangerous. 'I am sure it is just a passing ailment and it will wear itself thin soon,' he said, but throughout the night, he was kept from sleep by the sound of Martin retching and vomiting. The presence of illness never sat well with Courtney. He maintained a sailor's obsession with and fear of disease, certainly those that could strip through a vessel quickly and wretchedly. Eventually, he swung himself out of his cot, knocked upon the door of Martin's cabin and ushered the pallid, shivering man along to the sickbay.

Dr Archer still slept but Ellis was in the bay, awake. His eyes widened at the sight of Martin: not an ill deckhand but an officer.

'Shall I rouse Dr Archer?' he asked.

'I think it might be for the best,' Courtney replied.

Archer, arriving still in his nightcap, coolly observed Martin. The lieutenant had curled on one of the cots, obviously in some pain. Archer had previously said to Courtney of his confidence that the illness had been banished but he now observed Martin with a stiff, unhappy expression.

'It appears the same,' he stated. 'There has been a fever amongst the men affected by the malady and it runs itself through within a day or two.'

Something disturbed Courtney about it, certainly the fact that so few sailors had been struck down by it. He had seen the effect of yellow jack, scything through the crew of the *Scylla* and killing or maiming over half of the men.

'Could it be something they have eaten?' he asked again. 'Or…something related to the missing stores?'

Archer paused. 'Perhaps,' he said. 'It might be wise to inspect the victuals onboard.'

Courtney knew he should have considered such a thing before, but only Martin's illness had sparked it in him. The officers, he thought, did not tend to share the same food as the men. They had the luxury of supplying their own stores – but in the past days, due to the issues with the quartermaster, they had had to utilise the standard fare onboard.

He approached the topic with Captain Harrison who, to his credit, accompanied Courtney and Daniels, the purser, to the storerooms, a labyrinth of compartments and spaces tucked into the stern of the ship. Between them and the depths of the hold were the victuals to keep six hundred men fed and watered. The standing and petty officers had been turned out for Harrison's routine inspection of the *Lion* and all her innards, and Courtney felt their eyes as he and the captain stalked through their quarters.

Courtney looked over the casks and barrels, lashed together in the hold. One of Daniels's mates opened a number of the containers and Courtney knew that they would have to be meticulously sealed again. The pork and beef within some of them were deeply salted for preservation and carefully checked to ensure their suitability. But, as the lid of the next barrel was cracked open, even Courtney, from some distance away, smelt the inside.

'Good God,' Harrison choked, putting a hand to his mouth and nose.

It was obvious, even without looking within, that the meat had spoiled. Courtney delicately approached the cask and, screwing up his face at the odour, observed the brace of bass that had been brought ashore at Portsmouth under Harrison's orders. That had been four months before.

'This was meant to have been given to the men many weeks ago,' Harrison said. 'What the devil is it still doing here, and in such a wretched state?'

Daniels wrung his hands, obviously without answer.

'Has this been supplied to the men?' Harrison asked him.

'I...' Daniels stared into the putrid belly of the barrel, looking as horrified as Courtney felt. 'I believe so.'

'Well, there's the bloody culprit,' Harrison rasped. 'Who on earth thought this was edible?'

Courtney knew there was a large pool of men attached to the storerooms, petty officers and warrant officers with their own mates and teams, but not enough to cause a bureaucratic tangle that could lead to this.

'I am not certain how this occurred, sir,' Daniels said in a small voice.

'You are responsible for the stores,' Harrison accused. But, seeing Daniels's pallor, he shook his head. 'The others must be checked also. We are fortunate we have returned to the blockade. The storeships shall replenish our stocks.'

The laudanum, however, was not an item that was as easily replaced. Courtney tried to approach Harrison about it but the captain did not seem unduly concerned, even when Courtney said, 'The men may face grave injury and require surgical procedure or amputation. It would be remiss for Dr Archer to not have the facilities for all circumstances.'

'Are you a surgeon, Mr Courtney?' Harrison asked. The sharpness of his tone surprised Courtney. He had not heard that impatience in Harrison's voice before.

'I...' he began, unsure how to respond. As ever, in his uncertainty, a shocked anger broiled within him. 'I am merely concerned for the men, sir. There have been some issues I have noted and feel they must be kept on a tight rein. Lieutenant Appleton has been breaking up fights for many—'

'You allow me to fret about Lieutenant Appleton,' Harrison interrupted. 'And about the men's discipline. I'll hear no more about it. All is well.'

Harrison had not heard anything about it, but Courtney did not pursue the matter. Perhaps this was why Appleton had not informed the captain about the brawling: the dismissal, the false assurances.

Still, when the remainder of the stores arrived, Courtney kept a close watch. No other meat or bread or butter had spoiled but he thought he would adhere to eating fresh produce for the next weeks. He would even watch the killing of the poultry aboard if it meant confirmation its flesh had not festered.

He hoped that the issue of the ailments would cease now but still something did not feel correct about it. Daniels had clearly had no idea that the fish had spoiled, meaning it had not come aboard in that state. Courtney remembered Harrison himself touting the arrival of the bass, boasting of it to Nightingale. And Courtney had both heard of Daniels's diligence from Harrison as well as seeing it himself; the man did not even engage in selling supplies to the men, as other pursers sometimes did. The cask must have spoiled during the course of the *Lion*'s journey, accidentally or...deliberately.

The idea came to Courtney unbidden and unsettling. He had no reason to believe it but now the notion had struck his mind, he could hear the ringing of it always.

He tried to see it in context of the trouble hanging over him: the monotony of blockade, the disconnect he still felt from the crew. When word came that the *Lion* would be rotated from her usual position and sent to patrol further along the southern French coast, Courtney hoped it would administer a needed lifeline into the crew. He and Appleton had conducted the men through as many drills as could be attempted in her small patch of sea – setting and taking in her sails, running through the men's stations during battle, manoeuvres involving the *Lion*'s many launch boats – but there was little in the way of sailing the great seventy-four-gun beast through varying winds. As they departed under Nelson's orders further south towards the commander-in-chief's position off Sardinia, Courtney relished the strengthening breeze coming from the north-east. It blew favourably over the *Lion*'s starboard quarter, allowing her to sail large.

He told himself that the wind would usher away all his ugly thoughts and feelings. When Martin emerged from the sickbay, weakened but still standing, he hoped that would be the last of the problems, certainly as the offending cask had been tipped overboard. Martin picked delicately at his food when he was invited to dine with Courtney and Harrison in the great cabin. Courtney had run out of excuses to avoid dinner with the captain, another ridiculous notion that stemmed from the same source as his frets about the crew: his own troubled, mixed emotions. He did not want to hear of Harrison's in-laws. He did not want to wear false excitement for his own potential betrothal.

It seemed strange and fallacious to sit there and listen to Harrison's enthusiasm whilst the rest of the ship operated under a fog of difficulty. Harrison appeared as separate from his own crew as Courtney felt; the captain seemed an actor dressed in feathers and furs on a black stage. Courtney had anticipated voicing a reason to make his egress and starting another letter to Nightingale – guilt still weighed heavily on him over the notes – when Baker's bosun's whistle pierced the cabin. The familiar call interrupted Harrison's talk of London. He glanced to Courtney, and Courtney, feeling for some reason as if he were dictating events, stood from his chair. The call was no beat to quarters, but it still roused the off-duty men, who had recently left the deck for the second dog-watch, back to their stations.

Appleton occupied the deck. Harrison beckoned him to the weather side and stared out to starboard.

'Sails,' Appleton explained as Courtney tried to discern what they peered at. 'A possible squadron of them out of Marseille.'

A look through his glass showed flutters of white far out in the black night. Few stars peppered the sky, swallowed by a gathering of clouds that also fractured the waning moon. Perhaps the squadron had wagered they could evade the blockade because of the darkness. By the separation of the white sails, Courtney did not think these were ships of war, at least not the larger third- and first-rates that populated Villeneuve and Gravina's fleets. But the prospect of enemy vessels, no matter the size or purpose, stirred him. The goal of the British blockade was to entrap and intercept any ships of the French and Spanish, disrupting their capabilities for war and for trade.

'General chase,' Harrison ordered.

The wind still blew astern of the *Lion*, meaning she could easily maintain a course for the convoy. Courtney and Appleton set the men to their stations and by their orders, a reef was shaken out of the topsails. Courtney watched them closely, closer than he would have liked, but glad of it when the captain of the foretop did not notice one of the reef-points still tied. Before the topsail could be damaged, Courtney saw the midshipman of the top call to the captain. Courtney was pleased to see it was Fox – and then his vision dimmed as lights along the *Lion* were doused. Courtney knew, though, that any experienced merchant sailor would always have an ear out for the whistles and cries of a nearby ship. The *Lion*'s crew did not help themselves, though, murmurings and mutterings rippling irritatingly through the vessel as they heaved on the mainyard lee-braces to bring the spar to a better trim. He snapped for silence, only wanting to hear the creaking of the ship and the rush of the waves. Baker was ever on hand with his starting cane. His voice echoed Courtney's orders, though far louder than Courtney desired.

'Mr Baker,' he hissed lowly, approaching the man, 'keep your voice down.'

Baker opened his mouth, still in his guise of reprimanding the men. Then he steeled himself and nodded.

It did not take long for there to be a certain sign the convoy had spied them. By the time it came within eyesight unaided by a glass, Courtney could see the larger of the vessels separating to form a curtain about the rest. He could discern one three-master, only one true ship. The others were two-masted brigs and a sloop. Though he counted four of them, he knew the very sight of a ship of the line would put the fear of God into them. With multiple vessels to consider, their uniformity and cohesion might scatter. He calculated their potential firepower against the *Lion*'s but thought they may not even have to resort to cannonshot.

The convoy still beat to windward, following a sea path destined to converge with the *Lion*'s. Courtney caught sight of the names of two of the vessels: the frigate, *Canard*, and one of the brigs, *Caille*. They sailed well, but the mixture of tonnage and size would eventually hamper them. The vessels started to adjust their trim to bring the forward brigs five points large but they seemed to find the process laborious, certainly with a rising breeze on their hands. Courtney considered reefing the topsail which had so recently been shaken out.

'We will set the *Lion* on the starboard tack,' Harrison said.

Courtney thought that to wear would be a more proficient alternative. Although the action would be slower than tacking, they had time on their side with the convoy struggling to bear around and the men had not yet performed the manoeuvre in conditions other than an open ocean and favourable breezes. Now the wind strengthened, threatening to strain the lines that would be worked during tacking. If it caught the *Lion* at the wrong moment, they could easily miss stays and be clapped in irons, even. Courtney had seen it happen to the *Meridian* in the West Indies, staggering onto a sandbar, and then the *Lysander*.

But he had to obey Harrison's order.

'Stations to tack!' he cried down the deck. Further down in the waist of the *Lion*, he did not miss Appleton turning to stare at the two of them by the helm. But the lieutenant dutifully followed Courtney's example and repeated the cry. As the men found their places amongst the braces and in the tops, Courtney glanced towards the convoy. No guns had yet been run out. They intended to race for it. In succession, the *Lion* began to gain speed whilst the helmsman eased the wheel to leeward. Courtney heard the batter in the sails and feared that it was too strong.

The *Lion*'s head came around, nearing the sharp eye of the wind. She felt peculiar, the great weight of the ship heavy and stagnant whilst she approached stays. Appleton seemed to know this and delayed the mainsail haul before the yards were braced up sharp. Slowly, headway was made, as if given begrudgingly by the sea and the weather. The canvas filled gradually until Appleton could command the headyards around.

To Courtney's relief, the tack succeeded, the *Lion* swinging around into her new course moments before the first rain came. He realised he had barely breathed and sighed as the chase continued. Appleton caught his eye again, giving an almost imperceptible nod. The *Lion* crested the rising waves smoothly, ushered by the rising winds. She carried as much sail as she dared, too much for Courtney's liking, but the lack of reefing allowed her to gain one more knot on the convoy which appeared closer and closer through his glass.

There was another reason for their nearer position. One of the brigs was separating from the main force, turning to cut across the *Lion*'s path. As Courtney watched, another of the vessels echoed it, sailing closer into the eye of the wind. The cluster of ships in the midst of the convoy followed their original course, sails billowing.

'They are allowing the smaller vessels to run,' Courtney commented. 'They wish to draw our attack.'

Appleton hurried from the waist back to his captain. 'Who do we follow?' he pressed when Harrison did not respond to Courtney's assessment.

Harrison watched the situation unfolding. Each of the small squadrons represented a chunk of French trade to be harassed and stopped. They could not risk either one escaping, but Courtney knew what he would decide: the smaller starboard squadron should be followed and assaulted. The larboard ships would be forced to follow to defend their convoy, but for now their separation had lessened the threat towards the *Lion* and bolstered their own opportunity to attack.

'The larboard squadron,' Harrison opted for. 'We follow the larboard squadron.'

'Sir—'

'And Lieutenant Appleton, man the bow chasers. The gap is closing.'

Appleton looked to Courtney, as if he expected him to say something, but then gabbled a 'Yes, sir' and hurried towards the bow chasers, gathering their crews as he went. Courtney bellowed orders for the *Lion* to pursue the larboard squadron, whose larger weight made them sail sluggishly. The sea distance closed, enough that Appleton could fire off a succession of shots towards the sternmost brig's taffrail. Splinters flew off of it, raining about the surging waters. They had started to rise, the peaks and troughs of the waves increasing so the convoy bobbed and listed like corks trying to keep balanced. The brigs and sloops that surrounded the three-master suffered the most, tilting to starboard then larboard, rushing waves lashing about the gunwales. Courtney watched one entirely swamp a weather deck, making the matchstick figures of the crew slip and scramble.

The *Lion*, with her broader beam and longer keel, stood fast in the lurching seas. But the wind about her mounted as quickly and severely as the ocean, the twin elements whipping each other into frenzies. Above, the canvas started to strain. Courtney saw the yards pulling, upsetting their set canvas. As he watched, a sharp gust of wind suddenly snatched his hat from his head. He turned to try and grab it before it sailed overboard and almost lost his balance as the *Lion*'s entire frame jerked. Men in the tops were flung onto the yards, steadied and saved only by the footropes. In the din of the whistling breeze and the aching cordage, Courtney heard an awful ripping sound and watched in horror as the upper fore-topsail was torn from its spar. Its clew and the sheets stayed firm, stopping it from cleaving entirely into the wind, but the loss of the heavy body of it sent men scrabbling to hold on to stays and tackles and the *Lion*'s forward momentum staggered, thrown around as if she did not know what to do with herself.

'Double-reef the main-topsail!' Courtney shouted before Harrison could even open his mouth. 'And secure that fore-topsail!'

Even with other men, including Baker, racing into the tops, the men were too slow. The squall bombarded the canvas still aloft, straining the tacks and bowlines and sending clewlines flying from the men's hands as they tried to get a hold of them. On deck, they faltered as they tried to adjust the braces to bring the wind cleaner about the ship and the *Lion* was thrown like a child's toy over the waves she had so effortlessly crested before. Appleton, occupied at the bows, nevertheless stared backwards, obviously torn between staying where he was and aiding.

Courtney had never done anything other than launch himself into the heart of the danger. He hurried to the shrouds, dragged himself onto them despite the wind and rain, and joined the men in the maintop. Charlie Bowles was there and had bound himself to the yard by twisting his feet into the footrope. Courtney's stomach rose and fell as he bent over the spar which dipped and rolled with the might of the lurching *Lion*. The deck seemed a mile below, running with the water which sprayed up above the gunwales and over the waisters, Harrison, and Martin, who stared up.

Only Bowles seemed to work with any efficiency. They had not been drilled enough, Courtney cursed, but he had no time to damn such things now. The canvas filled, making it nearly impossible to grasp the reef-tackles, but with the rain striking his face, nearly stealing his breath, Courtney shouted along to the men at his side. Below, Appleton aided, bracing the weather yardarm to try and evacuate some of the wind from the topsail. It still rattled and squirmed and if the men had been jagged when reefing in good conditions, they were even rougher now. It took far too long to handle the lines and gaskets and at every moment, Courtney expected to hear the tear of more canvas.

As they steadied the sail, Courtney looked ahead to the foremast. For a moment, he thought his eyes deceived him. With the rain lashing down, obscuring his vision, he noted sailors pushing and jostling in their attempts to save the canvas.

And the succeeding moments happened in staggered flashes.

The stiff breeze rattled the backstays and rippled along the foreyard. The spar and cordage shivered. A shadow lost his footing, tried to clap onto a rope, and missed.

'Lieutenant Appleton!' Courtney heard himself shout to the deck below. Appleton whipped around, attempting to see who had cried his name.

Then, the thud of the body on the timbers silenced the entire ship. No longer did the sails groan in the wind, no longer did the yards ache, no longer did the sea score the hull. Courtney stared down, at that heap, blood spreading beneath its head, and felt his bones freeze over.

He did not know how he made it down the mast. Harrison stood at the foot of it, a shaking hand over his mouth. Appleton had run to the corpse but as Courtney rushed closer, he saw it was not a corpse – the boy was still alive. Fox's ashen expression gazed up at the sky. Shock and agony marred his face, mouth full of red, eyes two pools of glass.

Courtney dropped to his knees, stripping off his uniform coat and reaching to lift Fox's wounded head. He hesitated at the last moment, then did so, laying the mass of hair made sticky with blood and viscera onto the fabric. Fox seemed to be trying to say something, crimson lips moving soundlessly.

'Fetch Dr Archer!' Courtney ordered Appleton. A circle of men had surrounded them, including Baker, having rushed down from the top.

Within a minute, Dr Archer appeared, rushing over to kneel at Courtney's side. He took a single look at Fox and said, 'We shall move him to the sickbay. I can better assess him there and perhaps operate. He yet breathes.'

Courtney indicated Baker to come closer. 'Help me move him,' he said and between Baker, Archer, and Appleton, they manoeuvred Fox away from the staring eyes. Harrison hesitated, looking as though he was going to vomit.

'The convoy has escaped,' the captain said weakly.

Courtney ignored the comment, forgetting the French vessels. They reached the sickbay and Courtney could feel Fox's blood dripping over his arms, staining his shirt and waistcoat. Ellis immediately cleared a space on one of the cots and Fox was laid, with all gentleness, on the sheets. They steadily turned a vivid, ugly red.

'Mr Ellis, fetch my trephine and Hey's saw,' Archer said. 'I shall have to try and relieve pressure on the brain. I fear his skull has cracked.'

The gleaming saw ignited what little life was left in Fox, causing him to wriggle and cry in muffled yelps.

'Commander Courtney, hold him for me,' Archer snapped, and Courtney hurried to obey. He eyed the instruments with almost as much terror as he imagined Fox to feel. He had never witnessed a trepanning before. He had seen countless bloody injuries and surgeries but the idea of sawing into a man's head… Fox's pleading eyes stared up at him, saying what his lips could not. Courtney pressed down his own fright and with one hand, grasped Fox's head and with the other, he reached and gripped Fox's clammy palm. He was so cold, death-like, but at Courtney's touch, he clung on as though he were a rock that would stop him from drowning.

'Do we have no relief for him?' Courtney pressed.

Archer looked up, subtly shaking his head. The question of the laudanum lurched in Courtney, making him turn colder than he already was. 'Can we not give him brandy or beer? Something to ease him!'

'Time is against us, Mr Courtney. Come now.'

Courtney did want to look but he could not wrench his eyes away. Archer hastily hacked away chunks of Fox's fair hair and with a remarkably steady hand, began to cut into the top of his head. Courtney was no surgeon, had very little medical knowledge, but knew that the presence of so much blood already was not a good sign. Fox's skull had been cracked by the deck and relieving pressure on the brain beneath would not answer, he knew it in his gut. But he did not say so, and placed his faith in Archer's desperate attempts. His stomach rolled as he looked down at the bone, chips of it coming free under Archer's saw. Then, beneath, the wounded and fragile organ shone in the lantern Ellis had brought close. Courtney felt bile flood his mouth and he tightened his grip in the effort to stay upright. He could not help closing his eyes, and the sound was enough to make his skin crawl: the bizarre pop as the disc of skull came free, the dribble of blood onto the stained sheet, the rattle of Fox's groan.

Archer kept operating, kept trying to revive the boy, but with his sight obscured, Courtney could better hear the change in Fox. Beneath his hands, he felt the wetness of his blood and listened to the slowness of his breath. He knew when it had stopped, knew when there was no more existence left in the body he held.

Gradually, Courtney opened his eyes. He dared to look down, at the red-soaked hair and the exposed skull. Archer had paused, staring at the same point as Courtney.

'Doctor,' Courtney managed. 'Doctor, I think he's dead.'

The tension sapped from Archer's shoulders, as if a weight suddenly tumbled from him. The trephine in his hand drifted from Fox's head and came to rest, useless, on the cot. Gradually, he reached out and laid two fingers against Fox's neck. Courtney waited, looking down at the boy's still face. A trail of blood dribbled slowly from his open mouth.

Archer nodded. 'He's dead.'

Silence covered the sickbay, only broken by Ellis, who softly cried. Courtney lowered his head and slowly released Fox. He could feel the blood sticking to his shirt and as he raised an arm to wipe his hot face, a smear of it stuck to his cheeks. When he composed himself again, he noticed Harrison again, standing at the end of the cot. He looked as distraught as Ellis. He stared at Fox's corpse until turning and hurrying from the sickbay. A gang of men who had gathered stepped aside for him. Some of them had removed their hats, holding them solemnly to their chests. The other mids also stared in, all malice at Fox gone.

Courtney slowly stepped away from Fox, touching Ellis's shoulder and urging him to look up and present a stiff face to the world. He located Baker amongst the crowd.

'Mr Baker, would you see that Mr Midshipman Fox's effects are in order?' Courtney asked.

'I shall, sir.' Another midshipman entered the sombre space: Ramsey, who had teased Fox during the navigation lesson. He held his hat before him with shaking hands, looking between Baker, Courtney, and his dead fellow.

'That is very noble of you, Mr Ramsey,' Courtney said. 'I want you to arrange them and then aid Dr Archer with sewing

Mr Fox into his shroud. The rest of you,' he added to the gathering crowd, 'back on deck.'

Courtney's anger at them for allowing the convoy to escape cooled at the looks on their faces. They had been shocked into realising the power of the sea and the thin line between life and death aboard a man of war. Demise did not only come from the enemy. It stalked them, every day, striking down any man who did not respect the ship and the ocean. But Fox... He had not even been a man, but a boy, on his first voyage, with a life and career ahead of him.

Courtney found Harrison outside the sickbay, half-leaning against a bulkhead, distance behind his eyes. He barely looked at Courtney as he approached. Courtney wanted to guide him away from the rest of the men who did not need to see their captain so affected. He was meant to be a stoic, stalwart figure, never wavering, never questioning his own decisions. But Harrison murmured, 'I gave the order to pursue—' then cut himself off, trying to swallow the doubt and, evidently, the remains of his dinner that had been dislodged by the brutal sight of Fox.

Courtney decided to say nothing, subtly walking Harrison away from the sickbay. He thought of his words; true, Harrison had instructed the men to tack, to pursue the larboard ships of the convoy, not being expedient enough with his order to bring in the main-topsail. But the men had not responded efficiently either.

Courtney did not like the taste of such ideas, doubting Harrison's worth and his strength in making resolute choices. He and Appleton could work as determinedly as they were, but a lieutenant's word was only as good as the captain's above him.

It was simply his grief talking, Courtney thought. But the worries had been implanted since setting foot on the *Lion*. Now, they had spilled out onto the deck, seeping through the timbers as Fox's blood had.

PART II

Chapter Twelve: Ballast

Nightingale had not yet seen the new appearance of his *Lark-spur*. For the past week, launches had rowed back and forth with armaments, paid for from his own purse. He could have applied to the East India Company to underwrite the cost – it had not been long since they had agreed to provision non-Company vessels with great guns – but he felt his own money would secure a position he still felt was tentative. Though he did not occupy the naval list of officers, he received his authority as a privateer from the same set of men: the Admiralty and the Crown. It was no secret that the Admiralty did not hold him in as much respect as they had a mere decade earlier. A mere decade earlier, he had not burnt a very costly ship to the waterline.

But his letter of marque had been granted far more promptly than Nightingale had expected. He reconsidered the wording as he was ferried out to the *Larkspur*. As a merchant vessel, she already carried a slim armament, including two carronades on the quarterdeck: deterrents to any enemies who wished to try and carry away her cargo. With the recent Convoy Act stipulating that merchant vessels in coastal waters did not have to have a naval escort, much of Nightingale's work had taken him around Britain herself. But with the threat to the English coasts ever looming, and certainly with the recent action between Cornwallis's fleet and the French, Nightingale anticipated fights similar to those he had conducted in the service of the navy.

Rylance greeted him on deck, alongside Obi. They were observing the final twelve-pounder swung up by the means of the pulleys and tackles from the boat. A good portion of Nightingale's one-hundred-man crew were on hand to aid the perilous technique of bringing such a gun aboard and to secure the rest of the armaments in their positions on the flush weather deck. Nightingale looked with approval at the new array. Carronades were interspersed between the twelve-pounders, bringing the entire complement to eight guns a side. Swivel guns occupied the bows and stern, giving them additional manoeuvrability.

'Nearly complete, I see,' Nightingale said to Obi. 'She looks capital.'

'Yes, sir.'

'We shall soon have the tide. I believe we should test her new rig and balance and tour the north of the Isle of Wight.'

With additional iron weight on her, the *Larkspur* suffered a little during her first outing, despite the calm seas and fresh breeze. Nightingale and Obi spent time in the hold, shifting her ballast and weight to bring her back under familiar control. There was a time when Nightingale would have happily helped with moving the shingle and barrels but he found now that he struggled as much as the *Larkspur*. Moments such as these made him wonder if he had fallen out of suitability with this life, yet climbing back to deck and witnessing the *Larkspur* find a more comfortable position on the blue Solent made him smile. Since speaking with Louisa, a weight had dropped from his chest and he felt he could give himself to the service of the island. The *Lion* felt a little more distant; he thought he could submit her to Courtney's care.

Ryde's coastline passed to starboard. Nightingale believed they could soundly travel further south and round the foreland at Bembridge, but he paused at Ryde and went ashore. Mrs Woods occupied her usual position at the Catch, as did some of the regular Fencibles. She greeted Nightingale warmly and beckoned him to the bar. Nightingale was pleased they had made it to the point where she did not curtsey to him.

'You received my note?' she asked eagerly.

'I did. Have there been any further developments? Have the notes decreased further?'

'Yes, Mr Nightingale—'

'Please call me Hiram.'

'Hiram.' She blushed. 'Yes, Hiram. They have decreased. They have stopped altogether.'

'Are you certain?'

'Yes, yes, I am… Yes, mostly certain. We have seen nothing for at least a fortnight.'

'Those are good tidings.' He smiled. 'I have further good news. I submitted for a letter of marque and have recently received one. My *Larkspur* has been outfitted with great guns.'

He did not expect Mrs Woods to become enthused over the cannons, not as her former ward, Courtney, would have. Indeed, she seemed a little lost.

'What does this mean?' she asked, obviously trying to humour him.

'It means I can… Well, protect English coastlines a little more efficiently. I wondered if perhaps I could demonstrate the great guns to the Fencible men.'

He remembered Lovett's and Harry Castle's remarks about the men being less than enthusiastic about their maritime pursuits with the Sea Fencibles. He could not blame them, entirely. Lieutenant Osborne had not been much of an inspiring figure and had cast a black shadow over the reputation of the navy.

'They might appreciate that, Hiram,' Mrs Woods said. 'Allow me to speak with them.'

'Thank you, ma'am, but I shall. My steward has made friends amongst them.'

Nightingale felt as though he were a midshipman again, having to approach his captain with his journals and navigation work. He knew, even then, that many captains simply cast a bored eye over the work, not giving mind to their young gentleman officers. He half-expected a similar response from the Fencibles.

'Hello, gentlemen,' he greeted the table by the open door, hat in his hand. Faces turned towards him. He recognised Browne amongst them and was a little relieved. 'My name is Hiram Nightingale. You may...'

'We know you, sir,' one of them, not Browne, responded in a thick Island burr. 'Artie's friend?'

'Ah, yes, that's correct. It has been remiss of me not to make more frequent communication with you. I hear that you have given your service to the Sea Fencibles?'

The man did not respond, but Browne did. 'When we can, sir. But in these times, we do not have many hours to spare, not to service or to training, and we ain't often called upon.'

'I understand. I am... Well, I am not a Sea Fencible officer. I know that you have your men here, a captain that you answer to. It is humorous, in actuality, I knew him from a long time ago when... Well, never mind that. My past is not important. Recently, I have been commissioned as a privateer, which I realise may be a dirty word, but...'

'There are many dirty words here, Mr Nightingale,' Browne said. 'Many have been spoken of us too. Privateering is a small step to piracy and piracy is a small step to smuggling, which you saw is a thorn in us at the moment.'

'I did see so, yes.' Nightingale did not know what to make of that veiled statement. Were they supporting him? Finding common ground with him? 'I simply wondered, gentlemen, if you would enjoy seeing a ship of war in action. Apologies, no, not quite in action but... Well, a simulacrum of action.'

As ever, Nightingale felt more comfortable on the deck of his brig than in the Catch. His crew, many of them former Royal Navy men, knew the ways of the great guns intimately and had seemed overjoyed to mark the arrival of the meatier twelve-pounders. Nightingale felt the thrill as he paced the lines of them on the open weather deck. Seven men from the Catch had climbed aboard and, additional to their number, Lucy had appeared on the beach as they had been about to depart for the *Larkspur*. She followed Browne, observing the sleek twelve-pounders and carronades.

'In the service,' Nightingale said, 'a gun crew is expected to complete the entire process of running out, preparing, and firing the guns and so on in at least ninety seconds, ideally a minute. Often, we achieve two or three broadsides for every one of the enemy's.'

Nightingale was referring to the service as 'we'. He did not correct himself, knowing that his partner still gave his days to the navy. If Courtney truly were his spouse, he would still consider the navy as part of the family. The abrupt thought of such a thing filled Nightingale's heart. It gave him the enthusiasm and encouragement to speak to Courtney's friends as if he had a place amongst them too. He explained to them the motions of running out the twelve-pounders and filled in the gaps where lead shot was not being inserted into the barrels. Still, he had Obi direct the gun crews to demonstrate the rammers and the pouring of the powder from the horns into the pans. Then, with slow matches in hand, the gun captains lit the powder and one after the other, the cannons blasted, leaping back into their breech-ropes. Nightingale smiled at the smoothness and efficiency of the exercise: what he would expect from his crew.

His head still rang as the last of the guns fell silent. Though it had not been true shot, the din was just as real. He felt a curious pleasure to see the impressed faces of Browne and the others, hands protectively over their ears. Lucy had wrapped her shawl tightly about her head but seemed as awed as her companions. Nightingale did not know what they had thought of him before: perhaps as a quiet, timid man, softly spoken and a stark opposite of Courtney. The chaos of these guns in the quiet of the afternoon must prove differently.

Whilst Obi supervised the cleaning of the guns, Nightingale noted another vessel to leeward. He recognised the *Racer*, repaired after her tussle in the Channel. Lieutenant Osborne manned the deck, and Nightingale thought about ignoring him until he saw the flash of his spyglass, peering curiously at the *Larkspur*.

It was with gritted teeth that he allowed Osborne to come aboard, rowed across in a gig which Nightingale noticed was the same that had been shot at after Hodges's hanging. So the property of the Royal Navy that Osborne had complained about had not been as badly ravaged as he had claimed.

Some of the Ryde residents had departed on spying the *Racer* but Browne and Lucy remained. Obi put himself between them and Osborne but it did not stop Osborne's eyes roving over them both, lingering for a while upon Lucy. She did not look away but faced him with a straight back and defiant jaw.

'I assume that you have the relevant papers with you, Mr Nightingale,' Osborne said.

'Of course,' Nightingale said, not liking Osborne's gaze towards Lucy. He stepped forward to block Osborne's gaze. 'You may peruse them if you wish, if it is in your role as customs protector. But if you are of a mind to press my men into your service, you will be disappointed. We operate under a letter of marque now.'

'Yes, my uncle informed me. I do not need your men in any case. The navy patrols these waters and keeps a close watch on the Channel. Your support is welcomed but I pray you will not have to expend powder and shot, for your own sake. One does not wish for more bloodshed or to see vulnerable, aged men pressed beyond their capabilities.'

Nightingale smiled thinly. 'Thank you for your concern, Lieutenant. I shall take great care, certainly in my grand old age.'

Osborne looked him up and down, obviously having expected a more offended response. It took more than a young officer's arrogance to rile Nightingale. 'That is not why I am here, though, Mr Nightingale, despite being a little disturbed by your show of gunnery. My uncle, and Magistrate Castle, bade me to inform you that the man who fired the musket at my men was found and trialled quickly. Magistrate Castle wished for him to be sent to a gaol but he was shipped to the *Impregnable*, ready for transportation.'

Lucy and Browne reacted before Nightingale did, glancing to one another. 'Where was he found?' Nightingale asked.

'Hiding somewhere. I didn't see him again. Best that he rots on the *Impregnable*, where he cannot cause any more trouble.'

Nightingale pitied any man aboard that ugly hulk. He did not say so. 'Thank you for informing me. I hope that this lays the matter to rest.'

'We shall see.'

Nightingale watched Osborne walk to the side, about to return to his gig. Before he did, he looked again at Lucy and Browne.

'Ma'am,' he said, raising his hat to her. 'Can I expect to see you again?'

Lucy did not respond. For a moment her face curled and Nightingale thought she was about to spit at Osborne's feet, but thankfully, she did not.

With Osborne gone, Nightingale felt he could breathe a little easier again. He almost expected Lucy to explain Osborne's question to her, but about that, as with all else, she remained secretive.

'I shall see if I can alleviate the situation with this mystery man,' Nightingale said instead, referring to the circumstances on the *Impregnable*. He was unsure why he wished to. Perhaps it was related to his promise to help to protect these people and this island. The man with the musket had nearly condemned them all. Nightingale had been there when the shot had been fired.

'You shouldn't trouble yourself,' Browne said. 'He received what he deserved. We don't have any business with those prisoners, Frenchies or whatever breed they are. It is unfit enough that our work is shared with them in Cowes.'

But Browne's word could not sway Nightingale's ultimate decision. A dawning realisation crested over him: the notes had decreased in their frequency of coming to the cottage and then ceased altogether – simultaneously with the imprisonment of the shooter. Perhaps Nightingale leapt towards a conclusion that was not there, but he would be foolish to ignore such a potential connection. Who was this prisoner? And why, for all love, might he feel the need to send threatening notes to Courtney's cottage?

Now, though, the rig of the *Larkspur* had to be tested. He could not simply direct Obi to sail for Cowes without seeing how the brig sailed further – and with Lucy nearby, he wished to know her better, to determine for himself whether Mrs Woods's statement that she co-existed with trouble was founded.

'Well,' Nightingale said, 'I will return to that situation another day. Now these new guns have been tested sufficiently, I thought to sail about the island and trial her new manner. Are you occupied today, ma'am?'

Lucy seemed surprised with the question, but dutifully answered, 'Not much.'

'Would you accompany me, ma'am? It has been some time since I sailed south of the island and would value a knowledge-able pilot, seeing as I have heard that you were a resident of St Lawrence.'

Lucy frowned at Nightingale's knowledge of her past and glanced at Browne, hesitating. Nightingale wondered if he had said something out of turn.

'You shall be looked after, ma'am,' he assured. 'I will allow you leave of my cabin and my steward, Rylance, will cater to your every need.'

Browne assessed Nightingale with a critical eye. 'Captain Nightingale, sir,' he said firmly. 'We don't hold with our ladies being taken off by men. Lieutenant Osborne might think he can take some liberties but...'

'Oh, great God!' Nightingale rushed, reddening. 'That is not what I meant at all, I apologise. I have been married for over twenty years, and I...' *Have no romantic interest in the female sex.* '...I am the most upright, the straightest, of men, I assure you. But if it would allay your fears, you can also accompany us, Mr Browne.'

With arrangements made onshore and with Browne's companionship also, a lengthy journey commenced. Nightingale did not press the *Larkspur* too hard, for her own sake and for the sake of his passengers who had never been on such a long voyage. Fortunately, fair weather graced them and Nightingale was able to unfurl the full spread of canvas upon the *Larkspur's* yards, demonstrating her in all her glory. They neatly rounded Bembridge and travelled the south-eastern coast past Sandown, Shanklin and Luccombe. The evening came down upon them, the low sun soaking the craggy cliffs with red and gold. Secluded inlets and beaches passed them by until they could anchor safely off Ventnor for the night.

Only some way along the coast, Nightingale knew St Lawrence lay. He wondered how Lucy would feel, re-approaching the place of her birth from where she had recently departed. Before she could awake, Nightingale had the *Larkspur* leave the sight of the island and sail some way out into the Channel, without risking the wilder currents and conditions of that area. Ignoring Obi's looks which Nightingale knew meant 'Are you certain this is a good idea?', he shucked off his coat and shoes and began the steep climb up the *Larkspur's* mainmast. It was nowhere near as lofty as that of the *Lion*, or even that of the *Scylla* which Nightingale had unwisely scaled, but in the top, he still cursed himself. He had not clambered to a masthead for many a year. *You are nearly forty-five years of age, Hiram Nightingale*, he thought, *not a nimble midshipman any longer.*

But, as he heaved himself up, rising unsteadily to his feet and gripping a backstay for support, he took a breath and observed the deep blue bowl of the English Channel blooming about him. The day was as clear as a mirror, warm enough that a false horizon glittered. He could not see the coast of France from where the *Larkspur* lay, hove-to, some ten miles off St Catherine's Point, but tips of masts formed a cradle of sticks above the water. Nightingale felt for the glass in his coat pocket and trained it towards that mark. Cornwallis's Channel Fleet stretched from this strait all the way down the shores of France and Spain towards Gibraltar. The eyes of countless officers and men watched the movements of enemy shipping, blockading the war vessels into Brest. Around two hundred and fifty nautical miles was spread between the *Larkspur* and that important harbour. With the fleet strung out between England and the continent, it did not seem so distant.

There were fears of a French invasion of England. Yet, observing one of the hardy forces that prevented Ganteaume, Villeneuve, Gravina and Missiessy putting to sea, Nightingale could not see a passage for the enemy to threaten English shores. Previously, enemy squadrons had attempted landings in Ireland and Fishguard, only for weather and local contingents to repel them. Other French attacks had been schemed over the centuries, during the Indian Wars and further back into the times of the Armada. The last major assault had ended with the sinking of the *Mary Rose* in the Solent. Recently, French privateers had attempted to pick off merchant vessels but no wholesale strike had been forthcoming.

These histories both settled and unsettled Nightingale. They proved such an offensive was possible, but also that its repulsing was also attainable. Nightingale thought of the aggregation of vessels in Portsmouth, Plymouth and all of the docks along the south coast, and the Sea Fencibles trained as the final line of defence. They would ward off any attempt by the enemy. Now, with the letter of marque safely aboard, he knew he could join them. He could not help but wonder how it would feel using cannonshot again, this time in actuality and not simply for an exercise.

Obi met him at the foot of the mast. Nightingale tried not to show any trace that the climb had winded him, forcing that façade even more when Lucy appeared on deck. He hastily donned his coat and shoes again and tipped his hat.

'Good morning, ma'am,' he said. 'Did you sleep well?'

'Somewhat,' she said, but then smiled as she looked to larboard. 'I thought that we were off St Lawrence?'

'Indeed we were, but I wished to see the Channel Fleet. An old habit, perhaps, searching for other ships. Come, I shall send for Rylance and join you for breakfast.'

Despite Nightingale's frets, Lucy did not have any hesitation or uncertainty about their location. She joined him on the weather deck as they passed St Lawrence again and then raised St Catherine's Point. When they began the journey up the south-western coast, she talked with great knowledge of the various chines and beaches. Nightingale enjoyed the shroud of secrecy falling from her, reckoning she could be a stalwart pilot for these parts. They toured from the unstable, pockmarked cliffs of Blackgang and Chale up the isolated, sparsely populated bays of Brighstone towards Chilton and Brook. Here, the island appeared wild and moulded by nature and the forbidding gorges. The coast offered few places to land but those that existed seemed ripe for covert activity, providing a person knew them intimately.

That was no clearer than at Blackgang where the remains of a mainmast and destroyed timbers had been spat upon the shingle. Lucy, who had been observing through Nightingale's spyglass, slowly lowered it. It was there that Mr Hodges had been caught ferrying goods ashore. Nightingale wondered if that detritus composed the remnants of the wrecked ship he had taken them from. Lucy did not say anything about it, and indeed, fell back into silence for the rest of the journey.

Freshwater and the tall spires of the Needles marked the end of the rugged shores. The three great chalk stacks rose from the sea like sentinels, peculiar but eerily pretty. Nightingale directed the *Larkspur* to round the headland at a far distance, fearing both the visible and the hidden rocks. The wind and weather stayed on their side, a great relief as the brig navigated the narrow channel between Yarmouth and Milford-on-Sea where Hurst Castle watched over the waters.

It took some time to return to Ryde by way of Cowes. Passing the harbour, Nightingale looked at the foul form of the *Impregnable* and wondered about halting before swiftly changing his mind. If he was to do it, he would not go in company of Lucy and Browne. He had to consider his wishes first and ask more of Mrs Woods. He would not go aboard the prison hulk if he did not have to.

And another matter nagged at him after depositing Lucy and Browne safely back onshore. Though others came to the beach to help them out of the surf, making Nightingale hope he had gone some way up in their estimations, he could not stop thinking of Lucy's intimate knowledge of that south-western coast – far more detailed than a young woman might usually have. Perhaps it was innocent; she could have accompanied her father or brother out to fish or been accustomed to moving around.

But Nightingale could only remember Mrs Woods's idea that Lucy invited trouble. Perhaps that trouble was of the same kind that Mr Hodges had been embroiled in. Smuggling.

He could not make assumptions, not of a matter as serious as that. Now, he only thought of the day's experience of sailing a vessel, laden with great guns, on the open sea again. It existed in his blood; it always would. This, at least, had been the right decision. He hoped he could as easily shift the ballast of the rest of his life around, in an attempt to find an even keel again.

Chapter Thirteen: At Wit's End

Fox had been dressed in his best uniform. Courtney had watched as he was sewn into his shroud, the needle passed between the rest of the midshipmen's berth. Each of the boys had performed a ceremonial stitch. Perhaps as they worked, they thought of their previous teasing of the lad. Not a hint of hate or viciousness crossed their faces now. Tears dripped, noses were wiped on sleeves as though they were children at home rather than budding officers on a ship of the line. Ramsey wept the longest.

Courtney made himself listen. He could not shed the guilt which ached lowly inside of him, though he could not pinpoint the exact reason why. Fox had been trying to impress him, trying to be a respected officer-in-training. Now, he was dead because of it. Dr Archer had cleaned and neatened his wound as best he could, but the treatment did not quell the discomfort inside of Courtney.

At this, six bells in the forenoon watch, he stood beside Harrison before the complement of the *Lion*'s men and with each of the officers: Appleton, Martin, Simmonds, Archer, Moore, and all of the petty officers. The Bible was open in front of Harrison but the captain barely seemed to understand its verses. He read the words, staggering over some of them. Courtney could feel every judging eye on him. With each sentence, he tried to think how this burial united each man, no matter the cut of his coat or which berth he supped in, but the idea rang hollow.

Four seamen took a hold of the bier supporting Fox.

'We therefore commit his body to the deep,' intoned Harrison, 'to be turned into corruption, looking for the resurrection of the body, when the sea shall give up her dead, and the life of the world to come, through our Lord Jesus Christ; who at his coming shall change our vile body, that it may be like his glorious body, according to the mighty working whereby he is able to subdue all things unto himself.'

The formal words seemed almost callous. Neither Harrison nor Courtney had known Fox beyond the ship. They had no idea what his life at home entailed, who his family were. Now, his bier was lifted. Fox's white-shrouded body slipped from the support and dropped into the waves, churned up by the *Lion*'s progress. With a deep pit in his stomach, Courtney thought of how Nightingale must have once performed this task for his friend, Lieutenant Leroy Sawyer. This ship, Courtney believed, caused nothing but pain.

The splash marked Fox's delivery into the sea, back to the water which had only just started to shape him and his life. Courtney watched, waiting for that ghostly figure to sink. If he did not, the men would see it as a bad omen, one more to haunt the ship. Courtney could feel his skin drawing tight as Fox remained at the surface, bobbing lightly in the moderate waves. They had weighted him with roundshot, the required practice for burial, but perhaps, ridiculously, not enough. Perhaps the sea did not want him. It did not claim him, a life cut too short and at the wrong time.

Courtney noticed the men shuffling uncomfortably. He could do nothing but join them in their worry and fear as Fox was gradually carried away by the ocean. Slowly, the surface turned him about like a buoy, until at last, the power of the sea became too much and he vanished amidst the blue. Courtney breathed a sigh of relief. He relaxed the grip on his hat and placed it back upon his head. Beside him, he realised Appleton had his eyes shut, mouth in silent prayer. Courtney caught the repeated words:

'Lord, be merciful to us sinners and save us for thy mercy's sake.'

Courtney subtly touched his arm and he jerked.

'He is gone,' Courtney whispered.

Fox's loss seemed to carve a hole in the crew, though he had not made much of an impact in his life. The week, now back at the Toulon blockade, passed with interminable lethargy and lack of spirit, affecting each man. Harrison had been forced to admit the *Lion*'s failure to stop the French convoy to Lord Nelson, a job Courtney did not envy. Perhaps he imagined a slight where there was not one but the *Lion* was no longer entrusted to leave the loose line of the blockade, sitting stoutly and uninterestingly. Courtney felt a curious kinship with the ship. There was no rapport between the hands that worked the vessel and the soul of the *Lion* herself.

Courtney's letters to Nightingale became more maudlin, more yearning. He had since discovered that Nightingale had offered his services as a privateer, and Courtney respected the decision. He wished he could stand beside Nightingale on his *Larkspur*, the sprightly and nimble little brig that had doubtless now been fitted with more ordnance.

The one break in the oppressive atmosphere that lay over the *Lion* was the arrival of storeships. Since inspecting the spoiled barrels, Courtney held a suspicion of anything that came aboard. He stood beside Daniels, the purser, watching him note down everything that was heaved into the hold. His meticulous balancing of the *Lion*'s accounts did not speak to a man who had abandoned his duties, or perhaps it was harder work on his part now he had failed.

'I truly had no clue of the fish's spoilage,' he insisted to Courtney with his logbooks clutched tightly in hand. 'The captain was kind not to punish me.'

'Let us simply be glad worse did not come of it,' Courtney said. 'Lieutenant Martin might swear off all fish now, but there were no lasting effects.'

Daniels's insistence of his innocence, however, made those troubled thoughts stir in Courtney again. How did the fish come to be so rancid? Perhaps a mistake, perhaps not. Whatever the reason, Courtney kept a close eye as barrels from the visiting storeship brig were swung up. Harrison, allowing Fitzroy to scramble up and down the tackles and pulleys that supported the supplies, conversed with the brig's officers by speaking-trumpet.

'The *Victory* has received fresh food also,' he remarked to Courtney. Courtney wondered if the second-hand information from storeships was the sole means of knowing about the other vessels in the fleet now. The *Lion* had isolated herself with her failure.

'Sir!'

The voice of Mr Midshipman Ramsey suddenly echoed amidst the general din. Courtney turned to see the boy having hurried up a companion-ladder, now lingering uncertainly on the edge of the sacrosanct quarterdeck. Harrison waved him over. Ramsey seemed on the verge of spilling what he wished to say whilst looking askance at Courtney.

'What is it, Mr Ramsey?' Harrison prompted.

'The men, sir,' he gabbled. 'The men are fighting.'

'Fighting?' Harrison asked, as if the word did not make sense to him.

'Damn their eyes,' Courtney heard himself swear and, far more hastily and pettishly than he knew was right, marched to the boat supports, through which he could view the upper gun deck. He could see no disturbance there so hurried further down into the lower gun deck with Ramsey. Aft, a group of sailors clustered around the furthest guns of the larboard battery, jostling and murmuring. Two ruddy-cheeked, shaking mids tried to holler at them with high, thin voices. Mr Baker had already involved himself.

'What the devil is happening here?' Courtney roared.

A handful of the sailors separated. Courtney sighted Charlie Bowles and Donald McPherson, wrestling, shoving, gouging at one another. Appleton was embroiled in the midst of it, between the two scrabbling seamen, his coat stripped off and blood on his shirt-sleeves. Baker had his large hands about Bowles's upper arms, trying to wrench him away. McPherson's striped shirt had been half-pulled from his upper body, revealing a back livid with scars. Courtney had considered Bowles as one of the only sensible, diligent sailors in the *Lion*'s complement. He fought against his dark disappointment and shouldered his way closer to the two fighters.

They barely took notice of him. McPherson lunged again, breaking past Appleton's valiant attempt to snatch him, and punched Bowles savagely in the mouth. The man whined and crumpled, both hands slapping to his face. Appleton, nearly caught in the middle, physically grappled with the burlier, taller McPherson and raised a clenched fist as if to strike the man.

Courtney pushed his way in. He grabbed Appleton by the back of his waistcoat and the lieutenant span around, wild with anger. 'Take your hands off me!' Appleton shouted, then realised who he faced.

Courtney swallowed his shock, letting Appleton go. McPherson and Bowles had not realised the lieutenant's conduct and it took Courtney bawling, 'Every one of you, stand back!' for them to finally halt. Yanking McPherson away, Courtney continued, voice shivering with rage, 'All of you, kneel with your hands raised!'

Some obeyed, shocked at the stern order.

'Mr Midshipman...' For a moment, Courtney could not remember the name of the midshipman nearby. 'Harriet,' he recalled from somewhere in his head, 'fetch Dr Archer.'

Between himself and Baker, Courtney forced the men under tentative control, urging them to each side of the deck like dogs in a pit. Bowles, held back by Baker, groaned, blood dripping down his chin. He kept spitting it to the deck, trying to open his mouth.

'Not a word from you, lad,' Baker ordered.

'And not a single movement from either of you!' Courtney commanded. He still had his arms extended, keeping the sailors back and not taking his eyes from them. It seemed that it would only take one blink and they would surge forward again. The rest of the men stared blankly at him, as if they were unaccustomed to such harsh discipline. The disturbing notion, that they had been left to run amok, surged in Courtney again.

'Don't look at me with such half-witted expressions!' he exclaimed without thought. 'If you do not see your wretched behaviour, perhaps you should reconsider your place here. I would have hoped you'd have some respect for your ship after Mr Fox's death, after you allowed those enemy vessels to evade the blockade!'

It was not entirely fair to blame them, but the accusation had stirred in Courtney for a while and the emotion was scalding him.

'Sir...' McPherson began.

'Do not speak! Mr Baker, the next man to open his mouth will be started!'

'Yes, sir,' Baker responded.

The mention of the starting cane had not quelled the fighting spirit or produced any remorse. Clenched jaws and darkening eyes met him.

'You should be angry!' Courtney continued, heart now thudding with energy. He could not stop now he had started the reprimands. 'You should be angry at yourselves. Fighting, brawling, tardy seamanship! This ship will not be humiliated before the fleet. From now, we shall practise until your hands are raw and your feet cracked and your backs afire. I will not hesitate to use the cat o' nine!'

'Commander Courtney, that is enough.'

Harrison's voice shut him up. With Marine Lieutenant Farnham and two Marine privates at his side, Captain Harrison walked the length of the deck. He looked at the two fighters and at the other men who were still on their knees. Courtney could almost see the cogs of his mind turning, wondering how to respond.

'What is the meaning of this?' he asked softly. 'Why are you two gentlemen having a disagreement?'

'It is more than a disagreement, sir,' Courtney said.

Neither McPherson nor Bowles replied. It seemed Bowles might have made an effort to, but the mess of his mouth prevented it. Harrison turned to Courtney then back to Baker. 'Clap them in irons,' Harrison said. 'I shall have words with them later.'

Farnham obeyed, finally controlling the two men as they were arrested. With the disturbance ebbing away, Courtney's ire quickly turned inwards. Never before had he screamed at a crew with such unbridled fury. He had known many an officer who had been detested for cruelty and harsh behaviour towards his men and had sworn to never be one.

But he could not admit to such weakness, could not retract his statements. To do so would mean any respect he had tentatively gained would be lost in an instant.

Harrison watched the accused men ushered off by Farnham. He looked at Courtney, then Appleton, who was still finding his breath, clad in bloodied shirt-sleeves. Harrison said nothing, simply walked away from the horrid situation.

When he was out of earshot and the men sheepishly turned out to resume their duties, Appleton did not hesitate to approach Courtney, breaking the bonds of their hierarchy of rank. 'They are my men,' he said. 'I have the right to dress them down and instruct them in—'

'If they are your men, then discipline them,' Courtney snapped.

Appleton's eyes widened. Courtney could see he had been wounded, physically and internally, by the fight, affected by it more than an officer should have been. *More than an officer should have been*, Courtney thought. He was not one to speak of unofficerlike conduct. God, he had even threatened the men with the dreaded starting cane. He had hated that cruel stick when he had been a forecastle man, and as an officer, he knew that its efficiency was questionable. It was a bullying tactic. His enraged, screaming voice had reminded him of his father's, blaming the world for the problems he had caused himself.

Courtney had always considered himself as with one foot in the world of the common seaman, having spent his early naval career amongst them. Now, he had, however briefly, become the kind of officer he was disgusted by.

Chapter Fourteen: Impregnable

The *Impregnable* sat, dark and foul, just outside of Cowes harbour. It was the largest ship, by some stretch, so it dominated the other merchant and private vessels, looming darkly over them. Nightingale was accustomed to referring to ships as 'she', a loving and fond affectation that had passed through the ages. Yet he could not make himself see the *Impregnable* with that pronoun. It had been stripped of anything that gave it character and voice. No sails, no pennants and no armaments now adorned it and the portholes had been stamped with iron grates for prison bars. On the deck, a crude washing line had been hung between the timbers, and plain shirts and trousers wafted without privacy in the breeze. Every plank and knee and bulkhead seemed eaten by rot, barely held together.

Once, Nightingale thought, this ship had been a proud member of the fleet. No more.

He had gone alone, not even with Rylance for company, and had not mentioned to any, other than Magistrate Castle, that he would be attending on the ship. He had seen Browne's displeasure at potentially communicating with the prisoner, and Mrs Woods had stressed a similar uncertainty. But Nightingale knew he could not turn away from this meeting. He had to know whether this was the author of the threatening missives – and why.

Nightingale sat in a small gig which he noticed had bars attached to the shell, ready to lash prisoners to. As was the situation in Portsmouth, the inmates were used for labour in the dockyards and in the growing harbour at Cowes. Browne had mentioned people's discomfort at sharing their employment with the prisoners. It was already coming to the end of the working day when Nightingale approached the groaning, blackened sides of the *Impregnable*. Nightingale felt an itching tightness inside; he had never been onboard a prison hulk before, had never even been in the insides of a gaol. On his ships, there had been no brig, but the men had been clapped in irons for wrongdoing, awaiting reprieve, trial or the lashing of a cat o' nines.

Nightingale climbed the ladder, glancing at the portholes as he did. A number of faces pressed to the bars, men obviously not allotted for a work detail or men who had been punished. He felt their eyes raking over him, curious, perhaps even hopeful he was here to plead their cases.

A warden met him on deck, accompanied by the captain of the *Impregnable*. Nightingale guessed the captain was a little older than himself, but he seemed more haggard and lined, doubtless consequence of his presence on a hulk. Nightingale did not recognise him from his previous service, but he obviously recognised him for he offered a hand and greeted, 'Captain Hiram Nightingale,' then paused. 'Apologies. That is not your title any longer.'

Nightingale flushed. 'I still captain a vessel, though as a merchant master. No offence was given.'

'Ah. I am Captain Bartley. I and Warden Dixon shall accompany you around the ship. Do not stray from us or engage with any of the prisoners until we reach your man.'

Bartley seemed pleasant enough, but as they walked the deck, Nightingale began to see the signs of brutality. The *Impregnable* had once been a seventy-four-gunner and it still bore the spacious and wide beam of such a ship, yet there were things onboard that Nightingale had never once countenanced. Ringbolts were home to shackles, and great ugly awnings had been constructed over the weather deck, a wooden and unseemly shanty town that upset the line of the ship. As they approached the hatchway down, Nightingale could hear cries from that direction. At the foot of where the mainmast had been, a bowl had been sawed in the timbers. He noticed it had been filled with water where a man sat convulsing and yelling. Another prisoner, by the sight of his uniform and the brand on his right cheek, doused the victim with a harsh brush whilst another warden looked on.

'What is happening there?' Nightingale asked.

'The brine bath,' Bartley said with as much airiness as he had when greeting him. 'The man was lashed this morning. This cleanses him and ensures the wounds do not fester.'

However, as they descended into what had once been the upper gun deck, Nightingale did not see any further care for cleanliness and sanitation. The innards of the ship had been gutted, almost in the way of a vessel preparing for battle but in a far more permanent and barbarous manner. He looked forwards and astern and saw iron bars stretching almost the entire length. Inside the cages, crowds of men sat, packed almost atop one another. Nightingale had to remind himself that the *Impregnable* was currently at a lower complement, with some of the prisoners working ashore. The fetid smell of urine and excrement was like a cloak in the close proximity of the deck. Coughs and splutters somewhere in the musky shadows showed that the sick were mixed in with the healthy – if such health was possible.

As they walked along the deck, Nightingale could not help glancing into the cells. A mixture of ages stared back at him, from elderly men to boys who could not have been more than twelve. He wondered what crimes they had committed to find themselves thrown together in a stinking soup of wickedness. Voices murmured from the mass and he caught snatches of both English and French. Many prisoners of war occupied these hulks from Portsmouth to Deptford. When he had fought in America, he had known of others in New York and Halifax, and knew there were schemes to have British hulks further afield again in the colonies.

The next deck was no better, even though Bartley indicated the presence of a small hospital, screened off aft. He also pointed to a small schoolroom where a young chaplain currently sat. He did not say a word to them, only lowered his head towards Bartley.

'Where is our man?' Nightingale asked Bartley, wanting to finish this foul business as quickly as possible.

'He is further below, sir. He has been put in the black hole.'

'Pardon?'

'A single cell in the hold, sir. He has only boarded with us a few days but he has already tried to escape.'

'Boarded' seemed a callously euphemistic way to describe such a cruel imprisonment. Nightingale felt a pang of regret for coming here, knowing the sights and smells would not easily wash from him. A lifetime of atrocious pictures in the navy still simmered within him, though. He would deal with this in the same way he had dealt with them.

Down to the hold he climbed with Bartley and Dixon, the nauseating scent following them wherever they trod. The captain and the warden seemed used to such an aroma, barely wincing or turning up their noses. In the hold, casks and barrels still lined the timbers in the way of any other vessel and Bartley explained some of the slim rations the men lived on: the staple of ship's biscuit, pease soup, meat and potatoes. It was similar fare to an able seaman's, but Nightingale wagered there would be a vast difference between a prisoner's ration and the six pounds of beef and pork a sailor would receive, to say nothing of the eight pints of beer a day.

A cell had been constructed against the hull, stunted and isolated. Great bolts kept the wooden door rigidly shut.

'He has been put on reduced rations as further punishment,' Bartley said. The further they descended in the ship, the more heartless his light tone sounded. It was impossible not to feel a shred of empathy for these men and their squalid condi-tions. Nightingale imagined himself amongst them and his back itched with the burn of his scars. It had been a long time since they had troubled him. 'He shall be released from the cell in a few days, on the condition that he behaves sufficiently.'

Then, back to the horde in the upper decks with its rampant miasmas and dark filth.

'How do you know the prisoner, Mr Nightingale?' Bartley asked.

Nightingale had already had to discuss the situation with Harry Castle, who had wanted the man to be imprisoned in a gaol on land rather than the hulk. 'I do not, not well. He was involved in a fight involving a local officer and I helped to save him from a worse fate then.'

Bartley huffed. 'Better you had not,' he commented.

Nightingale chose not to say anything more, but waited silently for Dixon to draw back the bolts on the cell door. As he did so, he thought what a ridiculous notion this was, based on pure instinct and no factual evidence. Yet, so often during his career, his life had been saved by such an impulse. He knew he could not ignore this. He needed to know the truth and who this man was.

The door slid open and the man, propped up against the filthy bulkhead, winced at the light from Dixon's lantern. He held up a hand to block the glow which bled over the damp timbers. Every ship, whether fresh from the dockyards or in her twilight years, leaked, and Nightingale could smell the dirty bilge water that glimmered in the cell. The prisoner had been left there with only a bucket and the squeaking of rats. For a moment, he peered up at Nightingale, obviously adjusting to the new brightness.

'Is this the correct man, Mr Nightingale?' Bartley asked.

'Yes,' Nightingale said. 'That is him.'

'Stand, man,' Bartley snapped. 'You have a visitor, you can at least appear grateful.'

The prisoner slowly rose to his feet. His trousers were stained and ragged at the hem, his feet clad in old, threadbare shoes. A dirty waistcoat hung around his ill-fitting shirt. But as he looked into his face, Nightingale saw he was not much older than himself. His eyes still held a fragment of youth beneath their raw redness, a green iris flecked with brown. Perhaps once he had been handsome, but crime, poverty and drink, by Bartley's estimations, had worn him down. Nightingale again noted the harsh scar across his nose.

'You do not know me,' Nightingale started. 'But I...'

'I know you,' the man said, tone full of the accent of the island.

'Yes, we met briefly when there was the commotion over Lieutenant Osborne. You fired the shot at the lieutenant.'

'I did. Did he suffer for what he did?'

In the eyes of the law, Lieutenant Osborne had not set a foot wrong and had followed the legal code that prohibited smugglers. Perhaps he had followed it too stringently, too violently, but Nightingale knew he could not be convicted of such a thing.

'He has been reprimanded,' Nightingale replied, though his stern words to the lieutenant could hardly be termed that.

'That's not where I know you from though, Mr Nightingale. You stay in the cottage outside of Ryde.'

A shiver went through Nightingale's insides. Such a comment seemed to confirm his thoughts that the man may have sent the notes or, at least, knew where Courtney could be found. 'I do,' Nightingale said, choosing to not shy from the issue. 'I am known to the residents of Ryde. I assume that you do not live there? I have not seen you at the Catch before or amongst the company of the Fencibles.'

Nightingale's intention for saying thus was to show his respect for the island, even as an alien to it. He glided over any feelings the residents might have in return for him. Regardless, it did not convince the prisoner.

'I was born and bred there, Mr Nightingale,' he said. 'My life took me away from it but I am home now.'

'Home, in the *Impregnable*? It doesn't appear homely to me.'

'Where is your home, Mr Nightingale? Away from the island? Or here, at the cottage in Ryde? Reckon I know where you sleep.'

Nightingale tried not to react, though the comment made his skin tighten. He knew he was always one wrong step away from being unmasked. The appearance of the letters to Courtney had made that as plain as when his own father had bound him to an oak and lashed his back for his alleged sins. He prayed Courtney never had to experience such a pain, though he knew that Courtney had known about the notes. Did he fret and worry as Nightingale now did? For his sake, Nightingale had to remain firm.

'I don't follow,' he said, keeping his voice level. 'I am caring for the cottage in Arthur Courtney's absence. It was owned by the nephew of Mr Owen Woods. He submitted to fever in India and the cottage came to his uncle. But Mr Courtney now owns it.' Nightingale paused, knowing they stood on the verge of a sensitive topic. He steeled himself and continued, 'He has been receiving threatening letters. I wish to uncover who the sender is and lay the matter to rest.'

'No, Mr Courtney has not been receiving them any longer.'

Nightingale frowned. 'I have seen them myself.'

'They are no longer addressed to Mr Courtney, are they? Mr Courtney isn't here. I have said my piece to him and given him his warning.'

Nightingale paused. Questions revolved around his head. But at last, here was confirmation that this man was the author, whatever his connection. He said he had given 'warning' to Courtney. Did Courtney know him, or his identity? Was that another matter he had kept from Nightingale? Nightingale knew what that 'warning' may have entailed, judging by the short and sharp words on the notes: *Wives and Sweethearts. May They Never Meet.*

'Captain Bartley,' Nightingale said, trying to keep his voice from wavering. 'May I speak to the prisoner alone for a moment?'

'I cannot leave you alone with him, sir,' Bartley refused. 'Who knows what he may do to you? Or what you may do to him?'

'I assure you, sir, as a former member of your service, you have my word that I wish only to speak with him. Here, take my coat. You may even have my waistcoat if it proves I have no contraband on me or any methods to hurt the prisoner or help him flee. It is for my best interest that he stays here.'

Bartley paused, looking at the coat Nightingale had drawn from his shoulders. 'Keep it, Captain,' he relented. 'But Warden Dixon and I will be nearby.'

Once they had retreated to a darker space of the hold, Nightingale drew a step closer, lingering in the shadow of the cell's door. 'You wrote to Mr Courtney with these threatening notes?' he asked. 'Why? And you do not know me. Why would you then turn to threatening me, or...'

'He must have spoken of me.'

'Who?' If the man had not confirmed knowledge of the notes and the cottage, Nightingale would have thought him mad. Perhaps he was, after festering in this hellish ship.

But then the prisoner said, 'My son. I am John Courtney.'

The words barely made sense to Nightingale. Courtney had always said his father had died – no, he had said he supposed he had died, or been transported. He had escaped from home at a young age, living with his aunt and uncle until joining the navy on the *Grampus*. He had long thrown off the shackles of his troubled childhood, far more thoroughly and admirably than Nightingale had.

'You are Arthur's father,' he said softly, almost whispering it. It would explain the greenness of the eyes, the familiarity of the voice and face. For a moment, Nightingale saw the reality which might have come to fruition if Courtney had not forged his own path with Jane: condemned to rot in the hold of a prison hulk, every bit of his talent and skill wasted.

'I am Artie's father,' John Courtney verified.

'You neglected him when he was child,' Nightingale said, surprised at the sudden passion in his voice. 'He said he ended in the debtors' cells more than once because of your drinking and your gambling. He said he and his sister were worked from a young age and you squandered what pitiful money they made.'

'That is the life of the needy, Mr Nightingale. Perhaps you do not know that. I doubt that you have ever been hungry or poor in your life. Now, you come to the island and you tell us how to live and how to fight against our enemies when there are just as many enemies at home. When I heard that Artie had returned, when he had been living at a cottage in Ryde, I knew I had to warn him.'

'Warn him of what? Writing such horrid notes would not convince him.'

At least that was what Nightingale hoped. Or perhaps the messages had burrowed beneath Courtney's skin more than he had admitted, enough to unsettle him into considering Harrison's offer of marriage to Miss Sandham, enough to make him doubt... Nightingale could not begin to imagine the bewilderment which might have occurred in Courtney if he knew his father had been the author, confirming his living status after so many years.

'You know what it is I warned him of, Mr Nightingale,' John Courtney continued. 'I wrote to him with all kindness to begin with but he never replied, never acknowledged me. I know of his ways, knew of them when he was a child. I had hoped he had grown from them.'

Nightingale did not know what to say. To react, to argue, would confirm the truth of Mr Courtney's accusations. Did he also know of his own inclinations? Was that why he had reached out to Courtney, because he saw the truth of their relationship and wished to break them apart? It had to be the reason. The simple, threatening message on each of the notes would not stop running about his mind. Nightingale wondered what the other letters had entailed. And he also wondered, with a chill in his stomach, when Courtney had first shown the signs of the same inclination he had. As a child, like his father had said, closely watching other boys and desiring their companionship? Nightingale had known he was different from the youngest age he could recall. His own father had discovered it in him when Nightingale had been on the cusp of manhood.

Nightingale had to act, had to settle these troubles with John Courtney, but had no idea how to travel that path.

'Your son,' he said, 'is a good man. He has done very well and he has not allowed anything to hold him back. He does not need your warnings.'

'He has received them, though, and he has not written back to me. Where is he now?'

'He is…' Nightingale did not wish to reveal Courtney's location to this man. 'He has gone away. I am dealing with his affairs here. I command you not to write any further notes. It is upsetting people.'

'You cannot command me,' John Courtney said, almost with a chuckle in his raspy throat. 'You cannot decide what is best for my son.'

'What is best for your son is not for you to say any longer. He is his own man.'

'Did he heed my warning? Did he?'

'I…' Nightingale suddenly had no clue what to say. He had not imagined he would face this situation today, or upon any day. The intimate truth of so much threatened to surge to the surface and cause ripples which he was not sure he could stop. He fought for the words, fought for any shred of a façade, and only landed upon a pathetic, meek, 'I have no idea what you are talking about.'

It was clear from John Courtney's expression that he did not believe him. But before the man could press any more,

Nightingale turned away and called across to Bartley and Dixon, heart thudding sickly, 'I think I have heard everything I need to from this man. The matter is settled.'

Such a lie, but Nightingale needed time to sift through everything and consider his next steps. He could not do that in this horrid space rife with disease and suffering, the blackened bulkheads pressing too closely upon him. Dixon returned to shut the cell door again and Nightingale cast a last look at John Courtney, the father of the man he loved so terribly. He hoped that he wore a mask over the fright and also hoped that the bolt on his door had been thrown across with finality. Nightingale escaped the dark bowels of the *Impregnable* and breathed in shallow gasps until the launch boat deposited him back on secure, clean ground.

Perhaps he should have heeded the advice and avoided the shadow of the prison hulk. But he knew he could not have done that, for his own sake. He could not have had the wonder of the threats hanging over him. He had vowed to stay firm for Courtney; this had only complicated events.

Nightingale tried to stop with those spiralling thoughts. For what would come, he would need a clear mind.

Chapter Fifteen: A Loose Blockade

2 April 1805

As Courtney sat with Harrison in the great cabin, low heat leeching through his uniform, he thought of the other times he had participated in such an investigation like that which they currently had to wade through. He had interviewed Kieran Attrill with Nightingale on the *Scylla*, after he had been caught stealing and brawling, then he had spoken with Paterson and Arnold on the *Lysander* when they had been accused of sodomy. Courtney detested acting as a judge and jury, but these wheels had already been set in motion.

McPherson, hat in hand, had so far spoken in halting, ridiculous sentences, staring at a point on the gallery windows behind Harrison and Courtney, with Farnham lingering behind him.

'You say that you were brawling because you are of the opinion that this ship is cursed?' Harrison clarified. It bore a worrying resemblance to the jest he had made in Portsmouth.

'Yes, sir,' McPherson said. 'We've had some mighty bad luck, sir. The fish, sir, the convoy, sir, and then Mr Fox, sir, and how the sea didn't want him. Mr Bowles took offence, saying it was disrespectful to Mr Fox.'

'I am inclined to agree.'

'This ship is not cursed, Mr McPherson,' Courtney interjected. 'There is no such thing. If a ship experiences bad fortune, it is a result of her crew and the situations she finds herself in.'

'Sir, I mean no disrespect, but I've been on many ships and the bad luck follows some of 'em like a shadow. It soaks into the timbers. I fear we will lose the Frenchies or the Dons because of it.'

'That is dangerous language, Mr McPherson,' Harrison said calmly. 'It would be wise to not give voice to such superstitions.'

'But I've heard of this ship, sir. I know what happened to her last lieutenant. He died at the Nile and now his ghost is angry, sir.'

Courtney did not like this subject, certainly did not like to hear the shadow of Lieutenant Leroy Sawyer raised. His death had carved a hole in Nightingale's heart and had been the spark for so much of Nightingale's grief.

'There are no ghosts on this ship,' Harrison said. 'Lieutenant Sawyer's death was tragic but the way of the service. He would have known that, and he would be angrier to hear your irrational talk about him.'

'I hear the crying and the moaning at night, sir,' McPherson insisted.

'I believe that will be all,' Harrison finished. 'Lieutenant Farnham, please take Mr McPherson below and bring Mr Bowles.'

Harrison did not comment to Courtney about the proceedings, but waited for Bowles to arrive. Dried blood still coated his mouth and chin and when he spoke, Courtney saw his front teeth had been cracked or entirely wrenched from his gums. McPherson had been angry at him – and Courtney could not believe it was simply to do with the alleged 'curse'.

'Mr McPherson tells us,' Harrison said, 'that you were fighting over his superstitious beliefs.'

Bowles did not reply. Courtney was about to urge him to acknowledge the captain but Harrison continued.

'He said that you took offence to them and found them disrespectful to Mr Midshipman Fox.'

Still, nothing from Bowles.

'He seemed quite insistent upon there being ghosts and curses upon the *Lion*.'

'This ship ain't cursed, sir,' Bowles suddenly said. 'And there ain't any ghosts here either. Just evil men.'

Courtney looked to Harrison, who frowned in interest. 'Evil men?' Harrison asked. 'What prompts that accusation?'

Bowles shook his head. 'Can't rightly say it, sir. Makes me ill just thinking of it.'

'I don't follow.'

'I heard talk… Talk from the gunner's mates, sir—'

'Well, one mustn't pay heed to rumour, Mr Bowles.'

'What was the talk you heard?' Courtney asked.

Bowles fell into silence again. Courtney could see he was chewing the words in his mouth, trying to find the will to say them. What could be so terrible to shock a man of the sea? He knew, from McPherson's example and many others, that they were ones prone to superstition and fret, but they were also stalwart, bearing most experiences with a stiff spine. A man did not stare at his fellows being run through with cannonshot and emerge unchanged, yet it instilled a strength to face awful circumstances.

'Speak, Mr Bowles,' Courtney pressed.

'I heard talk, sir, that Mr McPherson had been…found with one of the midshipmen.'

Courtney paused. Harrison asked, tentatively, 'What do you mean by "found", Mr Bowles?'

'Doing unspeakable things with them, sir. That's all I heard, sir, but I have brothers, sir, around the ages of the midshipmen and if someone had…' Bowles shook his head again.

'Ah,' Harrison said, but seemed unable to comment beyond that.

'Where did you hear this rumour, Mr Bowles?' Courtney asked. 'Who spoke of it?'

'Mainly the gunner's mates, sir. It spread a little through the lower decks. I didn't have to hear much for it to disgust me, sir, to anger me.'

It was all that Bowles needed to say, and all that it appeared he could muster. Farnham also took Bowles away, back to his imprisonment, and Courtney turned to a shocked and bewildered Harrison.

'What are we to do, sir?' Courtney asked. 'If those rumours are true…'

'I…' Harrison fought for the words. 'I have not… It cannot be true. Why should anyone wish to interact with a midshipman, with a boy, in that manner?'

Was Harrison that blind to the world and its ugliness? Article Twenty-Eight encompassed it: sodomy with man, beast, or boy. Freely given love, rape, and pederasty were engulfed by the same clause.

'We must speak with McPherson again,' Courtney suggested. 'Put Bowles's accusations to him and see how he responds.'

'I cannot ask that of him!' Harrison rushed. 'It is… Not… Not something one should speak of.'

'The man may have harmed the midshipmen, sir. For that and the fighting, we cannot let him go unpunished.'

'Mr Bowles also fought, Commander. Article Twenty-Two states that any man who quarrels or fights with his fellows shall meet the judgement of a court martial. But I cannot apply for a court martial, not while we are on blockading duty.'

It seemed an ideal time to do so: captains were gathered, the admiral was present. However, the *Lion* had already drawn negative attention to herself, giving herself a name and reputation, and more would only solidify that discredit. Perhaps that was what Harrison referred to – yet Courtney could not stand by whilst boys were hurt. He had previously averred that seamen had strength to stoically face challenging circumstances, but not in this way. Such a thing should not be ignored with a brave face.

'We shall deal with the fighting first,' Harrison continued. 'The both of them must be punished. It is only fair.'

'Sir…' Courtney began but did not know how to finish.

'They must be lashed. That is the way of it. You, yourself, said that you would not hesitate to use the cat o' nine. Lashing, yes, that what the regulations say. Do you agree, Lieutenant?'

The use of 'lieutenant' rather than 'commander' stopped any rebuttal Courtney had. Harrison did not seem to realise he had said anything wrong. And neither did he retract his decision to flog both Bowles and McPherson, despite Bowles's misdemeanour being far less ugly than McPherson's alleged one. McPherson was not questioned again, but soon brought before the entire ship's company aside Bowles.

Courtney stood beside Harrison, the brightness of the low sun getting into his eyes. Surrounding the *Lion*, far distant, but still within sight through a glass, the rest of the fleet lingered. Courtney wondered if their eyes would too be turned towards the *Lion*, observing the ritual taking place. There was no shame in the punishment of flogging, not in the eyes of the codes that governed the fleet, but Courtney could not shift the unsettled feeling in his stomach. This felt wrong. They had not fully investigated the circumstances because Harrison had not dictated it.

Courtney tried to observe the expressions on the waiting sailors as Harrison read their crimes for all to hear: no reference to McPherson's hidden actions, but purely regarding the fighting. Bowles had said others in the lower decks had heard the rumours of harm to the midshipmen, and Courtney attempted to see any flicker in their expressions, any sign that there was more to this unseemly tale. No deckhand and no midshipman betrayed any hint.

Still, Harrison's voice had trembled a little as he spoke and now, next to Courtney, he seemed to sway on his feet, as if the heat of the sun caused him exhaustion. Hearing his harsh breathing, Courtney knew he himself had to remain firm and bear this exercise.

Baker came forth with his lash. Usually, this would be the duty of his mates, but Courtney did not know who to trust amidst the petty officers. He already suspected them after the incident with the spoiled fish, and these new rumours gave further cause. When Baker had offered his services in place of his mates, Courtney had agreed. The knotted cords of the cat o' nine tails drooped onto the timbers and the sinister sight seemed to move something within McPherson. He looked at it with widening eyes before being tied to the upright grating. His shirt was stripped from him and Courtney saw the patchwork of scars that lined his broad back. He had been lashed before. For what infraction?

'Mr Baker,' Harrison intoned. 'Begin.'

The whip lashed into the air, every knot coiling backwards and then, with a sharp flick of Baker's wrist, they each cracked into McPherson's shoulders.

McPherson gritted his teeth. By the look of his back, he was accustomed to such pain. But still he ground his jaw and winced as the next strike connected. Red marks appeared on McPherson's skin, blood welled and flew, and he remained silent. Courtney watched without reaction. The silence of the scene cut around him, the dismal quietude other than the slap of leather on flesh. Soon, it was split by a low growling from McPherson's throat, the first true sign of his pain. Baker did not cease his efficient, strong movements, continually opening the welts that spilled over McPherson's back.

With some strength, Baker administered the customary two dozen lashes. Harrison had not opted for more, though many captains did so. Witnessing his conspirator weathering such punishment had whitened Bowles's face. He went to his own discipline quietly but Courtney could see the shivering of his limbs. As his shirt was removed, Courtney saw pale, fresh planes of skin. He had not been lashed before.

'Mr Baker, begin,' Harrison said again, the words tumbling from him.

Courtney watched Bowles's expression. He did not tear his eyes from him as the knots of the cat o' nines first connected.

The man's mouth opened, though no sound emitted such was the shock. He barely had time to compose himself before the next lash tore a strip across his tender spine. This time, a high cry spouted from him. Courtney sucked in a breath, tightening his hands behind his back. Harrison, beside him, shifted his position.

Baker maintained a steady rhythm, directly whipping different spots on Bowles's back. It turned it into an ugly mess. Bowles choked out his groans, furiously trying to keep silent but only making the sounds worse, grovelling and tightening in his throat. Tears spilled from his eyes. He turned his face so he stared plainly up at Courtney. At first, Courtney thought it was defiance. Some men needed a target for their ire and he was not unaccustomed to being that. But the weeping and the pained sobs did not speak of fury and resistance. Desperation bled from his tense limbs and writhes as he tried to escape the lashes. Courtney kept his gaze. He had to remain with a stiff spine and firm countenance.

It was more than could be said for Harrison once the punishment had concluded. He dismissed the men by their divisions, settling them back under the authority of the midshipmen and petty officers, and exhaled a long, shivering breath which he had evidently been keeping in throughout the flogging. His face had turned a pallid green, eyes a little dark and sunken.

'Are you well, sir?' Appleton asked, and Courtney was glad he was not the only one to notice the problem.

'I am well, thank you, Lieutenant,' Harrison said dismissively, forcing a smile. 'I am not a flogging captain. The practice makes me itch, as though I am the one being whipped.'

'You are dreadfully pale, sir,' Courtney said. 'Shall I fetch Dr Archer?'

'No! No, I am fine. He has more important concerns.'

His brusque dismissal finished that topic of conversation. Courtney, however, still visited the sickbay. He wished to ensure it had returned to its normal standard, but also wished to ascertain the mood of McPherson and Bowles in their vulnerable periods after the punishment. Descending the companion-ladder, he passed men, scrubbing the remains of the blood from the timbers. They moved a few inches to let him through, looked up, and for a moment, Courtney did not think they would give the required salute. Not so long ago, he had bawled at them, blaming them for losing the convoy and for acting poorly. They saluted, but Courtney could not deter the feelings that had prompted such a doubt.

McPherson and Bowles had already made their way to Dr Archer's care. Ellis aided the doctor in soaking rags in vinegar and salt that would clean the wounds with vicious intensity.

'How are they, Doctor?' Courtney asked as he entered.

'They will recover, Commander,' Archer said.

Courtney looked over the men's red-raw backs where they lay on their stomachs. Blood had already been washed from their skin, so he could see the extent of the injuries. McPherson's wounds clustered about his shoulder blades, ugly lines that joined the patchwork of scars already there. Beside him, Bowles's back had been opened from neck to tailbone. Every subsequent movement of his would arouse the injuries. The man seemed to be in a dead faint, only wakened by the press of the cloth on his spine.

Courtney felt a spark of pity for him. He did not know whether to swallow it or not. He had trusted Bowles, had respected him as one of the only alert men when chasing the convoy, and now he had come to Harrison with the stories about McPherson…

McPherson barely stirred as he was attended. Courtney wondered if Harrison would imprison him again, pending further questions into his conduct.

Courtney lingered awkwardly whilst Archer dealt with the men. When he had finished, he took him aside, out of the curtained sickbay and to the quietest corner of the gun deck. With the noon meal approaching and some men aiding Cook at the galley with its preparation, attention was elsewhere.

'Are you well, Commander Courtney?' Archer questioned.

'I am well,' he lied. 'I… I wished to ask you something which might seem indelicate.'

'I find nothing indelicate as a naval surgeon, Commander.'

He had not heard Courtney's concerns yet and Courtney would not tell him all. But he had to know one thing. 'Have the midshipmen come to you with any ailments? I am…concerned for their health.'

'I would not like to speak of my patients, but no, I have had no visits from them. The only matter I have dealt with is from Mr Fox.'

'Mr Fox?'

'You did not know? He mentioned that he was going to speak with you.'

Courtney frowned. 'No, I did not know. He never came to me. When was this?'

'Two days or so before his sad death.'

A chill travelled down Courtney's spine. Fox had wished to speak with him? Had he uncovered something in the lower decks and had intended to impart it to Courtney? He would never know now. Fox's knowledge had gone with him to the depths of the sea.

'What did he come to you about?' Courtney asked. 'Was he ailing?'

'No, not in the body at least. He…' Archer paused. 'Commander, I do not enjoy discussing my patients outside the sickbay. I told you that I prefer to keep one side of the partition—'

'I'm aware, and I apologise. But something is occurring on this ship and I fear it is darker than I appreciated. If necessary, I shall have the captain ask it of you, but I…I must know.'

Archer considered him. They had served together on the *Scylla*, and Archer had given trustworthy testimony in support of Nightingale at the court martial. It was not as though Courtney was a stranger, pressing for untoward information. Eventually, Archer sighed.

'I understand,' he said. 'It unsettled me a little also, certainly in light of the missing medical stores. Mr Fox admitted that he had been having trouble sleeping. Something had shaken him, had meant he could not easily rest.'

That did nothing to allay Courtney. 'The missing laudanum,' he said. 'Do you believe Mr Fox had a hand in it?'

'No. No, he was a good lad.'

Courtney nodded in agreement. 'Thank you, Doctor. I appreciate your candour. Don't let me keep you from your patients any longer.'

Courtney did not go to Harrison with the information about Fox; he had not admitted to him that he had pressed the boy into service beforehand. The guilt flared up in him. Had his request to Fox led to his fatigue which in turn could have led to his fall? It only took a single slip in concentration to mean the difference between life and death in the tops. Knowing that Fox had wished to speak to him only made the remorse heavier.

But, before he could pursue this frightening theory, word came from the *Victory* that Admiral Villeneuve had again broken through the net at Toulon. At first, the same ideas spread as they had at the start of the year: Villeneuve would try to unite with Gravina's Spanish fleet and the rest of the French forces holed up in port and, failing that, he would retreat back behind the naval blockade. The same paths as before were travelled again. Nelson's Mediterranean squadron sailed south, investigating off Sicily and finding no signs of the Combined Fleet or any elements of it. The *Lion*, alongside two of her sisters, was sent further into the waters about Tunisia. There, close to the African coast, they watched the approach to Egypt in case Villeneuve attempted to make a run for Alexandria, that paramount location of interest for both sides. Again, as in January, he did not appear.

'Perhaps he is not in the Mediterranean anymore,' Appleton suggested one evening at Harrison's table. Courtney had not revealed Bowles's suspicions to Appleton. Instead, conversation had little strayed from the absence of the French and Spanish. 'Perhaps he has made for the Strait of Gibraltar and Spain.'

'Admiral Gravina is in Cádiz,' Courtney said. 'Admiral Orde has his eyes on them there. If Admiral Villeneuve passes through the Strait, he may seek to free Gravina from Cádiz.'

'Then where to?'

'Perhaps Ireland. The French attempted a landing in Ireland in the nineties, wanting to spark rebellion amongst the United Irishmen against Britain.'

'They would be fools to try again, knowing how disastrous their last trial was.'

Courtney could only agree with that. Gales, and the actions of Captain Pellew against the French squadron, had meant the planned French invasion was a resounding failure.

'What other areas does Britain control?' he mused. 'The east and India, parts of Africa, the Caribbean… Perhaps the enemy aims to sail for the Caribbean and disrupt British holdings there. The French have lost many of their possessions there, certainly after being thrown from Haiti, as the Spanish were too.'

'An entire fleet crossing the Atlantic?' Appleton asked.

'It isn't unthinkable. Admiral Missiessy escaped the Mediterranean in January and reached Martinique. Napoleon evidently has a scheme, or multiple schemes.'

'You would be returning to an old haunt in the Caribbean, Commander,' Harrison commented. 'As would I.'

Courtney smiled thinly. It had been three years since he had left the Leeward Islands Station, after the *Scylla* was broken up and her crew paid off. It had been almost five years since he had first met Nightingale, out there in Antigua's English Harbour. Such days seemed simultaneously an age away and also as though he had only recently experienced them. It would be strange to return, in Nightingale's old ship, no less.

Thoughts of Nightingale made Courtney determined to write to him again, to cover over the maudlin, grumbling mood of his previous note. He had much to speak to Nightingale of, but he knew he must talk to him physically, not through a pathetic letter. He loved him, and every hour spent apart from him made him realise the strength of it. He needed to see him, to hold him, to explain his actions over the notes, over Tabitha Sandham… Over everything Courtney had done, or tried to do.

But, within days, as if in reflection of the issues aboard, the winds turned against the ships. The fleet struggled against them in an attempt to set a course for Gibraltar and the gateway out of the Mediterranean. Courtney reckoned Appleton's theory was coming true and they spent more time in Harrison's cabin, troubling over the charts and inked maps of Spain and Portugal.

Then, Courtney's opportunity to write to Nightingale was scuppered by the confirmation, filtered through the fleet: Villeneuve had been seen passing the Strait of Gibraltar. The chase, once again, began.

Chapter Sixteen: Penance

For days, Nightingale pondered over John Courtney, rotting on the *Impregnable*. He had not shown how deeply his words and threat had cut into him, not to the man himself, not to Captain Bartley and certainly not to any other resident. He had not spoken to Mr or Mrs Woods about John Courtney's reappearance, though they would be of the best position to judge him. Nightingale wished to keep this all to himself until he decided what to do.

When the next batch of letters arrived from Courtney, Nightingale opened them with a pit of dread in his stomach. Courtney spoke of a convoy that the *Lion* had pursued and damaged, but by his morose tone, Nightingale knew they had let it slip. An older letter mentioned issues with the officers onboard the *Lion* and then, to Nightingale's consternation, referred to his own presence on the island. It could have been an occasion to mention his father, but Courtney did not. He kept that from Nightingale, as if protecting him from the information.

In their bedroom, Nightingale sat at the desk by the window. It overlooked the garden both he and Courtney had tended over the years, taming it, beautifying it. So much of this cottage was the product of their work together. That was what Nightingale considered their relationship: a union, where both the triumphs and the trials were shared. He could not help feeling a little hurt that Courtney had not revealed these dramatic events to him. Perhaps he had had his reasons, but Nightingale wished to aid him in anything, wished to be there for him.

He tried to write a response to Courtney but the words kept tangling. He tried to map out what he had done on the island, what he had discovered, but the idea of intruding upon Courtney's career stopped his pen a few times. Courtney, judging by his mention of the convoy and the officers, had problems already on the *Lion*. Nightingale did not want to add to them. But the notion of doing something without Courtney's knowledge or blessing…

It soon became apparent to Nightingale that he intended to do something, though he did not know the fullness of it. As he had thought, the letters no longer appeared at the cottage. But as the days went on and he mulled over John Courtney's vocal and written threats, he feared the power of the man over both himself and his son.

Even with the letter of marque safely with him and the promise of freedom of the seas with the *Larkspur*, Nightingale felt he had again taken two steps back on his journey. He did not want to return to the *Impregnable*, did not want to see the dire conditions and admit to the rattling of his nerves, but a fortnight at the cottage and Portsmouth, turning the locks of his mind again and again, frustrated him.

The closest to knowing the truth of the prisoner was Captain Bartley but even in his letter, permitting Nightingale's return to the *Impregnable*, Nightingale could read his surprise. Again, Nightingale steeled himself and made the journey out to the detestable ship alone. Its state had not improved and was not likely to unless there was a national outcry. Nightingale wagered people were content for criminals to languish here, beyond their sight in doomed hulks. He found it unconscionable not to have a shred of mercy for them, treated as callously as mongrels.

On the deck, Captain Bartley met him and informed him, quietly, 'Your man has taken ill. He has been removed from the cell and placed in the hospital bay.'

'Is it a serious condition?' Nightingale asked, pausing on the quarterdeck. A line of dirty clothes hung over them, their attempt at cleanliness not helped by the chimney belching smoke over the ship. Nightingale did not think the shape of the hospital would be any better.

'It is difficult to say with any certainty. Our surgeon believes it is a biliousness of the liver, perhaps a result of some underlying disease or the man's constitution. It has worsened these last hours and it was no longer viable to keep Mr Courtney in the cell.'

In a strange, harsh way, Nightingale thought his solitude in the hold might have aided him. Stuck in a cage with many other men, almost lying atop one another, would have spread disease of the body and the mind. A sailor's greatest fears were fire, undefined illness, and the prospect of an indecent death and burial. He was reminded of the state he had taken the old *Scylla* over in, her crew cut down by yellow fever. Captain Carlisle himself had succumbed; ailments knew no class or rank.

'I should like to see him,' he said. 'If he is in a well state, that is. Well enough to share a few words. I assume that your surgeon does not believe I will breathe in the illness in close proximity?'

'No. It is an internal matter, in his estimations, not a foul miasma that has caused it.'

The hospital, as Nightingale had expected, was almost as repulsive as the prison decks. Four patients currently occupied it: a smaller number than he had been expecting, but perhaps they fancied their chances in the cells instead of this bay, crammed in beneath the bows. A young surgeon, in a bloodied, stained smock and apron, attended the man Nightingale had come to visit. John Courtney was sitting up in his hammock and when he saw Nightingale, he gave a rattling, surprised cough. He appeared even more withered than when he had last laid eyes on him, so it had not simply been the dank conditions of the hold that had marred him. His skin shone with a yellow jaundiced hue, dotted with pallid patches from his miserable illness.

Nightingale approached him and tried to avoid looking at the other patients who slumbered with occasional fitful groans, dressed in their own emissions. The sole doctor already appeared worked to the bone, sallow eyes and skin from a life below decks or in houses of the dead.

'How is he, Remy?' Bartley asked with surprising familiarity. Shocking Nightingale more, the surgeon replied in a French tone.

'There has been no more vomiting or bloodied stools, sir,' he said, callously illustrating John Courtney's symptoms to the rest of the bay and to Nightingale's ears. 'The patient is as comfortable as I can make him.'

John Courtney huffed, though it could have been another cough.

'You are French,' Nightingale said to Remy.

'Yes, sir.'

'We try not to hold such a thing against him, Mr Nightingale,' Bartley interjected. 'He was plucked from amongst the prisoners. We are occasionally visited by doctors and medical students who wish to examine our men but they are more vultures and ghouls than men of science. We cannot be so proud as to reject the offerings of a surgeon's assistant, even if he is a Frog.'

Remy blinked and Nightingale knew it had not been through his generous offerings that he now served the ship. He had been pressed into service in the way of so many other able-bodied men.

'I would like to speak with Mr Courtney,' Nightingale said. 'You may stay to keep a watch on the patient if you wish, sir.'

Remy blinked again, obviously surprised at being addressed as 'sir'. With his letter of marque, Nightingale still fought Remy's countrymen, as he had done for many years, but he saw no point in being unkind to a surgeon who was evidently exhausted. Slowly, he sat beside Courtney's father, removing his hat and placing it in his lap for something to hold. Both

Remy and Bartley withdrew, the captain engaging Remy in conversation about the patients.

'I am sorry to hear of your condition,' Nightingale said. 'Bilious fever is a terrible thing.'

'You are not sorry to hear of my condition,' John rasped. 'You had no love for me when you visited last.'

Just as Nightingale pitied the young French surgeon, Nightingale found he pitied John Courtney too. 'You cannot blame me for that. You spoke harsh words to me and seemed out of sorts. Perhaps I should say this illness was the reason for it.'

John's red-dotted eyes roamed over Nightingale. 'My illness don't make me say things I don't mean. It never has.'

'This is a common complaint then? One you have experience of?'

'True enough. Since I was just out of my boyhood years. It'll always strike me down, but it won't kill me. I am sure you are sorry to hear that too.'

'I'm not a cruel man, Mr Courtney. I wish for no person's death.'

'Even that Corsican ogre?'

It was Nightingale's turn to huff, surprised at the astuteness of John's comment. He had barely expected him to keep up with the events of the world; people in his situation tended to stay within their small environment, finding it unnecessary to worry of politics and conflict until it touched them.

'Your son works tirelessly to curtail his influence,' Nightingale said.

John Courtney was silent for a moment, obviously pondering over that statement. Nightingale could see little of Courtney in his downtrodden, miserable father and was glad of it. Courtney had clawed his way out of the dirt, but was unashamed of his background, never hiding it in his accent and manner. He had turned into a fine young man without help from the people who had birthed him. So why was Nightingale stirring such things up? He wished to gain the same respect from

Courtney's homeplace as he felt from Courtney. Or perhaps, he thought disconcertingly, it was the aftermath of his own father's demise that influenced him.

'Where is my son?' John suddenly asked, disturbing his ideas.

'Your son is...' Nightingale did not know the precise location. Such was the life of a naval officer and the ever-shifting positions of Nelson's fleet. The last he had heard from Courtney was that he was at Toulon, but that could easily have changed. 'He is with the Mediterranean Fleet under Lord Nelson.'

'He won't be coming home?'

'He will come home,' Nightingale said avidly. He could not countenance a world without Courtney. 'Your son is one of the best officers in the navy. He may not always behave as a gentleman but he is talented and always takes his crews to heart.'

'He is an officer,' John repeated. 'I read his name but...could barely believe he had changed from a common sailor.'

'He has. He began as a forecastle man and...'

'I know that. He ran from home and took my daughter with him.'

'Jane is married to another naval officer. Did you not read of the incident of the *Ulysses* mutiny?'

'I did. I knew of my daughter's involvement with the mutineers but by that time, no one knew who I was or that she was a relation of mine. I have been away from the island a long time.'

'And you return now.'

'For my son,' John said as shortly as before. 'I know that he has returned to the island recently.'

'He has.'

'To marry?'

The question surprised Nightingale. He fought the shameful envy such a suggestion evoked in him, his mind immediately turning to Miss Tabitha Sandham whom Courtney had said Captain Harrison had pushed him in the direction of. Nightingale had been unable to turn Courtney away from that path. In truth, he knew he could or should not. Louisa, his friend, his confidante, was the shield that kept the prejudice of the world away. Courtney did not have that, and it was ever something which plagued Nightingale, raising its frightening head at troubling times. He wondered, not for the first time, if John Courtney's letters had affected his son's decisions.

'No,' Nightingale replied. 'Not to marry. What of your own wife? Arthur has made some mention of his mother.'

'She died.'

'Oh. I am sorry.'

'I have not touched a bottle for six months, not since she passed,' John insisted, then became racked again with coughs and splutters. Remy, who had been lingering by another cot, made a move to come closer but Nightingale held up a hand and attended the patient himself, stopping him from curling into a shivering ball and instead, easing him back in the hammock.

'Steady there,' he said.

John strained to continue speaking. 'Whatever it is that Artie said about her, I did not hate her. I loved her.'

'Arthur has never particularly spoken of her, or much of you. He has made his own way.'

'She died from the fever when I was away.'

'Away? Where were you?'

'We left Ryde after Artie and Jane ran away. We did not feel welcome there anymore, if we ever had. I did whatever I could for money. Would you believe it, I thought of joining the navy. I did not, but I had enough conflicts with men of the sea.'

'How do you mean?'

'You were there at Mr Hodges's hanging, weren't you?'

Nightingale frowned, before understanding dawned on him. He had thought of how smuggling was a part of so many people's lives here, a part of so many on the coasts of England facing France.

'Is that how you received your scar?'

John nodded. 'I protected those who ferried the goods ashore. Kept the musket for situations where I required it.'

'You were not required to use it against Lieutenant Osborne.'

'After he hanged one of our men? After what he's done to us?'

Nightingale did not respond. He knew that John Courtney could imagine himself in Hodges's position. Doubtless, many people in the crowd had thought the same of themselves.

'I would like to see my son again,' John continued. 'I wrote to him – do you know how long it took me to write those letters? – but he did not respond. I kept sending the notes to the cottage but he obviously went away – and then you took his place there. I thought the letters might convince you.'

'To do what? Insist to your son that he has to see you and hear your story? I do not know if that is a wise idea.'

But Nightingale knew, regardless of Courtney's knowledge about his father's return, he could not make that decision for him. As he had said to John Courtney, his son had made his own way and forged his own path. Although Nightingale had shared the experience of a troubled father and difficult childhood, he could not presume to definitively say what Courtney thought. He had closed the book on his past and with every year, every promotion, every success, he stepped further away from the boy he had been: struggling to survive, spending time in debtors' cells with this very same man, his father.

'He is not yours to command,' John said.

'I'm aware.' Nightingale glanced over at Remy where he was speaking with Bartley. Nightingale caught his eye. 'I believe I should leave you now. This excitement will only harm you more.'

Partially, Nightingale was glad to be away. He did not know what he saw when he looked at John Courtney: perhaps a man ravaged by his own condition and by the harsh situations he found himself in, not always due to circumstances beyond his control. There were many men like him, many men who turned to easy comforts to slake their own pain, and Nightingale could not look down on them for doing so. But John had made his choice not to support Courtney and Jane, had opted for the bottle over his own children's wellbeing. Perhaps there was something in his admission that he was no longer drinking, yet the effects of it had already done its damage, both in John's own body and in Courtney's youth.

Nightingale could not judge his worth in returning to society and into Courtney's life. He had already tried to shoot a naval officer, risking his neck and the reputation of his residence. His return had not been one of penance and remorse.

Captain Bartley stopped Nightingale as he climbed back to the deck. He looked Nightingale up and down as if he believed Nightingale had caught John's illness. 'He did not give you much trouble, did he, Mr Nightingale?' he asked.

'No. Not at all. I hope that he recovers.'

Bartley sighed. 'I am not certain and neither is Remy,' he said. 'Mr Courtney might say he has had the ailment for a long while, but he has not suffered it on a prison ship before.'

'He has had a harsh life. He will withstand it.'

'Perhaps not.'

Nightingale paused. He had told John Courtney the truth: he was not a cruel man, and he certainly did not wish for the fellow's death. He had seen the horrific state of the prison hulk and how even a man in the best of health could be ground down. But what could he do? And more, what should he do?

'I shall pray for his health,' Nightingale said, separating himself from Bartley.

The captain acceded, accompanying him to the side and seeing him safely down into the *Impregnable*'s launch. Nightingale again thought on the questions he had posed to himself. He could not choose a path which would upset or unsettle Courtney, not during this critical stage of his career, within touch of being made post. He knew Courtney already grappled with Harrison's offer, had seen it in his eyes when they spoke in London after Harrison's dinner. He did not know which timber to tread on for fear it would sag and rot beneath him. As much as he saw, and hoped, that his and Courtney's lives were entwined, he also knew that there were some matters which they would forever be apart on.

Forever, he thought, rubbing his wedding ring without thought. They could never have what Nightingale and Louisa had. The distance of more than simply the sea sat between them. With cold submission, Nightingale realised he had not felt so far from Courtney for a very long while.

Chapter Seventeen: Against Time

4 May 1805, Tétouan, Morocco

After months in the ever-pitching, ever-rolling ocean, Courtney relished the opportunity to leave the *Lion* and walk on the firm ground of Tétouan's harbour. The *Lion* was the largest ship he had ever served on and yet it felt the most suffocating, trapping him there with the worries about the crew and the captain. Conditions had not improved over the past month across the Mediterranean. Unfavourable winds had dogged the fleet, stopping them from making good headway, and a duty to cover an expeditionary force's convoy had done the same. Within the *Lion*, McPherson remained under arrest, Harrison unable to make a decision about him. Courtney had tried his utmost to press him to call for a court martial, to end this terrible uncertainty, but ahead of them lay the Atlantic.

Presently, further stores were being brought upon the *Lion* and Nelson's other ships of the line in preparation for a lengthy chase. With no indication from Cornwallis that Villeneuve's fleet had sailed north for the Channel, the steadily agreed-upon notion was that the French ships had crossed the Atlantic. As Appleton had suggested, they might yet be approaching the islands of the Caribbean, intending to sow chaos and discord. Nelson's vessels would set every sensible shred of canvas and crack on behind them.

His thoughts were interrupted by the reappearance of Harrison. Harrison, insisting he needed fresh air, had been gone a fair few hours, visiting other ships, convening with the other captains, but surely the proceedings had not sapped him as much as his appearance suggested. Deep circles blackened his eyes and his skin was pale, tinged with green. Courtney split away from Daniels to intercept him.

'Are you well, Captain?' he asked, extending an arm. Harrison refused it.

'I am well, I am well,' he rushed out. 'Are we nearly finished here?'

'Yes, I believe so. The other ships, sir…'

'What of them?'

Courtney did not know how to respond. He glanced to Daniels, thought that he could manage the rest of the operation, and said, 'Perhaps we should return to the *Lion*, sir.'

'Hm? Yes, very well.'

It took more than a bit of effort to help Harrison down into a gig. He looked inebriated and, though Courtney knew naval officers and deckhands alike needed no excuse to drink, he could not smell any port or Madeira on him. Still, he turned paler and paler, sweat breaking out on his cheeks despite the cool evening. He gave a pitiful moan and sank further into his seat at the stern, nearly disturbing the men heaving at the oars. Courtney looked sidelong at him.

'Lieutenant,' Harrison murmured, and Courtney did not correct him again, 'I think I am quite ill.'

'How do you mean?'

Harrison's state spoke for him. He put a hand to his mouth, and for a frightening moment, Courtney thought he would vomit over the boat.

'Perhaps the spoiled victuals have not yet run their course,' Courtney said, though it sounded a feeble reason to his ears.

'You are kind to me, Arthur. You're a good man. A good man who'll make my sister-in-law quite pleased.'

'We are nearly at the *Lion*,' Courtney reassured. 'I shall inform Dr Archer and have him attend you.'

It would not be the first time. Recently, Dr Archer had been a frequent visitor to Harrison's cabin. When Courtney called upon him again, he did not seem unduly surprised – and neither did Appleton, who had been below, looking over the ship's accounts.

'The captain has returned?' he asked Courtney.

'Yes.'

'Is he unwell again?'

Courtney gave a terse nod. He did not feel strong enough to argue with Appleton.

The days turned and Harrison only tentatively emerged from his cabin. He briefly came on deck during the fleet's time off Cádiz, hoping to gain more intelligence from Orde's frigates, which never arrived, then he disappeared again. He did not witness the *Lion* leave Cape St Vincent and pass Madeira in the second week of May. The fleet now consisted of eleven battleships, including the *Lion*. The eyes of the squadron were reliant upon the three frigates that they had. These would be invaluable when reaching the Caribbean and once again hunting for Villeneuve.

With the open water and the smatterings of kind airs, Courtney and Appleton drilled the men as often as they could manage. They improved slowly and Courtney attempted to concentrate upon what he could see on deck rather than the unknown below. He tried to keep the same cold and unfeeling mind with which he updated his journal and log, documenting the weather, the speed, and the progress. But, truthfully, with Harrison down, he knew he had to probe further into the dark underbelly of the *Lion*.

He had already conversed with Greene, the master gunner and McPherson's immediate superior, but had received little helpful information from him. McPherson's fellow mates offered the same, only saying that they had seen McPherson with the midshipmen sometimes. According to them, McPherson had even taken some of them to observe the guns, cleaning them and talking the boys through the procedure of running them out, after the poor exercise near the beginning of the *Lion*'s cruise.

Courtney knew he had to speak to the midshipmen again but his first attempts had not been successful, mainly due to his own hesitancy. He had tried to consider his approach, to dress it in the softest of terms; he could not simply walk in and bid them to unveil painful details in front of their companions.

He made a terrible job of it. Too frightened of upsetting them, too uncomfortable to go into detail, he edged around the questions and did not get to the heart of the matter. None of the midshipmen gave any indication that they had been harmed, although some of them did not speak at all. Only Ramsey spoke up, denying that he had seen anything untoward. Courtney was nearing the age that he could have looked on the boys as his own sons and the thought was unsettling as it was shocking.

As Courtney left the midshipmen's berth, none the wiser about what had occurred, he thought of his own father. He had tried to shove the feelings to the depths, hoping that the distance between John Courtney and himself would allow him to think clearly, but it had not occurred.

Instead, Courtney still sifted through the anger and the pain of his youth. He had consigned his father to death, or transportation, and to have so suddenly found out he remained alive, and wanted to speak with him again, had jarred him violently. His father, in his letters, spoke of remorse and regret, of the demise of his wife, of his struggle to put down the bottle and, moreover, his concern for Courtney and his friendship with Nightingale.

Courtney had no place for his father's concern or care. It would have been simpler if John Courtney had raged and spat at him through his letters, just as he had done during Courtney's youth. Courtney had sworn never to be like him, had vowed to shake off the hardship of his younger years, but here they were again. He feared they had burrowed into his decisions, into his perspectives, onboard the *Lion*, and for that, he despised himself.

And he intensely rued not dealing with the situation before coming aboard. Now, Nightingale had been left to pick up the pieces, and Courtney had not even been able to write to him of it beyond his previous note.

Courtney found himself drawn to the orlop and its labyrinth of storerooms. These small spaces split the deck into rough squares, separated by wooden partitions and each a compartment for the carpenter, the sailmaker, the cooper, the armourer and the ropemaker. McPherson had been imprisoned in one of these many rooms, its contents gutted and taken elsewhere. Courtney had spoken to the man a few times, but, without Harrison's guide, he did not know what to tell him, or what to ask him. Still, with the little information from the midshipmen and from Greene, there were few other people to interrogate.

To his surprise, Courtney heard voices as he approached. Appleton's soft, southern counties tone spoke quietly but urgently. McPherson responded, rougher, fuller with emotion. He stopped upon noticing Courtney's presence. Appleton, realising the prisoner had halted, turned and stiffened.

'Lieutenant Appleton,' Courtney greeted.

'Commander Courtney.'

Courtney thought Appleton was about to scurry off but, once the door had been shut and bolted again, he faced Courtney.

'I was not told of the reason for Mr McPherson's arrest,' Appleton accused.

'Captain Harrison and I thought it best to keep the matter as quiet as possible.'

'And yet you have kept him here, imprisoned, for many weeks, without trial and without investigation.'

'I have tried to ask… It is a delicate matter.'

'You…' But Appleton stopped himself, seemingly on the verge of propriety.

'Speak, Lieutenant,' Courtney urged, though. 'If there is an issue, then speak.'

'You reprimanded Mr Bowles and Mr McPherson soundly, you blamed them for the loss of the convoy. You then had them both lashed and imprisoned McPherson, investigating the matter of my men without consulting me, without—'

'They are not your men, Lieutenant, not solely. You are not the only one to care for them.'

Nightingale had said a similar thing to Courtney, not long after they had first met in the Caribbean. That seemed so long ago now. But it stirred in Courtney a sympathy for Appleton, for this man run to the bone by his duties and the weight of them.

'I was wrong to bawl at the men as I did,' Courtney said. 'It was poor conduct. I was angry at them, and other matters, and I should not have allowed it to cloud my judgement.'

Appleton frowned, obviously not expecting such an admission.

'What were you speaking to Mr McPherson of?' Courtney asked.

'I... I came to him after I heard of the accusations. He denies them.'

'I know. Of course he does.'

Appleton blinked. Courtney saw the rawness of his eyes, the depth of the passion within him, and wondered the cause. Was it simply due to his exhaustion, the burdens of this crew? 'I believe him,' Appleton said. 'At least let this come to a trial, to a formal investigation. This should be dealt with by a court martial. You know the regulations and the Articles.'

'I do. But...' Courtney could not bring himself to condemn Harrison's judgement, not aloud. It still tasted dangerous, and there were enough dangerous matters on the *Lion*.

'The captain,' Appleton finished for him.

Courtney nodded.

'Commander.' Appleton looked back at the door separating them from McPherson. He again hesitated but then steeled himself. 'He believes someone pushed Mr Fox.'

'What?'

'He believes someone murdered the boy.'

A dark chill rippled through Courtney. Murder. His instinct was to deny such a terrible idea, but then he considered what Dr

Archer had told him: Fox had had something to tell Courtney before he fell. Had Fox discovered evidence of the abusive behaviour and been silenced because of it?

'And the spoiled victuals,' Appleton continued. 'He says they targeted the gunner's mates, those closest to the gunner. He, himself, was affected by it. Mr Greene shares a space with the younger mids. To remove him from the gunroom, and his mates, it would...'

'Enough, Lieutenant.' The ugly accusations frightened Courtney more than he was willing to admit, though he had a similar unpleasant thought about the victuals. He had seen for himself how McPherson had been struck down by the ailment too. He needed to sift through the notions before arriving at a conclusion, before giving in to the high emotion of the case.

'Please, I beg you, call a court martial. Have this dealt with the proper way.'

'I wish to. But with the chase, the captain's illness, with the concentration on finding the enemy...'

They were weak excuses, and Courtney knew so. The lives and wellbeing of the *Lion*'s men were at stake, and the notion of justice, of allowing men their speech and defence at a formal trial, hung over them too.

'If the captain does not recover, then we must take action. Dr Archer must give his assessment, once we reach the Caribbean.'

Appleton nodded, appeased for a moment.

'Allow me to speak with McPherson,' Courtney continued, 'and I will bring the matter to the captain. Now, we cannot allow this matter to spread, you must understand that.'

'There is already rumour,' Appleton said. 'Ill feeling is rife.'

'I have seen. Let us pray that this swift chase and confusion to the enemy in the West Indies will be the tonic.'

But, as Appleton departed, Courtney felt the darkness around him, pressing in as if rising from the very keel of the ship. It unsettled him more than on any other ship he had served upon, even the ugly old *Grampus*. There, he had been able to try and solve the problems through his fists, through his anger, rolling over from the tyranny of his father. Now, the shadows were not above him, not from foul and dangerous superiors; they were below him, from men he should have been able to control and set in line. He felt alone in this large, forbidding ship.

Before he could enter McPherson's makeshift cell, another voice spoke from the blackness. He jolted, a hand racing to a sword that was not there. He cursed himself when Baker appeared from the bosun's storerooms.

'Apologies, Commander Courtney,' the man said obediently. 'Didn't realise you were down here, sir.'

'These are your rooms, Mr Baker,' Courtney replied. 'I was simply here to speak with the prisoner.'

'Mr McPherson, sir?'

All knew McPherson had been imprisoned. Courtney hoped the reason had not spread, as Appleton claimed, but there were few things a man could have been held for over such a long period of time, and Bowles had mentioned the lower decks' suspicion over the rumours.

'Ain't him who's necessarily the problem, sir,' Baker said, 'though he's a wrong'un, have no doubt of that.'

'What do you mean?'

'Wouldn't like to say, sir. Ain't my place.'

'And yet you insinuate it. I am growing weary of the secrets on this ship, Mr Baker.'

'I agree, sir, I agree.' He paused and looked along the deck, through the maze of storage and compartments into the darkness not touched by lanterns. No one disturbed their presence. 'The lieutenant ain't who he says he is, sir.'

'Lieutenant Appleton?'

'Yes, sir, the very same. I knew him from the *Eclipse* when he was young – younger, sir. He's earned quite a black record.'

Courtney frowned. 'It is not wise for a petty officer to accuse a commissioned officer, Mr Baker.'

Baker held up his hands. 'Oh, I know, sir. Apologies, sir. Was only saying what others don't know, what I thought might help your questions. The captain'll know it, sir, but he weren't a bosun on the *Eclipse* who saw the lieutenant's unfortunate actions.'

Courtney could not leave this perilous conversation now he had instigated it – and speaking to Harrison would not garner any results. The man presently did not know up from down. 'What happened?' he asked.

'It'll be on his sea service record, sir, but he was disrated as a middie. Sent to serve before the mast. Accused a poor man of something serious, something like to make your hackles rise. Something that I reckon our McPherson has had to answer to.'

Courtney said nothing, hating the taste of the air between them, suffocating and fetid.

'I've known since I saw him, sir. Heard all sorts about him since I came on at Toulon,' Baker continued.

'Why didn't you speak out?'

'Can't accuse a man without evidence, sir.'

'Evidence that I am sorely lacking.' Courtney sighed. 'Thank you, Mr Baker. As you were.'

Courtney did not know which way to turn. He had opinion from McPherson, from Bowles, from the midshipmen, from Appleton, and from Baker, and none of it matched together. This was not what he had expected when agreeing to Harrison's proposal to come aboard. He hated to think of it, but so far, he could not formulate a single reason that made him glad he had set foot on the ship's timbers. Once, she had been a capital ship, commanded by Nightingale, looked after by Lieutenant Sawyer, who Nightingale thought so highly of, and had crowned herself with glory at the Nile.

Now, she was but a shell of that former honour.

McPherson, as expected, barely spoke to him, not as he had Appleton. Somehow, the lieutenant had succeeded where Courtney could not. Courtney wondered if Baker told the truth, if Appleton indeed had such a gloomy record of sea service. If so, he would not be the only one.

A visit to Captain Harrison, holed up in his night cabin, also produced nothing. Dr Archer hesitatingly allowed Courtney to enter but lingered at the door, as if expecting reprimand for the state of the captain. Courtney, despite preparing himself, was shocked: Harrison lay on his side, green with nausea, sweating and finding it difficult to draw breath. He looked up at Courtney with glassy, unfocused eyes.

'Ca...' Courtney heard his voice hitch and only then realised what despair he was truly in. He swallowed. 'Captain, we must call a court martial. Lieutenant Appleton, Mr McPherson, and Mr Baker have made serious accusations.'

Harrison groaned. 'I cannot,' he managed to rasp. 'If I...call a court martial...they shall investigate me too.'

'Why would they ever investigate you?'

Courtney received no response. Harrison rolled over and Archer stepped in to return him to a safe position. For a moment, Courtney's gaze crossed with the doctor's and Archer shook his head meaningfully.

'It will be a long recovery,' Archer only said.

A long recovery, Courtney thought in agony. They did not have time for such a thing. They needed answers before the darkness on the *Lion* completely swallowed her.

Chapter Eighteen: This Side of the Sea

Each day, Nightingale expected to receive a note – no longer from John Courtney, threatening him, but from Captain Bartley on the *Impregnable*, informing him of John's death. Nightingale did not wish to visit again and stir up confused feelings about what he should and should not do. Yet the frustration and anxiety of not knowing ate at him.

So, feeling heavy with doubt, Nightingale visited the Fisherman's Catch. He felt he had acted behind their backs by conversing with John Courtney, a man whose children Mr and Mrs Woods had stepped in to care for. More and more, he feared the truth of what John had said about himself: he had come to the island, as an outsider, meddling in their affairs, trying to set a course he had no right to. Even Lovett's proposal seemed an ironic thing now. Lovett had suggested that Nightingale could bolster the enthusiasm and engagement of the islanders, but beyond a display of the *Larkspur*'s guns, Nightingale did not think he had done much. Every time he tried, another matter crested over him.

As ever, Mrs Woods approached him as he sat by the light of the fire, composing a note for Courtney. Although he knew he could not convey such a matter in bare writing, he could no longer stand the thought of the both of them thinking wrong things of the other's knowledge, not standing on the same level. When ghosts of Courtney's past had returned before, in the shape of Garrick Walker on the piratical *Barbarossa*, Courtney had struggled. Nightingale remembered soothing him after the destruction of the *Barbarossa*, learning more of Courtney's past than he had before. But through his strength, Courtney had laid it to rest and made his peace with it all. Nightingale hoped the same would occur with this situation.

'You are deep in thought, Mr Nightingale,' Mrs Woods commented, still refusing to call him 'Hiram' as he had tried to encourage her. 'I shall leave you to them.'

'No, it is fine. In actuality, I wished to speak with you.'

'Oh.' She looked towards the other tables but Walter was at hand.

'It is nothing to trouble yourself over,' Nightingale assured. 'It is a quandary I've been having.'

He folded over the letter and laid it aside with the pen. He had already addressed it to Courtney, but the knowledge of where the *Lion* might be meant he could not be very specific about the location. Such was the life of the naval officer, with the only hope of communication being at ports and when crossing a packet ship. Nightingale still tried to accustom himself to being on this side of the sea. As he had thought when leaving the *Impregnable* before, he had not felt so distant from Courtney in a long while, both physically and figuratively.

Opposite Nightingale, Mrs Woods took her seat, flushed and broad and seemingly nervous. Nightingale did not think he still bore the authority of a captain in the King's Navy – a merchant officer was not held in such awesome esteem – but perhaps there was a fragment of it left.

He wondered how to begin the conversation. 'I have visited the *Impregnable* over the last few weeks,' he said. 'The prison hulk out at Cowes. There is a man there who I have been speaking to.'

Mrs Woods appeared to sink away from her tense state, the chair creaking as she sat back. She looked down, nodded, and clasped her hands before her.

'You know of whom I speak,' Nightingale said, realisation dawning.

'I do. As soon as he came back to the town and fought with Lieutenant Osborne, I heard from the other men.'

'He is… Arthur's father. I did not even know he was still alive.'

'Nor I. After Artie and Jane left us, bound for their uncle and aunt in Portsmouth, I heard no more from John and Elizabeth Courtney. I assumed they were put in a debtor's cell or transported to Australia.'

'That is what Arthur has said as well. Mr Courtney says they left Ryde and became embroiled in other business.'

'I did not think to ask further of their whereabouts. Owen and I were pleased to have them away from our lives. A few times over the years before Artie and Jane left, they tried to find their way back into the children's lives. Owen and I had vowed to look after them and I did not think it would be a good idea to allow their parents to return. The last time they tried, Arthur claimed he could not stand their meddling anymore and ran away with Jane. I did not blame him, not truly.'

Nightingale nodded. He had thought the same now, doubting the sanity of allowing John Courtney back in, but Courtney was not a young lad anymore, needing shelter and responsible care. 'How was Arthur's life? When he was young? What did his father and mother do?'

'It wasn't so much of what they did do, rather what they didn't. John was a drunken sot who lost any money that he and Artie might earn. Elizabeth did not argue with him, never about anything. She allowed his behaviour and fell into a deep melancholy often. I felt sorry for the lass, sometimes, but the both of them neglected to provide any care or love for Jane and Artie. Artie raised his sister more than they ever did.'

'John claims that he has not touched a drop of gin or wine since Elizabeth passed.'

'She passed?'

'Yes, recently. It is why he has come back to Ryde. He wants to see Arthur again.'

'Ah.'

Nightingale smiled thinly. 'John Courtney says that he was in communication with Arthur. I know that you mentioned how Arthur was aware of the threatening notes but he… Well, he did not tell me of them and he certainly did not write of the return of his father. Arthur, he…'

Nightingale tried to think of a way to say how Courtney shared everything with him, without hinting at the true nature of their connection. But then, perhaps Mrs Woods knew. Nightingale had spent long weeks at the cottage, had always accompanied Courtney home after a meal at the Catch in the evenings. He shared all the day with him, did almost everything with the other man when on the island. To Nightingale, it seemed sometimes they were too blatant, but it was also true that others did not even think to see these things in such a light. The existence of men such as himself and Courtney did not cross some people's minds, as if they did not inhabit the same world as them.

'Arthur is a very dear friend of mine,' Nightingale continued. 'I thought I knew most parts of his life and he and I have often solved one another's problems. I do not know why he kept this from me.'

Mrs Woods was silent for a while. 'Perhaps,' she eventually said, 'Artie did not think you should involve yourself.'

'Have I done wrong by doing so?'

'No, that isn't quite what I meant. Perhaps he wanted to keep you away from his father and did not want to worry you. Mr Nightingale – Hiram – I know what the notes said. Perhaps he thought he could solve the issue when he returned and did not want to cause you pain. He did not tell Owen or I either about his father's return.'

Nightingale nodded. It sounded something in the way of Courtney's manner. 'Do you know I recently lost my own father?'

'I did know. Artie said he attended his funeral.'

'He was a horrid man. In ways, he was like Arthur's father. I never forgave his behaviour and he never tried to make amends for it. But I always wondered if one day, he would apologise and see me in a different way.'

'Would you have forgiven him then?'

Nightingale shook his head. 'No. It would have taken more than that. He would have had to prove to me that he had changed, and I don't believe he ever would have done so.'

Nightingale paused. He had been looking into the fire, at the flames crackling and rising from the blackened logs. The *Ulysses* had been the symbol of his past and present, the epitome of how people had pushed him down paths he had no desire for, the way such things had destroyed himself and others around him. He had burnt that ship and left it smouldering on a reef. And then after that, he had spoken against the tyrants in his life and severed all ties with his own father. He had told Courtney never to follow that example, not in such a dramatic and final manner, incinerating his career and the hopes for his future. John Courtney, in Nightingale's mind, was in the way of the anchor that had weighed Nightingale down. But perhaps Courtney did not see him like that. Nightingale could not truly dictate terms to it.

'I apologise,' Nightingale said. 'I did not mean to lay all of that in your lap. You hardly know me.'

'Of course I know you, Mr Ni— Hiram. You are Arthur's friend and we welcome you here.'

Nightingale was unsure about that but he decided not to say anything. 'I am trying to write to Arthur and express myself correctly. He obviously knows of his father and the letters. Do you think I should inform him that I also know?'

Mrs Woods did not need time to consider it. Nightingale knew she thought of Courtney in a way he could never truly understand: that of a parent, or with the love of a parent. Yet Nightingale adored him in other manners, as a friend, as a partner, with the intensity and union of a spouse. They both wished the best for him.

'I think,' Mrs Woods eventually said, 'that you should write to him of it. Circumstances have changed since he was last here and, as you say, his father may not survive the *Impregnable*. Artie is a long way distant. There is little he can do, so the least is to inform him.'

'The "little he can do" is what concerns me. I would madden myself with that news. But… He does already know of his father's return. Perhaps it will bring him some comfort to know that I am trying to handle the affair.'

He prayed that Courtney trusted him enough to do so. He thought that he and Courtney had become more similar over time, adopting each other's traits and pleasures and hatreds. He had once said Courtney was the other half of his soul; he truly believed it. But they still were their separate individuals and this was Courtney's business. His reaction, his decision, was his alone.

'Thank you for your aid,' he said to Mrs Woods. 'I will tell him the truth of it all.'

'What of Jane?' Mrs Woods asked. 'Shall you tell her also?'

'If I tell Arthur, I must tell Jane too. She has her own life now, with Lieutenant Wainwright and their home in Norfolk, so perhaps she will simply ignore the note but…that is her decision. He was – *is* – her father as well.'

As he began to commit the words to paper, Nightingale started to feel a little freer. He imagined Courtney sitting opposite him again, that soft smile on his face, knowing, understanding, and his heart filled with yearning. Sometime soon, he would be home, and Nightingale would rejoice.

Before perhaps losing him to Tabitha Sandham. The thought doused his hope for a moment. He paused, determined not to drown in those doubts again, and just as he was on the verge of writing once more, a disturbance sounded from outside the tavern.

Mrs Woods, at the bar, looked up. She quickly rounded the tables and urged young Walter away from the door. From the back of the building, Owen emerged and, in turn, ushered his wife away. Nightingale, too curious to ignore it, followed the man into the porch where the sound of raised voices echoed along the lane.

In the night, Nightingale could see two silhouettes, framed by the trees. A shaft of moonlight illuminated a shock of long hair worn loose and then glittered off the golden buttons and white decoration of a lieutenant's uniform.

Not caring for his own safety, Nightingale hurried over, leaving the growing crowd from the Catch behind. Lieutenant Osborne – for it was the man, in the midst of trouble yet again – had his back to him but the woman, Lucy, saw his approach. Her cloth cap had fallen from her head as Osborne had attempted to lift her strong form over his shoulder, which he now tried again. She, with no hesitation, brought her knee sharply into his groin and then, as he doubled over, groaning, she delivered a resounding slap to the cheek.

'Lieutenant Osborne!' Nightingale cried. The man turned, obviously only now realising where they were: in full sight of the Fisherman's Catch with many witnesses. 'Ma'am,' Nightingale addressed Lucy, 'come with me.'

She wasted no time in doing so, snatching her cap from the ground and marching over to Nightingale's side.

'You bitch,' Osborne snapped, and made an attempt to stand.

Nightingale held his arm protectively over Lucy. 'Return to your vessel, Lieutenant,' he said. 'Do not make me quote the Articles of War at you again.'

'You will answer to this,' Osborne threatened.

'Not without you voicing your role in it also,' Nightingale responded. 'I doubt your uncle, and the Admiralty, would be pleased to hear of it.'

Osborne chose not to reply to that damning truth. He finally rose to his height again, though with unsteady legs. Nightingale, without waiting for him to leave, escorted Lucy away, towards the safe light of the tavern. She was breathing heavily but seemed unhurt.

'Are you well, ma'am?' Nightingale asked.

'I'm well. But if I lay eyes on him again...'

'Come inside, ma'am.'

Inside, the Catch was silent. Nightingale saw that some men had crowded to the windows to watch the turmoil. He bid them to return to their meals and their drinks and then sat Lucy down at his table. Mrs Woods approached and Nightingale requested beer, which Lucy gratefully drank.

'Lieutenant Osborne is a dog,' she spat once she had set the tankard down again. 'He thinks, because of his uniform, because of his boat, he can do what he likes.'

'This is not the first time he has acted in this way?' Nightingale asked.

'No. And it won't be the last. I thought that he did wrong by hanging Mr Hodges, we all did, thought he only did it to prove to us that he *could*. He don't understand. The harvests have been poor and the trade that reaches us…'

'I have heard.'

'Now he thinks that he can take liberties with me, because I don't have a husband to protect me, because I am not one of the preened and pretty ladies of London, because I'm no gentlewoman… I don't need to be protected. If he'd have met my brother…'

Lucy silenced herself suddenly. She picked up her tankard again with a shaking hand and Nightingale saw blood on her fingers.

'You have been harmed,' he said.

'No. No, this ain't my blood. God, he's going to hang me now, isn't he? Let him. I ain't afraid of the gallows.'

'It won't come to that,' Nightingale assured.

Lucy thought of it but she seemed genuinely without fear of a hanging, as if she expected it of herself. Not for the first time, Nightingale remembered how Mrs Woods spoke of the trouble which followed Lucy, and reconsidered his own beliefs about her knowledge of the southern island. He did not voice it.

'Thank you for helping me,' Lucy suddenly said. 'There are others here that I think might have left me to him.'

'Oh, I like to think any man would have helped a woman in trouble.'

Lucy huffed. 'It was a man who tried to harm me.'

'Yes, I… Apologies, that was impolitic of me.'

Lucy shook her head. 'Men don't like it when we women fight back, just makes them angrier. I suppose you think I am some wild thing.'

'Not at all. I have witnessed women pushed to perform dramatic actions for their own safety and the safety of others. I once commanded a ship that hunted down a mutinous vessel in the Caribbean. That vessel was under the thrall of a brutal man. The one who ended his reign and helped to save the crew was a woman, your own Arthur Courtney's sister.'

'I have heard the tale. It was the *Scylla* and the *Ulysses*.'

Nightingale paused, surprised that she knew. 'It was.'

'You commanded my brother,' Lucy said, then hesitated, before continuing, 'He did not know you for long, but he wrote once and said how he respected you, even after you wounded him.'

Nightingale flushed. 'I apologise if I wounded him. The naval service is one of many pains.'

Lucy shook her head. 'He said that he deserved it. He was always finding himself in trouble when we were younger. We both did. And I suppose I still do now.'

'Where is he now?' Nightingale asked. 'The *Scylla* was broken up a few years ago.'

'He died.'

'Ah.' Nightingale cursed himself. 'I am sorry to hear that.'

'The naval service is one of many pains,' Lucy echoed him. 'He knew that he would have to give his life to it. Many of our men do not come back from the sea.'

'What was your brother's name?'

'You will not remember him.'

'I shall. I never forget my sailors.'

Lucy tilted her head. 'Never?'

'Not from the *Scylla*.' Nightingale had met Courtney on those timbers, now destroyed and moulded anew. A ship was not only its officers, though. They represented a small total of the men bustled into a vessel, sometimes forcibly pulled from their former lives, sometimes by voluntary action.

'His name was Kieran,' Lucy said, and instantly Nightingale's skin drew tighter.

'Kieran Attrill,' he said.

'Yes.'

'Of course I remember Kieran Attrill.'

When Nightingale had first encountered Courtney, he had sustained a lurid bruise from breaking up a fight onshore. Kieran had been the cause of that tussle after going ashore and being accused of stealing from a merchant for his friend. Nightingale had had to have him flogged and had felt a deep, ridiculous guilt for it, even though, as captain, it was his expected position. Nightingale had always felt uneasy with the expectations hanging around his neck. During the battle with the *Ulysses*, Kieran had pushed Nightingale down and away from a shot that would have snuffed out his years.

'Your brother saved my life,' he said.

'He did?'

'He was a good, sturdy man and a fine sailor. He was the sort of hand that every captain looks for in his ships: dependable, skilled, and obedient. I do not think he meant any true malice by the infraction I had to have him flogged for.'

'He would have been hanged for it if he had done it here. Mr Hodges ain't the first I've seen go to the gallows. The cliffs and bays at St Lawrence, where we used to live, are a smuggler's fancy and...'

Lucy fell silent again, obviously on the bounds of something. Nightingale did not press, regretting that such a sore subject had risen. He remembered wondering if Kieran Attrill had been involved in smuggling when he talked of his background. Nightingale now wondered the same thing about his living sister. Had she done what she could to survive, lending her hand to the free trade business?

'Again, thank you for aiding me, Mr Nightingale,' Lucy said. 'I will go home now and pray trouble doesn't find me once more.'

'I will accompany you. Lieutenant Osborne has proved it is not safe.'

'My thanks, but Mr Browne planned to meet me here tonight. It is why I was coming this way before the lieutenant… But I am visiting the workhouse in Cowes soon to call on my friend, Bridget, Mr Hodges's widow. I would appreciate the company then.'

Nightingale found he enjoyed her forwardness, her lack of qualms around the hurdles of their sexes. And he liked the thought of finding an ally; so often, he found the greatest companionship in those who did not fit into their societies. 'It would be my honour,' he said.

–

The visit to the workhouse was unpleasant but it showed, in stark colours, the truth of the poverty that existed on the island, across the entirety of England. Nightingale did not intrude upon Lucy and Bridget's meeting, only waited in the corridor with a porter and peered through the door to the large hall where the noon meal was being served. The inmates sat upon rows of long benches, gathered around communal tables. A number of others walked about, serving from ladles into simple wooden bowls. Nightingale recognised the kind of pease pudding which was given to sailors on certain days. All of the men and boys wore regimented, plain clothing, much of which seemed ill-fitting. They ate in near total silence, observed by porters and whom Nightingale assumed was the master of the house.

He thought of John Courtney on the *Impregnable*. Poverty and ill health robbed a person of choice and agency over their lives. So much of existence was driven by necessity. These people here may be fed and clothed, but at a bare minimum for survival. It was another world to him, a world John Courtney had been correct about: he had never been poor, never been hungry. But he was not blind to others about him, and neither had he been when he was a post-captain. Many men went to sea, not out of their own decision, but through obligation, whether running from hardship or pressed into service. They did not all have admirals as fathers, as he had.

Nightingale hated to think of his father, though with his passing out of the world, there was nothing more he could add to their story. He was gone, buried, never forgiven. What would Courtney do if his father also died, suffering on the *Impregnable*?

Sitting, watching the residents eat their small meal and then return to their places in the workroom, Nightingale decided what he had to do. Within the week, Captain Bartley responded to his next note, upon the same day that Nightingale also received word from Jane.

Chapter Nineteen: Adrift

20 May 1805, the Atlantic Ocean

Courtney was dreaming of Nightingale at the cottage. In his vision, they stood in the rubble of the bedroom. Some harsh strike had battered in the roof, sending masonry and scores of thatch tumbling amidst the downed rafters. Nightingale carefully moved through the wreckage, sifting past blocks and debris to try and rebuild. Courtney felt adrift. Each footstep seemed to threaten a fall through the unsteady ground. Why did he feel it was his own fault? He tried to lay a hand on Nightingale's shoulder but he did not respond.

'Hiram,' he said. 'Hiram. Hiram—'

About the cottage, surrounded on all sides, Courtney could feel the sea. It lapped insistently at the stone, making the ruined floors lurch and tilt. Below him and Nightingale, something stirred. A shadow stalked the house, stalked the ship, and he could not tell its form. If he could not understand it, he could not fight it.

'Hiram,' he tried again, but the man did not respond.

Somehow, he knew his father was outside the cottage, atop some bit of spindrift which Courtney thought had sunk long ago. He did not know what to concentrate on first: Nightingale, the shadows, his father, the besieged ship... Soon, the waves would roll in and he would drown, would be unable to keep his head above the surface.

'Hiram!' he shouted.

And then he was harshly shaken awake. For a moment, he thought he was back in his bed beside Nightingale, the man urging him out of sleep.

'Commander!'

But it was not Nightingale. Gainsborough's gnarled face peered down at him. Courtney jumped, clawing for the edge of his cot and the sword against the nearby bulkhead.

'What is it?' Courtney rushed to say, swinging his legs out of the bed. 'Is it the captain? Is he well?'

'It's the men on deck, sir. Lieutenant Appleton sent me. I was fetching some relief for Captain Harrison, sir, and...'

'Archer? Appleton?'

'He said to bring a tomahawk or axe, sir.'

Courtney shook the grogginess from his head and reached for his drawers and breeches, tugging them on beneath his nightshirt and hastily tucking the long tails of it away. With no time for anything else, he hurried out of the wardroom and towards the sickbay, past rows of sailors slumbering in their hammocks and slowly waking at the clamour. He clambered up the companion-ladder into a night bright with stars and moonlight, lanterns burning along the beam of the *Lion*. Men gathered beyond the foremast, clustered about the bows. He saw a few hands had climbed over the forward rail and onto the structure supporting the bowsprit.

Mutiny, Courtney thought. This had been the darkness that prowled the ship. But no one acknowledged his presence; no one fought back.

'You, there!' Courtney shouted. 'What the devil is happening? Make way there! Make way!'

Courtney shoved through the men. They all stared out along the spar, rocking up and down in the motion of the *Lion*'s passage. The jib-sails fluttered overhead, their stays straining healthily in the light airs. A man had crawled out onto the jib-boom, legs and one arm wrapped about it. A group of other sailors had stationed themselves outside the heads, leaning dangerously over the waters thrown up by the bobbing bows.

'Good God!' Courtney cried, realising the reason.

It was Lieutenant Appleton, stripped to his shirt-sleeves and with bare feet, out on the boom. He reached down beyond the footropes, fumbling in the bobstays. An additional line had been thrown over the spar, looped tightly next to the gammoning. The sorry, swinging form of Ramsey hung from the end of the noose.

For a moment, Courtney thought it was the movement of the ship which still made the boy twitch. But, in horror, he saw Ramsey still lived, choking and turning, writhing against the poor knot he had made about his neck. The surface of the sea loomed below him. It would have been more of a mercy to throw himself into it.

Courtney whirled about to face the gathered men. 'Mr Harriet!' he shouted. 'Take five men and swing a boat down! The rest of you, we will rig a jury-spritsail. Something to catch Mr Ramsey! And Mr Bowles, fetch a tomahawk!'

It was a risk to task Bowles, who had previously been lashed for fighting, with procuring a weapon, but Courtney still felt, somehow, he could trust him. Without thought, Courtney climbed out to Appleton, grabbing him by the shirt. He jerked and turned, Courtney stopping him from sliding off the boom.

'The men alerted me!' Appleton exclaimed. 'He was already hanging when I—'

'We'll save him, Lieutenant.'

For one of the first times, the men worked in unison to rig a spritsail. This kind of vessel was no longer of the ilk to carry such a sail but between the cordage of the flying jib-boom and the hanging dolphin-striker, they tied a loose canvas that hung below Ramsey's twitching feet. As they did so, Courtney and Appleton grasped Ramsey by his shirt, yanking him up so the rope was not lashed so tightly about his throat. He spoke no words, barely made a sound.

Ahead, the lights of the rest of the fleet burnt. They raced to the Caribbean, but now, the danger no longer seemed to be before them. The danger was here, festering in the *Lion*'s decks.

Within minutes, Mr Harriet and his small team had launched the gig. If the sail did not hold, at least Ramsey would not tumble into the churning waters. Harriet stared up at them through the blackness, directing his men to heave beneath the swaying bowsprit. It was a precarious position with the bows continually slamming into the surface, throwing up white foam and waves.

'I'm going to cut him loose,' Courtney said to Appleton, who had not wavered in his hold of Ramsey's shirt. 'Mr Bowles!'

The nimble young sailor was on hand with a tomahawk. Courtney grasped it in a fist which was slippery with what could be water or sweat. He looked at Ramsey's rope. It was taut but not taut enough. His attempt at a knot had slipped and not broken his neck as he had intended. Courtney saw the red rawness of the skin where it had cut in, but it no longer choked him so terribly. Ramsey, though, had not reacted. The air seemed to have been expelled from his lungs, withered by the agony and tension. *God, Ramsey, why have you done this?* Courtney questioned to himself, but he feared he already knew the answer.

'Hold him steady,' he ordered Appleton. There was no time to be gentle. He raised the tomahawk, slamming it into the rope. It had recently been coated in tar and so rebelled against Courtney's efforts for a time. He did not cease, plunging the blade harshly into the tough cord until frays appeared. One by one, they split, the innards of the rope coming apart. With one last endeavour, Courtney dismantled the cord and it unravelled from the spar. Ramsey dropped, falling into the cocoon of the canvas. Below, Mr Harriet leapt to attention, ready to grasp for his fellow midshipman if he tumbled further.

Courtney stared down, waiting for any sign that the boy was not dead: a twitch, a shiver, a noise. Nothing.

'Haul him in!' Courtney cried.

Gently, Ramsey was withdrawn from the sail and dragged over the rail to the heads. Courtney shimmied back off the bowsprit, helping Appleton to his feet. Side by side, the two of them raced down through the upper gun deck towards the crew's privies. Courtney pushed his way out into the round-house structure to find the men on their knees around Ramsey's stricken form. The way he lay in the white fabric was so reminiscent of Fox's final shroud. Appleton bent down, pressing his fingers into the bruised, mangled skin of Ramsey's neck. Courtney waited as the seconds seemed to turn into an age.

'He's alive,' Appleton said.

Courtney released the breath that had been stifled in his lungs. He nodded in gratitude to the men with them then offered Appleton his hand. He took it, rising to his feet.

'I shall take him to Dr Archer,' Appleton said.

'I shall remain on deck,' Courtney stated.

'No, I cannot ask you to do that.'

'I am not offering.'

With Ramsey safely below, Courtney tried to focus upon what would happen next. Fortunately, the rest of the first and into the middle watch passed without further incident. A quiet pall fell over them and, as if those experiences had fostered in them a newfound admiration and respect of the sea and its vessels, they worked the *Lion* with no troubles. Courtney, still in his nightshirt, breeches and bare feet, felt as though he was one of them again.

He thought of nothing but Ramsey. The boy had been hesitant when Courtney had gone to the midshipmen's berth. He cursed himself for not probing further into any discomfort, but he knew he had walked a delicate line. If McPherson had been the one to harm them, then his effects were still being felt. *Unless McPherson had not been the culprit.* Courtney had been unable to stop doubting, certainly with the nagging notions about the spoiled victuals and who they had affected. With frightening clarity, Courtney realised he could not handle this situation. He had always ploughed into difficult circumstances with no fear, no hesitancy, but this… He was out of his depth, and that scared him more than he cared to admit.

When Lieutenant Martin appeared, as first light dawned in the sky, Courtney left the deck. After a night with only two hours of rest, he knew he should return to his cabin but the tightness in his chest would not allow him to. With the cold morning seeping through his shirt, he found his way to Archer's sickbay. The men were still being roused by the quartermaster. Courtney saw Baker traipsing up from his compartment in the orlop and he seemed to start at Courtney's informal appearance. He quickly schooled his face, grasping his pipe to alert the men of their duties.

Word of Ramsey's state would doubtless spread but for now, the ignorance of it was comforting. Courtney reached the bows and after a polite knock on the timbers, was called through into the sickbay.

Ramsey lay out in one of the cots. He slept quietly, so still that Courtney feared the worst until he saw the rise and fall of his chest. Archer sat on one side of him and Appleton on the other. They both began to stand as Courtney entered, but he waved them down.

'How is he?' he asked.

'Alive,' Archer said simply. 'That is the best that we can hope for over the coming days. He has woken a handful of times but he will be confused and incapacitated for some time. The strangulation has affected his health and will do for some while.'

'I could not allow him to hang,' Courtney said, feeling he had to defend his actions. He had saved Ramsey's life, but at what cost to his wellbeing, both internal and external? *No*, Courtney thought. He had acted rightly. He would not bury another boy as he had Fox.

'I will do everything in my capacity,' Archer promised, 'but he may be here for some time.'

'I understand. Did he…speak of why he tried to… Why he acted as he did?'

'Not at any length.'

Appleton looked at Courtney and Courtney saw that the lieutenant, too, knew the reason. Appleton quickly glanced away.

'It is two bells,' Appleton said, changing the painful subject. 'I will supervise the holystoning on deck and then report to Captain Harrison.'

'I will do that,' Courtney offered.

'It is my role as acting first lieutenant, sir. I must.'

Regardless of Appleton's words, Courtney adhered to his side as he left the sickbay. Past the galley where Cook was lighting the fires in preparation for breakfast and the last of the men taking their hammocks down and moving them to be stowed, he followed Appleton and his hurried steps. Courtney was aware that he was trying to escape him; perhaps he still did not think Courtney worthy of caring for the men or giving them orders. He did not allow him out of sight, not even as he tried to ascend the companion-ladder. Courtney knew that one of his worst traits was being unable to let go of matters that he perhaps should, but he also knew that with the stability and health of a ship, he would not retreat. And more than Appleton, he knew the state of Captain Harrison.

'Lieutenant,' he said, stopping him from reaching the deck. 'I must insist that you let me speak to the captain.'

Appleton turned, shock crossing his features. His mouth opened without word, shut again. 'Sir...' he managed. 'I am the primary lieutenant.'

'I'm aware of that. But you have had a trying night. We all have. Do not make me order you to your cabin.'

'You cannot order me,' Appleton said, obviously without thought. Courtney could see he regretted it. The lieutenant glanced down the deck but no one was close enough to hear them. 'I mean to say...'

'I know what you mean to say.' Courtney took a step up the ladder so he was beside Appleton. He was a head taller than him and Appleton had to raise his eyes to look at him. 'I may be here on Captain Harrison's blessing but I still have a role and a position. I made certain of that.'

'They are my men. And I...I failed—' Appleton rasped. His voice wobbled and choked. With a convulsive swallow, he looked away and to his shock, Courtney saw tears in his eyes. Failure? 'Do you believe...' Appleton started. 'Do you believe that it was because of... That Mr Ramsey acted as he did?'

Courtney nodded silently.

'It cannot be McPherson,' Appleton insisted.

Suddenly, Courtney thought of what Baker had told him about Appleton, about his past on the *Eclipse*, about the accusations that had flown on that ship. He could not find the strength to ask him of it, not now, in these fraught circumstances.

Before Courtney could press on, Appleton shook his head and forced composure over his trembling features. 'They are my men,' he repeated. 'It is important that they see their lieutenants after such a distressing incident.'

Courtney nodded. It was obvious Appleton would not reveal more. 'I agree,' he said, softer. 'Put yourself among them. Allow them to see you and find some comfort. But permit me to go to the captain.'

Courtney did not have to ask Appleton's permission for anything, but he saw how the man appreciated it. 'Yes, sir,' he replied, and then disappeared to the deck. This time, Courtney let him go. As in his dream, he abruptly felt the weight of the water about them, the dark expanse that separated them from the land, from society, from comfort. Courtney had hoped that the open-water sailing across the Atlantic would bring a solution, but the problems were deeper than that, ingrained in each and every individual. He feared what awaited them in the Caribbean. If they missed the French and Spanish, the anger and the vexation would grow. But if they did meet the French and the Spanish, he did not know what state the *Lion* would face the enemy in.

Now, he had one matter certain. Before returning to his cabin, he made his way to Harrison, who only had

Gainsborough for company with Archer occupied in the sickbay. He told the captain what had occurred, watching his face turn paler and paler. Then, with finality, he said, 'I am going to call a court martial once we reach the Caribbean. That is the only way to resolve this.'

This time, Harrison nodded.

Chapter Twenty: Progeny

The carriage arrived a day before Nightingale had expected it to. No word had come forth to him and no notice, so as he met the vehicle on the little country lane that led to the cottage, he could not hide his surprise. Still, opening the door and seeing the familiar face in the small confines, he felt a lightness settle on his chest. The lady within was prompt and efficient, just in the way of her elder brother.

'Mrs Wainwright,' Nightingale greeted, offering his arm to her.

'Stuff, Hiram. Call me "Jane". We have seen enough of the world and of each other to use one another's Christian names.'

Jane, née Courtney and now Wainwright, took Nightingale's elbow and ducked out of the coach. It had been a long while since Nightingale had seen her. He tended to witness her in small images of her life, and those which were the most momentous. When he had first met her, she had been in a ragged dress, her wild dark hair unbound, skin flushed with rage and grief, and with a musket in her bruised hands. She had risen up against her tormentor, Ransome, who had driven the *Ulysses* into a cursed mutiny. His death had freed the ship from his oppression but had led to her trial for piracy and murder. Five years from that terrible incident, she had settled into her married life with Lieutenant Wainwright: a former officer on the *Ulysses*. They had walked the path of recovery together, in the same way that Nightingale and Courtney had.

The thick black curls of her hair were now primly gathered and styled amidst pins and blue ribbons. She wore a deep-green gown, simple but flattering, and in her hands she carried an oriental fan, defence against the rising summer heat. Scars of the mutiny still decorated her bare upper arms and one vivid white mark cut across her collarbones. She made no attempt to hide them.

'You are good to make the journey so quickly,' Nightingale said. 'But I did not mean to press you for such a speedy arrival.'

'You did not press me, Hiram. I wished to make the journey. I intended to wait for Eddie's arrival home but… In truth, I did not know how much time I had to spare. Your note made it sound drastic.'

'An old sailor's gift for hyperbole, my dear.'

He kept his hand upon her arm as he directed Rylance to bring the lady's luggage to the door. Rylance cast his eyes over Jane and bowed and scraped as if she were of the royal family, and not a girl who had grown up in abject poverty. Jane smiled at him but Nightingale could feel her fist about his. With every step closer to the cottage, her grip grew firmer. Nightingale wondered how long it had been since she had come home. Perhaps she did not see it in that manner anymore. She had made her own home in Norfolk with her husband and his seven sisters. The reappearance of her father was from a life long left.

'How is he today?' Jane asked now. 'I trust he is comfortable?'

It was the concern of a person who knew their fellow man was perhaps meeting death soon.

'Dr Harrow has treated him for the fever which seems to have broken. It has not troubled him these past few days. Do not fret, the doctor does not believe it is the kind that might be passed amongst individuals. His opinion is that it has stemmed from a lifetime of abusing a bottle.' A lifetime, Nightingale reminded himself, which was not so very longer than his own.

Jane took a shivering breath. 'That is something I can well believe. There are not many occasions where I can recall Father without…' She paused. 'There are not many occasions where I can recall Father at all. Arthur often cared for me.'

'I have heard. He was a good brother to you.'

'As are you.'

Nightingale glanced to Jane, but she did not seem to have considered anything amiss about her comment. She stared at the closed front door, surrounded by a trellis of vines and honey-suckles. The latticework, the floral decoration, the genteel rural appeal of the cottage had been a product of years of work and frustrated love. Courtney had, with Nightingale's financial aid and his own back-breaking labour, created a home for himself, just as Jane had made hers. But what lay beyond was a remnant of the time before they had forged their own paths. Nightingale could understand the shivering of Jane's hand in his own, and the flutter of her chest. She laid her other gloved palm to her throat and touched one of the long, healed scars.

She had survived the *Ulysses*; she could survive this.

Nightingale waited for her to open the door. She did, grasping the brass handle and pushing it back with some determined force. Nightingale felt her hand twitch in his own, beckoning him forth, and so he followed, eyes turning to where he had left John Courtney in the armchair by the window. A blanket had been thrown about his legs and there, with the bright June light filtering through the glass, he appeared older than his fifty years.

Jane stopped on the threshold. Her shoulders dipped and for a moment, Nightingale worried she might swoon. But a woman who had faced a Royal Navy court martial was sturdier than such shock, and she simply dropped Nightingale's arm and straightened her spine. Folding her gloved hands before her, she approached the back of the chaise lounge and carefully rounded it. The heels of her shoes clicked on the wooden boards and then deadened on the Persian rug.

'Hello, Father,' she said gently, the burr of her accent pushing through the softer tones she had adopted.

John sat up a little in the chair. The sun did not improve the yellowy hue of his skin. 'Jane,' he said shortly.

'Hiram wrote to me, Father. He said that you were unwell but had come back to Ryde.'

Every word seemed sharp and polished, as if Jane spoke them individually with no mind to the broader meaning. Nightingale could only imagine what she was feeling and thinking.

'You are no girl anymore,' John said, equally as terse.

'Not for many years.'

Rylance still lingered in the doorway. Nightingale turned to him as he shifted Jane's case between his hands, obviously debating the social etiquette of intruding upon this situation. 'I shall aid my steward,' Nightingale said to Jane. 'Then I shall return if you wish it.'

'No, it is quite all right, Hiram,' Jane replied. 'I shall call for you or Rylance if needed.'

Then, Nightingale could truly see the lady she had become, a mistress of her household and affairs, knowing how to conduct herself and how to present a face to the world. She had allowed the deck of the *Ulysses* to form a rigid, enduring core within her and she still stood upon those foundations.

'Very well,' he agreed. 'I shall leave you.'

Rylance had tried meticulously to dress one of the bedrooms in a manner befitting a woman, but had not succeeded much beyond potting a few flowers in the window. Nightingale had him lay Jane's case at the foot of the small curtained bed and fussily brushed down the corner of the quilt which had folded. No dust still clung to it, however, which was one positive mark. He and Courtney had little use for another bedroom and so had barely beautified this room more than a rug and airing the bed dressing. Now, Nightingale perched on the edge of the bed and stopped Rylance as he was about to exit.

'Rylance,' he said. 'We have known one another a long while, yes?'

Rylance smiled. 'Oh yes, sir. Twenty years this year, sir.'

Had it been that long already? Rylance had been a cabin boy on HMS *Marathon* whom Nightingale had employed as his own steward after the captain had fallen out with the young lad. As Nightingale had progressed from lieutenant to commander and post-captain, he had kept Rylance with him. He had been there when the *Orient* erupted; when Nightingale had crumbled to the floor of his great cabin, blinded, distraught after Leroy Sawyer's death; when he had gained the commission on the *Scylla*; when he had burnt the *Ulysses*; when he had faced a court martial and dismissal from the service. Rylance had even followed him out of that career, loyal to a fault.

'What do you think of Mr Courtney, Rylance?' Nightingale questioned, wondering if he was asking more than he should.

'Mr Courtney, sir?' Rylance reddened a little, rocking on his feet and twisting his hands behind his back. 'Commander Courtney, sir, is a fine man. I am…glad, sir, that you and he are on friendly terms still and…'

'Oh. No, I didn't mean…'

Nightingale chuckled before he noted the sincerity in Rylance's words. From the day he had shattered because of Lieutenant Sawyer's demise, he had always wondered if Rylance knew the secret he carried. If he did, he gave no cause to make Nightingale feel afraid of his knowledge. Though Nightingale often came alone to the cottage, Rylance had been in the navy since he was a boy and Nightingale knew the things that transpired between sailors on the lower decks. Rylance must, surely, have some idea of the depth of feeling between Nightingale and Courtney: why the former captain was still on such firm terms with his former lieutenant and why he spent weeks with him at his home.

Now, Nightingale collected his composure and clarified, 'I was speaking of John Courtney downstairs. What is your opinion of him?'

'My opinion, sir? That don't matter.'

'You have spent more time with him than I. You have been very diligent and accommodating by caring for his wellbeing as well as my own.'

Truly, Nightingale had not known how Rylance would respond to the other man. He had not known how anyone would. When Nightingale had written to Captain Bartley, requesting that John Courtney be moved from the *Impregnable*, with consideration to his dire health, he had expected a direct dismissal. Only officers could be given parole, under their word that they would not attempt to escape or act improperly. Mr Courtney had fired a shot at a lieutenant, brawled, and then tried to escape the *Impregnable* when imprisoned there. But, during the process of writing to Bartley, Nightingale had also involved Magistrate Castle and used every connection he could think would be relevant. The mention of his father-in-law, Sir William Haywood, a man who could be called upon to lean on any nearby MP, had evidently impressed Castle.

And with such a dire condition as John Courtney's, his release from the *Impregnable* did not seem as though he received a lighter sentence. Nightingale vowed he would drag the man back, regardless of health, if he set a foot wrong.

'I have flogged men for less,' he had told Harry Castle, hiding how little of a flogging captain he had truly been.

Rylance was silent for some time, perhaps considering these recent events. Then, he said, 'I think, sir, that he is trying to be true to his word. I ain't see him even eye a bottle of gin. Most likely a-feared of what it's already done to him. He ain't like his son, sir, but I've come across worse sods in my life. Better sods too, but many worse.'

'Thank you, Rylance. That is helpful to know.'

Rylance had once told him the curse of a steward was to hear everything that occurred on a ship. Nightingale could have pressed him to detail every shadowy and sordid event on the dim decks, but he never had, preferring to trust his men unless their behaviour disturbed the peace. Rylance was a good lad, obedient, quiet, and efficient. If John Courtney had stepped out of line, though, Nightingale knew that Rylance's loyalty to him and Courtney would mean he would tell all.

However, his concentration remained upon Jane now. When she had finished with her father, she emerged from the cottage into the garden where Nightingale had retreated to appreciate the June sun. Dappled light touched the creek which flowed behind the house. Courtney and Rylance had constructed a small bench with the skill of a ship's carpenter, and Nightingale sat there, watching the ducks which escaped the rising heat by dousing themselves in the water. He threw them crumbs of bread from the pantry, some of it disappearing into the reeds. He did not notice Jane approach until she lowered herself onto the bench beside him, smiling at the birds.

'I love watching the wildlife from our cottage in Great Yarmouth,' she said. 'We sometimes see fallow deer amongst the fields. Edward's little nieces and nephews like to name them.'

Nightingale smiled. 'I truly did not mean to startle you with my letter about your father,' he said. 'You have such a settled life now and I am ever so pleased for you. I feared telling you that he had returned would upset all of that. I assumed when writing that Arthur did not tell you of him either?'

Jane shook her head. 'He did not.'

'As I said in my letter, he did not tell me. I have written to him now, wherever he is, to inform him I know and what I've done but I worry what his response will be.'

'That is his decision. You have done your part. I know that, had you told me of our father's return a few years ago, when I did not know where I was heading, it might have unsettled me. Arthur, bless him, he did so much, but I was only in the Caribbean because of his presence. I would have followed him about the islands without a clue of my own future. Now, there is little that can turn me upside down. Not even my old father.'

'Old?' Nightingale chuckled. 'He is not very much older than I am.'

'Oh, you know what I mean, Hiram. He appears so very older than you. I will always see him that way because he is my father.'

She was silent for a moment, gazing at the dance of the ducks amongst the waterside plants. Nightingale tore off a chunk of bread and handed it to her. She turned it about in her bare hands for a while, then ripped it smaller and threw it into the creek.

'I did not think I would speak to him again,' she admitted. 'But I said my piece to him and was patient when he spoke of himself and Mother. I will be content to leave it in that manner if I am never to see him again.'

'You do not intend to?'

'I'm not sure. A mere week ago, I did not even know he was still alive and then, all of a sudden, there he is, sitting in my brother's cottage and ailing with a complaint which may kill him. He wished to make amends with myself and Arthur before that happened.'

'He spoke of it, yes.'

'I...' Jane sighed. 'I saw the evil of men on the *Ulysses*. I saw what they do to one another and to women. Ransome, the cur, deserved what I did to him. There is not a day where I regret wielding the musket and sword. My father, sat in that room with a blanket across his legs and the foulness of disease in him, is not of the godforsaken cast Ransome was moulded from. Not anymore. I feel that when I killed Ransome, I killed the hurt of my father also. That, I have no shame in saying.'

It seemed so peculiar to talk of such rotten things when the sun created beauty across the quiet garden and fields. Jane spoke her words with the certainty and detachment of a woman who had turned them again and again in her mind. Nightingale admired her sturdiness, as he ever had. He had thought the girl who had stood before an Admiralty court martial had vanished into her pretty gown and bonnet – but she still existed, would always exist, in a quieter, subtle way.

'Arthur will navigate this course in his own way,' she said. 'But I know he will wish to see Father as I have. There was no malice in what you did, writing to us both, Hiram, or having mercy on an old man. Rest assured that I will not carry this with any pain. I do not know how I shall feel in a few days, or a week, or a month, or a year, but now, I…I feel nothing heavy. It is hard to lay words to.'

'I understand.' Nightingale reached over and laid his hand upon hers, now curled in her lap. She smiled softly. 'Your brother was good to come to my own father's funeral. I did not feel many emotions towards my father then. I said farewell to him in Trinidad, just as you laid to rest your own pain for your father and mother. It is something none of us can dictate.'

Jane nodded. 'My brother thinks the world of you, Hiram. There is little you could do that would make him dislike you.'

Nightingale thought the same of Courtney. He even tried to remain firm in the face of Courtney's decision regarding Miss Sandham and Captain Harrison, though the idea tied his insides with shameful envy. He pressed such a reaction down now. 'Arthur is a good man,' he said. 'I do not know where he is and when he shall return though.'

'He will return. When we were children, we never truly had a home, only the small room in the back of the Fisherman's Catch. You have made a home here, in this cottage.'

Nightingale smiled. 'That was Arthur's doing. He is industrious.'

'And you are very kind to help him. I said that you have both been good brothers to me. I hope you take no offence in me speaking of you in that way. I have many in-laws from Edward's family, and it almost seems you are one of them from another side.'

A blush crossed Nightingale's face. 'That is very kind.'

'And it leads me to another matter I wished to speak to you of. I have also written to Arthur of it but, as you say, there is no definite answer to when he will receive the letter.'

'You may talk to me of anything, my dear.'

Now it was Jane's turn to take Nightingale's hands, cupping them in hers. 'I am with child, Hiram. Edward and I shall be parents soon.'

Joy filled Nightingale. He had never wished for children, knew that he and Louisa would not be attentive or skilled parents, but he would never dictate a path for other men and women. He saw the happiness in Jane's eyes and knew that she and her husband shared the same desire; it had not simply been a course taken for the sake of society and propriety, as it would have been for him and his own wife. 'Oh, Jane, my dear,' he said. 'That is wonderful news.'

'It is. I did not tell Father. He has not proved that he can be a stable part of my life, if he ever will be. But you… You are my family, though we do not share blood. I wish for you and Arthur, if you will be so inclined, to be the godfathers.'

It made the exhilaration in Nightingale crest over. He was not ashamed of the tears he felt in his eyes, as if he had just attained his post rank once again. 'Yes, my dear, of course. It would be my honour.'

'Yes?'

'Yes.'

He had begun the day with fear in his heart: that he had upset those dearest to him, that he had painted his own feelings for his father over someone else's. Yet Jane had touched him with her honesty and her request. He realised how deeply he wished to be part of her family, of Courtney's. Such a reality would never even have seemed possible when he had commanded the *Scylla*, as Courtney's captain and the man who had delivered Jane and the mutineers to trial. For every mistake he fretted he had made and every additional pain he had suffered, Nightingale knew he would not change the course of his life. He wished that he could remain in this position: Jane and Wainwright's child's godfather, Courtney's confidante and partner. Yet he knew times might change with Courtney's marriage. Perhaps that was pure selfishness on his part.

Now, he could not think of such a thing. Jane was here and she needed entertaining and joy after her trying day. He accompanied her to the Fisherman's Catch where Mr and Mrs Woods wept over her return to their tavern. She became surrounded by figures from her past, those who had never forgotten her. She was one of them, despite having left and made a healthy life elsewhere. Nightingale kept to her side, allowing Jane to tell her story, both of the *Ulysses* and of her time in Norfolk. The days of the mutiny seemed a different world now, a world she had made her peace with.

For that evening, Nightingale felt somewhat as though he belonged in the common room, privileged to witness both Jane's past and her present. He did not think of any more but what existed about him.

Chapter Twenty-One: Merciful

4 June 1805, Carlisle Bay, Barbados

Courtney, with an arm beneath Harrison's, walked out into warm Caribbean sun. It was as though he had stepped back five years, the sticky heat and sweat already gathering beneath his collar acting as an old, familiar trouble. The issues facing the *Lion* also echoed the old *Scylla*'s bane: the hunt for missing vessels again spread discontent and frustration about the ship's company. This time, however, it was an entire fleet which had vanished into the blue expanse. Once more, all that could be relied upon was the information and intelligence of port authorities and fellow ships. Only the day before, they had received their first confirmation that their enemies were in the West Indies – but where, it could not be pinpointed.

Now, though, in Barbados's Carlisle Bay, Courtney looked over a group of despondent and exhausted vessels. The chase across the Atlantic had passed in a blink of an eye with Nelson's entire complement making the crossing in just over three weeks. The *Lion*'s spars and canvas protested, and following Ramsey's grief and the other discontent, Courtney could not even find the heart to take pride in the momentously quick progress. As he observed the harbour, he spotted an equal share of carpenters, shipwrights, masters, and soldiers ferried across the water in launches. Soon, a contingent of soldiers would embark to be tended to by the fleet, perhaps in preparation of facing the French, but the additional duty muddied their purpose. In Courtney's absence, Appleton would direct them on the *Lion*.

Dr Archer followed Courtney and Harrison down to the captain's gig. He had not said a word about Harrison's condition, though Courtney thought the doctor knew the reality of it. Archer kept a close watch on his patient as they were rowed across the harbour. Stepping up onto the shore for the first time in weeks made Courtney's knees feel unsteady, but they were not as fragile and rickety as Harrison's. The man kept a firm grip on Courtney's elbow, skin entirely untouched by the hot sun, as pallid as he had been for a long while now.

'Shall I see you to the hospital, sir?' Courtney asked.

When Harrison gave a non-committal shake of his head, Archer interjected, 'I'll ensure he gets there safely, Commander, and that there are sufficient doctors and supplies there for his needs.'

'When… When do you anticipate his return?'

'Soon.'

Archer did not elaborate. As he guided Harrison up from the white sands and into the island's settlement, Courtney felt once again that other overly familiar sensation: that of the responsibility of a ship falling onto his shoulders. Too often he had received the duty, unexpected, unanticipated, and, if he was truthful, unwanted, considering the state of the *Lion* and her crew. He had led the *Scylla*'s men; he had led the *Lysander*'s men; he would now have to lead the *Lion*'s.

Appleton cared for the crew now. Courtney delayed his return, wandering to the shipyard and finding Master Moore. Together with the carpenter and his mates, they negotiated bringing the *Lion* back to a better trim and shape. Spars had been strained, canvas had been thoroughly wetted and abused in the mad chase, and the bowsprit still betrayed hints of Ramsey's grief, results of his writhing body and Courtney's violent attempts to save him. Returning to the ship, he supervised the work, all the while watching over the arriving soldiers and waiting for any information from any of their fellow ships, each one of them desperate for definite intelligence of the

French's location. After a muted and morose supper, Appleton tried to catch Courtney's eye and Courtney knew what he wished to ask: the state of Harrison was a shadow hanging over the entire *Lion*.

But there was no time to dwell. With the responsibility of the *Lion* in his lap, Courtney completed the task which should have been performed weeks ago. He sat at the wardroom table and by the light of the moon, dredged up his best handwriting to compose a note to Lord Nelson. A court martial had to be called, but Courtney hated intruding upon the commander-in-chief, knowing his present preoccupations about the enemy.

If he was honest, Courtney had not thought of the enemy for some time. But, when Harrison did not return, he was soon embroiled in the practice of holding the *Lion* together in the fleet's progress. They were drawn south by the suggestion of merchantmen and Rear-Admiral Cochrane who had been patrolling about Jamaica. He believed the enemy threatened Trinidad so, bolstered by further intelligence from Brereton, the commander of St Lucia, Nelson's squadron hurried to Tobago and further to the Bay of Paria. The excitement of finally facing their foes provided a distraction for Courtney and the crew. Eager to gain a sighting of them, and to avoid the dark mood below decks, he climbed the mainmast with Bowles again.

Balancing himself on the yard, Courtney remembered Trinidad well. It was there that Nightingale had nearly lost his position on the *Scylla*, there that Harrison had been on the cusp of gaining it, and there that the court martial of the *Ulysses* mutineers, and of Nightingale, had taken place. He regretted that another trial might have to occur. But none of those professional memories came to Courtney as he gripped a backstay and stared over the clear waters, the distant island. He had first kissed Nightingale there, in a little inn's bedroom in Port of Spain. They had spent the night with one another, embracing, touching, everything new and intimate and almost frightening in the emotion Courtney had already felt for him.

It had been the beginning of something Courtney never wished to end. But then, even sequestered in the very tops of the *Lion*, thoughts of Harrison, of Tabitha, rushed in and he almost felt the ground race up to meet him again.

The black tidings kept appearing. The French and Spanish had not been at Trinidad. Any prospect of repeating the Battle at the Nile, destroying the enemy fleet at anchor, disappeared. Courtney could sense the despondency on the *Lion* and even as they were drawn towards Grenada, relying now on information from fellow Caribbean officers, he doubted what they might find. When word came that HMS *Diamond Rock*, in actual fact an island off Martinique commissioned as a king's vessel, had recently surrendered to the French, further frustration simmered. It seemed their foes existed just over the horizon, only a short sail away, but constantly slipping through their fingers.

Courtney barely knew what to say to the officers around him. He had no answer to the disappearing enemies and he had no answer to Harrison's absence. But, as the *Lion* reached Grenada's St George's Bay, word came from the depths of the fleet. Courtney's submission for a court martial had been accepted. McPherson would be trialled and judged before a panel of captains. No more would Courtney have to decide the direction of his fate. He thought it might give him relief but it did not.

He broke the news to Ramsey. The boy had barely said a word since his attempted suicide. Courtney knew he would have to speak at the trial but he felt cruel for even saying he had to. Ramsey did not appear angry, or aggrieved, or hurt. Simply…empty.

The fleet journeyed northwards, peering into the islands of St Lucia and Martinique, en route to St Kitts and Antigua. Courtney conversed with the other ships as much as needed, knowing that soon he would be speaking to the illustrious captains in a tangled and dark trial. It was whilst returning to the ship in the vicinity of Dominica, sitting in the little launch boat and being dwarfed by the mightiness of the seventy-four-gunner, that he thought how terribly the *Lion* did not deserve this. She had survived the Nile, been patched together, and returned to the ocean. She should not suffer the blackness in her belly. Courtney realised, starkly, that he occupied the same position Nightingale had once; they had both been commanders of this vessel. Courtney dreaded bringing the ship back to England in such a state, admitting to Nightingale his failure.

And just as much as the ship, the crew did not deserve her reputation. They had behaved well in the lengthy pursuit. Courtney had spent hours on deck, adjusting the *Lion*'s trim and sailing capabilities, and the men had obeyed with barely a stagger or moment of hesitation. It was more than he could say for himself. Perhaps he had spent too long damning them, when the true problem was his own troubles.

In the launch boat, Courtney closed his eyes briefly, then, again pressing down his dismay, climbed back aboard. As the acting captain, Courtney entered Harrison's great cabin and ushered Appleton and Martin through. The place still bore marks of the absent captain: his logs and maps locked away, the writing desk with a sheet of paper ready to be used, Hephaestus's fur clinging to the seams of the timbers. Courtney rounded the table, about to sit at Harrison's chair, but at the last moment, he found he could not do it. He remained standing.

'We have been misdirected around these seas,' he said. 'Our foray to Trinidad, back to Grenada… The enemy has consistently eluded us.'

Appleton nodded, already knowing all of this. Martin glanced at him then shuffled on his feet, obviously uncertain how to react, if he should voice anything.

'Why was the fleet told such things if they were untrue?' Appleton asked.

'I don't know. Terrible intelligence, missightings… Now, it is considered that the enemy may be returning to Europe across the Atlantic again.'

Courtney sighed. It had been a long while since he had sailed as part of a fleet. He had forgotten the variables and the logistical problems of manoeuvring such a large complement of vessels and men. Failure was a terrible enough concept as a single ship, but amplified across a squadron, it became even more frustrating.

'Let us pray that the presence of Lord Nelson in the Caribbean has addled their minds and spirits,' Martin suddenly said. 'Perhaps they are running before the wind as quickly as they dare to try and escape his clutches.'

It was the first sensible thing Martin had offered. Appleton gave a nod of agreement and Courtney did also.

'There has been…no word of the captain?' Martin next asked. The lieutenant had never spoken so much to Courtney.

'Dr Archer believes he will make a full recovery but I have heard nothing else. It is best he is cared for…away from the ship.'

'What is…' Martin blushed. 'What is wrong with him?'

Courtney swallowed. Archer had not said, but Courtney had surmised that his ailment was no disease which might spread, and nor was it the lingering effects of the spoiled victuals. A disturbing notion had come to him when depositing Harrison in Barbados: Harrison's state had reminded Courtney unsettlingly of his father, in the fever of his drink or in the lull when he had been cast from it. As soon as he had realised that, he had thought of the missing laudanum. Perhaps it had not been the crew at all.

'He is suffering from a brief ailment,' Courtney said, hiding his worries. 'But it is not deadly. He shall return soon. In the meanwhile, we shall have to attend on Mr McPherson's trial. I have received confirmation that it shall be held at the earliest possible time. Until that time, it is recommended that the prisoner is transferred out of the *Lion* so his testimony is not corrupted by any inside influences.'

'He has been held here for many weeks without comment,' Appleton interjected. 'Why change that?'

'Only we knew of his condition. If the matter had been discussed previously, perhaps this would have occurred before-hand. But...' Courtney could not blame Harrison, not when the man was laid so low. He knew that he himself should have done more. 'I shall oversee his transfer during the first watch.'

The first watch arrived quickly. Courtney stood in his cabin, eyeing the box that contained his flintlock pistol. He did not anticipate trouble, prayed it would not be so, but regardless, he unlocked the chest. Holding the weapon in his hand, his heart suddenly throbbed in his ears. He remembered Lieutenant Hargreaves on the *Scylla*, released from his binds by the mutineers, breaking into Nightingale's cabin and shooting him. For a moment, Courtney saw a flash of his own fate.

He loaded the flintlock with a trembling hand. He gripped his wrist, made the trembles stop, and departed the wardroom. He would show that he was not afraid, would defend himself and the ship if it came to it.

Accompanied by Lieutenant Farnham, Courtney descended into the dim orlop. Lanterns had been lit along the length of the deck, throwing pools of orange glow. A handful of petty officers occupied the low area and each of them stared at Courtney and Farnham as they passed. To Courtney's surprise, Appleton awaited them. He looked darkly at Courtney and for a moment, Courtney thought there would be trouble, but he stepped aside and allowed Farnham to deal with the storeroom's lock.

McPherson emerged, pallid and broken. Courtney had treated him as humanely as his circumstances allowed, bringing him to deck for supervised exercise, having the stewards take him his rations, but he knew the man was hurt and subdued. The court martial would end this madness.

In silence, Courtney walked beside McPherson. Farnham flanked him on the other side, with Appleton behind. Up the lower gun deck they climbed and then to the upper. Moon-light shone through the next open hatchway. For a moment, McPherson paused, as if he believed it to be his last sight of that heavenly body. Farnham stepped forward to urge him on.

McPherson avoided him. Somehow, the man escaped the Marine's hands and ducked away, racing for the ladder.

'Mr McPherson!' Courtney shouted, grasping for him. The seaman turned and in the paltry light, something flashed. The blade of a dirk. It bewildered Courtney, almost stopped him dead. And McPherson ran.

'Stop him!' Courtney exclaimed as Farnham hurried forth. Appleton was close behind. Courtney took the steps two at a time, advancing onto the weather deck with his flintlock in hand. He looked forward, looked aft, searching for the escaped prisoner and saw him dashing for the stern, ploughing through a team of baffled waisters. 'Stop him!' Courtney yelled again.

Farnham's Marines pulled agog deckhands out of the way. Muskets glinted in the shine of the moon, the mere sight of them making McPherson weave desperately, but he was losing ground, forced into a tighter and tighter space. Appleton herded him closer to the gunwales, putting him between the sea and the weapons. Beneath the shadow of the mizzenmast, McPherson had nowhere left to run. Courtney approached, gripping his flintlock so hard he could feel it digging into his palm. Across the deck, his and McPherson's gazes crossed.

'Mr McPherson!' he cried. 'Drop your weapon and stop this! Lieutenant Farnham, seize him!'

Farnham came forth again but McPherson moved with the speed of a cornered animal. He grabbed Appleton, spun him, and, with one strong arm around the lieutenant's chest, aimed the point of the dirk below Appleton's ear. Appleton froze, hands raised. Blood welled and dripped over his stock as the blade nicked his flesh.

Courtney halted. He held McPherson's gaze as if by looking away, the man would lose all control. Agony was etched across

McPherson's face; his jaw clenched hard enough to break teeth, a vein pulsing in his forehead, his eyes shining with unshed tears, sweat slowly dripping from his hairline. The blade of the dirk trembled. One jerk and it could slip across Appleton's vulnerable throat.

'Mr McPherson,' Courtney found the voice to say, 'you have the muskets of the Marines on you. They will fire if you make one wrong move.'

But he knew if the muskets discharged, they could wound McPherson, shift his arm enough to slash Appleton's neck. Courtney tightened his grip on his own flintlock.

'Mr McPherson, you must stand trial. You have to answer for what you have done. The court will investigate you and make a fair judgement.'

'I did not do it,' McPherson suddenly spat. 'Ask the boy. I did not do it.'

'Then say this to the court. They will hear you.' McPherson shook his head so Courtney continued, 'Regardless, raising a weapon on an officer of the Royal Navy will not be favourable to you. Release Lieutenant Appleton.'

'I had a son,' McPherson suddenly said. Courtney could see Appleton's lower lip wobbling, in as much anguish as McPherson. 'He died whilst I was away at sea. I would never hurt a child.'

McPherson had not said this before. Courtney again felt he only looked at the surface of the troubles onboard, unable to see what lurked beneath. Everyone saw a different shadow under the water; everyone called it by a different name.

'They will hear your pleas and evidence. They will hear it from every one of us,' Courtney said, but knew, with an abrupt and heavy guilt, that he was making excuses for himself. He should have dealt with this situation in a better manner, should have acted quicker. Now, he was turning the matter over to other hands to avoid the judgement himself.

'I have been lashed many times for many infractions,' McPherson said. 'They will not believe me.'

246

'If you are innocent, then you will be acquitted.'

Courtney realised that might not be true. Lack of evidence did not always mean lack of conviction. He had seen innocent men lashed, accused, killed before. And the ignominy of being blamed for such an evil action would not leave McPherson. Even if he entered another ship, changed his mess and crew mates entirely, the shadow would still hang over his own mind. In the eyes of the Admiralty, he had sealed his fate by raising a weapon upon Appleton.

'I wish to be let go,' McPherson rasped. 'I want to leave this horrid ship. She's cursed! The convoy, the injuries, the deaths... This ship is why we cannot find the enemy! She's been damned!'

'I cannot allow you to leave,' Courtney said. 'You must stand trial.'

'I will not,' McPherson insisted and gripped the dirk tighter. Appleton struggled.

Courtney knew he had to act. McPherson, in his desperation, whether it was deliberate or not, would kill Appleton. He broke the man's gaze and looked towards Lieutenant Farnham. He was going to order him to advance, to arrest McPherson by any means, as long as he disarmed him quickly, but McPherson obviously guessed his approach. As Farnham stepped forward, McPherson whirled around towards the gunwales. His sudden movement slashed the dirk's blade across Appleton's neck. Courtney watched in horror as the lieutenant crumpled to the deck, a hand frantically feeling for the gushing wound. Courtney hurried to him, nearly missing McPherson leaping at the rail.

'Stop him!' Courtney shouted, and heard the report of Farnham's musket split the night. He did not see if the shot connected, but the sound of an echoing splash told him McPherson had reached the sea.

Appleton gasped, blood pouring through his fingers. Courtney wrenched off his own stock and wrapped it around Appleton's injury.

'Run out a line!' he ordered Bowles, who was standing nearby. 'Fish him back in!'

He listened to the attempts to reach McPherson as he urged Appleton to his feet. The lieutenant whitened, shock marring his features. Unbidden, Courtney thought of how Lieutenant Sawyer had died, on this same deck, choking and bleeding from a splinter which had punctured his throat. Dr Archer was not aboard; he still attended to the absent Harrison. But Ellis occupied the sickbay and it was to him that Courtney had Martin deliver Appleton. Once the lieutenant was away, Courtney rushed to the starboard gunwale and looked overboard. Pale moonlight touched the tops of the waves as they cascaded past the *Lion*'s hull. A paltry line had been thrown, far, far down into the darkness. Courtney could not see the end of it in the water and nor could he see McPherson. His form had been swallowed by the sea.

Courtney slowly stepped back from the rail. He gave the order for Bowles to reel the line back in.

'The sea will decide if he is worthy of mercy or not,' he said, and knew it would be the same for the rest of them.

—

Captain Harrison arrived back to a ship heavy with what had recently occurred. At Antigua, he came aboard with Dr Archer, ready for the next stage of the *Lion*'s voyage. After shedding the soldiers, word came that Villeneuve had also disembarked the French troops he had been ferrying around, in anticipation of amphibious operations. It seemed confirmation that Villeneuve had changed his schemes to cause disruption throughout the British West Indies and was retreating across the Atlantic. Perhaps Martin had been correct: Nelson's mere presence had rattled the French admiral and sent him scurrying away.

Harrison had been updated on all of that by the port authorities and now, he climbed the side of the *Lion* to the ceremonial clash of the Marines' muskets and the trill of the bosun's whistle announcing his return. Courtney had donned his dress uniform, the commander's epaulette on his shoulder gleaming in the sun and making him think what a failure he had been as a temporary captain. He tried to concentrate on Harrison, how the colour had bloomed in his cheeks again, his personality and character returning with his health. He nodded at the crew who had also turned out in their best, then his eyes roamed and Courtney could tell he was searching for Appleton.

Courtney had no choice but to tell the captain what had happened: McPherson's escape, the damage he had caused Appleton, his dramatic egress from the ship. The light which had briefly touched Harrison upon observing his quarterdeck faded as he heard of the incident. He had been absent for it, unable to offer a guiding hand as he should have in his role as captain. In a sense, Courtney was glad it had happened when he had been away. Harrison would have been of no use in his state of mind or body.

Neither, Courtney fretted, had he himself been.

Dr Archer, so recently finished with Harrison's ailment, now treated Appleton. Ellis had done what he could, stitching the grievous wound in the lieutenant's neck. An inch across and McPherson could have entirely slashed his throat open. Still, Appleton suffered. Courtney sat with him in the sickbay and watched his condition fester, even after the worst of the injury was dealt with. Archer observed him carefully, with Harrison and Courtney lingering nearby, and concluded that Appleton deteriorated under the pall of a fever. There was no time to land him, and the *Lion* could not be without their surgeon for the Atlantic crossing, so all that could be hoped for was a smooth passage and mercy for Appleton.

No one spoke of McPherson again. They let his memory sink beneath the waves and stay there below the surface. Appleton was not yet departed enough for another shake to the hierarchy and so Martin did not become the primary lieutenant, Simmonds stayed in his position, and the oldest midshipman did not climb up the pyramid into another acting command. That midshipman would have been Ramsey, in any case, and he was not fit enough to manage such responsibility, perhaps never would be now. As soon as the *Lion* reached continental Europe again, Courtney knew the boy would apply to leave the ship. He would support him in that movement and invent a viable reason for his departure.

And beneath it all, Courtney could not shift that other nagging doubt. Appleton had suggested, after Ramsey's near-death, that it could not have been McPherson who was the culprit for the upset in the midshipmen's berth. Courtney did not even know if the rumours had been true anymore. But if they were, had they rid themselves of the true root of the evil? Or did it still linger onboard?

For now, the Atlantic waited. On the thirteenth of June, not even ten days after arriving in the Caribbean, the fleet made sail again, preparing to catch the Gulf Stream and eventually return to Cádiz. Ahead of them sped the *Curieux* with dispatches for the Admiralty, informing them of Villeneuve's flight and Nelson's ongoing pursuit. Courtney looked towards the horizon, knowing that his judgement would come when arriving back in homelier waters: facing Nightingale, facing his father, facing the future, and perhaps facing Villeneuve.

PART III

Chapter Twenty-Two: Loyalty

Nightingale had been expecting no visitors. After spending a day or so back in Portsmouth, arranging matters with his bankers, he had carved some time to deal with John Courtney. His health had improved since entering the cottage, thanks to the care he had received from Nightingale, Rylance, and the advice of Dr Harrow, and Nightingale had started arrangements to settle the man into a cottage of his own once he had recovered: another in Ryde, but enough of a distance away from Courtney's to be comfortable. Nightingale had agreed to pay some of the finances towards it; he had inserted himself too deeply into John's existence to think of doing otherwise.

Now came a knock on the cottage door. Rylance opened it and, in the small kitchen, Nightingale listened to him greet their visitor.

'Pardon I, sir,' the steward said as he left the door and found Nightingale, 'Mr Browne begs leave to talk to you. Looks like he's been in the wars, sir.'

Rylance did not lie: Browne had a deep bruise about his jaw and his lower lip was cut and swollen. Nightingale halted at the sight. 'Mr Browne,' he said. 'Are you well?'

Browne turned his face away a little. 'It is no matter.'

'Would you like me to fetch you anything for it? My steward has become quite a medical man, after so many years on the sea.'

'It is no matter,' Browne repeated gruffly.

'Then how can I help you?'

'I, uh...' Browne hesitated, peering past Nightingale's shoulder. 'I've been sent by some of the lads to... We had heard...'

Nightingale understood. He stepped aside and allowed Browne into the cottage. In the parlour, John sat, as he had most days, looking out the window into the sunlit garden. Browne took notice of him before Nightingale guided the man into the kitchen.

'You had heard that I brought Mr Courtney here to the cottage,' Nightingale said as Rylance served them each tea.

Browne nodded. 'Some of us were angry,' he replied. 'That's why I offered to come and see the truth of it.'

'I understand. I thought that I might cause some offence by doing what I did. Truthfully, I have been searching for an apt time to explain myself.'

'He was imprisoned on the *Impregnable*,' Browne said. 'Maybe you don't know his past, sir, but we remember him and...'

'I know his past. I know it all too well.'

'You do?'

'Yes. It is a...rather complicated situation.'

'He deserved his place on the hulk. There are more worthy people to be given aid.' Browne paused. 'That was...what others have been saying anyway, sir.'

'You don't have to hide your true opinion,' Nightingale said. He knew that Browne thought of Lucy's friend Bridget and the others who suffered at the workhouse. They had not caused trouble; their only misdemeanour had been to be unable to support themselves, thus landing in a place somewhat akin to a gaol. 'I will explain why I acted as I did. My offer to Mr Courtney was not an arbitrary one. He is not an unknown man to me. True, I only met him for the first time when boarding the *Impregnable*, but I had been acquainted with him through word for a long time. You know his son well, as I do.'

Browne nodded. 'Artie is a good man. I was only a young'un when he was a young'un, but I remember how his father and mother acted, and I saw how Mr Courtney acted when he returned. We all did and decided to stay away from him. It was a good thing when he ran and was captured.'

'I know that. The father is nothing like the son.' Nightingale paused. 'Arthur and his sister thought their parents were dead or perhaps transported. But it seems Mr Courtney had been writing to Arthur for some time and Arthur had to leave for sea before he could conclude the business. The notes had become more threatening and I decided to investigate them, having no idea who they were from. I did not know I would uncover this. I had to navigate it without knowing what Arthur would want but… His father was very ill and not likely to survive on that hulk. I intervened where perhaps I shouldn't but with Mrs Woods's acceptance also, I wished to give Arthur – both he and his father – that chance.

'Since being here on the island, I have tried to act in a way that, I'm not sure, endears me to you or makes you respect me or is the least intrusive. I do not feel I have succeeded and for that, I apologise. I can see I have caused offence and upset a situation that was already troublesome.'

Browne was silent for a while. Nightingale hoped he had phrased himself correctly.

'None of us knew about the notes,' Browne finally said.

'Nor I, not until they kept arriving and bothering Mr and Mrs Woods. I barely knew how to deal with them. I have never been here without Arthur, not since I was a boy. It is his home, not mine.'

Another silence, one where Nightingale regretted his self-pitying speech, until Browne said, 'You intervened with Lieutenant Osborne recently. He's a bastard.'

Nightingale frowned, wondering how that linked to what he had said.

'I wish we had stood against him before. Miss Attrill has but I worry that's put her in more danger.'

'I won't see her hurt, you can be assured of that. I have experience dealing with unpleasant officers.'

'It was he who did this,' Browne admitted, waving at his injured face.

Even after seeing Osborne's behaviour, Nightingale was shocked at this low action. 'He wounded you this badly?'

'As I say, I wish I could have stood against him more. But I know what he did to Mr Hodges. I think he'd like to do that to me too, certainly now he has his eyes on Miss Attrill.'

'He should not act that way. He is bound by Articles of War not to act in an unofficerlike manner.'

But Nightingale knew Osborne had no care for how he treated these people. Nightingale had already quoted the Articles of War at him and it had not changed a thing about his behaviour. Nightingale wondered how far Captain Lovett was willing to protect him; he knew of his nephew's harsh actions and had not raised a hand against them.

'You quarrelled over Miss Attrill?' Nightingale asked.

Browne nodded. 'His attention has been on her for some time and he obviously thinks his position lets him approach her when he pleases.'

'I shall see if I can do anything,' Nightingale said. 'I know his uncle and shall raise the matter with him.'

He doubted it would have any effect but he wished to reassure Browne. He had gone to drastic lengths to aid a man the residents had strong feelings against, so he could make efforts to help them in a way they would be more pleased with. Browne did not say a word to John as he left, but Nightingale hoped he had explained himself well enough. He was about to speak to the man, to speak to him of the financial matters of the other cottage, when he noticed two more figures approaching the garden path. He recognised the uniforms before his eyesight could form the faces.

'Captain Lovett, Lieutenant Osborne,' he greeted. 'I did not expect you.'

Lovett gave a thin smile. Osborne did not react. 'Apologies, Mr Nightingale,' Lovett said. 'I would have sent word but it was thought best to visit you in person.'

'Come in.'

Nightingale ushered them through into the kitchen, again avoiding the parlour. Rylance stood at the door, looking as though he was about to man a gun deck. Neither Lovett nor Osborne noticed John Courtney's presence.

'This is quite a fine cottage,' Lovett commented. 'Do you live here permanently now?'

'No. Not exactly. I divide my time between here and Portsmouth.' *Between my two spouses*, Nightingale suddenly thought.

'Yet you have been here recently? You know of the...troubles we face.'

Nightingale looked between the two men. 'Which troubles are we speaking of?'

They sat at the kitchen table, Rylance now hovering around them with tea. Once he had served them, Nightingale directed his steward out but knew he would be lingering outside the door, and was glad of it.

'I have come, Mr Nightingale,' Lovett said, 'to make a request of you and to alert you to potential trouble.'

'What may I aid you with?'

Lovett hesitated. Next to him, Osborne appeared to want to say something but his uncle continued, 'There have been disturbances onboard the *Impregnable*. Captain Bartley has spoken with Lieutenant Osborne and fears a potential uprising. We are understandably concerned about this information.'

Nightingale frowned, trying to think through that information. His mind immediately conjured the ghoulish picture of the *Impregnable*, the men crammed into her decks and festering in their own diseases and effluents. There were many French prisoners of war locked aboard her. The notion of a rebellion did not seem inconceivable, but he had seen no threat of it when visiting John Courtney. More than revolution, the prisoners seemed to be driven by survival, barely energised for work, let alone anything else.

'I have recently been on the *Impregnable*, Captain,' Nightingale said. 'I saw no signs of rebellion.'

'You visited the prisoner, did you not?' Osborne asked.

'I did. I wished to ascertain a particular matter.'

'That matter was?'

'Mr Nightingale does not have to illustrate his personal activities to us,' Lovett interjected to Osborne.

'He might, if he saw something of worth on the *Impregnable* or has some information relevant to their potential rebellion.'

'Lieutenant, please,' Lovett said, raising a hand. 'Captain Nightingale is a trustworthy man, I can attest to that. If he saw something of note, he would have informed us.'

'I do not know many trustworthy officers who have willingly incinerated a king's ship.'

'Lieutenant,' Lovett reprimanded sharply.

'It is fine, Captain Lovett,' Nightingale said. 'I have heard it before. Many times before. It is not as much of an insult as you believe it is. And Lieutenant, before I incinerated that ship, I conducted a lengthy chase of her due to her mutiny. So I know what rebellion looks like. I have looked into the eyes of mutineers. I did not see them on the *Impregnable*.'

Nightingale bore Osborne's fierce, angry gaze. He did not balk from it. Perhaps there would have been a time when he would have. Not now.

'Regardless,' Lovett suddenly said, interrupting the tension, 'we must give this notion some credence. It would be folly not to.'

'What exactly are your fears?' Nightingale asked.

'An entire prisoner uprising,' Osborne said. 'You can understand why such a thing would give us concern, with the hulk in the Solent, and certainly with the recent issues over smuggling in these parts. Both troubles open the door to French agents and influences.'

'Forgive me, Lieutenant Osborne, but these people and the prisoners are only thinking of survival in these harsh times. It is hardly a French plot or collusion with the enemy.'

'I said I had a request for you, Mr Nightingale,' Lovett remarked before Osborne could retort. 'Come tomorrow, a ring of vessels shall encircle the *Impregnable*. We shall keep a tight blockade on her and a close eye upon her inhabitants. Captain Bartley knows of this plan.'

Nightingale could already guess Lovett's request. 'You wish for my vessel to be added to your complement.'

'Indeed, Captain. Your *Larkspur* has recently been refitted and you know these waters well.'

Nightingale had previously refused Lovett's notion of him joining the Fencibles. This request did not feel so far away from that, and he doubted the worth of his and Osborne's ideas. But he considered John Courtney's position in all of this. He had of late been on the *Impregnable* and thus would know with greater certainty if dissent had simmered on her deck. And Nightingale received the impression that this was not truly a 'request'.

'Very well,' he said. 'The *Larkspur* shall join you. There are also many other craft, fishing smacks and cutters, piloted by men who have used these waterways all their lives. I know their service could be invaluable.'

'We shall keep it within our ranks,' Lovett said.

'There has been little movement or training amongst the Fencibles,' Osborne commented. 'I am concerned for their loyalty.'

'Their loyalty? Do you suspect them of being revolutionaries too?' Nightingale knew he should not have said it, but it came to his lips before he could stop himself.

Lovett blanched. 'I think we should leave this matter. Thank you for your aid, Captain Nightingale. It is most appreciated.'

'There is one other thing,' Nightingale continued before he could lose his confidence against Osborne. 'I have heard that there has been some harassment of a local woman, Miss Lucy Attrill, and have seen evidence of it myself. Her friend, a Mr Browne, was recently injured in defence of her. I would appreciate if such a thing could be formally investigated and for some consequences to be enacted.'

Osborne, again, barely reacted but Lovett turned even paler. 'I...' he began and cleared his throat. 'I had no idea such a thing had occurred. Do you...know who the perpetrator is?'

'I do. And if he is a gentleman, he will speak up.'

Lovett glanced sidelong at Osborne, and Nightingale wondered if his insistence that he knew nothing was true. He, indeed, was aware of his nephew's harsh treatment of the populace; this was just another face of it.

'We shall...discuss this after the *Impregnable* is seen to,' Lovett rushed out. 'For now, that must be our priority.'

Nightingale was not willing to release the matter as easily as Lovett. As they approached the front door to leave, he was about to raise it again, to complain, when both of the men's notices were taken by John Courtney in the parlour. Despite being so without shock or remorse before, a range of reactions crossed Osborne's face. Nightingale decided to make no explanation until Osborne spoke.

'You removed the prisoner from the *Impregnable*?' the lieutenant accused.

'Captain Bartley gave his consent, as did Magistrate Castle. You may speak with them about it.'

'We were not informed of this.'

'The prisoner was not under your protection or your captivity. He was Captain Bartley's charge.'

Osborne turned to his uncle but Lovett had no rebuke for him. He seemed to not know how to respond to the situation.

'I must,' Osborne continued, 'ask if it is wise to involve Captain Nightingale in our scheme, considering these circumstances.'

'If you have concerns, compose them in writing to Captain Bartley.'

Nightingale could see Osborne had concerns, but if it was about his loyalty through his removal of the prisoner from the *Impregnable*, he could not tell. When he had shepherded them from the cottage, fully aware of the dissent and tension that still rippled between them, he knew that something did not feel correct. Osborne had not liked his actions with John Courtney, of course he had not, but Nightingale could not shake the feeling that it had been more to do with the alleged conditions on the *Impregnable*. He realised John Courtney would be aware of the lack of revolution onboard, something that Nightingale, too, was aware of.

Then, what was the issue onboard? Nightingale knew he would only discover that by following this strange situation.

Chapter Twenty-Three: Outside the Law

20 June 1805

The *Larkspur* had been positioned in the Solent within sight of Spithead and the forest of masts that crowded her anchorage. Nightingale had spent the last hours pacing the deck, finding new marks on the timbers which he knew he was marring with his shoes. He had already inspected the rows of twelve-pounders and carronades multiple times, checking their condition and cleanliness. They had not yet been fired in anger, only in practice with powder and shot paid for from his own purse, but he could feel the anticipation that pulsed about them. With every glance his crew gave them, Nightingale knew they veered closer to using their firepower.

Their target sat some two cables forward of them. The ugly, dirty form of the *Impregnable* seemed so far away but her presence loomed over the brig. A loose curtain of vessels surrounded her, in dire straits of waiting. Nothing had occurred over what felt like the interminably long period of watch. Such was the way of many blockades; perhaps Courtney, assigned to blockade Toulon, currently suffered in the same manner.

No strange movement had appeared on the *Impregnable* or anywhere around her. The only shift in the stilted tableau was the departure of one of the vessels in Lovett's command, a rotation or a request to take some other station. Nightingale kept expecting to be directed further into the broad veil of craft, but he remained on the outer rim, condemned to only watch through his glass. He could not rid the impression that it was because of his actions regarding John Courtney.

Obi joined Nightingale on deck. He looked out to the *Impregnable* and her abject silence. 'There has been nothing new,' Nightingale commented. 'No alarm has been raised from the hulk or by any of the flotilla.'

'Did Mr Courtney have any opinion on the uprising?' Obi asked.

Nightingale paused, wondering whether he should inform Obi of John's bewilderment. But there were few men Nightingale knew for certain he could trust: Obi was one of that select number. 'He said he had no idea of it. It's a putrid ship, full of decay and horrible conditions, but he seemed to agree with my sentiment. The prisoners only wish to survive. That is what drives them. Not outright rebellion.'

'Do you believe him, sir?'

Nightingale hesitated again, thinking over all that had occurred since John had exited the *Impregnable* and taken residence at the cottage. In the short while, he already appeared a different person to the one who had sent threatening missives. Nightingale could think of reasons he would lie – he owed no loyalty to the Royal Navy and perhaps he would delight in seeing the prisoners rise up against them – but something told Nightingale the man spoke the truth.

'I do believe him,' he said. 'But Captains Lovett and Bartley think differently, as does Lieutenant Osborne. It is true I saw the state of that prison hulk and its occupants.'

'Men don't like being kept in chains, sir.'

'That they don't.' Nightingale sighed. 'I want to trust John Courtney. I would trust his son with my life but they are so very different.'

'Fathers aren't always like their sons, sir. Your father would have shipped me back to Antigua without losing a second of sleep over it.'

'My father was a wretched man. Arthur's father… He at least appears to want to make amends. That, he claims, was the reason for his notes.' Nightingale shook his head. 'We shall see how this unfolds. I am going inside to eat something. Don't hesitate to send for me if there are further developments.'

Nightingale retreated to his cabin, a small space pressed tightly to the stern of the brig. He sat upon the locker and listened to the quietude of the vessel about him. He was accustomed to busyness and movement, the sweep of the waves past the hull, the footsteps of men on the boards and tramping aloft, the call of Obi and his other mates. Though the *Larkspur* had only recently become a ship of war, it was peculiar to hear her so silent.

He wiped a tired hand across his eyes. He did not know what to think. Since coming to the island, he had acted in the way he believed Courtney might want, though he was hundreds of miles distant. He had been unable to talk with him, to share his days and experiences with him, and it made him itch with worry and uncertainty. He had involved himself with Lieutenant Osborne; had convinced Lovett to support his application as a privateer; had tried to help the residents of Ryde but had invited a shunned man back into their presence and despite Browne's assurances, still felt he had upset them; had allowed John Courtney to intrude in the cottage Nightingale had become ever closer to his son within; and now, he observed a prison hulk which threatened to upset the way of the island even more. For many months, Nightingale thought he had caused more trouble than solution.

He had never felt he fitted into the world. Wherever he went, he knew he was different, knew he had to wear a thicker mask to hide the man within. With Courtney, and here in their cottage, he could lay that façade aside. What would he do when he had to say farewell to Courtney, when he had to relinquish him to another person?

Nightingale could not think in that manner. It was undignified and envious and pitiful. He stood from the locker, nearly cracking his head on the low timbers. Not since he had been a young officer had he done that, unused to the small spaces of ships. He had no Rylance to call upon to bring him something to eat – he had left him in the small hours to watch over John at the cottage – so he visited the galley himself and then returned to his desk. Courtney had not written for some time, had not acknowledged Nightingale's message about his father or about the situation on the island. Nightingale had no way to know if Courtney had even received the letters yet.

My dear Arthur, he wrote,

> *I offer my sincere apologies if I have offended or caused you any upset. It seems I have done the same to many people here, people who I have only tried to earn the respect and like of. I have not acted in a way I have been proud of for quite some time. I believed that by accepting a letter of marque, I would be able to steer my course a little straighter but life appears to have a way of laughing at me, amused at my attempts to move forward and grow. Each step I make, I feel I have then to make one behind me again.*
>
> *I miss your company, Arthur. Whatever path it is that you decide upon, know that you have my friendship, always. I must accept that of you, if this is what you desire and what you feel is correct for you. No one should ever dictate a man's journey but himself.*
>
> *I pray for your safety and good sense.*
> *Ever your friend,*
> *Hiram Nightingale*

Nightingale laid aside the pen, knowing that none of his words were any use to Courtney; they were simply a way to express his frustration and doubt. He wondered if Courtney felt the same way as he did, not only in the tedium of blockade, but in the desire to still want to prove himself to the world and to those around him.

Such a feeling had become a familiar companion to Nightingale. He wished he could do something but he felt as stifled, as sedentary, as the *Larkspur* in the blockade.

He had barely been thirty minutes away when an urgent rapping sounded on his cabin door. With a jolt in his stomach, Nightingale rose. Obi, stooping considerably with his tall height, entered.

'Captain, sir,' he said. 'A fishing smack is hailing us under a white flag. I think it is Mr Browne from Ryde.'

'Mr Browne?'

Obi was correct. Under the lee of the *Larkspur*, Browne stood on the stunted deck of his *Marian*, waving a white handkerchief above his head. With the *Larkspur* on the edge of the blockading vessels, he did not need such a drastic action, but Nightingale respected his foresight. He leant over the lee rail, calling to the man.

'Mr Browne, sir, are you well? What the devil is the matter?'

'It is Lucy Attrill, Captain Nightingale, sir! She has vanished with your steward and Mr Courtney!'

Nightingale hurriedly had Browne come aboard, Obi pulling him over the last bobbing few feet of the *Larkspur*. The three of them huddled in Nightingale's cabin, Nightingale's throat tight with dread as Browne rushed through his explanation.

'Lucy did not come to me this morning,' he said. 'I feared she was ill, or perhaps Lieutenant Osborne had visited her, so I searched for her, went to her home, but she was not there. Some of the other lads had disappeared too. I went to your cottage, sir, to ask you or perhaps your steward who has been a good companion to us at the Catch, but the door was open and the rooms empty.'

Rylance would not have been so careless. 'Did Miss Attrill mention she was travelling anywhere?' Nightingale asked. 'To the workhouse, perhaps?'

'No, sir. But I went to the Catch and asked Mr and Mrs Woods and they said they had heard the men speak of vessels coming past the south of the island, of...'

Browne paused, glancing between the two men looking so intently at him. 'Go on,' Nightingale urged.

'Lucy, sir, Miss Attrill... She... I know of her past in St Lawrence and that of her late brother. She left because of the dangers she'd faced there as a wrecker and a smuggler. Please, sir, I am only telling you this because I worry for her safety now. I fear she has gone to wreck these vessels, if they exist. I thought those days were behind her with Mr Hodges's hanging. It was the closest she'd come to...'

'Miss Attrill was there when Mr Hodges was arrested?'

Browne nodded. 'And many times before. She and some other lads here. They travel for miles to reach the wrecking sites.'

Nightingale fought through his reactions: the confirmation of his suspicions about Lucy's involvement in the free trade industry, the worry about Rylance and John.

'I have to speak with Captain Lovett,' Nightingale said. 'I shall invent some excuse of why we have to leave the blockade. I must stop them.'

'Sir...' Browne began. 'The prison hulk...'

'I do not believe she is any danger. Obi, we shall leave our position. Any retribution, I shall ensure it falls upon my head.'

Under his orders, the *Larkspur* approached Lovett's *Uriel*, occupying the closest place to the *Impregnable*. The *Larkspur* moved without haste, not wishing to upset the order, but Nightingale could feel the anticipation tightening in his chest. A brief interchange of signals passed and Nightingale was ferried over to the larger vessel. Lovett was not in sight as he climbed to the quarterdeck, but Nightingale was not deterred. He requested entry to the great cabin where the captain sat, composing letters as Nightingale had been.

'Sir,' Nightingale greeted, removing his hat. Lovett's eyes roved over him. He looked a tad pale in the cheeks, his colour wan even in the warm sunlight.

'Were you given permission to leave your station, Mr Nightingale?' Lovett asked. The question took Nightingale unaware.

'No, sir,' he said, steadying his voice. 'I would not have unless it had been due to a pressing matter. I fear it is.'

'We already attend on a pressing matter, Mr Nightingale.'

The lack of warmth surprised Nightingale. He had served with Lovett before, but in a time long past. Perhaps he had forgotten what the captain's behaviour was like when under the strain of encroaching battle. 'I do not believe the *Impregnable* is the issue, sir,' Nightingale said. 'While we have been watching her, the local woman I spoke to you of has gone missing. I believe something nefarious may have happened to her, or will.'

He knew he could not admit his true reason for wishing to leave the blockade, not without potentially incriminating Lucy and her fellows. But Lovett looked up, a streak of worry crossing his face.

'Missing?' Lovett asked. 'Are you certain?'

'Yes. What is it?'

Lovett shook his head. 'Was my nephew the one who harassed her?'

They had no time for this conversation now, but Nightingale said, 'Yes. He was.'

'He left the blockade some hours ago.'

Nightingale's stomach seized. Had that been the reason for Osborne's discomfort? Surely this could not be some elaborate deception for him to bring harm to Lucy? *Yes*, Nightingale thought. Men – certainly fragile men of Osborne's ilk, ripe to flare with anger over humiliation and rejection – had performed worse deeds with fewer motives. Lucy had hurt him, had evaded him – twice, if Browne was to be believed about her involvement with Hodges – and Osborne was embarrassed and furious.

'I must find her,' Nightingale said. 'If any harm comes to her, I shall never forgive myself.'

Lovett looked him over. Nightingale knew what he must be thinking: here was the man who had destroyed an English frigate, gutting her with fire and wilfully giving up her gold to the Caribbean Sea. It was all any naval officer thought of him. Any reputation he might have had had been stripped by that image. Here, on the island, with Courtney, he had not felt that way, for the first time in a long while. It reminded him how much he valued this place and its people. And it was why he had to leave the blockade.

Both Obi and Browne eyed him upon return to the *Larkspur*. Nightingale looked at them and understanding passed between him and Obi. 'We are leaving our position in the blockade,' Nightingale said. 'Lieutenant Osborne has left the blockade. I fear he has taken Miss Attrill.'

Browne's eyes widened. 'Good God,' he said. 'She hasn't left to wreck the vessels?'

'Obi, set a course for St Catherine's Point. Miss Attrill spoke to me of the beaches and chines there and to the west, prime locations for bringing ships ashore or wrecking them. If she is with them, then that is the lesser of two evils. But if she is not, we will continue searching.'

'I will accompany you, sir,' Browne said.

'Thank you for your bravery, Mr Browne. I plan to work along the southern coast, watching any of the harbours Miss Attrill mentioned before.'

'If Lieutenant Osborne has her, we will be pursuing a Royal Navy gunbrig,' Browne said, evidently afraid of its strength and speed. Nightingale smiled.

'Many of my men have braved the Southern Ocean and the infernal capes. I'm yet to see a challenge they can't face.'

–

The journey from Ryde, around the foreland at Bembridge and past the long stretch of coast between Sandown and Ventnor, took three and a half hours, hampered by the winds battering the tides against them. Nightingale spent much of the time riveted to the deck, watching for any signs of other vessels. He saw nothing of the *Racer*, nothing of any boats which may have been used by Lucy and her associates, and nothing of any approaching merchant vessels or their potential supporting convoy. As they sailed, he considered what may have happened. Possibly Lucy had gone south to wreck the incoming ships, or perhaps she had been forcibly taken. Either way, she was in danger, certainly if Osborne had departed, as Lovett said.

A smuggler, Nightingale thought. He had debated about her involvement in the trade, noting her recent departure from St Lawrence, and the Ryde residents' discomfort around her. She had been there at Hodges's hanging, and perhaps at his arrest, by Browne's estimations. There, she had been a step away from recrimination herself. If Osborne had known this, or if he had suspected it, it would be another bone of contention with her, another reason for him to desire her downfall.

But, as Nightingale had reckoned, bitter and cruel men had needed less reason for hurting women. The lieutenant had already fought with her, and with her companion, Browne. Nightingale prayed he did not arrive too late to spare her from whatever fate Osborne had planned.

The farther south they travelled, the more the barometer fell and the wind increased. The sun dipped, approaching the horizon, but by that time, the sky had already darkened, more than simply the dawn of night bringing deep shadows. It would be a perfect time for smuggling activity. Only a faint trace of moonlight struggled through the cover of clouds, and a rising sea promised a troublesome vista, ripe for deception and subterfuge.

The deep night found the *Larkspur* off Blackgang. Lanterns had long since been lit, the only illumination reflecting off the black waters. To starboard, Nightingale could barely see the craggy cliffs, though he felt their presence, the sailor's dread of a lee shore. Along the coast, he knew the chine cut a deep ravine down onto the shingle beaches. It was there he directed his spyglass, searching for any figures or vessels, the glint of torches or even white clothing. The entire landscape was deserted, secluded, eerie in the bleak hours.

He had pushed the *Larkspur* hard, determined to reach St Catherine's Point. But no vessel could be seen astern or forward. Nightingale remembered Lucy telling him how this entire south-eastern coast was pockmarked with bays and inlets. Towards the south-west, he had already searched the mouth of Shanklin Chine, Luccombe and Dunnose and now, he kept the *Larkspur* as close to the land as he dared, scouring the journey from Blackgang to Chale. He set a course to raise Atherfield Point, one eye for the shore and one eye for the wider seas to the east. There, the Channel enveloped the island.

Obi and Browne were at hand, tirelessly keeping watch. Browne had professed some knowledge of Lucy's smuggling past but had not given any indication of his personal involvement. His familiarity with the coast, however, helped Nightingale's course. With Obi, Nightingale maintained a steady observation of the weather and the sea state. He knew if the winds continued to rise then they would have to take the *Larkspur* into deeper waters. They could not risk a gale sweeping over them and blowing them onto the rocks.

After many hours sailing, Nightingale wondered if perhaps he and Browne had made a mistake. Perhaps there had been no intention to wreck merchant vessels; perhaps Lucy had not been taken. But until Nightingale saw Lucy safely back in Ryde, he would not cease – and they had made a further error in taking his steward, for whatever bizarre purpose. Rylance, he knew, would have not abandoned the cottage so suddenly or left it so unsafe. They had been together for nearly twenty years and Nightingale felt a deep affection for the younger man, another one of his many children of the sea. As for John Courtney... Nightingale did not know what to think of his departure. He had mentioned a former association with smuggling, had received the scar on his face because of that activity, but after the pains Nightingale had taken to remove him from the *Impregnable*, Nightingale had trusted him to stay at the cottage, as per the deal.

Nightingale did not know who would have his head first: Captain Bartley, Magistrate Castle, or Courtney himself.

He was wondering how he would explain this whole ordeal to Courtney when Obi spied movement on the land. Nightingale hurried forward, into the bows of the *Larkspur*, again sweeping his glass over the long, curving line of Brighstone Bay. Cliffs buttressed the beaches and at the foot of them, Obi with his young eyes had spotted the glint of something. As Nightingale peered, he noted a plethora of small boats, with larger fishing smacks and luggers hauled up onto the sands. Without a doubt, any person would have noticed his *Larkspur* coming in. He hoped they recognised her as not being an enemy.

But, still, as Nightingale opted for his course of action and settled into a launch with Mr Browne, he took armed men with him. He had informed Obi to signal to the shore if any vessels were seen out to sea, if anyone were to spot them on the shore. With anticipation tight in his chest, he leapt into the shallow waters and helped drag the boat the last way onto the beach. Wet, dark sand crunched beneath his boots. Ahead, he saw the remnants of a recent cliff fall. The abandoned boats, at first glance, seemed to be a part of the scree and debris. Perhaps, Nightingale suddenly fretted, it was not his target.

The click of a flintlock pistol made him freeze. Around him, his Larkspurs, almost as one, raised their weapons and Nightingale reached for his own sword, strapped to his belt. The mouth of a gun pointed at his head from the darkness. At the end of it, a figure wreathed in dark cloth, tied about their head and face, leered at him. Nightingale saw their filmy green eyes widen as he turned to them.

'Mr Nightingale,' John Courtney's voice, beneath the fabric, managed.

'Lower your weapons, men,' Nightingale ordered his crew.

No such thing happened with the men and women who now emerged from the shadows of the beach. Each one of them was also dressed in pitch-black clothing. There must have been around fifteen of them, many of whom Nightingale could not recognise in the disguises. He searched their forms, trying to ascertain if any were Rylance.

'What in God's name are you doing here?' Nightingale raged.

'Could say the same to you, sir,' John said.

'You're a damned fool,' Nightingale spat before he could restrain himself. 'I saved you from the *Impregnable* on the condition of your good behaviour, and yet here you are! You are ill, man. Do you want to die before you see your son again?'

This time, John did not answer. Slowly, he began to lower his weapon.

'Where is my steward?' Nightingale pressed. 'And Miss Attrill? They both best be here with you.'

Amongst the gang, someone pressed forward and, with a surge of relief, Nightingale recognised Rylance. His face was drawn tightly, streaked with panic, but he seemed unharmed.

'I'm sorry, sir,' he began to babble. 'I did not know Mr Courtney had departed. I went after him as soon as I realised and I tried to prevent him and the others… But they dragged me along with them.'

'You kidnapped my steward?' Nightingale accused the people before him. A deep sense of betrayal cut through him. He knew he had done wrong by bringing John Courtney back into their lives but this felt a harsh retribution towards him, towards Rylance who had had no say in the matter.

'You would have stopped us,' John said, though Nightingale could hear the growing weakness in his voice.

'You're damn right I would have. And I shall do so now. Where is Miss Attrill?'

No reply came. Nightingale searched the veiled faces before him but could not see her blue eyes or fair hair. Each of the gang glanced at one another.

'She is not with you?' Nightingale urged, his fears surging. Part of him had hoped she would be here, on a foolish errand but one which he could prevent.

'She did not come with us,' John said.

'We haven't seen her,' another voice remarked from the crowd.

Nightingale turned to Browne who looked as worried as he felt. 'We must return to the *Larkspur*,' he said. 'And you, all of you, return home. There shan't be a merchant convoy here, not in this worsening weather. You have been misinformed.'

Or deceived, Nightingale thought.

'What has happened to Miss Attrill?' someone asked.

'I fear Lieutenant Osborne has her. And if he is here, if he catches you, you shall all be hanged as Mr Hodges was.'

Nightingale did not know how they had heard of potential vessels to wreck, but he feared a deeper conspiracy here. Osborne wished for revenge, not only against Lucy but about this entire community who had evaded punishment for hurting him and his men. Nightingale felt caught in the middle, torn between his duties as a privateer and the lingering shade of the Royal Navy, and his desire to be useful to these people. All he was certain of was that he had to find Lucy.

Before Nightingale could do more, Browne suddenly grasped his arm. He turned to the man, seeing him pointing out towards the *Larkspur*. A beacon flashed on her deck: Obi signalling to them. Vessels had been spotted out to sea.

Chapter Twenty-Four: The Needles

The first traces of dawn broke the blackness, slivers of a pink and purple sky, but the shadows still clung to the sea. Nightingale had been staring through his glass for some time now, the *Larkspur* bobbing in the disturbed waves off Brighstone. Across the waters, he could see sails, hull-down on the horizon. From what he could see, the vessel resembled Osborne's gunbrig, *Racer*, but the rig had been adapted. She sailed in a north-westerly direction, and since coming into sight, had veered further and further from the coast.

There was only one way to be sure of the brig's identity and that was by pursuing her. If it was truly Osborne, if he had Lucy onboard, Nightingale would chase him to whatever end. As a captain, Nightingale did not hold with rash decisions. Until the day he had burnt the *Ulysses*, he had never strayed from his directives, had been a conscientious and compliant mariner in all of his commissions. To command a ship was to sit in a rigid hierarchy, with the eyes of the Admiralty ever at his back and the mercy of the sea ever at his front. Tide and weather did not respect hasty resolutions.

But a sailor's instinct – the kind that knew when something did not feel correct about the sky or the swell of a sea beneath a hull; the kind that intuitively felt for rope and line – pulsed inside of him.

Obi, beside him, watched the horizon as keenly as he did. The first mate waited for the order which Nightingale had thought he would never give again.

'General chase,' he said. 'We must keep him in sight.'

By the information from those onshore, they had expected merchant vessels along the south-eastern coast, and had planned to draw them onto the rocks or to await their troubles in the growing heavy weather. They had gathered at Brighstone to meet the ships, or at the least sight them and follow their progress, but now, the brig avoided the sheltered bay. Nightingale knew he could not keep to the shadows, so he continued burning the lanterns on the *Larkspur*. Around him, a flotilla of illumination bobbed through the black waters. The order of 'general chase' also now included the panoply of skiffs and luggers from the beach. Though they were light and had lithe manoeuvrability, they would not keep pace with the *Larkspur* – but they had insisted upon following.

John Courtney sat at the *Larkspur*'s taffrail with a coat draped about him. He claimed the smuggling contingent had allowed him to accompany them, owing to his past as a batsman, protecting those coming onshore with the goods. So far, he had offered Nightingale, and Rylance, no apology.

'I am not sure who I shall be in more trouble with,' Nightingale had said. 'Captain Bartley or your son. Or my wife! You are fortunate I don't clap you in irons and keep you below as on the *Impregnable*.'

But John could not be set down now and neither could the other would-be smugglers. Nightingale would have to deal with the consequences later. As Nightingale stood beneath the *Larkspur*'s mainmast, his back to John, he hated the position he had found himself in. He felt betrayed by the people he had tried to ingratiate himself in, as if he were no better than the Royal Navy officers who would hunt them down for their activities.

Perhaps he should not have come to the island.

Now, the heaving of the lead showed they were making a steady five knots. Nightingale and Obi kept a close watch on the helmsman. He tried to press down his dismal thoughts and focus on what was ahead. It had been many years since he had felt the thrill of a pursuit and the uncertainty of what awaited him. The last time he had been in action, he had started in the captivity of Barbary pirates, not knowing if he would see the light of England again. He had watched the *Lysander*, under Courtney's command, close in on the piratical *Barbarossa* then board the *Fantôme* which he had been a prisoner on. Courtney had saved him, had saved them all. Obi had been at Courtney's side. Now, he adhered to Nightingale's.

'The brig hasn't hailed us,' Obi said. 'They must know we are pursuing them.'

'If it is Lieutenant Osborne, he will know the appearance of the *Larkspur*. And if he has Miss Attrill, he will run for it.'

'He has adapted his rig,' Obi commented. 'To what purpose?'

Nightingale looked at the makeshift convoy trailing the *Larkspur*'s wake. 'How well do you think they know the *Racer*'s form? Certainly in a storm, she would be easily disguised. Has Lieutenant Osborne spread the word of a convoy, in the hopes of catching them in the act of smuggling? Perhaps that is why he has Miss Attrill as well. He wishes to ensure she is there and he can incriminate her afterwards.'

'Putting his own vessel in danger? That breaks many Articles. It is foolish.'

'I did not say it was an intelligent scheme. Just a dangerous one, from a dangerous fool.'

Gradually, the light increased, like a curtain being slowly pulled from the eyes of the world. The lanterns were steadily doused as the forms of the vessels were revealed. There could be no mistaking the identity of Nightingale's squadron now. Nightingale had seen the *Racer* before, and, as a man who had served the sea for more than thirty years, never forgot the appearance of a vessel. He hoped that the brig's adapted rig would not have fooled the smugglers; it certainly did not fool him now. The *Racer*, a gunbrig, was of the kind of vessel designed with this express purpose in mind: cruising coastal regions, watching for convoys, guarding dockyards with its shallow draught. It could carry heavy guns, including the weightier carronades that the *Larkspur* currently held, and would be a significant force to match, certainly with Osborne's knowledge of the waters and the smuggling routes.

Did he think they would engage in action? It would be folly to discount such an event. Nightingale was not sure what the lieutenant would be willing to do.

Nightingale obsessively watched them as the *Larkspur* pursued the brig past Brook Bay into Compton. Still no signal came from the *Racer*. Nightingale knew, more and more, that he trod the fine line of the law in this pursuit. If the smugglers had been caught, they would have been hanged, without a doubt. They would not hang him.

At least he thought they would not hang him.

It was too late to return now.

Nightingale had been awake for nearly twenty-four hours since rising preposterously early to join the blockade around the *Impregnable*. His bones ached but he did not allow himself the rest he had urged his crew to take intermittently. He ate at the helm, keeping a close watch on their course.

The further they sailed, the worse the weather turned. Nightingale had to order reefs in the main and foresail, though kept the trysail on the foremast. He kept a firm eye on the large fore-and-aft sail on the spanker boom, making the calculations of balance that he had for so many decades. They needed enough driving force to keep up with the convoy but not enough to send them reeling. The ragged coast still loomed beside them, now marginally further away due to the distance Nightingale had put between them. The same horror of that shore would be on Osborne's mind also.

Past Compton's shore they sailed, heading towards Freshwater. They had nearly crossed each of the possible landing sites and were driving towards the protruding eastern arm of the island. There, they would have to round the perilous Needles, which Nightingale had not relished even in the fine conditions that he, Lucy, and Browne had travelled in before. From that point, it would be further north into the Solent, hugging the coast of the mainland and passing through the small gap which split Milford and Yarmouth. If the tide was not right, they would be at risk of beaching.

Nightingale pressed on, even as the first rumble of thunder shivered through the heavens. Rain soon drizzled over the *Larkspur*, turning the timbers slick. What had been a pink sky dimmed to grey, the colours draining into forbidding smears. The wind, blowing one point on the *Larkspur*'s starboard quarter, urged them forward, ever so slowly closing the distance between her bows and the *Racer*. *What are you doing, Lieutenant Osborne?* Nightingale wondered.

The jagged points of the Needles split the distant horizon. The white chalk faces of the three stacks could be seen, bright against the stormy sky. Before them, a grim reef lurked beneath the water, a dangerous stretch of shingle that would scour any vessel approaching too close. Nightingale did not like the state of the sea, the bracing winds, but he knew he had to pursue the *Racer* wherever she went. Osborne was relentless.

The smaller boats, though, might be battered to bits in the lurching waves. Scratchell's Bay could be a safe landing point for them. Nightingale found Browne, who had been keeping a firm watch on the flotilla, still some way astern of the *Larkspur*.

'The conditions are not safe for the boats,' he said to Browne, feeling the wind start to whip at his coat even as he spoke. 'I do not want to push them around the Needles. It will be warm work for us to round the point. And I do not know what Lieutenant Osborne intends to do. I would rather the others are not caught and punished.'

'What of you?' Browne asked.

'I shall take the risk of what awaits the *Larkspur*. I do not want to see any of you harmed.'

'I will inform them,' Browne said. 'But I won't leave, not until we find Miss Attrill.'

'Sir!' Obi's voice echoed over the deck. Nightingale returned to the bows where his first mate had been observing the *Racer*, now only a few cable lengths away: close enough to be observed plainly through Nightingale's spyglass. He saw the glint of the *Racer*'s guns, including one in the stern, before a wave lifted her and dipped her into the trough. The close presence of those great guns sent a cold dread through him. It had been a long while since he had been in the midst of flying iron shot and fire. He thought of Lucy, possibly on that brig, and the desire to shoot upon the *Racer* drained in Nightingale.

'I am going to hail her,' Nightingale said. 'Osborne is a naval officer. He will know his signals.'

There were no former signalmen in Nightingale's crews, so he drew on Popham's codes and his own knowledge as a midshipman, learning his flags, and cobbled together a number of pennants, hoisting them quickly. If there was to be no reply, then Nightingale would fall back on semaphore.

His answer came. The *Racer*'s stern gun ignited, the spit of fire flashing before Nightingale heard the report. No ball spat from the mouth of the cannon, but without a doubt, Nightingale received the message. A warning.

'He does not want us to approach,' he said to Obi.

Obi did not respond, though Nightingale could see he stared at the *Racer* with as much determination as he did.

'He thinks we will give up the chase,' Nightingale continued. 'But he forgets I burnt a king's ship to the waterline. Obi, clear for action. Run out the guns. We will make him think we will fight, but until we know Miss Attrill's safety...'

'Yes, sir.'

With Obi directing the men to their stations, a procedure Nightingale had carried over from his days as a post-captain, Nightingale found Browne again. He had followed the last few minutes, observing the change of the *Racer*'s attitude.

'I am going to engage the *Racer*,' Nightingale informed him.

'Miss Attrill—'

'I know. I shall not bring her to harm. I promise you this. Now, you and Mr Courtney need to go below. I do not know how far Lieutenant Osborne is willing to fight. Perhaps he will not at all, now he has fired his warning shot. But I do not trust him.'

'I will not go below,' Browne insisted. 'I will stay.'

'Mr Browne…'

'I will stay.'

Nightingale saw he could not shift him. The man wished to ensure the safety of his friend, perhaps the woman he loved. If Courtney or Louisa had been on that other vessel, Nightingale knew he would not be moved, either. So he nodded and bid Browne to arm himself with the weapons brought up.

Nightingale paced the weather deck where the guns had been manned. He directed the helmsman to put the *Larkspur* further out to sea, avoiding the jagged teeth of the Needles. In the bows, he looked at the carronades, thought of the damage they would do, alone, against Osborne's *Racer*. With the *Racer*'s carronades, they may be more or less evenly matched.

As if setting the stage, the storm broke over the wild coast. A resounding clatter of thunder seemed to shiver through the *Larkspur*'s bones. Lightning split the sky, dashing the horizon. Nightingale kept his eye firmly on the *Racer*, directing the helmsman. The braces had been adjusted, easing the *Larkspur*'s head away from the shoals, her bows taking the brunt of the waves. Nightingale's stomach dropped and fell with the lurching rhythm, but he knew what this little vessel was capable of. She seemed more spirited since the cannons had come aboard, as if their additional weight had given her a burst of enthusiasm and life. Nightingale felt again the thrill of the pursuit as she approached the *Racer*.

In the bursts of the lightning, the *Racer* seemed transformed. Her size bloomed as she scaled the waves, masts scraping the sky. She approached the Needles, intending to round the sharp headland. Nightingale looked between the farthest chalk pillar and the *Racer* as another flash split the morning. Again, the *Racer*'s stern chaser had ignited – and this time, Nightingale heard the cry of a ball, scything through the air and splashing some fifty yards away from the *Larkspur*'s bows.

The first true shot had been fired. Nightingale carried a letter of marque, permitting him to wage war against Britain's enemies. He had not imagined he would be fighting his countrymen again, not after the *Ulysses*.

'Obi, run out the guns,' he said. 'But wait for my command and my command only.'

Nightingale personally manned the carronade in the bows. If Osborne was willing to fire warning shots, then he knew he must be, but he would not aim for the *Racer*'s hull. He would not risk Lucy's safety. Feeling the power of the wind in the *Larkspur*'s topsails and with her foremast trysail eagerly taking the brunt of it, he had his bow chaser crew load the stout little gun with an eighteen-pound shot. He stood back, observed them prime the carronade and heave it to its elevation. Then, acting as gun captain, he fired the terrifying thing. The recoil nearly took his breath away, the deafening roar creating a fog of ringing in his ears. The projectile fell far short of the *Racer* but that had been it: Nightingale's first shot, fired in anger, since leaving the *Scylla*.

He watched the *Racer*'s deck through his glass. Men waited at the guns, but none of them responded. Nightingale found Lieutenant Osborne, beneath the mainmast, mouth open in a shout Nightingale could not hear. He grasped his sword and pistol, gesticulating wildly with them. The gun crews seemed to hesitate. They did not want to obey, Nightingale thought.

Regardless, the two vessels approached the fringe of the Needles, that jagged line of danger and lashing tides. Finding Obi, Nightingale called out to direct the *Larkspur*'s head further out to sea. The neat manoeuvre, bracing up to ease the yards, manipulating the cut of the wind upon them, moved the brig away from those gnashing teeth. Nightingale placed a hand on the gunwale as he felt the bows lift in the rising seas, dropping with a suddenness that made his stomach roll. But the *Larkspur* bore it handsomely.

The *Racer* now sat between the *Larkspur* and the craggy shore. If Nightingale could cut off her advance, he could have her. *Sink her, burn her, take her as a prize*, he thought, the old rhythms finding him again. But no, he did not want to blast her to pieces, only to threaten her into submission.

The *Racer*'s carronades gaped at them from the weather deck. Osborne would not have enough hands to man both sides, or even one side. Nightingale swallowed his fear at the sight of those great guns. Speaking-trumpet in hand, Nightingale bellowed over to Osborne. He found he had to shout even louder due to the driving rain and wind. With each wave, the two vessels drew closer, the weather threatening to do more damage than either one of them could. Following the *Larkspur*, the *Racer* tried to move out of the maw of the Needles and the deadly reefs below. The wind was against her, refusing to lessen its grip.

'Lieutenant!' Nightingale cried. 'Heave-to and surrender!'

'Surrender' seemed the wrong word, but it was all that came to Nightingale's lips. He wished for Osborne to cease, to avoid any more conflict. But the lieutenant's answer came with a shout Nightingale could hear even without Osborne using a speaking-trumpet.

'Fire at will!' he cried. 'Fire as she bears!'

For a moment, no one obeyed and Nightingale thought he had won the victory without unnecessary bloodshed. But then Osborne ploughed amongst his small gun crews, forcing his way to the carronade at the waist. Cajoling his men, between them they pushed the squat gun into ignition. Shot soared overhead, lashing the *Larkspur*'s mainmast. As it connected, the ball burst, scattering a hail of smaller roundshot. Nightingale heard the cry of men aloft but the mainyard stayed firm, keeping the brig on course. Grapeshot. He meant to kill or maim.

Nightingale caught Obi's eye across the deck. The shock raced across the first mate's face. In response, each gun captain at the twelve-pounders and carronades readied for Nightingale's order.

'We shall fire a broadside across your deck!' Nightingale shouted, knowing he could not for Lucy's sake, but not allowing Osborne to feel his hesitation. 'I repeat: heave-to and surrender!'

'Fire at will!' he heard Osborne roar again. 'Goddamn you all, fire at will!'

'Good God,' Nightingale breathed to himself. His next order became lost in the hail of fire from the *Racer*, two carronades booming simultaneously followed by the pop and crack of two others in succession. Nightingale felt the impact, some shot directed towards the *Larkspur*'s hull, some catching the cordage and spars again. The foremast suffered, part of the trysail yard flying off. With the damage, the gaff-rigged sail sagged, knocking the *Larkspur* off a point. Nightingale stared through the smoke as the brig's bowsprit arced to starboard – and there to meet it was the *Racer*, forcing herself around, setting herself on a collision course.

For a moment, Nightingale admired Osborne's bravery – then thought of the crew beneath the man who would suffer.

'She means to board us!' Nightingale shouted to Obi. 'Prepare to repel them! Obi, raise the trajectory! Aim for the rigging only!'

Now, the *Larkspur*'s own guns came into force. Nightingale heard his twelve-pounders nipping the *Racer*, making snags and holes in her cordage and canvas, as she swung further into the *Larkspur*'s path, bursts of illumination flaring along her gunwales. He felt the timbers quake at their blasts, that old sensation of standing on the deck of a ship of war. He breathed in the choking haze, the stinging salt of the sea, the dense pall of the storm. Wiping rain from his eyes, he watched the *Larkspur*'s roundshot churn up a mess of the *Racer*'s main chains and mainyard. Splinters rained down and men below staggered away, some groping at limbs and faces. Nightingale's skin tightened. He did not have the stomach for this anymore. And so he could not bring himself to order the fire of the carronades. They would slaughter the men on that deck, and bring Lucy to harm if she was nearby.

Osborne had no such qualms. As the remaining carronades were run out again, other deckhands rushed to the waist, boarding pikes and axes in hand. Yet, even with the close-quarters fighting, near enough now to discharge a musket, the *Racer* did not part from her course. Osborne allowed her to lurch and sway in the swell, targeting the *Larkspur*'s bows.

'Helmsman!'

Nightingale hurried aft. He would meet the *Racer*, play Osborne's game.

'Two points to starboard!'

The *Larkspur* strained, so Nightingale grasped the wet spokes of the wheel himself, aiding the helmsman, bringing the *Larkspur* about. With an unceremonious yank on the braces, she obeyed. A wave lifted her, made her list a little, her main and foremast tilting. The water passed under her, struck the *Racer*, and the gunbrig rocked like a cork. She too heeled and the yards came perilously close. In the near proximity, Osborne took his chance. Grapnel hooks streamed across the passage that split them, catching on the *Larkspur*. Nightingale looked up, saw the *Larkspur*'s main yardarm glance the *Racer*'s futtock shrouds and held his breath. The next swell heaved both vessels and with a resounding crunch, the starboard side of the *Larkspur*'s bows slammed into the *Racer*. The collision course the *Racer* had been on suddenly crippled her; faced with the force of the *Larkspur*, larger, weightier, she teetered, as if struck by a battering ram. Her masts arced and then lifted once more in a mighty rolling wave.

'Brace!' Nightingale heard himself roar as the *Racer*'s mainyard sliced through the air, plunging deeply into the labyrinth of cordage on the *Larkspur*. It did not matter that the gunbrig was partially dwarfed by the *Larkspur*; she raged and fought in her crisis. The deck tipped beneath Nightingale's feet, yanked furiously by the gunbrig. He looked across to the other vessel, saw Osborne staring directly at him. The screaming storm scythed about the vessels, enveloping them. But beyond the struggling, ensnared *Racer*, he viewed the tall, forbidding white rocks, the awful reef that surrounded them. They were too close. They would be drawn into jagged, violent death like in a maelstrom.

'Cut her free!' he shouted to the men at the guns, to those remaining in the tops. From the previous damage, the foremast already hung at an angle, further entangling them. The grapnel hooks, still attached, tugged and pulled at the *Larkspur*. Obi, hastily ushering a gang of his men, armed himself with a boat knife, ready to dash the tethers back to the *Racer*. The cordage and spars could not so easily be disengaged. It was as though a great monster of the deep had grasped them, shaking and groping relentlessly, empowered by the tempest. Upon the *Racer*, he saw a cluster of men race for the stern. A terrified look overboard showed the mauling of the gunbrig's rudder. The helm span wildly, the entire vessel lurching, heading for the rocks. Osborne had condemned them all.

Grapnels and tethers flew free, plummeting into the churning waters. At the same time, the *Racer*'s mainmast toppled, scattering men on each vessel in an attempt to escape the spar. Nightingale pulled three sailors to safety as the great pillar smashed into the *Larkspur*'s waist. It cracked the gunwale and nearly entirely hacked off the fore-trysail yard on the way down before completely obliterating a twelve-pounder and its carriage. Now, the *Larkspur* was truly at danger of sharing the *Racer*'s roiling, grisly fate. The reef approached, the gateway to the high, serrated Needles.

Across the connected decks, Nightingale caught sight of Osborne again. Nightingale knew he had to make a decision, knew he had to save as many men as he could, and moreover, knew he had to find Lucy.

'Lieutenant!' he bawled through the speaking-trumpet. 'Have your men come across to the *Larkspur*!'

He could not decipher Osborne's expression but the man gave no order to his crew. With no time to waste, Nightingale signalled to Obi, who came running.

'I am going to board the *Racer*!' he shouted to get above the wind and rain. 'The gunbrig is doomed, but I must find Miss Attrill! We can still save the crew!'

'And Lieutenant Osborne, sir?'

Nightingale did not answer. He knew it was much to ask his men – boarding a vessel destined for abject destruction – but a contingent of fifteen came to him. Browne was at their head.

They rushed to the downed mast. It was a tenuous link to the *Racer*, bobbing and slippery in the rain. Nightingale bottled his fear and clambered onto the spar. He could feel the shaking and lurching of each vessel so, without glancing down at the beating waves, he half-scrambled, half-slid onto the lower deck of the *Racer*. As his Larkspurs followed, he found Osborne, near the fallen spar. No more orders had come from his mouth; his men seemed to not know whether to meet the Larkspurs with violence or resistance.

Nightingale, not in the frame of mind for hesitation, grasped Osborne's arm and shouted, 'Where is Miss Attrill?!'

Suddenly jerked into life, Osborne shoved Nightingale away, nearly making him lose his footing on the unstable deck. Browne was at his side in his instant, flanked by his Larkspurs. Osborne raised his flintlock, the barrel of it quivering, but Browne stepped before Nightingale.

'Where is Lucy?!' Browne exclaimed through the storm.

'You have destroyed my vessel!' Osborne accused. 'I shall have every one of you hanged!'

'Lieutenant Osborne, lower your weapon!' Nightingale ordered.

'Damn you all!' Osborne answered. The crack of his flintlock boomed through the storm and Nightingale cringed, tugging

Browne out of the way. He expected someone to fall, or even to feel sharp pain through his own body – it would not be the first time a lieutenant had shot him – but nothing came.

Osborne staggered. Redness bloomed on his white waist-coat. He looked down in shock, raising a hand to touch the wound. Nightingale whirled around to see Lucy at the mouth of a hatchway, musket in hand. A black bruise ringed her eye and dried blood marred her forehead and loose hair, but she seemed otherwise unharmed.

'Lucy!' Browne cried. He rushed over to her, encircling her in his arms, and checking her for any other injuries. Nightingale looked from her to Osborne as he sank to his knees, expression dulling, skin paling.

Before he could do a thing, the *Racer* gave a great lurch. Before Osborne, a ragged crack appeared in the timbers. Nightingale pulled his men away as it deepened like a ravine, the worn vessel starting to surrender to the merciless waves. Behind Osborne, he could see the men who had run for the stern to check the *Racer*'s destroyed rudder. They, and their lieutenant, were being severed from the rest of the brig. The *Racer* had not been built for these extreme conditions. With every swell, the chasm enlarged and would soon be split entirely asunder by the looming reef.

'Mr Browne!' Nightingale exclaimed. 'Take Miss Attrill to the *Larkspur*! Men of the *Racer*, abandon ship!'

The thirty or so men who could reach the downed mainmast rushed for it under Nightingale's orders, but he ploughed his way astern, slipping on the timbers. It was not only rainwater now; the sea bubbled and foamed at the *Racer*'s rail where she listed and suffered. It seethed against Nightingale's ankles, soaking his breeches. He would have stripped off his shoes, in the way of a common sailor, but the splintered deck would have cut him to shreds.

With Larkspurs at his side, he reached the deepening chasm, staring into the uncovered wooden bowels of the gunbrig. Even as he looked, he heard the creaking and cracking of the vessel's innards. In sharp clarity, he thought of the old *Fénix*, struck by lightning and then split asunder by the sea.

'Men!' he shouted across the gap, using a voice he had never had to employ in the merchant's service and digging into the wells of his career in the king's service. 'Go for the *Larkspur*!'

The two vessels still bobbed and knocked together. With the mainmast down, a mesh of cordage and sail united them. It would be a short jump from the *Racer*'s lower deck up to the *Larkspur*'s. Over on his own brig, Nightingale watched crew come running, there to help the struggling Racers. Lucy and Browne had already made it across, safe in Obi's care. Nightingale stayed, observing the twin exodus of the sailors, only occasionally glancing backwards towards the looming Needles. They were close, too close, but if the crew of the *Racer* could be saved, they could throw the gunbrig off and head for open waters. He counted them off as they left, nearing the full complement of fifty or so. Finally, enough had departed for Nightingale to urge his own men back to their brig.

He looked over at Osborne. The man had been unable to stop his men leaving and not a single one of them had halted to check on his welfare. Now, the lieutenant struggled to his feet, bleeding heavily but leaning on his sword. Nightingale stared at him across the widening gap and wondered if he could leave him, if he had the heart to abandon a man, as guilty and wretched as he was, to the elements.

His decision was stolen by a mighty roar. Nightingale looked in horror towards the *Larkspur* as a wave lifted her and the *Racer*, pulling the two vessels away from one another. In the swell, the *Racer*'s mainmast slipped, caught on a shredded gunwale, then, with finality, toppled into the sea. The fall imbalanced the *Racer*. She lurched and listed, the chasm that split the gunbrig completely fracturing. Nightingale watched a wedge of the stern get carried away, swallowed by the angry waters, and Osborne went with it, staggering into the rising water. Now nothing but a chunk of timber, uncontrollable, unsalvageable, the *Racer* almost heeled entirely over.

Nightingale heard his name, shouted on the wind, but could not answer. He grabbed for whatever he could take a hold of, the deck spitting him out. He hit his back on something, sending raging pain up his spine. A wave lashed the *Racer*, spilling over the rail, swamping him, and the doomed gunbrig was thrown onto what beam-ends she had remaining. Nightingale stared up as the sea rushed down and suddenly, he could see nothing but white foam and black water. The power of it nearly banished his sense. A shadow of what had been the *Racer* rolled up and away from him, tossed like flotsam.

Turned about and around, Nightingale's head finally broke the surface again. He gasped for air, sucking in rain and the spray of the breakers. From touching timber, his feet now floated in the churning deep. He blessed all the times Courtney had taken him into the river, into the shallow sea, reminding him how to swim, teaching him how to stay alive. Courtney. The image of the man gave Nightingale determination and strength. Nightingale forced himself to adhere to the surface, trying not to fight the insurmountable force of the sea, allowing himself to be carried along with it.

Fragments of the *Racer* plunged and reeled. Over the next wave, Nightingale caught sight of her fallen mainmast. It rolled and dropped within touching distance and he reached for it. For a moment, he slipped, lost contact with it, then managed to drape his arms over its stout pillar. He trembled, teeth chattering. The shock of the plunge still coursed through him, but beneath it, he felt the freezing water seep in, making his teeth chatter, his limbs cramp. He had to hold on to the mast long enough for rescue.

He could barely see the *Larkspur*, only the heights of her tops. They could not approach in this wind, not without risking the same fate as the *Racer*. Now it was only him, the raging storm, and the forbidding rocks. If he could not be reached, the sea would swallow him, as he always knew it would.

Chapter Twenty-Five: Resolute

Nightingale remembered the darkness of the deep. He recalled clinging to the *Racer*'s mainmast. In his delirium, he thought how ridiculously symbolic it was: he had tried to take a step away from his life in the navy, jarred and frightened by the reappearance of the *Lion*, but there, in the freezing pull of the tides, it was the only thing keeping him afloat.

He knew he could not let go.

The waters, the blackness, swept over him. He tried to face it bravely, but the sea scoured away the veneer. He was a man, constantly lured back to the deep, constantly measuring himself against it.

It nursed him, cared for him, ravaged him, left him empty and irresolute.

The shadow of the *Lion*. The wraith of the *Scylla*. He was there again, waterlogged and shivering, on the decks. Such very different vessels, but one and the same: each forming him, each moulding him. Nightingale walked the timbers alone. He ran his hand along the gunwales, touching the belaying pins and lifting his fingers into the shrouds. The ship slumbered in silence, her canvas catching no wind, her helm without motion. If he looked overboard, he knew he would see white sands beneath her keel, grounding her, never allowing her to sail again.

Then, a lightening sky. It rose over the familiar frontage of the cottage. A single flower had fallen from the trellis about the door. Nightingale could no longer reach out a hand to pick it up and he despaired. Courtney would want to come home to a perfect place, a neat place, a safe place.

Someone else spoke at his ear. Perhaps it was Courtney's voice, perhaps someone else's. Nightingale's name echoed about the empty rooms. A veil separated him from responding.

Hiram. Hiram. Hiram.

Had he and Courtney said their final words to one another? Would he never hear Courtney's familiar tones saying his name again?

Hiram. Hiram.

He had been a fool, coming to the island and trying to make a place for himself. He had condemned them all, may have killed everybody on the *Larkspur* and *Racer*.

Hiram.

These were not brave thoughts to go to death with. Had he ever been courageous? Had he ever been worthy of the ships he commanded, of the people he tried to help?

Nightingale opened his eyes.

Above him, the rafters of his and Courtney's bedroom shimmered with a soft glow. For some time, Nightingale could not unite his vision with his thoughts. He expected the sea to pour in again. It followed him everywhere he went, no matter where he tried to escape. But beside him, the window let in only sunlight, orange and gentle.

In small increments, he turned and faced it. Outside, swathes of fresh green fields covered the land from here to the sea. The upper branches of a pear tree bent over the glass. Nightingale recalled the raging eye of a storm, one which could be seen in the damage to some of the lush leaves. Now, though, the sky was blue and no water, no sea, no tempest, intruded upon him.

'Hiram?'

His name came again, this time whispered by a woman.

'Hiram?'

He knew that voice. But he could barely shift to turn towards it. Instead, a figure moved before his sight. Blue muslin, hastily tied ribbons, bare hands. Louisa, her face drawn with worry, crouched before him.

'Hiram,' she breathed. 'I shall fetch Dr Harrow.'

'The flower,' Nightingale managed, his throat feeling as though it had been scrubbed with a holystone. 'There is a flower by the door. And the pear tree…'

'Do not fret,' Louisa said. 'You are safe.'

A moment passed and then a shadow who must have been Dr Harrow appeared. He pressed and prodded Nightingale, examining him with a far colder touch than his wife. But by the time he stood again, Nightingale could better see his form. He looked harried, fatigued, but pleased. He nodded to Louisa and Nightingale heard 'He seems well. The worst is over, as I promised'.

Louisa sighed and seemed on the edge of collapse. As her shoulders sank a little, Rylance appeared from nowhere and set her down in the armchair by the bed. Nightingale, jolted from his lethargy at the sight of her distress, tried to sit up. Rylance seamlessly changed his focus and helped him.

'My dear,' Nightingale croaked to Louisa. 'I thought… I thought I had drowned.'

'You damn near did, Hiram,' Louisa cursed. 'If you had not been found when you were, if Obi and Miss Attrill had not aided you, then I…I do not think you would be here.'

Nightingale paused. The events suddenly swept over him as the water had. He recalled the *Larkspur* and the *Racer*. He remembered his lack of courage in the waves.

'I am sorry,' he said. 'I do not know what I was thinking.'

'I came as quickly as I could with Dr Harrow,' Louisa explained. 'But it is these people who you should thank. Miss Attrill, Mr Browne, and Mr Courtney have cared for you. They have barely left your side.'

'They… They have cared for me? They survived?' Relief flooded Nightingale, only tempered by the bewilderment he felt at being on the receiving end of their aid. One name amongst Louisa's list gave him the most cause for confusion. 'Mr Courtney also? He helped me?'

'Yes,' Louisa said. 'I have been told that he was grateful for your care of him and wished to return the favour.'

'Ah.'

Nightingale had prayed there was good remaining in John Courtney. He had berated him for accompanying the smugglers, had berated them all, but then had pushed everyone to their limits by pursuing the *Racer*. Unbidden, Nightingale felt tears rush upon him: solace, appreciation running over.

'Well,' he said. 'I owe them my eternal gratitude, and my apologies.'

Louisa looked up and Nightingale noticed another figure at the door. Lucy slowly approached, having obviously been waiting outside. Her head was bare, long curls hanging about her waist. A bandage had been tied about her forehead, though her black eye remained. Nightingale wondered how long he had been slumbering, close to death.

'Come in, Miss Attrill,' he said. 'I must speak with you.'

'You are exhausted and weak, Hiram,' Louisa warned.

'I must, my dear,' Nightingale insisted, and Louisa saw she could not argue. She stood, brushing down her skirt. The fierce protectiveness of him vanished from her eyes for a moment and affectionate warmth crossed her.

'I shall be outside, Hiram,' she said. 'I am glad you are well.'

When the door had closed, Lucy gingerly took the place where Louisa had been. Nightingale felt vulnerable and exposed lying there in what he now saw was his nightshirt but, by Louisa's account, Lucy had seen him in a worse state.

'I hear,' Nightingale started, before clearing his throat and trying again. 'I hear that you and my first mate rescued me from the sea, and you have since been caring for me.'

Lucy nodded. 'I…I thought you had died.'

'As did I. I was quite certain of it. And I…' He paused, not wanting to illustrate his tragic notions to her, not wanting to reconsider what he had thought upon dying. But he had to dredge up some of it. 'I apologise for my actions. I did not mean to endanger you. I certainly did not mean to bring the *Racer* to destruction. I do not know what I was thinking. I wished to aid you here and I feel I have behaved quite appallingly at times.'

'Mr Nightingale...' she started to say.

'No, I...I know that I did not win favour for myself by opening my home to Mr Courtney. I tried to explain myself to Mr Browne but I still feel I was disliked for it, and people were within their rights to feel so. For many months, I have tried to act in a way that helped you, because I... Well, I care for this place, and for you, and Arthur is a very dear friend of mine. I believe I have made the situation worse.'

Lucy still did not speak. Nightingale felt her gaze, weighing him, until she asked, 'Have you finished?'

Nightingale could not hide his surprise at her boldness. 'I... Yes, I have.'

'I don't know what you are apologising for, Mr Nightingale. Lieutenant Osborne was the one who kidnapped me. He wanted to pretend his ship was in distress and deceive the...the smugglers. He wanted to incriminate them and make it seem I was involved too. You stopped him.'

Osborne had wished to pretend his *Racer* was in difficulties. Nightingale had made that true. 'I could not allow you to be harmed,' Nightingale said. 'I spoke harshly to the wreckers but I felt they had behaved badly to me, certainly taking my steward and with Mr Courtney supposedly ill...'

'Mrs Woods has spoken some harsh words to them for that.'

At that, Nightingale could not help laughing. 'I am sure she has. That carries far more weight than what I could do, I wager.'

Lucy smiled and Nightingale realised he had not seen that expression from her before.

'You were not harmed by Lieutenant Osborne?' he asked.

'No. Not beyond this,' she said, waving at her black eye. 'But I gave him a greater wound. He deserved it.'

'Yes. I believe he did.'

She reminded Nightingale of Jane, unafraid of standing up, unafraid of taking action though it would not be seen her proper place. Nightingale did not give a damn about expectations, not here in this cottage he shared with the man he loved.

'We do not think badly of you,' Lucy said. 'You did come here with no true idea of our situation, of what would help us, but you have done much that we appreciate. I know these people did not like me either, but...'

'They all came to rescue you from Lieutenant Osborne.'

Lucy nodded, obviously as touched as Nightingale was for the residents' aid. 'They did,' she said.

Nightingale found himself smiling again. 'I am pleased that you, and the others, are well, Miss Attrill. That is all I wanted.'

'You don't have to do grand things for us,' she said. 'The others... They say how you're Arthur Courtney's friend and any friend of Arthur Courtney belongs here.'

A sickness swirled in Nightingale's heart for a moment. He hoped terribly that he remained Arthur Courtney's friend. But now, he could not voice that to Lucy. She had been kind to him, soothing his fears, nursing him back to health with the other residents. When she rose to leave, John Courtney lingered in the doorway. Nightingale caught his eye, wondered if he would enter, but he appeared not to know if he would be welcome. Nightingale nodded towards him. He, obviously in echo of his son, in echo of the career he knew Nightingale had had, put a knuckle to his forehead in salute. The gesture made Nightingale's throat squeeze. He blinked away more tears, the exhaustion, the fright, the doubt rolling over him.

He had survived, and so would press on, holding the sea's mercy close.

—

Dr Harrow wished for Nightingale to stay abed for a few more days but Nightingale, as much as he loved the bedroom he and

Courtney had nurtured and furnished, felt a prisoner in the soft quilt. He tentatively walked down the rickety stairs, into the kitchen and the parlour that Rylance had been tending to, and on the third day, exited into the sunlight. The first thing he did was to attend to the flowers on the trellis, picking up the fallen ones, beautifying those remaining. For some reason, it made him feel closer to Courtney, to what they had done here. This was their home, he thought, and it had given him purpose, given him a place to retreat to. For that, he would continue.

Nightingale lasted a bare five minutes outside before Rylance came running with an overcoat, but, soothing Rylance's fussing, he insisted on staying outside by the creek. The fresh air calmed him, helped his aches and fatigue. Dr Harrow said how he had gained a foul-looking bruise on his back, result of whatever debris he had tumbled into, alongside a number of cuts and gashes, but nothing that would trouble him in the long term. The salt water had relieved the worst of them.

Within the next day, he was able to make the journey into Ryde and show his face at the Fisherman's Catch. Mrs Woods hurried to him and, forgoing all her previous hesitance, embraced him like a son. Nightingale kept a firm façade but the joy simmered through him. *Any friend of Arthur Courtney belongs here*, he thought, and truly felt it.

From believing he had no place there, Nightingale experienced the other far end of the range of the situation, almost overwhelmed by their care and good wishes. He discovered how much they had done for him when he had been away from the world. He had thought the worst, as he often did. But here, he was glad to be proved wrong. The love he had always sensed from Mrs Woods extended to all of them, evoking a sensation not unlike when he had stood before his crews, knowing they would follow him. Now, though, they were not there for obligation or orders. He dared to think he belonged, an unfamiliar sensation.

The only aspect he had not braved questioning yet was the professional consequences he feared would come his way. Regardless of Osborne's actions, he had again destroyed a king's vessel. Nightingale did not want to learn any information that would rupture his newfound ease but he soon had his answers from Captain Lovett. The man made the journey to the cottage, surprising Nightingale by his appearance at the front door. Nightingale had been preparing to travel back to Haywood Hall, but Louisa had been called away from their home, going to her father in Bristol. Obi had gone with her, preparing to meet with Robert Haywood, the owner of the *Larkspur* and many other merchant vessels. Fortunately, the little brig would be spared but would require a costly repair and refitting.

So, when Lovett arrived, Nightingale was briefly taken aback and must have showed it, for Lovett removed his bicorne hat and apologised.

'Captain Nightingale,' he said and then, resorting to familiarity, 'Hiram. I meant to send word but my business has been relentless this past week. I hope you do not mind my intrusion.'

'No,' Nightingale said. 'No, you are quite welcome. Would you care for some tea?'

Lovett assented and Nightingale felt a curious relief. He had believed the navy would despise him all over again. If that had been so, surely Lovett would have rather thrown the tea in his face. Instead, they sat in the parlour together and Lovett looked around at the furnishings with some pleasure.

'This is a homely place,' Lovett commented as he had before.

'It is. It is somewhat of a…an investment of mine. I am caring for it in the absence of Commander Courtney and it offered a good location to stay whilst helping on the island.'

'I see. Well, in regards to that help, I wished to offer my explanation to you.'

Nightingale waited, cradling the warm mug.

'There was no uprising on the *Impregnable*,' Lovett said. 'It appears we were misinformed by Captain Bartley, who was mistreating the prisoners, worse than their already abysmal conditions. He shall be replaced in due course. As for the *Racer*, she was lost. Her crew was saved on your *Larkspur* but my nephew disappeared into the sea. I...' Lovett paused. 'I fear he was also involved in stirring the idea of discontent on the *Impregnable*. I have heard he did, indeed, capture a local woman.'

Nightingale nodded. 'He did. She is safe now.'

He was not about to tell Lovett about the other strand of Osborne's nefarious schemes: aiming to make the would-be wreckers incriminate themselves. Lovett did not need to know of the smuggling undercurrent in this community.

'I feel a hard mixture of sensations,' Lovett admitted. 'Grief, but also bewilderment and no small degree of shame. I was so blind to my nephew's actions. I simply thought he was a little heavy-handed with his dealings on this island, but not that he could stoop so low.'

'I did not truly know what I would find by pursuing the *Racer* and I certainly did not reckon on so destroying the gunbrig. I simply wanted Miss Attrill to be safe.'

'That is an understandable motive, Mr Nightingale. You have behaved more honourably than my nephew who was a commissioned lieutenant in the Royal Navy, and yet you were dismissed from that service.'

Nightingale inclined his head. 'I feel no regret for that,' he said, and honestly this time. These recent incidents had solidified that surety in his mind. 'But I expect there shall be an investigation of trial into the loss of the *Racer* and these circumstances.'

'You are correct, Hiram. But I shall tell you that there have been people already speaking in praise and support of you and your actions.'

'The islanders, yes. They have been very kind to me.'

'Not only them. Many of my own colleagues have expressed their admiration for what you did. Lieutenant Osborne's own crew are very grateful. They did not wish to obey his orders. I suspect much further and they may have turned to mutiny.'

'Oh. I am…surprised. Well, not about their disobedience; I saw how they hesitated to fire the guns. But, at the gratitude of the Royal Navy. I thought I was quite beyond that. I annihilated a king's vessel.' *Again*, he did not say.

'No, the storm did that,' Lovett said meaningfully, and Nightingale heard the firmness in his tone. That, he knew, was what would be passed around. There he had been, fretting over the perception of himself – a perception which had already been marred in the navy – but the world had seen him in a different light.

'Well, I shall give my testimony to any court martial. I have experience before them.' Nightingale sipped at his tea, feeling greater at ease now.

'Indeed. Well, I thank you, Mr Nightingale, for what you did and for also thrusting me into the light again. Us old captains, we shall do anything to make it so, shan't we?'

The final jest made Nightingale laugh. He said his farewells to Lovett, knowing it would not be the last he saw of him but willing to face whatever circumstance arose. He watched him walk down the garden path, heading back towards Ryde and his command, and left the front door open, allowing in the light and the soft breeze. *An investment*, he suddenly thought. Not only had he invested in this cottage, but his entire time on the island had been an investment too, trusting in the place and the people and in himself, though that latter faith had often been shaken. For the first time, he could see it succeeding, and in the way of his old career, it had come as a result of blood and grief and hardship. Yet, for those things, it was all the more rewarding.

Now, he only wished to see Courtney returned. He had thought of him in the cradle of the sea, thought of speaking with him again, holding him again, and even as he imagined he was on the verge of death, he had lamented the idea of their parting. Soon, he hoped, he would come back. The sea had turned Nightingale about, devoured him, and spat him out again. He prayed it would not take Courtney.

Chapter Twenty-Six: Overcome

18 August 1805

A batch of letters from Nightingale and Jane reached Courtney when the *Lion* docked in Portsmouth, but he had no second to even open them all the way to London. Courtney knew they would be regarding the same subject as before: the threatening notes, Nightingale's hurt over Courtney's misinformation to him. His mind was consumed with Harrison. So very recently recovered, the captain seemed on the verge of another break with the news from his wife: the moment of her childbirth dawned and Harrison spent hours fretting and musing so much that Courtney felt he played nursemaid. His frantic worries churned up the very same things in Courtney's breast and he felt nauseous every time he attempted to open the dense packet of notes. By the time he reached Harrison's house and found that Jennifer was not so near crisis as anticipated, his bones were heavy with fatigue. He tried to peruse the letters but stumbled on Jane's only recently improved handwriting, contenting himself with her assurance that all was well.

The following day sapped the rest of his dwindling energy. Since leaving Antigua two months before, Courtney did not think he had stopped moving. The fleet had flown across the Atlantic, reaching Cape St Vincent in the third week of July. Villeneuve, again, had not been in their net. No news came forth until intelligence from the brig-sloop *Curieux* suggested the Franco-Spanish fleet aimed for the Bay of Biscay. Further orders for the squadrons to reconvene off Ushant drew the *Lion* and her sisters north. And there, scoured and worn down by years at sea, Nelson had departed for Portsmouth. The *Lion*, urged by Harrison's news and the need to refit, followed.

London had been no more relaxing. The contingent of Sandhams, Jennifer's family, descended upon Harrison's house and Courtney had to confront the looming spectre: the reason he had left the *Lion* in Portsmouth and travelled with Harrison to the capital. With Harrison's encouragement and that of his parents-in-law, he did his duty.

At last, in the lingering pain of his actions, he returned to the package of letters and wanted nothing more than to comfort himself with Nightingale's news. But the words only darkened him further.

Nightingale had met with his father. The man had been held on a prison hulk at Cowes but, ailing, Nightingale had been caring for him at their cottage. Courtney could not believe it. He cursed himself for the packet not arriving to him sooner, and then for not opening the packet, and once again, not revealing things to Nightingale. In his discomfort he blamed Harrison, but the man immediately let him leave, taking the fast coach away from London and south to the coast. Courtney, in a fit of self-hatred and regret, did not rest but travelled through the night and day, boisterously cajoling a captain into giving him passage across the Solent on a packet vessel.

The journey lasted an almost insufferable age. He was twice foisted by tides and then, finally upon the island, had to loiter and bide his time for a carriage to Ryde. When it came, the rickety old thing had been nearly filled with passengers and so he sat with the driver at the front, crammed on the thin seat. Thinking his close proximity required talk, the old driver would not cease chattering to him, looking at his uniform and asking him question upon question of the navy and Nelson's actions in the Mediterranean and Caribbean. Not for the first time, Courtney hated his commander's epaulette and shining buttons.

What would his father think of it? He had not written back to him, had not told him of any of his new life. When Courtney had left home with Jane, he had been wearing oversized clothes that Mr and Mrs Woods had given him from a previous ward. He had been as thin as a waif, a lad growing into lanky, ungainly limbs, but had still been driven by a burning fire inside. That fire had driven him onto the *Grampus*, had made him survive her sinking, and then had seen him through his career on the *Scylla* and *Lysander*. He had never considered it would bring him home, back into his father's gaze.

Now, here John Courtney was again, crawling back, allegedly without a bottle in his hand, apparently trying to form a better picture of himself, and Nightingale had found out about him, perhaps that Courtney already knew of his return. Courtney could not set a definition to the emotion in his chest, if it existed. He told himself it would be as if he met a stranger, a man who had never existed before. He did not need his father's approval and blessing anymore; neither did he have to give his forgiveness.

But when he walked up the garden path, his feet quickening, his chest tight, and opened the unlocked door, he tried to tell himself where he stood. This was not in the way of being before a sailor who harboured mutinous thoughts. This man held no power over him anymore, not like the other one who suddenly hurried in from the kitchen, face flushed at their reunion. Nightingale looked at Courtney, smiled, and Courtney was almost overcome with affection. Every letter he had not sent to Nightingale, confessing the truth; every secret he had kept from him; every time he had thought Nightingale would not bear it – they all dropped away. He could believe, for a moment, that Nightingale was not angry with him.

Then, his father rose from his seat by the window. He had always looked elderly, even though he had sired Courtney and Jane at a younger age than Courtney was now, but now he seemed as ancient as the walls around him and not as lovingly treated. A dearth of fortune and of anything but gin had sapped his years, bending his back and stiffening his limbs. The aftermath of his illness still pulsed in his yellowing skin, sallow hair and dark teeth. That fragility nearly stopped Courtney's mouth.

But still he said, 'You dare to continue sending threatening notes? After I did not reply to you?'

Old John Courtney did not snap at the accusation, not like the baited dog Courtney had built him to be in his head. He merely nodded. 'I did. I wanted to warn you, Arthur. I wanted to make sure you were not making a grave mistake. I would say that it was out of my character but you know it was not.'

'Damn right it was not.' Courtney had not schemed on being this angry. He was almost ashamed of it after his insistence that his father had no authority on him. 'It has been seventeen years.'

'I heard that you had returned to the island,' his father said, still refusing to rise. 'I heard of your career upon the sea and how you were at this cottage.'

'You had no right to come here. I had not responded to your letters.'

'Mr Nightingale has been kind to me and made arrangements with Captain Bartley of the *Impregnable*. He offered me a place here.'

Courtney looked towards Nightingale and saw the uncertainty on his face. He had made the decision without consulting Courtney, but Courtney had not spoken of his father at all, had not mentioned he had known of his return. Nightingale had discovered that for himself. Courtney could not find it within his heart to blame Nightingale. His kindness was not a detestable quality. It was Courtney's fault; he had treated him terribly.

'I had everything in its place,' Courtney said, voice wobbling. 'And then you wrote to me, and I was placed onboard the *Lion*, and I...'

He could not finish. The damage had been done, both now and before from his youth. He bound the ire up within him, pressing it down so ferociously that tears clogged his throat. The emotions of the past few days, his exhaustion, his remorse, ran him through.

His father had not noticed, but Nightingale had stepped forward. Courtney waved him off.

'I regret many things, Arthur,' John said. 'Mr Nightingale has cared for me, though I have done some unforgiveable things. He has made me realise that I perhaps don't deserve your forgiveness, and if it is never given, I will understand. But I had to return here. It is my home as well as yours. Mr Nightingale is a good friend to you. I know now that you do not need my warnings.'

Courtney could feel the pressure of his tears, the edge of composure wobbling inside of him. He swallowed, unable to process the meaning of what his father said. And then, as if he were the same thirteen-year-old lad again, he rushed from the room.

Even alone, with the door shut on his and Nightingale's bedroom, he could not find the bravery to weep. The act seemed as if it would make all the heartache crest in him and he would never be able to return to the person he had been before boarding the *Lion*. He paced the floorboards like the listing deck of a ship and pressed the heels of his hands into his eyes. When his knees became too weak, he sank to the bed and breathed in ragged gasps. A deep panic had bound his chest in knots and his head pounded. It was all of his own doing. He had caused this turmoil. If this was what the rest of his life would entail, he did not know how he would bear it.

It could have been a minute later, or perhaps an hour, when gentle hands touched his arms. He had been clinging rigidly to the quilt and jerked at the touch.

'I'm sorry, my love,' said Nightingale's soft voice. 'I did not mean to cause you any pain. I did not take the decision lightly and I wanted ever so much to discuss it with you. Did I do the wrong thing?'

'It isn't you,' Courtney managed feebly. 'I am as unforgive-able as he is. You will hate me.'

'There is nothing you could do to hurt me, Arthur. Tell me what I am to do to heal this.'

Courtney wanted to sink into Nightingale and find the comfort he always had, but a wall of his own making prevented it. 'I cannot speak of it. Not now. And I cannot... I cannot talk with him in this state. It is a bad time.'

'I can send him away. There is a cottage we have been looking at these past weeks. His standing has quite increased recently because... Well, I shall speak of that later, if you wish to hear it.'

'And so I am unreasonable for not wishing to see him.'

'No. Of course not. No one would dare think such a thing. Come, my love, tell me what ails you.'

Courtney shook his head. 'I cannot. I must think of how to say it. I just... I am sorry for not telling you of him. When his letters came, I thought I could deal with it alone. I did not want to upset you after the death of your father. I was a fool.'

Silence spanned the room. Nightingale squeezed his arms and laid a soft kiss on the top of his head. Courtney closed his eyes.

'I do not blame you, dearest,' Nightingale said. 'This past year has thrown many challenges at you. Now, I shall have Rylance accompany him away. You are tired from your journey. We will speak when you are recovered.'

Courtney nodded silently.

'I love you completely, dear heart,' Nightingale insisted. 'You know that, don't you?'

'I do.'

And that was what made everything all the more painful.

–

Courtney quietly opened the door to the bedroom, softening his feet on the bare floor. A tallow candle still burnt low, throwing orange illumination about the homely space. The curtains had partially fallen open, so he drew them fully and perched on the edge of the large bed. Nightingale slept quietly on his back, an arm over his eyes. Courtney watched him with a gentle, slowly dawning smile on his face. The man was as handsome as he had ever been, auburn hair now shot slightly with silvering strands, the white of the scars around his eyes and forehead now a dull pink, lines made tougher from a sailor's life appearing about his mouth. Courtney wanted to spend his life waking next to him, but he knew it could not be. Nightingale had his home and his wife, and Courtney knew that soon, so would he.

Courtney felt even worse after hearing of what Nightingale had done recently. He had been ever so unfair to him.

He looked away before the sadness could touch him again. As he shucked off his coat and shirt, he heard movement and Nightingale shifted beneath the quilt. A hand reached out to him and stroked his lower back.

'Arthur,' Nightingale said, voice laced with sleep. 'You returned.'

Courtney had been spending his time at the Fisherman's Catch, hiding from himself and from Nightingale. He had spoken unceasingly with the two people he still considered his true 'Ma' and 'Pa', Mr and Mrs Woods, and the both of them had maddeningly told him to follow his own heart with regards to John Courtney. Courtney had not wanted that answer: he had wanted someone to tell him what to do, as selfish as it was to admit that. The two nights away from the cottage had not calmed his mind and he knew he was making himself suffer for the self-pity of it.

'I missed you,' Courtney said, reaching for Nightingale's hand and cradling it. 'Can I join you?'

'Of course.'

Courtney pulled on his nightshirt and, flooded with relief, sank beneath the bedding. It was heated by Nightingale's body and a luxurious bed-warmer, both things Courtney had sorely longed for on the *Lion* and at the Catch. He wrapped his arms about Nightingale for the first time in months and eased him into a tender, lingering kiss. Nightingale did not release him when he tried to lean back, pressing his mouth to his again and stroking through his hair to free it from its ribbon tie. Courtney sighed and buried his face into his shoulder. Before he knew it, tears overcame him and he wept.

'Oh, my dear,' Nightingale whispered. His hands rubbed soothing circles on Courtney's spine. 'Do not cry so.'

Trembling, Courtney tried to keep a hold of his voice. 'I'm sorry,' he managed. 'I did not intend to be so harsh to you.'

'You did not mean any malice by it.'

'It does not make it acceptable.' He raised his head and wiped his face on the cuff of his nightshirt. Nightingale tutted and found his handkerchief for him to use. 'I do not like the man I've become these past months. I've been a brute. I always condemned men for imparting their pain on their crews and acting the tartar but there I did it myself. I made some terrible decisions and men, and boys, were hurt because of it.'

'I am certain it is not as bad as you think. I always reprimanded myself, wondering how I could have acted differently.'

'No, I was dreadful, Hiram. I have spent my career wishing to become a captain, a commander, and then once I have the chance, I…' He shook his head, but if there was any soul in the world he could admit it to, it was Nightingale. '…I hate it.'

Nightingale did not speak for a moment and Courtney feared he was going to sob again. He instead lay against Nightingale's chest and selfishly held him close.

'There is no shame in that,' Nightingale said softly. 'I too had such thoughts. The step between a lieutenancy and that of a commander is very steep.'

'I have been given it before my time. I felt I was ready and always desired it and worked for it and then…' He swallowed, hating that he had to tread through this quagmire again. Instead, he asked, 'Why did you not tell me what you had done here? About Lieutenant Osborne and the *Racer*? About how you... You nearly died.'

Courtney felt the tears come upon him again, the idea of nearly being wrenched from Nightingale twisting in him like a knife. His throat squeezed, ridiculously pathetic noises choking from him.

'Dearest, come now.'

Nightingale sat him up and found a handkerchief. Courtney, trying to compose himself, grasped it.

'I'm sorry, I didn't... I could not lose you, Hiram. After I heard of what you did, the danger you were in. I would have returned if I had known.'

'You were at sea.' Nightingale paused, taking the handkerchief from Courtney's shaking hands and wiping at the wet mess of his cheeks. 'I weighed the risks and pursued Lieutenant Osborne, perhaps to a greater degree than I had intended but... I was spared. And I thought of you as I was spared, thought of how much I wished to see you. I knew I would forgive any reaction you had against me. I told my wife about you, about our bond, and I knew from then – no, that is not right, I knew from a long while ago, but now I know with even more certainty – that I want to be at your side for as long as I am able.'

'I wish that too.' Courtney swallowed his emotion, feeling it rise again. Nightingale smiled and pulled him close, embracing him tenderly. 'But I have been such a fool,' Courtney forced himself to say.

'Arthur, do not doubt yourself. I know where that road leads.'

'No. No, I must speak with you.'

'Speak. I shall not judge you harshly.'

Courtney took a breath, preparing himself for the anguish and the disappointment. 'I went to London with Captain Harrison. His child is to be born very soon. Whilst I stayed

at his house, the Sandhams visited for Mrs Harrison and I…
They assented to my marriage to Miss Sandham.'

The calming motions of Nightingale's hand upon his back ceased. 'Ah,' Nightingale said in a small sigh.

'I'm sorry. We have spoken of it before but it feels so wretched. I promised Harrison and Miss Sandham and… Christ, he even bought a ring for me to give to her. I suppose that I hoped we could find an arrangement somewhat like you and Mrs Nightingale, that perhaps she would not care if I…I don't know. I would only break her heart and mine, and yet… God, I still did it. I thought it should be what I needed to do to keep us safe and to keep a position I should crave.'

His head had not been facing the right way for many a month. He had acted in ways he hated and was ashamed for. Now, he had made irreparable mistakes that did not deserve any pardon or excuse. Nightingale would detest him for his lack of faith.

'You are correct,' Nightingale said softly. 'We did speak of it before. And I have often thought of it. I was foolish. I told you before that you should follow your heart but… Oh, it is so selfish of me.'

'No. No, tell me.' The same impulse Courtney had felt when speaking with Mr and Mrs Woods churned up in him: he wished for someone to decide a path for him, though he knew they could not. This was his own road to travel and more than at any time in his life, he felt the terror of its shadows and bends. But still, he said, 'I wanted you to beg and plead with me not to do it.'

'You know I would not do that. Yet I…I wish to be with you. I wish it so much. I wish the world were different and I could love you as a spouse.'

The admission broke Courtney's heart as much as it filled it with joy. Tears threatened him again but now he pushed them away angrily, knowing that weeping would get him nowhere.

'I wish the same,' he said. 'But it is a ridiculous hope.'

'And doubtless a familiar one to men such as us. We always yearn for a soul who shall accept and understand us. I have found that in you.'

'And I, you. Yet I fear I cannot go back on my vow now. I do not know what to do.'

Courtney, as Nightingale did, yearned for a world where he did not have to force his will towards a person he could not fully love. Miss Sandham was a kind creature, pretty and intelligent, but he could not imagine his life at her side as he could with Nightingale. It was not fair on either of them – on any of them. Yet the wheels had been turned now and would not cease easily.

All he could pray for was that innocent, deserving lives did not become mangled in the course.

Chapter Twenty-Seven: The Admiral's Cabin

30 September 1805, off Cádiz

The enemy fleet could no longer be seen. Nelson's squadron had been moved fifty miles outside the harbour of Cádiz, strung in wide lines with broad distances between each vessel. Frigates and smaller ships surrounded the blockading fleet and the coast, the watchful eyes ever searching for movement amidst the Spanish and French. It reminded Courtney of the long, painful days outside Toulon, almost willing for the foe to take their chances and run the siege. The wind, he knew, was against the enemy, keeping them holed up as much as the chain of third- and first-raters.

More vessels were due to arrive over the next couple of weeks, including the *Agamemnon* and the *Royal Sovereign*, fresh and prepared. Ships had been rotated about the line, sent away to be re-victualled and then returning to take their place again like birds coming back to roost. For every store and supply that was swung onboard the *Lion*, Courtney knew the equivalent would be draining away quickly in Cádiz. Word had spread about the British fleet: if the enemy would not come out, they would be starved out.

Each entry in Courtney's logbook recycled the same words. Recently, the *Lion* had arrived at Cádiz with the *Victory*. As if the Atlantic chase and the short time in England had refreshed the vessel and allowed Courtney to view her in a warmer light, he finally felt a difference aboard her. The men and officers had come to know her more closely. He hoped the dismal events had come to a head in the Caribbean, in the open sea off Guadeloupe and Dominica where the *Lion* had suffered in the eye of the storm. Ramsey had been alighted in England, returning to his parents, and Appleton had taken a brief leave to recover from the worst of his fever. He now took a more personal care of the midshipmen, supervising their education and spending time with them during their navigation lessons on deck. With a livid pink scar around his neck, it was impossible to forget his ordeal, but in the way of the rest of the vessel, he seemed bolder, revived from a terrible peril.

Harrison's appearance in the wardroom marked a new event. Courtney immediately shot to his feet, nearly cracking his head on the low timbers. Harrison had much improved since his visit home: his skin with more colour, his hair again curled and preened, the boyish roundness of his cheeks returning. He had not acted out of sorts since taking his place at the helm again and Courtney thought he recognised the man he had first met in Trinidad five years before. Mr Fitzroy perched on his shoulder, playing with the gold lace of his hat.

'Commander Courtney,' Harrison greeted warmly. 'You are to make a journey with me.'

'A journey, sir? Are we required in another port?'

'Of a manner of speaking. You are coming onboard the *Victory* with me.'

Courtney felt his stomach roll, as if he stared down a broadside. 'The *Victory*?'

'Yes, my dear man. The admiral's flagship. The large one.'

'Why, sir?'

'Lord Nelson is inviting all of his captains to dinner. Doubtless he has something astonishing and clever to tell us all.'

'I'm...' Courtney swallowed. 'I'm not a captain, sir.'

'You are a commander. But such hierarchical questions are not under debate. Lord Nelson has asked specifically that you join us also.'

'Me?'

Before the present moment, Courtney had not even considered Lord Nelson would be aware of his existence. Nightingale had served under him at the Nile but that was the closest connection Courtney had to him. He had not joined Harrison in going aboard for the admiral's forty-seventh birthday dinner. Yet, within the half-hour, he sat with Harrison in the captain's gig, dressed in shining lace, brushed blue wool, scrubbed white breeches, silk stockings, and polished buckled shoes. Fitzroy insisted on continuously leaping onto his lap and he had to keep encouraging him off lest he make a mark. Courtney wondered if the monkey had been particularly invited also; perhaps that was the level he sat at, next to a primate.

The *Victory* towered over them, a beacon where other launch boats were being drawn. Her flanks beamed in pale yellow and black, which the rest of the fleet had recently mimicked on their own ships. Courtney, still with no head for heights, determined not to look down as he climbed the tall sides. The *Lion* was not a particularly small vessel, but the *Victory* was a behemoth in comparison, a floating town. On the wide, spacious quarterdeck, a Marine guard waited with weapons clashing in ceremonial greeting. Masts that seemed to reach the very clouds loomed above them, the waning sun kissing the timbers and dressing the canvas in pinkish light. Courtney, as though he had never walked upon a ship of the line, stared down the deck towards the broad bows. Seamen had lined the gunwales, donned in their best clothes. Hats came off in his and Harrison's presence.

Then the attention shifted to the next captain ascending the ladder. Harrison greeted Captain Duff of the *Mars*, grasping his hand warmly and familiarly. Courtney had met with a few of these men in the Caribbean, but his mind had been elsewhere then. He tried to act as a more cheerful man this time, speaking with Captains Fremantle of the *Neptune* and Codrington of the *Orion*. A whirlwind of names came his way and as he ever did, he wished Nightingale were there. Nightingale had always had the correct poise in these formal situations. The thought of him, at the cottage, doubtlessly stewing over their disagreement, knocked what little appetite Courtney had.

The worry soon had to be pressed down when the officers were ushered below to the admiral's cabin. Courtney adhered to Harrison's side and again fended off Fitzroy's attention, not wanting the monkey to draw eyes to him also. The great cabin, astern of the upper gun deck, had its doors thrown open as if the partitions had been lowered for battle. Courtney felt as nervous as if he entered a smoke-strewn battery. He clenched his trembling hands into fists behind his back and tried to quell his shaking knees, but upon going inside, he found the space empty. Stewards guided each officer to his place and Courtney found himself, terrifyingly, near the head of the table, beside Harrison and Duff.

Hardy, the captain of the *Victory*, entered: an immensely tall man who had to stoop beneath the low timbers. Courtney, following everyone else, rose to his feet and barely saw the slight, thin figure who appeared with Hardy. Lord Admiral Horatio Nelson, the commander-in-chief of the Mediterranean Fleet and the hero of all England, would not have attracted gazes in a crowded room if not for the medals upon his breast and the fine uniform. He was a frail-looking man, white-haired and marked by a life at sea and illnesses. One eye, blinded at Calvi, did not seem to take in the men before him, and one blue sleeve was pinned across his chest, result of the Battle of Santa Cruz. But Courtney still found himself in awe, perhaps even more so because of the underwhelming appearance.

One by one, Nelson greeted his guests, knowing every man closely. Harrison dipped a little to acknowledge the smaller admiral and then he was before Courtney. At least a head or more taller, Courtney looked down and plastered a nervous smile on his face.

'Commander Courtney,' Nelson said, and Courtney felt an unexpected pleasure that his accent was so tinged as his own countryman's tone, heavy 'r's and vowels. 'Captain Harrison has told me of you.'

'Thank you, sir. Yes, sir. I am Lieutenant…' Courtney fought the urge to wince. '…Commander Courtney, sir. N–not Lieutenant-Commander, sir. Simply Commander Courtney.'

Nelson smiled, as if accustomed to this fuss and nerve in his companions. 'I confess I knew of you already. You played a role in the capture of the *Ulysses*.'

'Yes, sir. With Captain Nightingale, sir. Who served with you at the Nile.'

God, was he incapable of speaking in full sentences?

'I remember Captain Nightingale. A good man, I was sorry to hear what happened to him. He was a recipient of one of my Nile medals, he and his lieutenant, Sawyer.'

'Yes, sir.' Courtney was not about to tell Lord Nelson what Nightingale had done with the medal. Weighed down with sore memories as it was for him, Nightingale had thrown the medal into the sea. Recovered by fishermen afterwards, it had been returned to Courtney. Nightingale had insisted on Courtney becoming the proud owner of it, instead of keeping it himself. 'Captain Nightingale is a good friend of mine,' Courtney commented.

As they sat, Courtney breathed a sigh of relief. His cheeks blazed and he knew he would spend the rest of the night considering and reconsidering his words to the admiral, doubtlessly finding fault. Harrison turned to him and said, quietly, 'You speak very highly of Captain Nightingale. I appreciate how you value your captains.'

Courtney wondered precisely what Harrison meant by that. Perhaps it was a mark of gratitude towards him for the way Courtney had acted around his ailment. Courtney still did not know precisely what it had been but Courtney appreciated how Harrison had returned to his former self. During the dinner, he drank healthily and without embarrassment. Fitzroy demonstrated his one talent of tying a variety of knots on command

and became the centre of attention more than once when he clambered over Nelson's shoulders.

'The *Lion* must be a ship of mirth,' Duff muttered to Courtney during the next round of port.

'Oh, you do not know, sir,' Courtney responded, which was apparently a humorous comment.

Conversation veered to Cádiz and the prospect of luring the enemy out of the harbour. Starvation was the word of the day, but other tactics had been suggested and continued to be. The topic of fire ships emerged and Harrison clapped Courtney on the shoulder and announced that he had played an important role in the previous year's raid on Boulogne: the reason, Courtney suspected, of his invite to dinner.

'Oh,' Courtney said, reddening. 'My role was…not so significant. My *Fearnought* caught ablaze at an incorrect time and erupted before anticipated.'

'You have experience with fire ships, though,' Harrison insisted.

'I have experience with ships which come to be on fire.'

In the end, however, Lord Nelson did not need to hear any further talk or debate on how to pull the enemy into their embrace. When plates and cutlery was cleared and more port was brought into the dining cabin, he beckoned them closer about the table. Hardy, evidently Nelson's most trusted companion, disappeared to return with a sheet of paper which was spread on the tablecloth. Courtney, for all his exhaustion brought about by social niceties and interaction, could not help drawing nearer, curious. Harrison did not seem to be any wiser than him.

With the aid of salt and pepper pots and cutlery, Nelson created a diagram of two lines of battle: the Combined Franco-Spanish Fleet and that of the British Navy. Many fleet actions occurred with the enemy craft parallel to one another, firing broadside to broadside. Blood would be shed and lives gutted by cannonshot until one side gained the upper hand. This, to begin with, seemed to be what Nelson illustrated. But, as Courtney leant over Harrison's shoulder, the admiral turned the line representing his Royal Navy vessels by ninety degrees. With the position he set them in, they pointed directly at the enemy.

Staring at the paper, Courtney listened to Nelson's methods. His fleet would split into three: a weather column, a lee column, and an advance. Nelson would lead the weather column, Vice-Admiral Collingwood would lead the lee. The enemy line would be split at its centre and rear, with the might of the British vessels punching ragged holes in their formation. Once through, the British could rain hellfire upon all angles of the Spanish and French ships.

But, for a prolonged period of time, the enemy would be firing upon Nelson's columns without their ability to respond.

Such a plan turned on its head the convention of battle tactics. It ensured that there was no chance of the kind of incomplete victory that could occur during traditional line of battle engagements. The effect of this irregular scheme rippled through the listening captains like a rip tide. It crested over each in turn: the awe, the enthusiasm, the energy. Courtney caught Harrison's gaze as he turned back to look at him and for a moment, in contrast to the zeal of the others, Courtney did not know what he saw in Harrison's face. He did not know what he felt in his own chest but, after a moment, found himself swept up in the fervour. He smiled, nodded, shook hands, all the usual motions of an officer staring in the face of grandeur. Again and again, he remembered what he had thought when first joining the fleet in January.

For a man like himself, a grand naval victory was the only chance for promotion and for that hallowed post rank.

Harrison was quiet when they returned to the *Lion*. The night had fallen, a chill dressing the waves and leeching through Courtney's uniform. Any effect of the port on the both of them had vanished, chased away by Nelson's vivid scheme. Courtney stared ahead at the looming sides of the *Lion* and thought of how she had survived the firestorm of the Nile, but only by a margin. Lieutenant Sawyer had breathed his last on the deck and the vessel had been burnt and scarred and ravaged. So she would be again. In the quiet darkness, he imagined the noise of the guns and the crunch of timbers as they rubbed and lacerated each other.

'He is extraordinary,' Harrison suddenly said. His voice sounded very small.

'Lord Nelson, sir?'

'Yes. I have never heard of such an incredible plan before.'

'It is a bold one.'

'What do you think, Commander?' Harrison turned to him. Courtney recalled the other times Harrison had asked such a thing of him.

'The *Lion* has borne worse, sir,' Courtney replied. Not only had she experienced conflict from the outside, but a festering rot within too. Both times she had emerged. 'She will bear this.'

Harrison nodded. 'I agree,' he said quietly.

She would survive, Courtney thought, but it would be an annihilation. A complete and utter annihilation.

Chapter Twenty-Eight: Vanguard

18 October 1805, late evening

For days, the entire fleet had been waiting, endlessly looking for the signal that the enemy was leaving port. Within the wardroom, Martin had suggested placing wagers on when it would come, something that Courtney had quickly dampened down to avoid accusations of unlawful gambling. But, whenever Courtney dined with Harrison, the captain seemed on the verge of the same thing. Courtney knew Harrison was torn between two things: the duties of the *Lion* and the news from back home. As they had reached Cádiz, his child had been born. Courtney was not sure which event was the more terrifying – that or meeting the enemy which had long evaded them.

'We are still puzzled over a name,' Harrison said now in the great cabin, finishing the last of his plum pudding. He had been eating more substantially, his round, ruddy cheeks returning after the gauntness of his illness. 'We have considered "Henry", but I did so resent my parents for calling me that. Harry Harrison.'

'Your son, sir?' Courtney asked.

'Yes. I do regret not being there to see him. I'm sure I shall see him soon.'

Harrison quietened for a moment, the gravity of that statement cresting over them both. A great battle awaited the fleet. It seemed too much to tempt fate to speak of a future after it. But still Harrison continued, 'I am so pleased for you and Miss Sandham. She is a lovely girl, is she not?'

Courtney nodded.

'She knows all there is to know about the King's Navy. She has been hoping to be an officer's wife for many years. I remember in the Caribbean when I used to teach her the names of the sails and each rope. I dare say she remembers it all.'

Courtney smiled thinly. 'She is very charming,' he said.

Harrison looked at him sidelong and Courtney wondered if he should paint false enthusiasm onto his face but could not find the energy or will. All he could think of was his final parting from Nightingale at the cottage, embracing him and selfishly never wanting to let him go.

'You are…pleased with your match?' Harrison asked with some hesitation: the first time Courtney had ever seen him read his demeanour correctly.

'I…'

Courtney knew he should speak up. He tried to find the words but was interrupted by the sound of footsteps hurrying to the cabin. Harrison rose as the Marines outside the door opened it to reveal the master gunner.

'Are you well, Mr Greene?' Harrison asked, and Courtney thought for a moment that the signal about the enemy had come.

But Greene said, 'Pardon me, Captain, Commander, sir. It's the midshipmen's berth.'

Courtney turned cold.

'Again?' Harrison urged. 'What is it now?'

'Lieutenant Appleton, sir…'

Harrison listened to no more explanation. Courtney adhered to his side as they hurried through the ship to the after gunroom where Greene had his berth along with the younger midshipmen. It was there that Courtney feared the mids had been hurt and abused. There had been no more complaint since returning from the Caribbean but the accusation and the threat still simmered about the young boys. Now, Courtney brooded again that the entirety of the awful proceedings had not vanished to the bottom of the sea with McPherson.

But Lieutenant Appleton… What part did he play? Courtney remembered Baker's words: that the lieutenant had once accused a man of such vileness on the *Eclipse*. The lieutenant had been a skilled officer onboard, if a little hostile at times. Had Courtney been wrong about him?

Harrison reached the gunroom first. Courtney rushed after him and froze. Appleton had pressed Baker against a bulkhead, the shining point of the dirk which had once threatened him in his hand. He now shoved it tightly against Baker's throat. The midshipmen huddled by their small mess table, expressions utterly agog.

Courtney, with no regard for his safety, grasped Appleton and tried to wrench him off the bosun. Baker had blood smeared on his chin and gushing from his nose. One of his eyes, swollen and black, streamed. He shoved at Appleton, and Courtney managed to drag the lieutenant away, trying to wrestle the dirk from his fist. Appleton writhed and freed himself for a moment, shouting, 'Take your damned hands off me!' just as he had when Courtney had pulled him from McPherson and Bowles's fight, but Courtney did not let go.

Greene had stepped between Baker and Appleton, an arm over the bosun's front. Harrison stared between them before finally finding his voice and accusing, 'What the devil is happening here?!'

'Captain, sir,' Baker rasped, hands raised. 'The lieutenant, sir, his mind has cracked!'

'I'll crack your head apart, you fucking bastard!' Appleton shouted and lurched forward, only for Courtney to snatch him about the waist and nearly tackle him to the timbers.

'Drop the weapon, Lieutenant!' Courtney cried.

Appleton did not. In his struggle, one of the sutures on his neck had burst and a shock of red decorated his collar. Still, he thrashed and twisted. But Courtney had dealt with stronger, burlier men than the lieutenant before and did not shift. It did not stop Appleton spitting and swearing towards Baker, who looked as shocked as Courtney felt. Appleton had been a thorny officer, perhaps hard to work alongside or be friendly with at times, but he had been an honourable, steady gentleman. A mask seemed to have been wrenched away from him now, exposing a raw and angry underbelly.

Lieutenant Farnham arrived quickly, sent for by Harrison. By the time he appeared, Courtney had managed to wrench the weapon from Appleton's grip. Realising Courtney was not about to release him, some of the energy had drained from his tense and shaking body.

'Lieutenant Farnham, take Mr Baker away,' Harrison ordered. 'Lieutenant Appleton, you will be confined to your cabin. Are any of you young gentlemen harmed?'

The midshipmen, headed by Harriet, shook their heads.

'Lieutenant, you have behaved disgracefully,' Harrison reprimanded. 'I do not expect to see my officers fighting with the crew, certainly not in front of the midshipmen they are meant to guide.'

'S-sir...' Harriet managed to say. 'It wasn't Lieutenant Appleton, sir. He... He helped us.'

'Helped you?'

Harriet nodded.

'Commander Courtney,' Harrison said. 'Take Lieutenant Appleton to his cabin. I shall speak with him there. And Private'—he addressed the Marine still at the door—'keep a watch on the midshipmen. Ensure they are guarded from any further upset.'

Courtney helped Appleton back to his feet from where he had half-fallen. Dirk safely in his hand, he shepherded the lieutenant along, relieved when he composed himself and acted as though nothing had occurred. It would help settle the minds of any man who saw them or had heard them. But the three of them had not gone far when another din rose from the lower gun deck where Baker had been taken. Harrison turned and seemed on the verge of cursing.

'I shall go, sir,' Courtney offered.

'No,' Harrison rejected. 'You take Lieutenant Appleton to the wardroom. I shall be there as soon as I can.'

Harrison departed quickly. Satisfied for the first time that Harrison could manage the situation, Courtney took Appleton to the wardroom and sat him down at the mess table. As soon as they were alone, Appleton's ire turned to anguish and he began to weep in choking, guttural sobs. He slumped and put his head in his hands. Unsure how to act, Courtney lowered himself onto the bench opposite him.

'Lieutenant,' he said quietly, 'are you well?'

Appleton shivered, as if still in fever, and nodded. 'I am well now, yes,' he managed. 'Perhaps better than I have been in many years. I should have acted in that way a long while ago. It would have solved many problems. It is my fault. I am to blame for what happened to Fox and Ramsey and McPherson...'

Appleton sniffed and wiped at his cheeks, at the blood and tears there. Courtney handed over his handkerchief. Appleton took it and tried to make himself more presentable.

'You are bleeding,' Courtney said, indicating the damaged suture on his neck.

Appleton dabbed at the injury and pressed the handkerchief to it. 'You must think me some wild thing,' he said.

'No. I am not innocent of brawling or behaving in a way others would think crazed.'

'You are a commander. Officers do not act in such a way.'

Despite the dire circumstances, Courtney chuckled. 'I am not an officer who was placed upon a vessel as a midshipman by a kindly uncle or father,' he said. 'I came aboard the *Grampus*, my first vessel, as a thirteen-year-old lad running away from home and joining the forecastle men. I was that way for what felt like a long time. I am certainly no gentleman and have never professed, or tried, to be.'

Appleton frowned. 'You were an able seaman? Not a midshipman?'

'I joined in the way of most men in the fleet, escaping home and poverty. I am a tarpaulin officer through and through.'

'I thought… Well, it does not matter what I thought.'

Courtney realised that Appleton had thought he had attained the position of commander onboard the *Lion* through Harrison's patronage. Courtney had never believed he would have such an accusation shoved upon him: connections and favouritism did not play a role in his life, and he had condemned those who solely relied on it.

'I too served before the mast,' Appleton suddenly said. 'It is how I joined the navy and how I thought I would end, after I was disrated as midshipman.'

Courtney knew this from what Baker had told him. 'I have heard of your past,' he said carefully.

'From who? From Baker? What did he tell you? That I behaved badly and that was why I was caned, why I had my rank stripped from me?'

Courtney did not want to bring up what Baker had told of Appleton's past, but he had been afraid to mention unsavoury things when speaking with the mids. He had not confronted the terrible situation and Ramsey had then tried to kill himself. 'He said that you accused a man onboard of something heinous.'

'And who do you think that man was?' Appleton spat. 'It was *him*.'

A long silence stretched. Courtney tried to think through what Appleton had said. The man accused of terrible acts had been Baker? Indeed, Baker had said he had served on the *Eclipse* as the bosun. So too had he been present on the *Lion* in the midst of its wretchedness. Had Courtney truly been so blind?

'There were three mids on the *Eclipse*,' Appleton said, squeezing the bloodied and damp handkerchief in his hands. 'I was the youngest at fourteen, the same age as Mr Fox. They didn't like me. They treated me as an outsider. Mr Baker was so kind to me. He protected me from the mids and from the other horrid officers onboard.

'At first, I...' Appleton's voice hitched. Courtney did not press, knowing how to act from the periods of Nightingale's worry. The rest of the ship had quietened, the tumult of before fading. 'You understand that I have never told a soul this. I was so ashamed. That is why I could not act.'

Courtney said nothing. He knew he did not want to hear the next words out of Appleton's mouth but he made himself listen.

'At first, I thought that...what happened was a part of it. I had never been away from home before, I did not know how boys were supposed to act around other men. Mr Baker told me it was the way of the ancient Greeks. But it hurt me. I came to dread seeing him.' Appleton sniffed and blinked away more tears. 'I tried to go to the captain...'

'Go on,' Courtney encouraged. 'It is all right.'

'I intended to bring Mr Baker's true character before the captain. But the captain did not like me, did not like any of us mids. Mr Baker painted me as a bully and a tyrant to the other mids, and he called me a liar, intent on ruining other men and their careers. The captain believed him. He ordered me to be caned and Mr Baker delivered it, not allowing anyone else to do so. Then I was disrated and it has been a black mark on my sea service record, one I cannot run from.'

It sounded familiar. Baker had been the one to administer the flogging of McPherson and Bowles, and had planted the doubt in Courtney's head about the lies onboard. Ramsey had seemed a bully to the midshipmen's berth, but perhaps he had not been; Courtney had certainly seen no recent evidence.

'When I received my commission here,' Appleton said, tone trembling, 'I had no idea that he would be the bosun. In fact, I cannot believe that the fate of our previous bosun had nothing to do with him. I had hoped that Baker had died but here he was... I do not know how many people he has harmed, how many times he has evaded justice. Still, I did nothing. He still frightened me. I know he could still break me.'

'It was not McPherson,' Courtney said, giving voice to the doubt which had nagged him for some time.

Appleton shook his head. 'It was why I begged you to call a court martial. I thought they would see the truth of it, that I would not have to admit anything. I knew he was not guilty. I deserved what McPherson did to me. I do not know how he got hold of the dirk, but that is the kind of weapon Baker carries. Perhaps he gave it to him, convincing him he was helping but really, wanting him to cause trouble when he was moved. I thought I would die because of it, and perhaps I should have.'

'Lieutenant…'

'No. I allowed an innocent man to suffer. I did not stop Baker as he abused Ramsey, when he poisoned the stores to remove the gunner's crew from his way… I fear he even pushed Fox if the boy found out about him, just as McPherson said. I finally stood against him but it is too late.'

Courtney fell quiet. Suddenly all the information, all the misinformation, all the truths and the lies settled into place. He truly had been a fool. The answer had been before him since the very beginning and he had not seen it. Appleton had witnessed it but his foul treatment as a child had stitched his mouth. Courtney understood the anger in him now, the anguish of his attack on the bosun. The ire bubbled up inside himself too; he would not let Baker walk away.

'Why,' he began, 'why did you…'

'Why did I not say anything? I should have. But I couldn't. Not when I was still so afraid of him and his power over me. I was terrified of what more he could do. He knows what I am, and he knows what I have done. Perhaps he shall still try to hurt me but I could bear it no longer. After I became invalided, I vowed that I would do something.'

'No, I wasn't going to ask why you didn't say anything. I was going to ask why you are telling me. What do you wish me to do?'

'I don't know. But I…' He paused and seemed to be finding his next sentence. 'I saw you, at Portsmouth, with the captain.'

327

'Captain Harrison?'

'No. Captain Nightingale. And I observed you when he boarded the *Lion* last year. You treated him with such respect, even though it was clear he was… Well, there was talk after the *Ulysses* incident that he was not in his right mind. I know that others would think the same of me. You and he are still dear friends, are you not?'

Courtney nodded.

'Now I know of your past also… You are a good man.'

'And you also, Lieutenant. You have courage I could not even dream of.'

'It is not the same as facing a mutineer or a battle.'

'No, it is far greater.'

Appleton sighed. 'I do not feel it, or believe it.'

'I will ensure that Mr Baker faces justice and that your role in it is unknown, if that is what you wish.'

Appleton nodded. 'Thank you, Commander.'

Proving the strength Courtney now saw in him, Appleton occupied the deck the next day into the forenoon watch. Dr Archer had bound his suture again but the wound acted as a reminder of what had occurred and what Appleton had confessed to Courtney. Harrison came to Courtney soon after the lieutenant appeared on deck again and said, 'Mr Baker has been placed under arrest. He fought with the Marines and anyone who came close to aid them. Did Lieutenant Appleton speak?'

'Yes, sir. It was a…personal matter between the two. Mr Baker must stay in irons and be taken to a court martial, damn his experience and skills.'

Harrison, to his credit, did not question such a request or statement. Other pressing matters soon raised their head. During the forenoon watch, a signal came from Captain Duff's *Mars*, relayed throughout the rest of the fleet from the frigates stationed close to Cádiz. Signal No. 370: the enemy were leaving port. It prompted action throughout the blockading squadron as the *Victory* hoisted her signal for general chase. Every detail of the pursuit, notwithstanding weather, had been spread amidst the captains of the fleet.

But rain and fog dogged every ship around the harbour of Cádiz. The rumble of excitement and anticipation that throbbed with the sighting of the enemy's movements dwindled as the French and Spanish languished in their attempts to get to sea. Courtney watched for any glimpse of them and their actions, but worsening damp haze frustrated him and the other officers. He remained on deck with Appleton. Poor visibility stretched between the ships of their side, so much that even the man at the masthead struggled.

As they had during the weeks of blockade, he, Appleton, Harrison, and Moore debated where the enemy fleet might go. The British ships would follow them towards the Strait of Gibraltar where it was assumed their foe would break through in an attempt to be reinforced by further vessels at Cartagena and Toulon. Throughout the dreary Sunday, sightings of the French and Spanish placed them to the north then the west, but always with their heads in a southerly direction. Updates from the frigates – lights burning blue in the fog – signified that their enemy remained within sight.

Uncaring of the fleet's movements, the wind shifted throughout the day, meaning each vessel had to wear around. Afternoon and evening shifted into ominous night, made darker by the prospect of what would soon occur. Courtney, in the chase, could not help thinking of what lay ahead, not only the battle. He wondered if he should even consider the future. It was a morbid thought. He had participated in countless skirmishes and fights upon the sea and had only suffered one major injury: a stab-wound from falling upon a knife. As the *Lion* sailed onwards, he condemned himself for musing so disastrously and ghoulishly. Before, as a lieutenant on the *Scylla*, as a seaman on the *Grampus*, he had few people to think of. He had survived for Jane and sometimes, for Jane alone. Now, he had a family in England. He had Jane. He had Mr and Mrs Woods. He had Nightingale. And soon, a wife.

Courtney found his hands trembling as he wrote notes to those distant shores. England was so far away. England was beyond the line of French and Spanish ships. The only way back was directly through them.

Chapter Twenty-Nine: Hellfire

21 October 1805

Courtney tried to eat the food before him but every bite tasted like ash. He forced himself to swallow through a tight, dry throat, frequently sipping at the bitter coffee. He did not know how many he had supped, but the fizzing energy inside of him said that it had been many. Across from him, the places were empty. Dr Archer had been chained to his sickbay in the orlop for days, walking on sand-coated timbers and with surgical instruments gleaming. The lieutenants had adopted their places on their respective gun decks. Courtney had not told Harrison of the extent of Baker's evil actions, only insisting that a court martial must be called once the battle had concluded.

And soon, it would be.

The men ate a hasty breakfast as the time approached the forenoon watch. Courtney had only come below on Harrison's insistence he ate something. Giving up on his food, Courtney walked the decks again, observing the final motions before battle. Hammocks had been taken down to provide additional protection from cannonshot and splinters; canvas had been wetted as fire-guards; animals had been stowed out of the way with other effects and belongings; partitions had been hauled down. And finally, the great powder-store and armoury were opened, shot and weaponry and every method of destruction at hand. Courtney supervised as much as he could, even helping to man the pumps to soak the fearnought screens. As he did so, he thought of that fire ship he had commanded at Boulogne with the very same name. *Fearnought*. She had ignited in a halo of decimation, and had not been a stepping-stone to promotion.

This battle, some twenty miles off Cape Trafalgar, would be his crucible.

If he survived.

Once, he looked at his letter home but had left it there on his cot. He had written all that he could. No more would explain his feelings any clearer.

Light airs greeted Courtney on deck. The harsh conditions of the last day had withdrawn but the rolling Atlantic swell dogged the fleet, foretelling an approaching gale. Since the middle of the morning watch, the British ships had formed up in their two columns, both weather and lee. The planned-for third column had not materialised due to the required ships still being off Gibraltar. Both of the columns had been slow all morning, due to the bare breeze, but at last, Courtney could see the formation of the fifteen ships of Admiral Collingwood's lee line. Astern of the *Lion* sailed the two-decked seventy-fours *Leviathan* and *Conqueror*. The *Lion* sat prettily between them, not quite a sister but sharing the same gunnery and approximate size. Ahead of them Courtney viewed the mighty sterns of the *Neptune*, *Temeraire* and at the very vanguard, *Victory*.

Courtney looked past the *Victory*'s canvas – every inch of it on her grand masts – and towards the Combined Fleet of the French and Spanish. They stared back at the British vessels in a bunched crescent formation. Since Courtney had last viewed them, the ungainly swell had troubled the enemy's seamanship and some vessels had settled behind the loose line. He had known such a sight would be waiting for them but seeing it again made it clear how much of a tumult this fight would be. The British vessels, when breaking through, would be fired upon at all angles.

Courtney joined Harrison on the quarterdeck, staring down towards the *Lion*'s bows. Echoing the *Victory*, every sensible sail had been set, a great bird opening her wings to catch even the lightest wind. Harrison greeted Courtney with a small nod.

'Lord Nelson on the *Victory* is raising another signal,' Harrison commented. 'Mr Simmonds, might you read it aloud for us.'

Harrison gave Simmonds his own spyglass and the boy peered towards the impressive form of the *Victory*. 'England expects,' he narrated, 'that every man will do his duty.'

'Well, that is a stirring sentiment,' Harrison commented. 'I believe that calls for a cheer.'

Each man had seen the signal flags dress the flagship. Alongside Harrison, they cheered and waved their hats, a motion echoed by the rest of the surrounding vessels. Courtney joined with them, but he could sense the anticipation thundering within his chest.

'Men!' Harrison called as the huzzahs died down. He had turned towards his crew, the one who had not, at all times, treated this ship with respect or admiration. Now, on the cusp of fighting, a new fire burnt in them, a new spirit. 'We go towards a battle the like of which we may never see again. I have not always been with you but in this, I will stand through it all. I cannot say it in a better way than Lord Nelson himself. Do your duty – to your country, to your ship, and to each other. Let us hear "Heart of Oak"!'

Three men struck up the rousing tune, drums and fife echoing over the waters. Now the *Lion* had been cleared for action, each battle station manned, there was naught to do but wait. The great seventy-four's progress clawed by, struggling and straining even with all canvas aloft. Courtney stood upon the quarterdeck, one hand behind his back in a tight fist. Harrison kept commenting on the columns' advances but each time he tried to reply, the words clogged in his throat. Noon came and passed with the chiming of the afternoon watch's bell, a routine that continued even on the cusp of battle. Courtney focused his eyes on the grand enemy vessel slightly to the northeast of the *Lion*. Even from some distance, she towered over the other ships, four red-painted decks packed with heavy guns.

'The *Santisima Trinidad*,' Harrison said. 'She is the largest ship afloat. One hundred and forty guns.'

The entire enemy crescent bristled with cannon, ready to receive the British fleet which slowly but inexorably approached. When the first shot flashed, down to the south, Courtney barely registered it. It seemed unbelievable that after such a long and eventful pursuit that the fight could at last be starting. His disbelief was shattered when the other guns opened. They ranged their fire at Collingwood's lee column, smoke beginning to broil. Collingwood's flagship, the *Royal Sovereign*, pushed through the haze, almost swallowed by it as he out-paced the rest of the line.

Courtney's attention wrenched back as a shot tore through the *Victory*'s main t'gallant sail. He stared at the ragged gap, just a pinhole from where the *Lion* was astern of her. But it seemed to draw a curious hush over the weather column. Courtney became aware of Harrison's breath beside him, his own shivering in his lungs. The world dropped into silence. He moved his hand out of its fist, gripped his sword as if it alone could fend off the enemy. For a moment, he closed his eyes, aware of his blood, his heartbeat, every one of his tense limbs. The music faded into the distance.

And then hell opened its mouth.

The scream of enemy guns poured upon *Victory*. She inched within their range now, open to raking fire. Ahead, the gargantuan *Santisima Trinidad* loomed. The foremost of her one hundred and forty guns now directed their fury upon the British ships, sailing into that realm of death. Courtney watched cannonshot sear about *Victory*, then about *Temeraire* and *Neptune*, but still the vessels pushed on. No fire could be returned; the vessels were at the wrong angle so had to sit and take it with a stiff spine and firm legs.

To the south, Collingwood had engaged. His *Royal Sovereign* appeared like a phantom through the fog and plunged into the heart of the enemy line. As he did, Courtney saw the damage to his flagship, but with a mighty roar, the *Royal Sovereign* slammed beside her targeted enemy vessel and Courtney felt the broadside in his own chest. The *Lion* crept forward, shot churning up the seas before her, and Courtney looked between his own vessel and those of the lee column. To his horror, he saw the *Royal Sovereign* alone, but she fought and writhed against the grip of a crowd of enemy ships. Each of them pressed so close that there barely seemed room to move, only pour cannonfire at pistol-range into one another.

'Good God,' Harrison spat out. 'It's carnage.'

Courtney counted off the yards as they travelled in the *Neptune*'s wake. Every minute dragged into an age. Alee, the *Royal Sovereign*'s masts teetered like trees battered by a hurricane. In amongst the swarming fog, he saw the flashes of her cannon-fire. *Belleisle* sailed astern of her, creeping to her aid.

Courtney watched the battle and knew the same butchery awaited the *Lion*. She followed *Victory*, *Temeraire* and *Neptune* into a tempest of smoke and flying debris, yards and rigging whirling chaotically. But with every shot connecting with the *Victory* ahead, every piercing fire, she kept driving relentlessly forward. The *Lion* mimicked her, fearless of the screaming metal, snapping cordage and breaking timbers that would be her fate too.

With startling suddenness, the *Lion*'s fore-topmast crossjacks erupted, sending Courtney's heart into his throat. Splinters scattered about the deck and for a moment, the mast shuddered. The line of Farnham's Marines cringed as a wooden hail-storm pelted down upon them. Courtney barely had time to think before the next shot came, barshot ripping through the halliards and eviscerating the starboard topmast studdingsail boom. Union Jacks, recently tied onto the stays to distinguish British ships, fluttered down around him.

'Get them aloft!' Harrison called. He already had to raise his voice and with fierce clarity, Courtney realised they had entered the eye of the storm.

No sooner had the men moved to obey Harrison did a barrage explode from the *Lion*'s larboard side. Every topmast took a beating, canvas and ropes flying loose. Courtney watched the foremast cap pinwheel into the air with a great chunk of the fore-topsail yard, cartwheeling into the shrouds and main chains and thudding onto the deck. Those at the waist scattered with seconds to spare, but their shelter did not last for long; now the larboard studdingsails, stretched to try and make the most of the paltry airs, streamed from their spars as they were shot away. A cloud of splinters rained over the men. Ridiculously, the drums and fife continued, straining through further rounds of 'Heart of Oak'.

'Commander!' Harrison shouted. 'Have the men lie down! We'll not lose men before we have to!'

'Men!' Courtney shouted, the first time he had used his voice in an age. 'Lie down! Down, now, down!'

The crew on deck, many of them stripped to their waist, neck-cloths and bandanas tied about their heads, sweat glistening already, lowered themselves to the timbers. Below in the gun decks, Courtney knew Appleton and Martin's men would be doing the same. But the officers and the midshipmen remained standing, facing the oncoming slaughter. Courtney pressed down every clenching, awful terror and walked along the deck, letting every man see him and seeing every man himself. Their stoic silence filled him with inspiration, and he hoped he did the same for them.

Ahead, behind the shredded canvas of the *Temeraire* and *Neptune*, the *Victory* suddenly shifted to larboard. She had nearly reached the enemy line and now she aimed towards a grand vessel near to the French flagship. Courtney held his breath and then with a crash that could have woken the devil, Nelson's *Victory* smashed into her. Her carronades roared into life, followed by a broadside at such close range that Courtney could almost smell the death. The *Victory* dragged a pall of smoke and fire from her cannons as if she wore a cloak of destruction, and *Temeraire* and *Neptune* followed in her mad wake.

'Set our course south of the *Temeraire* and *Neptune*,' Harrison ordered the *Lion*'s helmsmen. Half of the spokes of the double wheel had been shot away but enough remained for the two men to grasp on and urge the *Lion*'s head towards the enemy ships Harrison indicated. Through a halo of slaughter she sailed under ragged canvas, trailing *Temeraire* and *Neptune* which both passed intrepidly under the sterns of their foes, delivering horrific raking fire.

And so came the turn of the *Lion*.

Courtney looked to starboard, looked to larboard, heard the screaming of men, ships, and weaponry, and then stared at the gap the *Lion* aimed for, nestled beside their allies so brutally fighting. The *Lion*'s bowsprit targeted it, bouncing in the rolling swell, and he knew she would have to force herself in, just as the others had done.

A rain of cannonshot raked her bows, tearing down a line of Marines and finally bringing 'Heart of Oak' to a discordant end as two of the drummers were torn in half. The force of the fire threw Courtney off his feet, missing him by mere inches. He felt the wave of it in the air and collapsed against the ladder to the poop deck. A helmsman dropped to the deck beside him and once the shock had passed, Courtney saw the man was dead, felled without a scar on his body. The mere passing of the ball so close had struck him down. Across from him, Harrison clambered to his feet, unharmed. Courtney felt himself and found no injury.

'God above!' Harrison cried and leapt for what remained of the helm. It had been nearly destroyed; barely anything was left to steer the *Lion*'s bulk. She missed the ship she aimed for, which Courtney now saw was named the *San Leandro*, and scraped along her hull. In the barrage which erupted from her side, the *Lion*'s mizzen-topmast toppled and took away with it the spanker boom. The cat's cradle of pulleys and cordage flung around, severing themselves.

A cluster of ships had been stationed astern of the French flagship. A Spanish vessel, with a huge wooden cross hanging from her boom, stood directly in the *Lion*'s path. Courtney caught her name briefly on her stern: the *Mistral*, appearing through the smoke, one deck higher than the *Lion* and bristling with armaments. The *Lion*, out of control without her helm and with her sails tattered and yards damaged, fell upon her, all one thousand and six hundred tons smashing headlong into her starboard side. Her bowsprit crumpled as weakly as if it were paper and Courtney watched in horror as the bows nestled beneath the embrace of the *Mistral*'s shining guns. Though she was taller and weightier than the seventy-four-gun *Lion*, the *Mistral* staggered in the water at the impact. For a blessed moment, she appeared incapacitated.

'Lieutenant Martin! Lieutenant Appleton!' Harrison screamed through the chaos. 'Angle the guns! Return fire!'

It would be a tough movement. Courtney did not stare over the side to see if it could be achieved as to starboard and to larboard, the *San Leandro* and what he now identified as the *Redoutable* towered. The *Lion* had managed to batter through the line frightfully close to Collingwood's melee. Cannonfire still rained over the ship's vulnerable deck, surrounded at all angles. Every inch of the starboard gunwale had been churned up and the base of the entire foremast had been eaten away at so it seemed a hit away from collapsing.

Ahead, Courtney stared at the *Mistral*'s guns. She would have a range of guns from eight- to thirty-four-pounders, spread over her decks and forecastle, and the entire starboard battery now stared at the *Lion*. *Good God above*, Courtney thought and then a scourge of iron ripped through the foremast. The upper fore-topsail yard wrenched off entirely, chunks of it pirouetting through the air in a deadly hail. It caught in the main course, still set, and gouged great holes in it. Musket shot sliced the rest of the canvas which was quickly becoming as tattered as lace.

'She's coming down!' somebody shouted, and Courtney stared as the huge foremast surrendered to the fire, lurching, crossing the shadow of the sun, and toppling in a cloud of cordage and sail. It caught on the hull of the *San Leandro* and then, mercifully, crunched into the sea.

With the loss, their hope of steering the *Lion* waned. The helm had been wrecked too. Courtney raced for the taffrail and peered over the side. He could almost feel the heat of the enemy guns, aiming down the length of the *Lion*. Below, the rudder had been dashed and as he stared, a ball pierced the gallery façade, explosively entering the wardroom.

'The rudder has been shot to pieces!' he called back to Harrison, then, when the captain signed that he could not hear, ran to the ladder to the poop deck and shouted it again.

'We'll have to bear the fire then!' Harrison cried, and winced when the *Mistral*'s broadside sang again in a scream of metal and gunpowder. It destroyed two of the boat davits and pierced the mainmast before scything through a group of forecastle men. Courtney watched in horror at the spectacle. Blood and gore splattered the newly painted mast-rings and tainted the timbers. Those who lived staggered to their feet, heaving their comrades, limbless and disembowelled, over the side.

'We must increase our rate of fire!' Harrison shouted. 'We cannot sit here waiting to be destroyed!'

As if answer to Harrison's cry, Martin appeared at the forward hatch. He was wreathed in smoke, skin blackened already. Red stained his white waistcoat.

'Mr Martin, below!' Harrison ordered.

'The guns, sir—' Martin began but his loud voice was interrupted by the next storm of raking fire. The ladder rung beneath Courtney's foot shattered and he found himself falling through the air, hitting the quarterdeck with a firm thud. His breath rushed from him as he jammed his chest against a ring-bolt. Behind, he heard bulkheads splinter and the clanging of iron. Something rolled against his arm and he thought it was a cannonball, red-hot and soaked with something clammy. He shoved it and found Martin's frozen expression staring back at

339

him, eyes wide and lifeless. The rest of his body, decapitated and spurting from the severed neck, still twitched on the wet timbers.

'God!' Courtney rushed to his feet, jerking away from Martin's head. To larboard, Harrison had been thrown against the gunwales and tried to stand with unsteady limbs. One arm hung loosely at his side. 'Sir!'

Courtney hurried over but Harrison waved him away. 'I am not hurt, Commander,' he rasped. 'I was not hit.'

Blood soaked through Harrison's coat, seeping over the blue wool near the shoulder. The gold lace of one of his epaulettes had turned red. Shocked, Courtney helped him remove it and found something protruding through the skin: part of Harrison's collarbone. The limb twisted foully, a hunk of wood jammed near the armpit.

'You must go below, sir!' Courtney shouted.

'It is nothing! I still have my other arm! Dr Archer will be occupied enough! These men must have their captain!'

'Sir—' Harrison would lose the arm if something was not done.

'Go below, Commander!' Harrison ordered sharply. 'See to the guns! They will be down one lieutenant! And Commander, release Mr Baker from his irons. He needs to be on deck. There are few men who know the rigging better.'

Courtney wanted to argue, but could not, certainly not as Harrison shoved him away with his one working arm. He regretted not telling Harrison everything about Baker. Surely the captain would not have had him released if he knew. Courtney rushed towards the hatchway, willing himself not to give into instinct and duck at the popping of the muskets and howling of the great guns. The entire sea seemed afire with shot and battle; everywhere he turned flames fizzled in the smoke and timbers smashed. Ahead, the *Lion*'s bows still jammed squarely into the *Mistral*, each heave of the ocean grinding them together. He could see men through the open portholes, a charnel house of darkened faces and men fighting to stay alive.

The *Lion*'s upper gun deck seethed with death. Courtney stepped down a ladder slippery with blood, having to leap over some of the missing rungs. The evisceration of the *Lion*'s armaments and stores awaited him: guns blown from their carriages, gaping voids opened in the *Lion*'s flanks, powder horns spilled, bits of the capstan thrown to the four winds. The entire galley had ripped apart with fragments of the black stove scattered about the floor. Butchery painted the deck, dead and dying men as far as he could see through the acrid smoke. Gun crews worked around their slaughtered mates, continually sponging out the cannons, reloading, wadding, running them out and firing. Courtney remembered every time he and Appleton had drilled them, the efforts of the officers and the crew bearing fruit. Boys acting as powder monkeys raced past Courtney, dancing around the limbs and torsos that covered the timbers.

'Lieutenant Appleton!' Courtney shouted and a man, stripped to his dirty shirt-sleeves and smothered in sweat and blood, wrenched himself away from the starboard battery. Appleton's hair was blown in a fair halo about his face, chunks of some unknown substance dripping through it.

'Sir!' his mouth said, but Courtney could not hear him above the pounding of the guns. The men set a punishing pace but it was not enough: the devastation came from everywhere, reverberating through the entire ship.

'Martin is dead!' Courtney screamed. 'The captain is wounded. The *Lion* must be moved – she's jammed against the Spaniard and her rudder is shot away! The captain orders that Mr Baker has to be released!'

Even in the fury of the battle, Courtney saw new dread strike Appleton's face. 'He cannot be released!' he screamed.

'There are many men dying, Lieutenant!'

'I won't allow you to release him!' Appleton raged, an ire that surpassed rank overcoming him.

'I said: there are many men dying, Lieutenant!'

Suddenly, Appleton caught his meaning. The fear dropped from his expression, replaced with determination. He nodded and Courtney ploughed astern, groping through bodies to get into the orlop. There, below the waterline, no shot had pierced the *Lion*'s hull, but blood still dripped down the companion-ladders. A few corpses lay at the foot of them and Courtney had to step over each one. Dr Archer and Ellis laboured over a heaving sickbay, men groaning and crying out as their lives hung in the balance. Courtney ignored the sickbay and found Baker, unguarded because of the need for Marines on deck, but still bound in chains.

'Commander!' he cried, as if about to beg for mercy or wear an innocent act.

'Not a word, you fucking dog. I know who you are. You're going to face the battle.'

Baker's expression curled into a sneer. 'Lieutenant Appleton told you, did he? Or did he not? The fucking dirty bugger, the catamite. You should be wary of him. He's accused men before—'

'I ordered you not to say a word.' Courtney had loosened the shackles. As soon as Baker was standing, he let the fear and dread of the battle turn into anger and he slapped Baker across the face, making him reel. When the bosun raised his own arm, Courtney gripped him by the collar and hissed, 'I could have your throat out, you bastard. You are the worst kind of man. You're a coward and a wretch with nothing but evil in him.'

'You are no gentleman officer,' Baker spat.

'And I am proud of it.'

Grabbing his shirt tightly, Courtney forced Baker towards the ladder. He had no intention of taking him to Harrison and would gladly lie about what would transpire, if he survived this fight. Amidst the carnage above, Appleton appeared. His gaze crossed with Baker's and without hesitation, he ran down the rungs.

'You son of a bitch!' he cried, and this time Courtney did not hold Appleton back from attacking the bosun. He watched, ensuring no one saw as Appleton punched and kicked at Baker, laying him low onto the blood-soaked timbers. Baker tried to react, tried to grope and grasp at Appleton, but the lieutenant had nothing to restrain him now. Every time Baker attempted to escape, rolling over to crawl pathetically away, Courtney rushed into his path.

'You ruined me!' Appleton shouted at Baker. 'You ruined me and the lives of other midshipmen! Fox died. Ramsey tried to kill himself. McPherson took the blame for you. You took everything from me!'

'Commander,' Baker gasped, mouth full of blood. 'Commander, please, won't you do something?'

Courtney responded by slamming his foot into Baker's shoulder, pinning him to the deck. He looked at Appleton and nodded.

Appleton unsheathed his sword. The point of it glinted and for a moment, with the fight raging above him, he stood there above this wretched, sickening tyrant. Then he plunged the blade deep into Baker's stomach. The bosun howled, hands flying to grope at the sword and for the wound Appleton opened. Cursing him, sobbing out years of torment, Appleton stabbed again and again at Baker's torso for every life he had wrecked. His blood flew, his screams rose, until Appleton lifted the blade and forced it one final time into his neck. Baker's shouts immediately trailed into gargling chokes, before dying completely.

Appleton crouched there, panting. He stared down at the dead man, observing his frozen, anguished expression. Then, as Courtney gave him his hand, he stood, finding his feet.

'If I am to die,' he said, 'I will have no regrets.'

Courtney nodded. 'We shall heave him overboard. He is just one more victim of the battle.'

It was an easily performed task, shoving Baker over the side as so many others had been during the fight. It still roared, consuming the *Lion*. Courtney found his way to the lower gun deck once Appleton had returned to the upper. The ship was so close to her adversaries now that it was impossible to elevate the upper guns high enough to blast the enemy rigging, but the lower guns could not miss, hurling roundshot into hulls. Part of the forward reach of the gun deck had been carried away, a gaping hole letting in smoke and choking air. Courtney could only see that far, but no more; a gunpowder-infused haze roiled throughout the timbers. The men resembled phantoms, blackened and wounded and drenched in sweat from the constant firing and reloading of the cannons.

They did not need his help. Mr Midshipman Harriet cried orders and each gun captain, those who remained, led his crew over and over, the battle making perfection of their efforts. It was a world away from the disastrous exercise Courtney had overseen; their skill had been birthed in blood and fire now. Still, he prowled along the lines of the crew, trying their utmost to man both sides. Sailors opened their mouths to shout, but he could barely hear them. As he observed the men, he saw some of them had tied rags about their heads, red liquid soaking through from bleeding ears. The King's Navy was led by officers, by lieutenants and captains and admirals, but its beating heart was here: in the workforce of the men, whether they were able or not, toiling, sailing, fighting. In war, their presence made all the difference. Courtney was a commander now, but once, he had been one of them and that respect would never die.

'Don't stop, men!' he bawled, though he knew they did not notice him. 'The *Lion* will survive this! Keep firing, do not—'

It was as if the world erupted. Portholes all along the starboard side suddenly imploded in on themselves as the outside of the *Lion* became her inside. An entire gun crew turned to mist before Courtney's eyes as he was thrown across the deck, bouncing on shattered wheels and linstocks and overturned carriages. He nearly cracked his head open on a gun. Above, he heard a deep groan as if the *Lion* herself cried in agony and then a lurching whine as something heavy soared overboard.

He coughed and spluttered, smoke swarming in his eyes. For a moment, he could not see, could not move. Bodies had fallen over his splayed legs and he kicked at their hefty weight. Darkness pressed in. His stomach heaved as he breathed in the scent of fire and gunpowder and annihilation.

Retching, gasping for air, he turned over and gripped the knotty ridges of the deck's timbers. He dragged himself away from the pile of debris and corpses he found himself under, trying to locate where he was. His ears rang, his head pulsed. Inch by inch, he clawed through the carnage. He could taste it, feel it sticking to his arms and chest, the blue sheen of viscera replacing the caulking in the deck's seams. Another eruption knocked men off their feet but he barely heard it, the entire ship becoming distant and muffled.

This is hell, he thought. *This is hell come to earth*.

Courtney had to rise and stand firm but he could barely feel his legs. Suddenly terrified, he looked down, fearing he would see bloodied stumps. His feet were still there, a buckled shoe missing. His stockings and breeches were torn. He would never, he thought, rinse out the stains. Nightingale would chide him.

Nightingale. The face of the man suddenly appeared in Courtney's mind. He would be at home now, in Portsmouth, perhaps in his garden. Courtney imagined the chill of an approaching English winter, the long nights drawing in. He and Nightingale had spent so many together, safe in their bed with miles of silence between them and the horrors of the world. Abruptly, Courtney remembered their times in each other's company. The *Scylla*. First meeting Nightingale in his great cabin, the sting of a bruise on Courtney's cheek. Arguing with him about the man Nightingale assumed him to be. Defending him at his sham trial. Fighting alongside him to capture the *Ulysses*. Their first night in one another's arms. Days and days in the cottage. The *Lysander*. Rescuing him from the *Barbarossa*. Telling him how much he adored him, how much he wished to spend his life with him…

The images and memories assaulted Courtney, raining upon him as though they were the last thoughts of a dying man. No, he would not die. He would return home. To Nightingale. To the one he loved.

Courtney pushed himself up, straining to get to his feet. He slipped once but steadied and forced his legs to move. His commander's coat suddenly felt too heavy, so he stripped it off and threw it somewhere to the deck. Something was grinding against the ship, making her shiver and buck. For the first time in an age, Courtney could feel the water beneath her keel. He struggled to get up the nearest companion-ladder, needing to know what had happened, what state the ship was in.

Pushing through seething, sweating bodies, Courtney reached the deck, only for a sailor to appear from nowhere and shove him out of the way. He groped for the ruined gunwales and for a moment his back arched over the churning sea. Above, through the blinding smoke, the main-topmast plummeted, a trail of cordage raining with it. It caught in the tattered shrouds then fell yards away from Courtney with an immense crash. The central spine of the mainmast shivered, shot so many times it seemed an army of insects had gnawed it through. Scraps of canvas covered the deck like a shroud.

But, remarkably, the *Lion* moved. Her stern was swinging as if pressured by a veering wind. With shock, Courtney saw the reason: the *Temeraire* had collided with the *Lion*'s larboard quarter. The strike gave the *Lion* the momentum she needed to inch away from the incandescent *Mistral*. Buffeted by the *Temeraire* and the surrounding vessels, the *Lion* eased out of the raking fire of her foes, her broadsides gradually coming to bear.

At the bows of the *Lion*, men worked the mighty carronades, now able to aim them up into the flanks of the *Mistral*. Courtney groped his way forward to them, spying Harrison's tall form through the haze. As he approached, he saw the man was leaning against a gunwale. His weak, ragged voice directed the carronade crew and with his right arm he waved his sword.

'My God!' Courtney cried. A tear had ripped apart Harrison's shirt at the collar and beneath, he could see an open, gushing wound in Harrison's flesh. His left arm now hung on by mere sinews. 'You must go to Dr Archer!' Courtney shouted.

'No… No!' Harrison tried to protest but his face was white, eyes unfocused. 'I must stay on deck!'

'You cannot stand!'

'I can! I must!'

Harrison wrenched himself away from the gunwale but overbalanced himself and fell. Courtney caught him beneath the arms, or what remained of the left one. His body sank in a dead swoon, head tilting. With nothing more he could do, Courtney shouted to one of the crew. It was Bowles, his face illuminated with fire. Between them, they grasped Harrison and carried him below, manoeuvring down dangerous companion-ladders. Despite the battle raging, men turned to look at the insensible figure in Courtney's and Bowles's arms. Courtney ignored the stares, only thinking of reaching the cockpit.

Dr Archer's ward teemed with crying, broken men. Sand had been scattered over the floor but the blood still soaked through, making feet slip. Ellis, bandaged about his head, helped Archer. He held a man from the afterguard down on Archer's table, willing him to be still and silent as Archer sawed at his arm. Archer did not look up as Courtney entered, focused entirely on his work. But other eyes swivelled to stare and even the groans of the wounded ceased when they saw the captain.

'Don't,' Harrison suddenly mumbled, jerked back to reality for a moment. 'There are…other wounded. Let me…sit.'

Courtney obeyed. He carefully deposited Harrison amongst the scores of men who made way for him.

'I will be with him soon, Commander Courtney,' Archer called, still without raising his head.

These men would lose their captain. Looking at Harrison's pallid face, the amount of blood he had lost, the terrible state of his arm, Courtney knew he would have to bury him. He

347

thought painfully of Harrison's child back home and his heart ached.

Then the booming of the guns interrupted him. Without further comment, he and Bowles clambered back over the prostrate bodies of wounded seamen and rose back through the smoke onto the quarterdeck. The *Lion* had shivered herself free from the fiery snare and with a severed helm and ragged sails, staggered wildly over the waves that had been churned up from two fleets of ships of the line wearing and firing. There had to be some way to guide her, even just a jot. The foundations of the wheel remained: the tiller ropes stretching below decks where Courtney prayed the steering mechanisms would still be operational.

'Mr Bowles,' Courtney snapped. 'Get ten men and have them go to the tiller flats. We'll steer the rudder by hand.'

Courtney remained on deck, splinters and metal hurtling around him. He heard the whistle of it, searing close to his head, and felt the heated wind, perilously near to his limbs and torso. But the drive to rescue the *Lion* and bring her back into the fray steadied him. Someone had found him a speaking-trumpet and he clutched it strongly. Pulling a voice from the very depths of his lungs, he screamed as loudly as he could to the men below.

'One point to starboard!' he shouted. There was a moment where he thought they could not achieve it, that the *Lion* would not capitalise on her miraculous collision. But then, with the strength of her tiller and by yanking her unceremoniously by her braces, her great, injured bows ached about. The bowsprit snagged a tear in the chains of the *Mistral*, bringing a veil of cordage down. They would have to sacrifice the spar to get her fully around. It resisted, catching on porthole lids and hull, then with a grinding crunch, the jib-boom snapped and the *Lion* was free. The jerking movement wobbled Courtney on his feet and he groped for the rail. But there – there was a sliver of open water, a gap for the *Lion* to nestle into.

'Ahead! Ahead! Keep her steady!' Courtney yelled, willing that space to draw nearer.

A broadside knocked into her larboard side, a stream of fire wailed from the *Mistral*'s waist guns, but the *Lion* kept on, driving towards her freedom. Every sail was still set and, despite the loss of the foremast, half of the mizzenmast, and the devastation to the canvas, she strained to use the light winds.

It approached, the moment where she could turn against her foe. She forced her way towards the *Mistral*'s high stern and with a resounding crunch, collided with the starboard quarter. Her bows scraped off paintwork and wood, sliding through blood which poured from the aft gun ports and scuppers. The open channel widened before her and she struggled into it – at the same point that another vessel, the *San Leandro*, loomed. But the *Lion* had her space now and she beat relentlessly towards it. The *Mistral*'s stern, the *San Leandro*'s bows, towered to either side of her.

Courtney, heart thudding in his breast, hurried down to the upper gun deck. Some of the men had been heaved over the side now but the timbers were still slippery with gore. The carriages which had been overturned now stood proudly again. The crews had been working without end, fighting for their survival, fighting for the fleet. That was what throbbed through a sailor's chest when in the heat of battle. Thoughts of king and country became buried beneath the goal of breathing for another second, the yearning to support their fellow men. Courtney had been a forecastle seaman, and an officer, and now, with sudden clarity, he realised he was in command of this seventy-four. This ship which Nightingale had led through Battle of the Nile.

'Men!' Courtney shouted, his voice cracked. 'You have gone through suffering which no man should witness! You have served this ship when your fellows died around you and when weather and tide have been against you. I know that you believe her dogged with misfortune, I know you fear she is cursed! But look how she still sails! Look how you still live! Men—'

And ridiculously, faces amongst the hellish smoke were looking at him. He had to speak quickly, had to bring them back into the fight, but not without these words.

'We shall not lose this ship! You, my lions of England, treble shot these guns!'

'Treble shot!' Appleton screamed in response and again down to Harriet on the deck below. 'Quickly now!'

Appleton met Courtney's eyes across the deck. Without thought, Courtney rushed to join in with the nearest gun crew, who had been cut down to four men. They loaded the cartridge, the shot, three eighteen-pound balls, jammed it with wad, then ran the cannon out, heaving it between them to the port. It mattered nothing for elevation or targeting now; they could not miss.

And then, with the stern of the *Mistral* to larboard and the bows of the *San Leandro* to starboard, two perfect raking shots, Courtney screamed, 'Fire!'

'Fire!' Appleton wailed.

'Fire!' shouted the gun captains.

Deafening booms nearly split Courtney's eardrums. Every gun at the *Lion*'s waist on the upper and lower decks ignited, three eighteen-pound balls blasting from each. He imagined he heard the impact, finally striking revenge on the *Mistral*. There was no time to think of more. As soon as they had fired, he ordered the men to reload and deliver another devastating storm across the two enemy ships. The explosive energy fizzed inside of him too, the sensation that he had to be here, amongst these men, on this ship, defending them, leading them. At last, through all of the pain and grief that had struck the *Lion*, he felt they were united: officers, midshipmen, and crew with one sole purpose.

'Sir!' Simmonds cried from above, sticking his head down the hatchway. 'Sir, the *Mistral*!'

Courtney raced up to see the *Mistral* suffering. Her entire stern had been decimated, gaping holes that blurred where one deck began and one ended. The raised poop deck was a broken and jagged heap of timber. Her mizzenmast had been severed and broad voids had appeared in the mainmast. The foremast tilted to starboard, the entire ship lurching dangerously.

'Mr Bowles!' Courtney cried down to the makeshift helmsmen, still at the tiller. 'Bring her around! Four points to larboard! Lay us alongside the *Mistral*!'

The hasty, ungainly manoeuvre drove them broadside onto the *Mistral*. Their sides collided, yardarms tangling. Each ship was pulled inexorably together and apart again, grinding and shattering.

'Fire, all!' Courtney screamed and at a range so close he felt he could almost touch the enemy ship, the *Lion*'s larboard broadside erupted. Simultaneously, the *Mistral* fired and rattled the *Lion* to her very keel. She was taking a violent beating; she could take more. 'Fire!'

It went on and on, a firestorm which Courtney knew he would never be able to scrub from his mind and senses. When he returned to England, he might be deaf, blind, wounded… *When he returned*. He thought of Nightingale, there at the cottage, the only person he wished to spend his life with. There was no one else, only Nightingale.

The cannons of the *Lion* suddenly fell quiet. Every eye on the ship stared as through the smoke, the great tower of the *Mistral*'s mainmast teetered. Courtney stared up, watching it begin to topple. Then, with a roar, it came down, smashing into the *Lion*'s waist.

'Lash her down!' Courtney ordered. 'Don't let her escape!'

Straining against exhaustion, the Lions did so, binding the great spar to their ship, tangling her in the detritus which swamped the deck. The pops of muskets sounded from the *Mistral*, echoing all around Courtney's head as he helped his men. Flashes and explosions sounded in the short distance between the trapped ships, hand grenades erupting. Farnham's Marines cut down their opposite number, keeping the enemy crew from harassing the Lions as they worked.

And then, suddenly, the *Mistral* was silent. Courtney wondered if his ears had been destroyed, but about him, he could hear other vessels engaging in their fiery chaos. He looked over at the Spanish ship, watching as the gunsmoke wound around what remained of the masts and spars. His gaze drew to the Spanish colours, still hanging despite the ferocious struggle. There was no shame in their action as through the haze, they suddenly dipped and were lowered. A cheer rose from the *Lion*. Courtney closed his eyes for a moment, letting out a trembling breath. But there was no time to hesitate. Gathering men around him, Courtney leapt onto the *Mistral's* downed mast. The two ships remained locked together, hulls knocking. It was a short dash across their spar onto the other ship's deck.

Courtney jumped down onto the timbers. After the din, the *Mistral* seemed eerily quiet, everything dampened beneath the pervading gunsmoke. Courtney walked carefully, hand gripped around his sword. Dead bodies littered the floor, buried beneath fallen spars and canvas, impaled on broken timbers, many with ragged holes torn in them, missing limbs and heads. It was carnage. Courtney knew he had done it, had ordered the broadsides which had devastated these men and their vessel. But his own men had paid in blood. The lives of countless souls still clung to Courtney's uniform, red and black with gore and fire.

Ahead, a figure suddenly loomed. It walked with an unsteady gait, dragging one leg behind it. Courtney stopped before his boarders, the muskets of the Marines pointing over his shoulders. He held up a hand to still them.

The captain of the *Mistral* appeared. Courtney sucked in a breath.

'Allende!' he gasped.

The man who had escaped the inferno of the *Fénix* five years before stared back at him. Courtney had dined with him on the *Scylla*, had sung as he strummed a Spanish guitar, and had then delivered him, as a prisoner, to the authorities in Trinidad. He had occasionally wondered what had happened to him, if he had been exchanged, if he had returned to Spain.

'Lieutenant Courtney,' Allende greeted, just as surprised. Without his commander's coat on, Courtney assumed he still resembled a lieutenant. He did not correct the other officer but watched as Allende grasped his sword, turned it from him and held the hilt towards Courtney. 'I believe this is the second time you have overseen my surrender, sir.'

Courtney reached out to take the sword, but stopped himself. 'Keep it,' he said. 'You have behaved honourably and bravely. I trust you will continue to do so.'

Allende nodded. 'You have my word.'

Courtney ordered the Marines to round up the Spanish crew and keep them under guard. In the same way as many battles, Courtney did not feel he looked upon an enemy once he saw men face to face. It was hard to believe the slaughter he took part in. Foes existed in many guises, often times on the same side, as Baker and Garrick Walker and Lord Fairholme had proved. Courtney wondered, not for the first time, why he fought, why he still served the navy. He was good at it, he thought. He had grown up in the walls of naval ships, in cradles such as these battles, on the open seas. He fought for the ships and their hearts. He fought for the men he served alongside and for those at home.

The war off Cape Trafalgar had not run its course yet. Courtney's duty awaited him and the others in his crew. He would not lose the *Lion*.

Chapter Thirty: The Lee Shore

The battle was over. As the sun began to descend onto the horizon, the French *Achille* ignited and erupted in a halo of destruction. Her almighty explosion marked the end of the fighting, as if the roar of her demise deafened all else. By that time, Villeneuve had already surrendered and was being held captive on the British *Mars*. The enemy vessels which remained seaworthy strained to bear away to Cádiz, the grand Spanish flagship, *Principe de Asturias*, opting to salvage those still breathing rather than press on with the brutal battle.

Then the word spilled through the fleet. Soon into the conflagration, Nelson had been shot and been taken below. After being informed of the resounding British victory, he had quietly died in the orlop of his flagship.

Courtney had no more emotion to react. His bones ached with exhaustion, his limbs seemed to move as if through treacle. He had escaped with only ringing ears and minor scrapes, aside from a cut across his face he could not even remember receiving. After the capture of the *Mistral*, the *Lion* had manipulated what little canvas she had intact and fallen upon the foes in her vicinity, pressing and shoving through the blood-soaked crush. So tight and fierce had been the throng that she had elevated her guns at ridiculous angles to fire over the decks of her allies and into the enemy. Courtney had lost sight of all else but the men before him, their force, their ferocity, their will to survive.

Now, he staggered through those same decks, taking stock of the damage and the dead. Every timber had been christened in blood, every seam clogged with gore. Each of the *Lion*'s masts had been cut down to some degree; nearly all of the canvas shredded; the bowsprit entirely severed; the rudder ravaged; holes gouged in her hull; her bows shot away. All of this could be repaired, although with strenuous effort.

The lives of the men could not so easily be returned.

Courtney had spent months learning each man's name. So it was with knowledge of their identities that he saw who had perished. Those he could no longer identify were still counted and noted down, but he knew there would be others who had been unceremoniously slung overboard during the battle. By his estimate, they had lost sixty, alongside three midshipmen and one lieutenant, and another eighty had been wounded. Appleton accompanied Courtney on his rounds, helping him to heave bodies into the sea after they had been sewn into their hammocks. There was not enough time to deliver services to each man but Courtney offered a silent prayer for them as they tumbled into the waters. Harrison had not yet emerged from the sickbay and Dr Archer's reports were unfavourable. The doctor had seen many men die during the battle and many men afterwards too, and it seemed Harrison would become one more of them.

The enemy had lost eighteen ships of their thirty-three. Nelson's fleet, now commanded by Admiral Collingwood, had lost none. No British vessel had dipped their colours or been lost to the French and Spanish. It was a dear victory, one which would be felt across families in all ends of society.

But the lowering of night brought worsening weather. The swell rose with the winds. Ships already torn apart fretted over more damage. Sense would dictate that they should anchor, but the *Lion* was just one of many vessels that could not do so, her cables shot away during the battle. Orders came down from Collingwood to take the sea, risking its mercy, and head for Gibraltar. Though his body throbbed and his mind twisted with the horrors of the day, Courtney kept to the deck, ordering the men to get the *Lion* under a jury-rig. Commanded by

Appleton, a crew made the perilous journey to the surrendered *Mistral*, the Spanish prisoners put to work to save what was now the prize of the British. Allende, as Courtney had expected, behaved as honourably as he had in the fight, not stirring any unrest amongst his men and only meaning to save the beautiful timber and hempen creation, regardless of her colours now.

As the storm rolled in, Courtney felt it like no other. The *Lion* could not take much more turmoil. It was as if her old scars opened too, ravages from the Nile splitting again. If they could only stop her from being blown towards the dangerous shoals around Cádiz, she might survive. In the way of praying a deadly fever would break in the night, Courtney wished for a bright and steady morning. It did not come; the gale raged, as if the battle which had turned the sea red was now being fought in the heavens, the souls of the dead repeating their end. Courtney had not slept a wink for an interminable length of time and he found himself drifting for a second or two on the tilting deck.

With the topsails close-reefed, Courtney prayed for the wounded *Lion* to stand firm against the ever-shifting wind. She and the fleet could not force their way to Gibraltar, the weather pushing them nearer and nearer to that dreaded lee shore. Throughout the two days after the battle, he barely ate, barely rested, having to watch what remained of the masts and spars ravaged by the hurricane. The already-abused main-mast shook and whined, rigging and stays ripped and snarled, and during the second day, the mizzen-topsail nearly cleaved entirely from the yard, threatening to take the *Lion* aback. Courtney witnessed prize ships split from their tows, some of them devoured by the rocks or the rising seas. The captured vessels hampered the fleet, dragging them down like the anchors which had been lost.

But side by side now, the British and enemy crews worked themselves to the bone, continually manning the pumps and cutting away wreckage. Courtney joined them with Allende, toiling until he could barely stand. He hardly knew what had happened when after days of terror and desperate seamanship, another order came from Collingwood. Threatened by a counterattack, the British fleet once more prepared for battle, straining to shield the damaged vessels and their prizes. The fight did not come, but the fear remained.

Three days after the grand victory, Collingwood directed for the hard-won prizes to be destroyed. Their final surrender was not to the British but to the sea. Courtney, knowing he broke the hearts of his men and his enemy's alike, watched the *Mistral*, which had battled so bravely, ignite into golden fire. He ensured every prisoner, every member of Appleton's prize crew, had been taken off her before she turned into a pyre, but across the waters, on other prizes, some captives, too wounded or aggrieved to be removed, remained behind. The ignominy of loss – and of loss without meaning, now their vessels turned to ash – struck them down.

Even free from her prize, the *Lion* still struggled. Many of the third- and second-rates, and the *Victory*, had to be towed by the smaller vessels, but the churning seas put them at risk of collision. Courtney prayed for calmer weather, for kinder waters. Mercy came to some of the injured sailors when they were able to be landed in Cádiz. The Spanish treated their enemies with compassion and for some time, Courtney could barely believe they had been battling each other so brutally mere days before.

It was only through writing in his logbook, lamenting how dryly he had to write of the extraordinary conditions and experiences, that Courtney knew what date it was. An entire week and more had passed before they gained some reprieve whilst struggling towards Gibraltar. The arrival of a handful of frigates provided relief for the battered vessels. When a sturdy thirty-six-gunner offered her services to the *Lion*, Courtney could have wept. He supervised the great cables stretched between the ships, ready for the third-rate *Lion* to be towed. With pleasure, he noted the frigate's name – the *Reliant* – and hoped she would stay true to it.

As he observed the officers of the *Reliant*, he thought of the *Scylla*, long gone but ever appearing in his mind. She had resembled the *Reliant* in her frame and appearance. And whilst he watched the *Reliant*, he frowned, wondering if she was alike that old ship in another way. When he realised his eyes had not deceived him, the first joy for many days overcame him.

'Mr Smythe!' he called across to the fair-haired lieutenant at the *Reliant*'s taffrail. The young lad – no, he was no longer a young lad – looked up and shielded his eyes against the low sun. He seemed to search around for a moment and then found Courtney.

'Commander Courtney!' he shouted back, no mind for decorum in his joy.

Courtney located a speaking-trumpet and continued, 'Captain Nightingale told me that you had been made lieutenant! Congratulations, sir!'

Even across the distance, Courtney could imagine Smythe blushing, as if he was being praised by his mother in front of his peers. 'Thank you, sir! And to you also, sir!'

During the battle, Courtney had abandoned his commander's coat in the debris of the lower gun deck. When he had found it again, it had been damaged beyond all saving. He still captained this ship though, regardless of uniform. The word about Harrison was still dire; Dr Archer feared the fever he suffered under.

'Are you well, sir?' Smythe exclaimed.

Courtney paused. Was he well? The reality of the battle had not seeped into him yet and nor had the exhaustion of the gales. He had simply stayed standing and alert because that was his duty. He had no time to grieve, no time to give in to rest. Perhaps in a day, perhaps in a week, perhaps in a month, the horrors and the destruction would crest over him. He could not time it, could not measure it. Now, in that moment on the *Lion*'s deck, he still breathed.

'All the better for having the *Reliant*'s assistance!' he shouted across the gap. 'I shall meet with you more formally in Gibraltar, Lieutenant Smythe!'

Smythe waved his hat in salute. Courtney smiled as he returned to his work. He could not wait to tell Nightingale of the meeting. At the thought of him, his heart clenched. He found his eyes momentarily fogged with tears. He could have never seen Nightingale again, had the sea taken him off the Needles. He, himself, could have been wiped from existence at any second during the battle. But both of them survived. Courtney could not wait to be home, even if meant facing his father again. He would go to the reunion with more openness, more heart. He simply wanted now to be back in England, safe and dry, and with Nightingale, the man he loved. The man he would always love.

–

Courtney was awoken by a gentle petting on the face. He groaned, trying to bat whatever it was away. The touch continued insistently. Suddenly fearing that some part of the ship had come loose and now assaulted him, he cracked open an eye. A little, furry paw smacked his cheek.

'What the devil are you doing here?' he questioned Mr Fitzroy, who sat on his chest.

In response, the monkey thrust a note into his gaze. Courtney sat up, carefully putting Fitzroy aside. The light was still dim but he deciphered a scrawled hand on the paper: *Mr Fitzroy requests your presence in the orlop.*

Courtney had no choice but to leave the cot he had so longed for. He followed Fitzroy, who tugged incessantly at his stockings, threatening to tear them with his claws. Through the decks he walked, noting the better state of them. The result of tireless cleaning, the blood and gore had been stripped from the timbers but the smell of metal and gunpowder was not so easily scrubbed away. When they had been able to, they had fumigated the ship and struck open every porthole lid to cleanse her. With immense toil and strength, the men had bonded to save their ship, the one thing that united them throughout their entire journey. They had done their best to repair her in the turbulent seas and, still under tow by the *Reliant*, Gibraltar's safe haven became closer and closer with every mile travelled.

The petulant monkey guided Courtney to Dr Archer's sickbay. Courtney pulled back the fabric partition and Fitzroy charged in, leaping up onto one of the cots – straight into the embrace of a smiling Captain Harrison.

'Captain!' Courtney cried, realising he had come along without properly brushing down his clothes and hair which still hung in dirty curls about his face.

'Hello, Commander.'

Harrison helped Fitzroy up onto his left shoulder, but Courtney's eyes drew to his right one. Just below the armpit, nothing but the cloth of his shirt existed and that had been tied in a neat knot. As on the decks, the blood and viscera had been cleaned. A healthy flush had returned to Harrison's cheek, a far cry from the pallid greenness of his expression days before. Courtney had never expected to see him alive again, certainly not after Archer had said fever had sunk its awful fingers in.

'Are you… Are you well?' Courtney managed to say.

'Tolerably. Dr Archer is a skilled surgeon, but I am sure you know that. He extracted the ball from your Captain Nightingale after he was shot, didn't he? It's a shame there was no ball here. I would have liked it as a souvenir.'

'Your arm, sir…'

'Clean off. It is a pity I needed that arm to write – apologies for the scrawled note – but it is no matter, Fitzroy is my right-hand man now. Ha!'

Courtney looked over to Archer, who stood at a respectful distance. The surgeon smiled.

'I am satisfied that Captain Harrison shall make a full recovery,' Archer confirmed, 'though it shall take some accustoming to use the left arm.'

'Dr Archer tried to insist I leave his sickbay to more private quarters but...' For the first time, Harrison's smile faltered a little. 'I wanted to be amongst my men. I hear you took very good care of them, Commander.'

'I shall see to my other patients,' Archer said. 'I am glad to see you well, Commander Courtney.'

Archer swept past him, leaving them alone in the small curtained bay. Courtney took a seat next to Harrison, unable to stop looking at his wound. Only a man like Harrison could find himself in such a momentous, painful occasion and accept it so heartily and with humour. *Only a man like Harrison*, Courtney repeated in his mind. The captain had returned to the person he had once been. Courtney did not know what had prompted either his descent or his ascendancy again.

'I wish to give you my thanks, Commander,' Harrison said softly. 'You saved my ship. I did my all to stay on deck but this damned arm got the better of me.'

'There is no shame in that, sir.'

'Perhaps not that but...in other ways. I have behaved abysmally.'

Courtney did not comment on that. The incident during the battle had not been the first time he had stepped into the role of a leader, a commander. In truth, he felt he had been acting that way ever since setting foot on the *Lion*. But it was impossible to feel malice for Harrison after how strong he had stood in the hellfire of the fight. He had tried to reach beyond what was humanly possible of himself.

'May I tell you something personal, Commander?' Harrison asked. 'I do not expect it to justify some of my behaviour but you, of all men, deserve an explanation.'

'You do not have to ask my permission, sir. You are my captain.'

'Even so, it is a weight that I could not, in all good conscience, lay upon your shoulders without consent.'

Whatever it was, it could not outweigh what Nightingale had admitted to him, whispering his grief in the dark of the night, sharing it with a man he knew he could trust. Courtney wished he could bear every burden of Nightingale's, wished he could reach into the past and change all of what had hurt him.

'You may tell me, sir,' he said.

Harrison smiled, though with a distant sadness in his expression now. He let Fitzroy scamper down from his shoulder and handed him a spool of bandages to play with.

'I have been a very weak man, Commander,' Harrison admitted. 'It has made me ashamed of myself. When I married Jennifer and was accepted into her grand family, I vowed that I would be a worthy husband to her and a valuable son-in-law to her parents. You know of the Sandhams, yes, but perhaps you do not know in what high circles they live in.'

'Oh, I know, sir,' Courtney said, thinking of how Nightingale had tried to convince him of a potential marriage into such a family. 'They are far above me.'

'Oh, Commander. You do not know the irony of those words.' Harrison chuckled. 'They are one of the foremost families in London. Jennifer's father has the command of Parliament as much as her uncle has the ears and eyes of the Honourable East India Company. I knew that I would have to stand amongst those lauded folk – I, a mere post-captain of the King's Navy.'

'You led the flotilla at Trinidad, sir, and you are a knight.'

'With all respect to Captain Nightingale, who was initially suggested as the commodore at Trinidad, it was a position in some far-flung corner of the empire where men feared to tread because of the disease. And as for my being a knight… Well, I only gained that title after I wed Jennifer and stepped into her family.' He sighed. 'If I speak the truth, Commander, it unmanned me more than any ship I have captained or served in, more than any battle. I could never fly the same flags as my wife's family, and the notion of our bringing progeny into the world… It was an anxiety which ate away at me and caused me to doubt every word and every action. I had more to lose now.'

Courtney knew that sensation too well. Before the battle, he had been terrified of never seeing Nightingale again, of leaving him to the world. The man would not have been alone, he knew, but the idea of their separation tortured Courtney. He wanted to touch him, to embrace him, to kiss him, to spend long years with him.

'Commander,' Harrison said. 'I am a seventh son, the youngest of a tribe of brothers. The only occasion I had to be near the kind of life Jennifer has was…' He paused, obviously strengthening himself for more. Courtney patiently waited. 'Well, perhaps when I accompanied one of my brothers to walk my mother home from her time as a kitchen maid.'

Courtney had not expected that. He had assumed, by Harrison's accent and his gregarious nature and his ease of talking to others, that he had been born to that life. He, of all people, should know not to judge by appearance and attitude. If he was to do so, he never would have come to respect and adore Nightingale as he did.

'We came from Hull and my father and elder brothers were involved closely with the whale fishery. I did not want to join them – I had no stomach for the stink of the profession – but I knew how to sail and how to manipulate a rig. It was mere fortune that saw me into the King's Navy. I saved an officer from drowning in the Humber and he vowed to vouch for me. He helped me gain a position on his vessel. Slowly, I befriended every officer and important man I could and climbed the pyramid. But I still fret that men can smell the ambergris and tryworks on me.'

'Sir,' Courtney began. He did not know where to start. 'If there is one sole thing I have learnt from this service, it is that men have a myriad of backgrounds. Princes' and merchants' sons share one ship, alongside rich folk and illiterate men and poets and bastards. I was a forecastle man once and I came from nothing.' Courtney thought of his father in Ryde, the life he had thought he had left behind but which still shaped him and influenced him. He continued, 'But during battle and on the sea, we all have one united goal. The ocean does not care where a man comes from. She has no discrimination.'

'Only men's hearts make that discrimination.' Harrison shook his head. 'It made me ashamed of myself that you were so unapologetic about your heritage. You do not disguise your voice or your behaviour. These timbers have always been my stage. I am an actor more than a captain.'

'Every officer is an actor to some degree, sir.'

'And yet not every officer turns to the shameful things that I turned to. I tried to take comfort in drink and then, when that no longer worked…' Harrison paused, bracing himself for what was obviously further confession. 'I turned to laudanum. It numbed me for a while but when I attempted to cut it out of my life, it made me feel so wretched. I found myself stealing it from Dr Archer's stores and allowed it to be believed that the men had done so. It was awful of me.'

Courtney remembered his bewilderment, and concern, over the missing medical stores. He had realised something was wrong but, in the way of McPherson and Baker, he had not seen the truth of it. He knew the effect of an addiction to such substances – perhaps not laudanum, but drink had cut down his father and mother.

'I had Dr Archer help me,' Harrison continued, 'but God, I was so weak. It led to me evacuating the ship when she needed me the most in the Caribbean and…I was a terrible example of a captain.'

'That is not true, sir. You returned and ensured the ship conducted herself gloriously in the battle. You refused to leave the deck even with half your arm hanging off.'

Harrison smiled, but Courtney could still see he did not believe him. 'It is a ridiculous notion but I simply wish for the men's respect,' he said. 'It must be earned and not expected or demanded. Yet I still seek it, and I know that this journey has not enamoured me to them.'

'Oh, sir, I…'

'No. It is a childish desire, Commander. I know it and I have accepted it. I am simply grateful for my life after such a fight and after such a wound. I shall go home to Jennifer and to my child and perhaps the loss of my arm will allow me to gain something else.'

Courtney smiled. He had come to have a newfound admiration for the captain and a kindred spirit in him too. Both of them came from the depths of poverty; both of them had risen through the hierarchy on fortune and unlikely circumstances, only with different faces. Now, they were here, on the *Lion*, survivors of the battle and tempest, leading other men who came from many backgrounds.

When Harrison emerged from the sickbay, the arm of his captain's coat pinned across his chest – 'like Lord Nelson himself, God rest his soul,' Harrison had commented – Courtney ensured he arrived on a deck which had been holystoned and swabbed and was manned with well-presented sailors. Harrison cast an approving eye over all of them, smiling. He walked to the weather side of the quarterdeck and seemed to breathe in the air, cleansed by the previous storm and now fresh and bright. Courtney, who had been standing with Appleton, far more content and free after his actions during the battle, turned to the men on duty.

'Three cheers for Captain Harrison!' Courtney called.

Harrison's face glowed as a panoply of 'Huzzahs!' and wordless cries echoed through the *Lion*. He kept his officer-like façade, bowing his head to the men, but Courtney could see the tears shining in his eyes when he looked up again. He glanced over to Courtney, nodded in gratitude, and Courtney smiled back. The battle off Cape Trafalgar had forged every one of them, transforming the ship and all her inhabitants. They had pushed through the line, had suffered greatly, and emerged on the other side, baptised in the blood and fire. Now, home, the safety of England, would be the reward.

Chapter Thirty-One: Return

Courtney counted each minute as he travelled down from London. The scenery changed from the close, crowded architecture of the city and to greenery dappled with the frost of an approaching winter. He rested once, in a coach-house on the outskirts of Guildford, and then pushed on, thinking only of his destination. Time and necessities had meant he had not been able to pen any notes, so his heart throbbed with anticipation as the farmland turned to village and then back again. Eventually, each time the door opened and another passenger joined, he could smell the scent of the sea. The south coast approached: the south coast and home.

The return from Gibraltar had been interminably long. The *Lion*, patched up for days on end, still licked her wounds in the harbour, side by side with other victims of the battle off Cape Trafalgar. Harrison had been indefatigable, despite the loss of his arm. He had dined with other captains, seen to business ashore, and then travelled back with Courtney to England. Soon, the *Lion* would return to Portsmouth and all her men would be paid off and treated as heroes with the spreading of the news. Courtney had already tasted it in London, visitors aplenty flocking to Harrison's home and wishing to hear of the events.

Yet every joy was tempered with a note of sadness. Nelson's death had carved a hole in many Englishmen's and women's hearts. The way they spoke of him appeared to make it seem he was a saint already. His loss, in the arms of victory, was as a martyr to the naval cause and to the sea. His body would soon return home and his funeral would attract the masses.

Now, Courtney thought of his own loss. He knew, with the events in London at Harrison's house, he had killed a part of his future. He had shut the door on a life which he knew he would not be able to return to. He did not know how it would have unfolded, but he could not think of that now. Portsmouth – and Haywood Hall – awaited him.

As the carriage deposited him upon Portsdown Hill, Courtney felt the same anticipation he had when visiting this spot three years previously. He had come home from the Caribbean and, dressed in his best uniform, adorned with scent from the barber's, had reunited with Nightingale, so recently his captain, his friend, his partner. Then as now, Nightingale had not known of his visit. So much had changed since then, across the wide tapestry of the world, within their careers, and in their union. Yet, at the heart of it, Courtney felt the same. His love for Nightingale had never ceased and he still sensed the same thrill as he climbed through the fields towards the hall.

The butler met Courtney at the door. He admitted him into the grand house and into Mrs Louisa Nightingale's presence. She smiled at him with open affection and wished him joy of his victory. Her words, however kind, washed over Courtney. He only heard when she directed him through the parlour and drawing room and out the wide doors into the fine garden.

Nightingale sat there in the softly warm autumn afternoon. He was alone, away from the household and servants. He faced the meadows which stretched beyond the stone wall of the house, a book upon his lap. Courtney walked quietly over the paved stones, the scent of the flower beds washing over him. This was the peace he had fought for, the image he had kept in his mind on the bloody decks of the *Lion*, throughout the din of the battle. It smelt all the sweeter for the pain and grief he had suffered through, so others would not have to.

Beneath a trellis archway, he paused. His heart pulsed in his ears. He took a steadying breath.

'Hello, Hiram,' he said.

Silence followed. Nightingale stiffened and slowly turned about. Across the garden, his eyes met Courtney's. His mouth fell open as words obviously fought to find it. Instead of speaking, he began to weep, his face crumpling into tears.

Courtney hurried towards him. Nightingale rose, rushed forward, and swept him into a tight embrace. Courtney sank into his arms, the fright of the battle, the exhaustion of London, the nerves of the journey rolling over him. He buried his face into Nightingale's hair and felt his body shivering as he cried. He did not want to let go, wanted to stay this way in the heat of the low sun and the fresh scent of the outdoors.

But finally, Nightingale pulled away and, with a hand still cupping the back of his neck, looked into his eyes. He traced the scar across Courtney's cheek, tears clinging to his lashes.

'You... You are not hurt?' he whispered.

'No,' Courtney managed, overwhelmed with adoration.

'Oh, when I had not heard... I thought... I was mad with worry.'

'I meant to write to you, but Captain Harrison took me to London again and...I wanted to see you to explain it to you.'

'He is well? And the *Lion*?'

'He lost an arm during the battle. He was very courageous. The *Lion*... I did not lose her. I could not lose her.'

'You are more important than the ship,' Nightingale said, and to hear such a thing from him ignited the love inside of Courtney. Nightingale, whose life had centred around these ships and that service, who knew how glory and honour dictated the careers of men, spoke the truth of their connection. He had emerged from the Nile on the *Lion*, and the ash of that battle had always clung to him. They understood one another, in this, as in all things.

'I am alive,' Courtney said, 'and I know what it is I must do to make you and I content.'

'My dear, I am content, always, with you.'

'I went to speak with Miss Sandham,' Courtney spoke quickly before he could wither from the conversation. 'I needed to speak with her about our…proposition.'

A shadow of doubt crossed Nightingale's expression. Courtney felt his hold around him loosen. 'And did she… Did she accept?'

Courtney nodded. 'She did. She accepted that I cannot marry her.'

'Arthur…'

'I cannot. It would break her heart – and mine. I will not… I will not marry anyone if I cannot marry the one I love the most.'

Nightingale stared at him a while longer. Courtney felt his heart, beating near to his. He steeled himself and reached into the pocket of his coat. There he found the velvet box containing the ring he had intended to give to Tabitha Sandham. She had looked at him with disappointment in her eyes, but she was young, intelligent and pretty, from a settled and ambitious family. She would find a far better partner than Courtney would have been to her. Her grace in accepting his dismissal had done great credit to her.

Nightingale's eyes followed his movements. Between their close bodies, Courtney opened the box's lid and revealed the contents: the satin bed and the silver ring.

'I wish to…' Courtney started and had to find his voice again. 'I wish to give this to you. I know that our bond can never be as spouses, not in the material sense, but it would be a great honour and joy to me to know that you had this, from me. It can be a small token. You do not have to wear it – in truth, I do not think it will fit – but…'

'Arthur.' Nightingale's hand closed around his on the box. He breathed out and Courtney felt him tremble. 'You are wrong. It can be material. I have named you in my will. When I die, all of this will come to you and Louisa. And I wish to be named on the lease of your cottage. I want to help you pay for it. It has been a great pleasure to me to stay there and be amongst your fellows. I have already made motions to aid with the workhouse there and other institutions. You and I… I would value it if we owned that cottage together.'

'Hiram, you do not have to do that.'

'I want to. For all the reasons that you say.'

Courtney could not deny him that. There had been times where he had felt embarrassed at Nightingale's offers of payment and gifts. He had felt it was Nightingale pawning off his old life in the navy, but he knew that it came from a place of goodness in Nightingale's heart. He had not fully considered that it was the man's attempt at unifying them, putting them closer together.

'And this,' Nightingale continued, squeezing his hand about Courtney's on the ring box, 'I cannot accept.' He paused. 'Not without giving you one as well.'

Courtney smiled. Hope and fulfilment flooded his chest, the feeling of his days leading to a moment where he needed to be. 'I would treasure it,' he said.

Chapter Thirty-Two: The Lion

The *Lion* had returned to Portsmouth. Nightingale could see her from the top of Portsdown Hill, looking down over the town and the distant harbour. He had watched her for some time through his spyglass and had expected her to look wounded and broken, the aftermath of the devastation she had suffered off Cape Trafalgar. But she had been repaired and refitted so her masts stood upright, her hull without penetration, her figurehead still that proud roaring lion. Men, whom he once would have commanded on that deck, flitted about her in the tops and about her boat davits and appeared from the hatchways. A decade before, she had been assembled in Portsmouth. Now, she had come home, perhaps one day to be broken up, perhaps to be sent on her next voyage.

Nightingale had not asked. Though she resembled a new vessel, he knew she would always feel the effects of the Nile and Trafalgar. Within himself, he felt the same. He had been patched up, treated, soothed, but that past would never leave him. From his days as a seasick midshipman to now, five years out of the service and yet still sailing, the days he had lived and the pain he had borne would not ever vanish. It dictated his actions and his ways, the places he travelled to and the people he shared his life with.

Despite the trials, he would not have changed it.

For coming to meet him here was the man he never would have met had he not been put aboard the *Scylla*, had he not relented to going out to the Caribbean. Their paths had been intertwined through the suffering and the joys and each of them had stood firm, beside one another, understanding each other's minds and experiences.

Nightingale pulled his coat further about himself as the chill of winter swept over him. December had its grip firmly about the world, present in the cold weather, the frost on the grass, and the low sun. He could not believe it had been nearly a year since he had waited for Courtney outside the George Inn, ready to accompany him to the *Lion*. Recently, Lord Nelson had been brought back to England, his *Victory* sailing slowly and mournfully past Portsmouth. Nightingale had watched that ship as he now watched the *Lion*. He had served under Nelson at the Nile and now Courtney had served with him off Trafalgar, each on the same vessel. It felt as though history had travelled in a circle, closing itself around them. Nightingale would go to London with Courtney and attend the admiral's funeral, an event that would draw the masses. Naval affairs were still written closely in the hearts of every Englishman and woman.

Yet, with the destruction of the Spanish and French fleets, Nightingale did not know how time would move on for the King's Navy. The war still raged, but the seas felt more firmly in their grasp. Battles would ravage the lands now, as they ever had. He and Courtney would give their service where they were needed.

Footfalls crunched on the grass behind him. Nightingale turned to see Courtney climbing the hill. His heart swooped with affection. Courtney wore his dress uniform, his one commander's epaulette shining, gold lace and white fronts gleaming on his coat. He would soon have his own sword, a token of his participation at Trafalgar, but now he wore Nightingale's. At the sight of Nightingale, he swept off his decorated hat and held it beneath an arm. Nightingale smiled. He looked every inch as handsome as he had when they had first met in the cabin of the *Scylla* – no, more handsome, his looks growing with his age and experience. He paused and bowed, black curls bouncing in their ribbon tie.

'Hello, sir,' he said sweetly. 'May I join you?'

Nightingale laughed. 'It has been a long while since you called me "sir".'

'Apologies, Hiram. I thought that would sound a good deal more romantic than it did.'

'I was remembering when I was your captain,' Nightingale said, accepting Courtney's arm and beginning to walk the last distance up the hill. 'I cannot believe it was five years ago.'

'It seems so far away and yet as though it occurred yesterday. I had been trying to wrangle Kieran Attrill after his theft onshore an Antigua and then I came aboard the *Scylla* to find out that you had already arrived. I was not pleased.'

'I know you weren't. Just as I was not pleased with you and your insolence.'

'You would not change my insolence,' Courtney said with a smile, digging his elbow affectionately into Nightingale's side.

'No, but you did yourself. I am so proud of what you have become, Arthur, and what you have achieved, how you treat others.'

'Oh, hush, you sound like my father.'

Nightingale huffed. Courtney had spent more time with his father over the last month, visiting him at his new home on the island. Though past hurts would never be entirely cured, John Courtney had done much to try and make a smoother future for them – and Courtney was meeting him on that path, if only tentatively to begin with. Nightingale had faith in Courtney to act as he saw fit; he was talking truthfully when mentioning his pride.

'I appreciate what you have done for me, Hiram,' Courtney said, more serious now. 'You are good to me. I had doubts where I would fit into your life but I do not believe we have ever conformed to what society puts down for us. There is little in us which is of the traditional.'

'Oh, there is some,' Nightingale said with a smile. 'I wish to be at your side, I wish to help you through all of your days, I wish to see old age with you.'

'And I, you.' Courtney pulled him closer, leaning his head on his shoulder for a moment. 'We have seen enough together to almost fill an entire life already. The *Scylla*, the court martial, peace across Europe and war again, the *Lysander* and the *Barbarossa*, your adventures on the island and I at Trafalgar… Soon, we shall be old men by the fire, reminiscing to anyone who will listen.'

'I thought I was an old man already,' Nightingale teased. 'I should be careful at my great age.'

Courtney laughed at the reminder of what he had said when they had first scaled the mainmast of the *Scylla*. 'You will never allow me to forget that, will you?'

'Mm, no. Because as much as you have changed, there are parts which are the same. Your spirit, your passion…'

'Save some of this kindness for me to put upon you, Hiram! I cannot have you speaking such sweet things without returning them.'

'Let me hear them then.' Nightingale chuckled.

'Here.'

Courtney stopped. They had reached the summit of the hill beneath the cool sun. The world was quiet, away from the busy docks and the bustling town. Not a soul existed for miles. Courtney faced Nightingale and, comfortable in their solitude, took both of his hands. Nightingale squeezed them firmly.

'My life has not always been happy, Hiram,' Courtney said. 'I was born to a very poor family who had nothing. I was shown kindness by two people who did not have to care for me. When I ran away from home, I thought I was taking my first steps to manhood and to my own ends. But I did not know myself, not as a forecastle man and then not as a lieutenant. I was angry at the world and felt I had been treated very wrongly and very unfairly. I thought the same when you gained command of the *Scylla*. But then you made me see the truth of it, that my own expectations and assumptions were as flawed as the ones I condemned people for thinking of me. You have helped me more than you know and more than I can express, Hiram. You made my life happy, you made me happy, you still do. I would not be standing here without you.'

Nightingale smiled, tears rushing to his eyes. 'You speak the same words in my own mind. You have given a new meaning to my days.'

'I love you completely, Hiram. Completely and in every way. I always shall.'

Courtney released one of Nightingale's hands to search in his coat pocket. He found the same box he had pressed into Nightingale's hands a month before, but now, the ring inside had been adjusted. When he held Nightingale's palm, the metal slipped easily onto his finger. His own blessed, official ring from his marriage to Louisa sat on his other hand and though he would not be able to wear Courtney's amongst other people, for this one moment, they could pretend this intimate ceremony was true.

Keeping Nightingale's gaze, Courtney lifted his hand and pressed his lips to the metal. Nightingale felt his breath shudder, his chest swelling with emotion.

In silence, he pulled a box from his own waistcoat and opened it to reveal the ring he had bought for Courtney. Relief soared through him as it fit perfectly onto his finger. It looked so very apt there, a small symbol of their connection. As Courtney had, he cradled his hand and kissed the silver band. He wanted to kiss his mouth too but that they would do afterwards, in the safe privacy of Courtney's cottage.

'I love you completely, Arthur,' Nightingale echoed back to him. 'Completely and in every way. I always shall.'

Courtney smiled and pressed Nightingale's hand to his chest, thumb rubbing over the ring. For a moment, with the *Lion* so far below, with the world so far away, they stood there, quietly, thinking of all that had come before and all that was still to come.

Then Courtney whispered, 'Come, let us walk together,' and they left the view of the harbour behind, out of the shadow of the *Lion*.

Acknowledgements

Writing this book conjured a mix of emotions: frustration, joy, sadness, and not a small deal of fear. Although all this series has required extensive research, *A Merciful Sea* needed that times ten as Courtney's story so closely followed the route and events of the Trafalgar campaign. Tackling such a momentous few months in British history, culminating in perhaps *the* most famous naval battle, was very intimidating. Therefore, I must first mention the sources I used, scouring each for the fine detail as well as the large threads. *The Campaign of Trafalgar* from Chatham Pictorial Histories was invaluable, as well as *Trafalgar: The Men, The Battle, The Storm* by Tim Clayton, *Nelson and Napoleon* by Christopher Lee, and *Nelson* by Andrew Lambert. Because the battle is so extensively covered in sources, it was simple to come across information, but extremely difficult to sift through.

I also fell back on the sources that have helped me throughout the series to get detailed insights into the lives of both officers and men in the Georgian-era Royal Navy. Stephen Taylor's *Sons of the Waves* remained helpful, as well as the *HMS Victory: Pocket Manual* from Osprey Publishing. My trusty *Seamanship in the Age of Sail* by John Harland provided extensive guidance in the complex world of historical sailing. One of the most difficult scenes to write was the tiny part where Courtney joins in with the midshipmen's navigation lesson. For this, I used countless YouTube videos of how to determine latitude and longitude with period-appropriate instruments.

For Nightingale's plot, I was very happy to set it on the Isle of Wight, where I am from. Although the individual Sea Fencible officers were made up for this story, the Isle of Wight Sea Fencibles did exist. The island's link with smuggling was also true, though of course the plot details were invented. The website *Smugglers' Britain* was invaluable for research into this. Roger Knight's *Convoys* also gave helpful background details for merchant shipping.

Thank you of course to Canelo, to Kit, to Miranda, and to my agent, Francesca, for supporting me throughout *A Merciful Sea* and the entire Nightingale & Courtney series. It has been a whirlwind to bring these books into the real world and I have been over the moon to hold them in my hands. Thank you also to all my writing friends online and in real life, and to the bookshops that have stocked this series — still such a bewildering thought for me! I particularly appreciate Medina Bookshop on the Isle of Wight which is such a fantastic champion for local authors and creatives. I want to also mention the lovely Anmarie Bowler and everyone involved in the *Hear Me Now* project in 2024 which gave voices and opportunities to queer writers and artists on the Isle of Wight.

Again, thank you to all my friends and family who have continued to be there for my highs and my lows. Your support and love has meant so much, whether it's my dad being my early reader, my mum giving me words of encouragement, or my partner George listening to my ideas and being a nerd about naval history with me.

And thank you to every reader who has given this series a chance. I was incredibly intimidated to enter the nautical fiction world — and I still am! — as I did not know how these stories would be received. I appreciate the response and your love. I did feel sadness while coming to the end of *A Merciful Sea* as it was the last in the trilogy for Canelo and it seems as though Nightingale and Courtney have been in my life for so long. I've absolutely adored bringing their story into the world.